LS

PASSI SSION

Julie Ellis i
other nov
and *Far* T
and a full-time w
Publishers Weekly han
genre'.

BY THE SAME AUTHOR

The Only Sin
East Wind
The Velvet Jungle
Glorious Morning
Rich is Best
Maison Jennie
Loyalties
No Greater Love
Trespassing Hearts
Lasting Treasures
Commitment
Far To Go
A Woman for All Seasons

JULIE ELLIS

Passionate Obsession

HarperCollins*Publishers*

This novel is a work of fiction.
The names, characters, and incidents portrayed in it are the work of the author's imagination.
Any resemblance to actual persons, living or dead, events or localities, is purely coincidental.

HarperCollins*Publishers*
77–85 Fulham Palace Road,
Hammersmith, London W6 8JB

This paperback edition 1998

1 3 5 7 9 8 6 4 2

First published in Great Britain by
HarperCollins*Publishers* 1997

ISBN 0 00 649900 7

Set in Postscript Linotype Sabon by
Rowland Phototypesetting Ltd,
Bury St Edmunds, Suffolk

Printed and bound in Great Britain by
Mackays of Chatham plc, Chatham, Kent

In memory of Arthur McBride, Jr,
a fine and talented young man who died tragically young
– and for his parents,
Rae and Arthur McBride, Sr.

Chapter One

On this sharply cold eve of November 9, 1938 – in Berlin, Germany – small, delicately lovely, 13-year-old Vera Mueller walked towards the family flat in the four-storey house at the corner of Wilmersdorfstrasse and Kurfürstendamm with a hand tucked firmly in one of her father's. Her lush blonde hair was tucked beneath a knitted cap of the same dazzling blue as her eyes. She walked with quick small steps to keep pace with her father, who towered above her in the bleak twilight.

Mature beyond her years because of the cataclysmic upheaval in her life these past five years, Vera was conscious of the blanket of doom that seemed to hang over the Jews in Germany these past two days.

On October 28 the Nazis embarked on a brutal action – grabbing thousands of German Jews of Polish extraction from their homes, children from the streets at play, thrust them into trucks and trains and deported them across the Polish border, where they were abandoned in bitter cold to a hostile country. Then two days ago, a 17-year-old in exile in Paris – distraught over this latest atrocity, his parents among those displaced – shot a German official in Paris.

Here in Berlin – as throughout Germany – the tension was agonizing as the official hung between life and death. German Jews feared that even more Nazi rage was about to explode into fresh horror for them. Papa said they must be honest, Vera remembered. '*Vera, my love, not all Germans are Nazis. There are many who live in fear themselves... who hate what has fallen upon Germans who happen to be Jews.'*

But not for one minute of a day could Vera brush aside the upheaval in their lives since Hitler had steamrollered into power. Papa had lost his position as professor of languages at the university. He was not allowed to teach except in the classes for Jewish students, which he – along with another teacher – had organized in a meeting room of their synagogue. The books he'd written had been burned – along with the books of other Jewish writers.

The family had lost its beautiful apartment 'to the needs of the German economy.' They lived now in three tiny rooms in one of the few Berlin buildings where Jewish tenants were accepted. Papa said that Frau Schmidt was taking a risk to allow them to live in the building owned by her husband and herself.

'Say nothing to Mama and Ernst about what we've just heard,' Papa cautioned Vera when they arrived at their door. She understood he referred to the news – ricocheting throughout Berlin – that the German official shot by young Herschel Grynszpan had died in a Paris hospital early this afternoon. 'You know how Mama worries.'

Vera nodded. Mama was so scared that Ernst, who would be 17 in a month, might be drafted into the German army.

The family's closest friends had left or were trying to leave Berlin – but how could the Muellers survive when no more than 10 marks could be taken out of the country? They had no family in other countries to receive them. And Vera knew that her father was determined to remain in order to teach the Jewish children forbidden to attend German schools. Mama complained that Papa was obsessed about the importance of education – but she knew her mother was proud of this obsession. Mama was proud that her two children spoke French and English almost as well as their native German.

Encased in prescient foreboding, Vera walked into the small foyer of their apartment house and followed her father up the three flights to their own front apartment. The rear was at the moment without a tenant. The Schmidts occupied the two floors below their own – the ground floor was occupied by an elderly woman who took in boarders. The only child living in the building other than Vera and Ernst was Frau Schmidt's daughter Alice, a few months older than Vera. Since August, Alice had lived with her grandmother in Switzerland because her parents were anxious about conditions in Germany.

'Vera, remember. Not a word to Mama and Ernst,' her father repeated as he reached to unlock the apartment door.

But before he could turn the key, the door was pulled open. White and trembling, Lisl Mueller hovered before them.

'Viktor, you've heard?'

'I've heard.' He nodded with fatalistic calm.

'We can't stay here,' she whispered, reaching to pull Vera into the apartment. 'It's suicidal!'

'Where can we go?' He closed the door behind them. 'Where would we get the emigration taxes? Who is there in another country who would take us in? Only rich Jews with bank accounts in Switzerland leave. But this insanity will run its course,' he soothed. Would it? Vera asked herself fearfully. 'This madness can't continue.'

'Viktor, we still have some money,' her mother tried again. 'Perhaps if you talk to the right persons –'

'What remains will get us nowhere.' His face was grim. 'They tell us to go, but they rob us of the means to do this. Enough of this, Lisl. Give us our supper.'

*

Because of the anxiety that permeated the atmosphere, the Muellers retired for the night far earlier than normal: Her parents in the small bedroom, Ernst on his cot in the kitchen, Vera on the sitting room sofa. As though, Vera thought as she huddled beneath the blankets, the darkened apartment provided them with some safety. It would appear that nobody was home.

Even the children at school today had felt the fresh dangers that threatened them, Vera admitted reluctantly, lying awake in the darkness. Everybody knew the terrible Nazi rage. With a German official assassinated by a young Jewish boy, how could they not be afraid of repercussions?

Eventually Vera fell into troubled sleep. She awoke to an urgent pounding on the apartment door.

'Mama,' she called in alarm and leapt from the sofa. Moments later her mother rushed into the sitting room. The pounding continued.

'Don't turn on the lamp,' her mother cautioned and hurried towards the door. 'Who is it?'

'Lisl, open the door,' Frau Schmidt pleaded. 'We must talk!'

While her mother hurried to comply, Vera groped in the darkness for her robe. She was conscious that both her father and Ernst had come into the room – summoned by the middle-of-the-night invasion.

'Lisl, there's terrible trouble!' Frau Schmidt's voice was harsh with alarm. 'My sister just phoned to tell us. For almost an hour – since 2:00 AM – shop windows have been smashed, fires started!' In the distance they could hear the ominous sounds of shattering glass. 'The Gestapo and the SS are breaking into Jewish homes and dragging them away. Let Vera come with us. If anyone asks, we'll say she's our daughter Alice.'

'Mama?' Vera turned to her mother, then her father. Her eyes beseeching. 'I don't want to go –'

'You must,' her father ordered, his face taut. Sounds in the street warned them a mob was close at hand.

'Throw some clothes in a bag,' her mother said. 'Take –'

'No!' Frau Schmidt interrupted. 'There's no time. Vera, come with me.' She reached for Vera's hand. 'They mustn't find you here!' Subconsciously Vera remembered that the Gestapo knew about her father's organizing the school and disapproved, knew that they lived here in 'an Aryan building.'

With one last supplicating glance at her parents and her brother, Vera allowed their compassionate landlady to pull her from the apartment and down the stairs to hopeful safety.

Inside the exquisitely furnished Schmidt duplex, Vera clung to the foyer door – discreetly locked now and in total darkness.

'Vera, we must be quiet,' Helene Schmidt warned. 'Say nothing.'

Galvanized by fear Vera listened to the menacing sound of feet climbing the stairs, heard shouting on the floor above. She heard her father's rebellious retorts and shivered. Her heart pounded as she listened to the noisy descent from her family's apartment. She'd heard terrifying stories about what happened to Jews who were dragged off in the night. *What would happen to Mama and Papa and Ernst?*

Now the hallway was quiet. The sounds of shattering glass continued in the night-dark streets. In the distance were sounds of shots. Helene Schmidt pulled Vera into her arms, murmured words of comfort.

Herr Schmidt came into the foyer.

'Helene, make tea,' he ordered. In the streets SS men and the Gestapo rounded up Berlin Jews, and Hitler Youth gangs continued their wanton vandalism. 'Let's go out to the kitchen – the lights can't be seen from there. Let nobody know we're awake.' The SS would hesitate to awaken an important businessman like Herr Schmidt, Vera understood.

Numb with shock, too stunned to be afraid for herself, Vera sipped at the hot cocoa Frau Schmidt placed before her. Traumatizing sounds continued in the distance. Relentless smashing of glass. The sirens of fire trucks howling through the streets. Obscene shouting. Though Helene and Anton Schmidt knew their voices could not be heard, they spoke in muted tones.

'You'll stay with us,' Frau Schmidt told Vera. 'If anyone asks, you're our daughter Alice.'

'Let's try to get some sleep,' Herr Schmidt said at last. *How could she sleep? Vera asked herself – recoiling from the prospect.* 'I must go in to my office in another four hours.' Vera knew he was a very successful exporter. 'But neither of you is to leave the house tomorrow.' His eyes focused first on his wife, then on Vera. 'It won't be safe. But I must go in to the office as though nothing happened tonight. Life must go on as usual.' He flinched in rejection. 'If anybody comes to call, Vera – which is unlikely in these conditions – you will stay in Alice's bedroom with the door shut.'

'Anton, *drive* to the office tomorrow –' She paused. 'Drive this morning,' she corrected herself. 'It could be dangerous to take public transportation.' She sighed. 'I wish you would stay home for the day.'

'That would be unwise,' he objected. 'Also, I need to make arrangements for a business trip to Copenhagen.' Vera sensed a silent conversation between the other two. 'Now,' he reiterated, 'let's try to get some sleep.'

Obediently Vera allowed Frau Schmidt to take her upstairs to Alice's bedroom, accepted one of Alice's lovely nightgowns. But how could she sleep when she didn't know what was happening to her family? Where were Mama and Papa and Ernst? *What was happening to them*?

Twice during the morning and again in the afternoon Helene Schmidt talked with a woman-friend on the phone. The phone was a stranger to Vera these days – Jewish homes were denied phone service. After each call Frau Schmidt reported on the latest news of what was being called *Kristallnacht*. Crystal Night. Not only Berlin was experiencing this carnage. It was happening in every city, town, and village in Germany.

'Gerda says we wouldn't recognize Kurfürstendamm. Plate-glass windows have been smashed from one end to the other, the shops vandalized. You know the wonderful Margraf Jewellery Store on Unter Den Linden? It's in shambles. Even the branch office of Citroën – a *French* company, Vera,' she emphasized, 'has been wrecked.'

Despite the horror still erupting through the city at dusk, Helene Schmidt went about preparing dinner while Vera set the dining room table. Tantalizing aromas emerged from the large, comfortable kitchen – lending a specious air of well-being – as though nothing untoward was happening. On schedule – as on any other business day – Herr Schmidt arrived home.

While Vera listened in muted terror, Frau Schmidt plied her husband with questions.

His face etched with pain, he reported on what he had seen in the course of the day.

'You would not believe the fires that are still raging in the city,' he wound up. 'The broken glass that litters the streets.' He hesitated, his eyes resting compassionately on Vera, yet some compulsion forced him to continue. 'The beautiful Great Synagogue is a burnt-out shell. I suspect not one synagogue in Berlin still stands intact.'

'What's happening to the people they took away?' Vera asked in an anguished whisper. She remembered the shots fired in the streets at regular intervals. 'When will we know?'

He sighed before replying. 'Thousands have been taken away to camps. We –'

'Nobody does anything to stop them?' Vera interrupted in a surge of rage. But she knew the answer before he replied.

'People are afraid for their lives,' he said gently. 'To object is to be an enemy of the government. We won't know for a while what will be done with those in the camps. Perhaps they'll be released in a week or two,' he said with an effort at optimism. 'But it isn't safe for you to remain in Berlin. We'll wait another two days, Vera, until the violence simmers down. Then you'll go with me to Copenhagen.' Her eyes widened in disbelief. 'You'll pretend to be Alice. I have a friend in Copenhagen – a high-level government official. You'll live with his family and help with their two small children. You'll be safe there.'

'But I have to be here for Mama and Papa,' she protested, dizzy with shock at the prospect of leaving Berlin. 'And Ernst –'

'They would want you to be away from Germany in these times,' Helene soothed. 'We'll keep in touch with you. When we know where they are, we'll write you.'

Three days later – with no way of learning the whereabouts of her family, still encased in shock – Vera went with Anton Schmidt to the Anhalter Bahnhof, the largest of Berlin's railway stations. She wore clothes that had belonged to Alice and altered to fit her more slender frame. Herr Schmidt carried a forged passport, identifying her as Alice Schmidt.

Vera's eyes swept about the bustling railway station.

Her heart pounded. It was terrifying to be going so far from home – to a foreign country. Alone. She had never spent one night of her life away from Mama. *Would she ever see Mama and Papa and Ernst again?*

'How will I talk to the children?' she asked Herr Schmidt when they were at last seated in their train compartment. She knew that she was to live with a Danish government official and his wife and was to help care for their year-old son and three-year-old daughter. 'I don't speak Danish.' Where would she go if they didn't like her?

'You're fluent in English,' he pointed out. 'The Munches – like many Danes – speak English. And they're eager for their son and daughter to learn the language. You'll have no difficulty,' he promised.

Frightened for her family, suffering an aching loneliness, Vera strove to make herself acceptable to Mr and Mrs Munch and little Nils and Krista. The household included a cook-housekeeper and a part-time nursemaid. Vera would care for the children when she came home from school each day and over the week-ends. She was relieved that she would be allowed to attend school. Papa would be very upset if she didn't continue her education.

She was grateful that the Munches brought English newspapers into their house. They were eager to perfect their knowledge of the language. But she was stricken by what she read there. The British newspapers told of 20,000 Jews being held in three camps: Buchenwald, Dachau and Oranienburg-Sachsenhausen. Where were Mama and Papa and Ernst? Those last moments together would be forever etched on her memory. There had not been even a moment to kiss them goodbye before Frau Schmidt snatched her away.

Helene Schmidt wrote that she was struggling for

information about Vera's parents and brother. Thus far she had been able to learn nothing.

'But we keep trying, Vera. When there's word, we'll be in touch immediately,' she promised.

Vera was astonished at the warmth and compassion she felt in the Munches. She was conscious, too, of the sympathy she felt in the Danish people towards the refugees from Germany who came into the country. Nowhere did she see any sign of anti-Semitism.

At the end of her sixth week in Copenhagen, Vera was alarmed when Mrs Munch called her from her room after she had put the children to bed for the night and was engrossed in homework for school. Panic drained her of colour as she joined Mrs Munch in the family sitting room. They were unhappy with her, she thought in terror. *Where would she go? Where would she live?*

'Vera, you must be brave,' Mrs Munch said gently when they were seated. 'We've heard from Herr Schmidt in Berlin –' She hesitated. Vera was all at once ice-cold, knowing what she was about to hear. 'He has finally been able to get word of your family.' Vera was aware of tears in Mrs Munch's eyes. 'Your father was shot to death on *Kristallnacht*. Your mother and brother died in Oranienburg-Sachsenhausen. Through special channels – since he's not a relative – Herr Schmidt was able to collect their ashes for the regular fee.' The dead were cremated, Vera interpreted in a corner of her dazed mind. 'The ashes were buried in synagogue ground and a service conducted for them.' Mrs Munch reached to bring Vera into her arms. 'You'll stay with us,' she said gently. 'You'll be safe here.'

Vera awoke each morning with reluctance – dreading to face a world devoid of parents and brother. She went through each day in an aura of painful unreality. She ordered herself to focus on the wishes of Mr and Mrs Munch. They were her new family, and Copenhagen was her home. But she listened every day to the reports on the radio, read the news in the English newspapers that came regularly into the house, and she was fearful of the relentless onslaught of the Nazis. And with devastating frequency she relived in nightmare dreams that November night in 1938 when all she loved was wrested from her.

On March 15, Nazi troops occupied Czechoslovakia. On August 31 – anticipating war with Germany – the British government evacuated women and children from London. The following day the Nazis invaded Poland. On September 3, Britain and France declared war on Germany. But soon, Vera told herself defiantly, the British and French would put a stop to Hitler's march across Europe.

A few months later – on April 9, 1940 – the Nazis invaded Denmark and Norway. Denmark had declared itself neutral, Vera remembered in shock. Mrs Munch was so proud of that. But on the night of April 9 – in a surprise move – Nazi forces invaded Denmark.

What had happened in Berlin would happen in Copenhagen, Vera thought in rising terror. *Would she be sent to a concentration camp or shot dead on sight?*

The Munches tried to assuage Vera's fears.

'Denmark won't be like Germany,' Mr Munch explained. 'The Danish government realized it was futile to fight. We've made an agreement with Germany. They recognize our sovereignty. We've become a kind of protectorate. We'll negotiate those matters that concern both Denmark and Germany. Vera, it won't matter in Denmark that you're Jewish,' he said forcefully.

But Mr Munch bought a gun to keep in the house – locked up, he pointed out, so that Nils and Krista could never find it. But if Nazi soldiers ever came into the house to take her away – or to hurt the children – she would use the gun, she vowed. She would fight back. Papa would have done that if he'd had a gun in the house.

Chapter Two

On this sunny late May day in 1940, Paul Kahn left his room in the John Jay Dorm at Columbia and strode across the summer-garbed campus towards the West End Bar to meet his roommate for a late lunch. Every corner of the campus exuded an aura of pleased excitement as students prepared to take off for home for the long summer vacation. But Paul was acutely conscious of the news this morning that German armoured columns were arriving at the English Channel – trapping 400,000 British and French troops at Dunkirk.

Slim, handsome – his dark hair rumpled, brown eyes sombre today – Paul wrestled with the decision he must make within the next twenty-four hours. It was a decision his roommate – Chuck Jourdan – had already made. A third-generation of French descent, Chuck carried on a personal vendetta with the Nazis. Paul sighed. Dad would be shocked and upset if he went to Canada with Chuck and enlisted. But he was 19 years old, he thought defiantly. Wasn't it time he called the shots in his own life?

Chuck was waiting for him in their usual booth.

'Hey, you're late,' Chuck scolded good-humouredly. 'I'm starving. I ordered burgers and coffee for two.' His cool grey eyes searched Paul's – but Paul's provided him with no answers. 'Hear this morning's news?'

'Yeah.' Paul nodded sombrely. 'It's grim.'

Like most students their age, Paul and Chuck had been brought up to believe that war was to be avoided at almost any cost. Yet they realized that Hitler was a madman who must be stopped. When a group of Columbia students – like the thousand at Dartmouth – sent a telegram to President Roosevelt to keep the United States out of the war, Paul and Chuck had not been among the signers.

'I can't get over some of the crap that keeps turning up. Like that character who said, "Why doesn't the British government give up the British Isles and just retreat to Canada?"'

'You're dead set on going to Canada to enlist?' Paul asked, knowing the answer.

'Look, we're going to get into this war. Everybody's saying we'll have a military draft within ninety days. Why wait? The sooner we get in and get it over with, the better. We're going to have to fight. I don't know why Roosevelt's not moving ahead. Let's stop that bastard Hitler. Right now,' he wound up. 'I'm leaving for Canada tomorrow. My folks are carrying on like mad. They want me to stay on in college and get my degree. But that's two years away. The war can't wait.'

Half-listening to Chuck's monologue, Paul considered his rebellion at having to settle on his major. He didn't *know* yet what he wanted to do with the rest of his life. He'd chosen engineering because it sounded kind of adventurous – travelling to all parts of the world on assignments. Deep inside he knew he'd chosen engineering because it meant getting away from Eastwood – and his father.

He loved Dad. And he knew how deeply Dad loved him, wanted the best for him. But he could never truly forget that Dad was responsible for Mom's death. He'd only been six – the whole awful tragedy was cloudy in his memory. All that remained clear in his mind was the devastating image of his adored mother falling to the floor dying from a gunshot wound inflicted by his father. A horrendous accident – the whole town had mourned for Mom and felt compassion for Dad. *Why couldn't he forgive Dad*? He loved him so much – but he couldn't forgive him.

Their hamburgers and coffee arrived. For a few minutes they focused on eating. But Paul's mind was racing. Dad expected him to come into the business this summer even though he was an engineering major. '*It's time you got your feet wet in the business. Eventually it'll be yours.*' Four generations of Kahns had been gunsmiths. His great-great-grandfather had set up the Kahn Firearms Company in the tiny upstate New York town on the Vermont border. Dad had gone through tough times, but now – with the Depression over – he was doing well. He'd just hired new workers. The fighting in Europe had opened a new market to him. Dad figured he'd play awhile at engineering, then settle down to learn the family business.

Dad didn't know how he hated guns. Only his sister Doris knew how he dreaded the hunting season each year. He'd grown up in a town where every man and boy hunted and fished. To folks in Eastwood it was strange – *unmanly* – not to hunt and fish. He'd been ribbed plenty about that, he remembered wryly.

It was weird, he mocked himself, that he would even consider running up to Canada with Chuck to enlist in the Canadian Air Force. Still – each time he went home from school – his father talked with such anxiety about the way country after country was falling before the Nazi onslaught. Dad was sure America would be sucked into the war. '*Why is Roosevelt dragging his heels? With France and England under attack, how can we stay out*?' And Dad – who considered himself an American 'who happened to be Jewish' – felt a new, strong awareness of his Jewish heritage and a horror at what was happening to Jews in Hitler's path.

'If we enlist together, we have a real chance of serving together.' Chuck interrupted his introspection. 'Come on, Paul. Let's do this together. Or would you rather go home and learn all about how to manufacture guns?'

Paul hesitated – his mind assaulted by the craziness at Dunkirk.

'I'll go with you,' he agreed. 'But I'll have to stop off at Eastwood for a day so I can break the news to Dad.' He sighed. 'Oh God, he's going to be upset.'

Paul and Chuck were jubilant when they were accepted for training in the RCAF – the Royal Canadian Air Force. Most of those enlisting were eighteen or nineteen or twenty – and proud of the white tabs on their overseas cap that identified them as aircrew students . . . all of them anxious to emerge as pilots – a role glamorized by Hollywood movies, fiction, and comic strips.

Paul and Chuck began their training at a manning depot, remaining there for three weeks for intensive physical training, learning to march with the high Air Force swing. Then came a dreary month of walking a post at an RCAF station until they were given places in a five-week class at an Initial Training School – where they were subjected for long hours each day to arduous training, both impatient for actual air experience. Still, both Paul and Chuck felt triumphant when they were advanced to 'flying' in a synthetic plane – the Link trainer.

Paul and Chuck emerged with their wings – to their joy – with commissions, plus the knowledge they were headed for combat training in England. They understood they would be assigned to the RAF, per arrangement with the British government, desperate for aircrews. Landing in England, Paul and Chuck were assigned to the same

Operational Training Unit. In fifty hours they must be prepared for action.

'Hey, we're making it!' Chuck chortled when he and Paul settled down for their first night on British soil.

'Yeah.' Paul patted the coveted double wings pinned above his breast pocket with affection.

The 'O' with a single wing indicated the wearer was a bombardier navigator – in Air Force slang, the 'flying asshole.' The rear gunner was labelled the 'Ass-end.' Yet every pilot knew that the bombardier navigator and the rear gunner were as indispensable as the pilot. They depended upon one another for survival.

Months blended into a year and then it was yet another year. Their lives – night and day – revolved around flying. They flew a seemingly endless stream of missions over northwestern Europe. Then on the same mission – in the early summer of 1943 – both Chuck and Paul were hit with their respective crews. Chuck's plane burst into flames before Paul's eyes. He knew Chuck and his crew could not have survived. And a few minutes later his own plane was crippled – his gunner and himself badly injured. He managed to fly back to their base in England, but he and his gunner spent long weeks in recovery.

At last Paul left the hospital for a recuperation centre, then was released from active duty with appropriate medals for his valour. On the day of his dismissal, he offered his services to the American army. He was welcomed with enthusiasm.

Now his train was pulling into Waterloo Station in London.

He was to report for a special assignment – secret, dangerous, but of utmost importance. He wasn't sure what it involved, other than some intensive non-military training.

He was assaulted by fresh anguish as he strolled from the train, through Waterloo Station, and into the September twilight. He and Chuck had thought themselves invincible – together they'd survived the unbelievable. Until that last mission. What about this special assignment? Paul asked himself with new ambivalence. Was he insane to take this on, when he could be going home? But he wasn't ready to go home, not with the war not yet won. At least for a little while he would sleep in a decent bed, be able to shower at regular intervals, maybe even eat decent meals.

Now he glanced about for a taxi to take him to the small hotel where he was to stay. London taxis – small enough to turn on a dime – had never ceased to operate despite the war. London, he thought in a moment of whimsy, had become his home away from home. He and Chuck had spent many leaves here.

While he signed the register at the hotel desk, Paul was conscious of the clerk's curiosity.

'You in the RAF?' he asked, reaching for a key.

'That's right.' Paul smiled faintly. He still wore his RAF uniform.

'You talk American,' the clerk said.

'That's right, I'm an American. I enlisted in the Canadian Air Force before my country got into the war.'

'Hey, mate, you're all right.' The clerk's smile was broad, approving. 'Together we'll lick those bastards.'

Paul sat across the desk from the colonel who was now his immediate superior and listened intently to what was being said.

'You don't have to accept this assignment,' the colonel stressed. 'God knows, with your record you've gone far beyond the call of duty. We won't think less of you for turning it down.'

'I'm accepting it, sir,' Paul said, almost with detachment. He wasn't ready to go home. His job wasn't finished.

The colonel's smile radiated relief.

'We're pulling all the pieces together for this operation. We're set to move on the groundwork now that you're in place. You're scheduled for eight weeks of rigorous language study. You'll spend eight hours a day learning German. We know you have college French behind you –'

'It's not great,' Paul warned, his smile wry. But Chuck had spoken French as a second language, and some of that had rubbed off on him.

'You'll know enough to get along when you're dropped into French territory. It's what you can pick up with the knowledge of German that's important to us. You don't have to worry about speaking it,' he emphasized. 'We need you to be able to understand what you hear. Give yourself a week off, then report to this department and expect to work your rear off. We've arranged for you to take over a small flat close by. In London today, that's a real accomplishment.'

They talked a few minutes longer, then Paul was dismissed. One week from now – at 7:00 AM sharp – he was to report to a room where a communications instructor would be waiting for him. At 8:00 AM, he'd go to another room to study with a German tutor who must in eight weeks stuff his head with that language. That would be his schedule for eight weeks. Today he'd renew his acquaintance with London. He'd have dinner at one of the great restaurants, then go to the theatre.

With rationing what it was in England, anybody who could afford it ate out, Paul reminded himself. Though the government decreed that no restaurant meal could cost more than five shillings, plus a fancy cover charge for special spots, no ruling existed to prevent restaurant hopping. He'd eat well tonight. It was amazing, he thought humorously, how preoccupied Londoners were with eating.

For a week he'd forget the ghastly war. It was incredible how there were sections of London which showed little of the devastation that affected so much of the city. Trafalgar Square, Bond Street, much of the West End. He'd live in that London for this week, he promised himself with defiant gaiety. Make it a small, luxurious respite from reality.

Chapter Three

Despite the passage of time – and the continued reassurances of Herbert and Margrethe Munch – Vera never felt totally at ease in Copenhagen, though she'd come to love the bright and shining city. How could she not be fearful, she asked herself at painful intervals – when they lived surrounded by Nazi police? Since the German takeover, it was almost impossible to learn what was happening to the Jews in other parts of Europe. Mr Munch no longer received British newspapers – Denmark was now a German 'protectorate.'

But the Danish government permitted no anti-Jewish measures, she conceded. The synagogue remained open. The Jews in Denmark lived normal lives except for the constant awareness of the Nazi presence.

Yet – as with all Danish citizenry – Vera was aware that the situation was deteriorating. The underground Resistance fighters were becoming bolder, their numbers increasing. Though the Danish government called for law and order, acts of sabotage continued, infuriated the Nazis.

In late September 1943 – three afternoons before Rosh Hashanah Eve, the beginning of the Jewish New Year – Vera sat in the family sitting room with Margrethe Munch and watched while her benefactor applied the finishing touches to the dress Vera meant to wear to the synagogue services on that High Holiday eve. The family maid had gone to bring Nils and Krista home from school.

'You chose the perfect material,' Margrethe said with

pleasure. 'This blue velvet is lovely, the colour just right for –' She paused at the harsh sound of the front door of the house being opened and slammed shut.

'Vera!' Herbert Munch called out in agitation from the foyer. 'Margrethe!'

'We're in the sitting room.' Margrethe Munch laid aside her sewing and rose to her feet. Her face was drained of colour. Normally her husband was a quietly spoken, reserved man. 'Herbert, what has happened?'

'The Nazis have executed saboteurs. In reprisal, the Danish government has resigned. The king is under house arrest. Martial law is about to be declared.' In the past two weeks sabotage and strikes had brought brutal reprisals that had enraged the Danish people. He drew a long, nervous breath. 'And there's more. A German attaché with a conscience has warned us of a roundup of all the Jews. They're to be deported to camps outside of Denmark. It's to happen on the eve of Rosh Hashanah,' he told Vera, 'when they expect Danish Jews to be at home or in the synagogues.'

'What do we do?' Margrethe demanded, instinctively drawing Vera into her arms.

'We're making sure the word is spread. Vera, you'll go to Sweden and –'

'Herbert, you know how the borders are guarded,' his wife interrupted. 'And the Swedish are protective of their neutrality.'

'That is about to change.' His face was grim. 'Already negotiations are under way to make Sweden understand that it must provide sanctuary. We have to establish escape routes immediately. Over 7,500 Jews must be rescued!'

'But can this be done quickly enough?' Margrethe clung to Vera. Both were trembling, ashen.

'I've already made the first arrangements.' His face was

encouraging as he turned to Vera, yet she was terrified. 'Tonight you'll be admitted to a private sanitorium for a supposed emergency appendix operation. At dawn you'll be driven to a house on the coast – presumably your family's. You'll be told when a fishing vessel is to take you to the Swedish coast.'

'I'll go with you, Vera,' Margrethe said instantly. 'I'll stay until you're on the boat.'

'It's better that you don't,' Herbert told her. 'But we must sit down and work out the plans. I've already talked with a friend in Sweden. He'll be there to receive you when you're across the Sound, Vera. He'll help you get to England. There another friend attached to the British government will see that you have employment as an interpreter. You speak fluent German, English, and French – this is a valuable asset. You'll be all right.'

Margrethe accompanied Vera to the hospital as her 'aunt.' It was clear that the staff understood what was happening but was determined to rescue the Danish Jews who came to them. Then – with a hospital gown over her clothes – Vera was bundled in blankets, placed on a stretcher, and carried to a waiting ambulance. Earlier Margrethe had wrapped a scarf about her waist and whispered that money had been sewn into the folds.

Vera was taken by ambulance to a modest cottage right on the sea. An elderly Danish couple received her with compassion and a determined optimism. Here she would be hidden until fishermen could take her across the Sound to Sweden. She understood now that, with astonishing swiftness, massive Danish rescue efforts had been set in motion.

Two days later – on a cold, cloudy night when the lack of visibility was on their side – a pair of Resistance workers appeared to escort Vera and another escaping Jew to a waiting fishing vessel. Vera was conscious that each man held a gun. Minutes later she froze in terror when a young harbour policeman suddenly approached the fishing vessel when she was about to climb aboard.

'Who goes there?' the policeman demanded brusquely.

'You don't wish to know,' one of the two underground workers responded and pointed his gun at the policeman. 'Talk to your superior,' the other added with a chuckle – but he, too, held his gun ready for action. 'He'll explain.'

Stumbling in her haste, Vera climbed into the fishing boat.

'It's all right,' the other fugitive told her gently. 'The police know to look the other way. This one will learn fast enough.'

From what was said, Vera gathered that Danish fishermen had been involved in shuttling refugees across the Sound for the past two nights and this would continue as long as there were Jews who needed to be rescued.

Still, she understood the danger that lay ahead of them. Would there ever be a time when she lived without terror?

On this – her third morning in London – Vera came awake in her drab, shabby 'bed-sitter' with an instant realization that today she was to begin her first assignment, as arranged by Mr Munch's London contact. She must do well, she told herself anxiously. She was on her own in a strange city. The most expensive city in the world right now, she had read in a London newspaper. She was nervous about money – she'd have to learn to budget, the way Mrs Munch had instructed her.

In a corner of her mind she remembered that she had been told few bombs were falling on London of late. Still, her first sight of London had been unnerving. Copenhagen had not prepared her for what she found here. The shattered buildings, whole blocks reduced to rubble. The FAP – first aid signs – everywhere. The signs for day shelters, night shelters, huge tanks labelled 'static water' for use in fighting fires. The anti-aircraft guns in Hyde Park, brick blast baffles positioned to protect doors and windows, rotting piles of sandbags.

She left her bed – shivering slightly in the morning chill. It didn't matter that she had arrived with only an extra change of clothing beyond what she had worn on the nerve-racking dash from Copenhagen to Sweden, across Sweden and Finland to England. Her British benefactor – who had helped her obtain the necessary ration card as well as her tiny flat – had assured her that in London everyone except for the rich appeared slightly shabby.

'*When you can find what you want, clothes are dreadfully expensive,*' he warned her. '*Plus we have all these restrictions.*'

She put up water for tea, decided to heat up a roll left over from yesterday: No butter in London, she thought wistfully, remembering the rich, creamy butter in Copenhagen. A dab of margarine. That would be quicker than making herself a dish of porridge – unappealing with powdered milk and no sugar.

While she ate, she considered what lay ahead of her this morning. She was to report to the room in an American government building where she would meet the American military man who was to be her pupil. For eight hours a day, six days a week for the next eight weeks she was to try to cram as much German as possible into the mind of this military man.

'*You'll be provided with a textbook, but you may deviate as you see fit. Don't concern yourself with the quality of his accent. It's comprehension that is of utmost importance.*' The colonel knew she had learned English and French from Papa – on a one-to-one basis.

It had been explained to her that she was not to discuss the assignment with anyone. It had something to do with

Allied security, she understood. It was like being part of the war effort, she told herself with a flicker of pride. *The Nazis must be defeated.* She knew vaguely of the war being fought in the Pacific – but that seemed too distant to visualize.

At 8:00 AM sharp – in her freshly pressed blue wool dress made for her by Margrethe Munch – Vera presented herself per instructions. The colonel who had interviewed her sat behind a desk. In a chair beside the desk sat a young man in what Vera guessed was an Air Force uniform. He rose quickly to his feet as the colonel made the introductions. Now, she reminded herself, she was Vera Miller – the English interpretation of Mueller.

He was polite, Vera thought, but Paul Kahn was shocked that his instructor was someone so young. She intercepted the colonel's smile of mild amusement.

'I'll leave you two to settle down to work,' the colonel said briskly. 'Take an hour's break for lunch – whenever you decide.'

Vera forced herself to focus on the task ahead, earnest about fulfilling her obligations. If she pleased the colonel, instinct told her she would find other assignments. But she was conscious every moment of the nearness of her handsome young student.

His name was Kahn. That was German or German-Jewish, wasn't it? She remembered Papa saying that Americans were not bi-lingual or multi-lingual like many Europeans. But how strange, she considered in a corner of her mind, that if his family had emigrated from Germany he had made no effort to learn the language.

For most of the morning, Vera and Paul concentrated with mutual determination on his introduction to the German language.

'I'm a little ahead of the game,' he chuckled at one point. 'I know about eight words of Yiddish – which is closely related to German.' *Did that mean he was Jewish?* 'I learned them from my grandfather.' He paused, his eyes bright with curiosity. 'I can't quite figure out what's your native language. Your English is terrific – and you wouldn't be here with me now if your German wasn't great. And the colonel says you're fluent in French –'

'I was born in Berlin,' she told him, all at once self-conscious. 'I managed to get out when I was thirteen. *Good* Germans helped me –' She saw the sudden compassion in his eyes. He was sensitive; he understood that she alone of her family had escaped. 'I was taken in by a family in Copenhagen, where I helped with the children. I'm sure you know what happened there.' She gestured eloquently. 'A wonderful Danish couple got me out of Denmark and to London.' She paused, fighting against recall. 'I've been here just a few days.'

'You've been through the mill,' he said gently and smiled at her blank glance. 'That means you know what the war is all about,' he interpreted. His face was taut now. 'I flew with the RAF on more missions than I want to remember. Then my luck ran out somewhere over Germany.' Her eyes clung to him. 'We managed to limp back to our base, but I spent weeks in the hospital. More weeks in a recuperation centre. I won't be flying again – my right arm isn't as good as it should be to handle a bomber.' He shrugged this off with an air of impatience. 'I was released by the RAF and signed up with the American forces. I'm on a special assignment now. Later I'll join my regular unit.' Vera knew they must not discuss this.

'We'd better get back to work.' All at once she was conscious of a special bond between Paul Kahn and herself. She felt less desperately alone in London. 'We'll be taking – how do you say it?' She fumbled for the right words. 'Taking a break for lunch soon.'

'We can go for lunch now. There's a great pub two

blocks over,' he said impulsively. 'Let me take you to lunch there.' His smile was ingratiating.

'Oh, but – but –' She was startled by his invitation.

'I'm bored to death alone in London. I don't know anybody here anymore. Take pity on me,' he coaxed. 'Colonel Brett won't mind.' He'd read her thoughts.

Vera and Paul left their 'classroom' and walked out into the crowded London street to the nearby pub. It was as though she had suddenly moved into an exciting new world, Vera thought with heady delight. Paul Kahn was so nice. *And he liked her.*

She'd known few young men in her life. None who was so warm and understanding, she decided. None with whom she could laugh as she was doing now. Since she was eight years old and Hitler came to power, a pall had hung over her life. She'd always known a sense of fear that had been elevated at times to terror. Paul had flown planes over Germany. He'd been shot down by Nazi guns. But he knew how to laugh.

The pub was busy, as Paul had warned it would be, but they found a table. He joshed about the red leather and chrome chairs, the chandelier that was reminiscent of another time and another place.

'I know you've only been in London a few days,' he said with a light, conspiratorial smile, 'but that's long enough to know that food in London in these times is limited.' He uttered a mocking sigh. 'The eggs are powdered and so's the milk. Forget about sugar or butter or fresh fruit – and oh those hard, grey rolls! But we survive.'

'In Copenhagen, we survived,' Vera conceded, 'though much food was shipped out of Denmark to Germany.'

'Thank God, bread isn't rationed – but, of course, there's that constant reminder that we should eat potatoes instead of bread. Everybody in London claims to have lost weight in the course of the war – but they all admit that's healthy.'

Vera was relieved when Paul suggested he order for them. '*I know all the pitfalls.*'

In truth, she hardly tasted the food when it was served. She was mesmerized by Paul's ebullient conversation, his high-spirited teasing. Back in the room where they'd worked together, he'd seemed charming but so serious. This new mood was ingratiating, contagious.

'Do you know how long we've been here?' she asked in astonishment as they dawdled over their custard and tea. 'We must get back to work!'

'So I'm dealing with a slavedriver,' he drawled. 'For that, you have to go with me to the theatre tonight.' Her eyes widened in astonishment. 'We'll go straight from the classroom to queue up. Because of the blackout, curtains have to come down by 8:00 PM. Then we'll go out for dinner,' he plotted in high spirits. 'But I promise you'll be home by ten o'clock. London's night life is on a weird schedule these days.'

'But I – I can't let you –' How did she explain that she couldn't permit him to spend so much money on her?

'I've got all that back pay piled up! Somebody has to help me spend it.' *He'd understood her reluctance, she thought tenderly.* 'We've got eight weeks of intensive work together. So let's have a little fun with it, too. It's your patriotic duty,' he said with a flourish. 'Help entertain a member of the Allied forces.'

They returned to the office – both determined not to shun their obligations. Promptly at five, they left to join another of the endless queues that were part of London wartime life. Paul had decided they would see a Shaw play, 'The Doctor's Dilemma.' For an instant Vera was caught up in anguished recall. *Mama's favourite play.*

In Berlin – before Hitler – her family had attended the theatre often. Though she was a little girl, she had gone with them because Papa considered this part of her education. In the Copenhagen years, there had been no such diversion. They'd lived under a constant cloud – presumably safe yet ever humiliated by the Danish defeat. It amazed her that here in London – where the people had suffered so from the bombings – life went on as usual, though with an amended timetable.

In the queue at the theatre, they exchanged lighthearted conversation with the young couple ahead of them.

'Night life in London isn't dead,' Paul pointed out, an arm about her waist as the queue advanced.

Yesterday, Vera recalled, she had gazed into shop windows that displayed elegant jewellery. She'd walked through the aisles of the fine department stores. Here and there a shop-window sign announced some shortage. But life these last months – with few bombs falling now, Paul said, seemed almost normal. Even the children were being brought back to London.

The stage performance was superb, Vera thought, exhilarated by the small adventure. But how strange to be leaving the theatre at 8:00 PM! They found a nearby restaurant – where the waiters knew Paul from earlier leaves – and ate amazingly well in the face of the shortages and restrictions. But best of all about this evening, Vera told herself with awe, was that Paul had brought laughter back into her life.

It was as though in the rush of London they lived in a private world of their own, Vera thought at the end of their first week of daytime study and evening play. Observers of that other world around them – isolated from that world by a kind of magic. For eight hours they were teacher and student – both dedicated to the job at hand. For the next four or five hours Paul showed her London, which he clearly loved. From 7:00 AM to 8:00 AM Vera understood he was receiving technical instruction that had to do with his mission.

They strolled along Piccadilly and through Leicester Square – both populated day and night by young men and women in uniform. Young people in search of romance. They visited Trafalgar Square, remarkably unscathed, with Lord Nelson still atop his column and the National Gallery still open to the public, though its priceless masterpieces were hidden away in bomb-proof safety. They saw the serious damage meted out to Westminster Abbey and the House of Commons, where its members had met for almost a century. Big Ben had been hit in a heavy raid two years earlier but continued to tick.

On their seventh evening together, Paul began to talk about his father and his sister Doris. His mother, Vera understood, had died when he was six.

'Eastwood's a tiny little town in upstate New York. My great-great-grandfather emigrated from Germany in the early 1800s. I know,' he joshed, 'in Europe that's being newcomers.'

'I don't understand.' Vera was apologetic. 'If your family came from Germany, how is it you don't know the language?'

Paul chuckled. 'When immigrants from Europe arrived in the US, they were consumed by a desire to be full Americans. Their first priority was learning to speak English. From toddlers to grandparents, they flooded the classrooms so they could speak like other Americans.'

'Yes.' Vera's eyes glowed. 'This I can understand.'

'My great-great-grandfather looked around for a good place to practise his trade and raise a family. He settled in Eastwood and opened up a gunsmith shop. It's been the family business ever since. It was tough during the

Depression years. Dad had to fight to hang on. But once war broke out, the business took off. Dad's the major employer in Eastwood now.'

'An important business,' Vera said respectfully.

'Doris says he's working sixteen hours a day, always fighting to fill orders. He's so proud of being part of the war effort.' He paused, squinted in thought. 'I think we first became truly conscious that we were Jews after *Kristallnacht*.'

So he was Jewish.

'We knew five years earlier.' Vera was sombre. 'All of a sudden we weren't Germans. We were Jews – the enemy.'

'Everybody back home has always thought of the United States as the great "melting pot." Generations of foreigners poured into the country and became *Americans*. Why should ethnic roots divide us now? But to some people back home, Americans of German descent, of Italian descent, of Japanese descent are suddenly enemies.'

'I don't understand these things,' Vera said. 'My father would have understood. When he could have gotten out of Germany, he stayed – to help provide education for Jewish children who couldn't go to the Berlin schools. To him, education was so very important.'

'Enough of serious talk,' Paul ordered and reached for her hand. 'Let's go for a walk along the Thames Embankment. On a moonlit night like this, the river is magnificent.'

They strolled in silence, enjoying the spectacle of moonlight upon the Thames. And when they paused, it seemed only right that Paul should draw her into his arms and kiss her. A soft delicate touching that sent her heart into chaotic racing. And then his mouth released hers and she felt the warm closeness of him moving away.

'Let's find a place where we can have a cup of tea and a piece of cake, and then I'll walk you home,' he said gently.

Chapter Four

In the days ahead, Vera waited wistfully for Paul to take her into his arms again. Those few moments when he'd held her, kissed her, lingered in her mind in exquisite recall. Her last thoughts before drifting off to sleep each night, the first on awakening each morning.

Was he sorry that he had kissed her? Was there a girl back in that town he called Eastwood whom he loved? *Had she disappointed him*? But she knew she loved Paul Kahn with a love that would be eternal. She hadn't expected it to happen. She wasn't ready for it to happen. But she understood that in a handful of days her whole life had changed yet again.

When they were together now, it was as though those moments in the moonlight along the Thames Embankment had never existed. They shared a warm camaraderie – nothing more. But she longed for so much more.

They spent exhausting hours working on his comprehension of German. They played after hours just as determinedly. On Sundays – supposedly their day away from the improvised classroom – they were together for hours that included her ordered conversations in German.

Italy had declared war on Germany. 'Three years late,' Paul declared. She'd hoped – naively, Paul chided – that this meant the war would soon be over.

'We have far to go yet,' he told her tenderly. 'But now we're on the offensive.'

She had no conception of what Paul's special assignment was about, yet she was convinced it was very dangerous. Once it was over, he'd confided, he would join the Army Air Force unit to which he was now officially attached. Secretly she was relieved that his flying days were over.

At the beginning of their third week of working together, Vera spent a half hour in earnest conversation with Colonel Brett. She was appalled that he was having afterthoughts about her ability to provide Paul with the knowledge of German he required.

'Perhaps we should split the day with someone more trained in rapid instruction,' the colonel said uneasily.

'It would be unproductive to divide Paul's teaching that way,' Vera objected, quoting her father's words in a similar situation. 'Paul doesn't need perfect grammar – he needs comprehension.' Now she quoted the colonel himself. 'We work so well together,' she finished lamely, all at once aware that the colonel suspected some romantic involvement and was disturbed by this.

Vera returned to their improvised classroom and told Paul it was his turn to confer with Colonel Brett.

'He's worried that I can't teach you enough,' she explained, her eyes desolate. 'He talked about your working with me in the mornings and with somebody else in the afternoons.'

'Nobody can do better than you,' he said, his face taut. 'I'll make Colonel Brett understand that.'

He stalked out of the room, returned fifteen minutes later with a complacent grin.

'Nothing's changed,' he reported and reached for her hand. 'We're in this together, baby.'

But something had changed, Vera realized. She felt a soaring protectiveness in him. His eyes told her what he had not put into words. It was difficult to focus on their work. *Paul returned the love she felt for him.*

The morning had been unseasonably cold, depressingly

grey. By the time Vera and Paul left the office for the day and ventured out into the street, an icy rain had begun to fall. Paul reached for her arm.

'We'll never find a taxi at this hour in this weather. And we'll be sopping wet if we wait for a bus.' He hesitated. 'My place is close by,' he reminded. Her heart began to pound. 'We could make dinner there. I keep a few tins for emergencies.' His eyes pleaded for agreement.

She hesitated for a second. 'All right.' Nothing was going to happen.

Paul's smile was dazzling. He reached for her hand as the rain assaulted them. 'Let's make a dash for it.'

Paul's flat was small but larger than hers. A tiny sitting room and another room – his bedroom, she guessed – right off it. In a corner of the sitting room was a makeshift kitchenette.

'Let me take your coat – it's dripping wet,' he said solicitously. 'And your shoes are sopping. Kick them off.'

They made a small ceremony of hanging away her coat and depositing it along with her wet shoes in the bathroom. Paul reached into a closet for a flannel shirt and held it for her.

'Not your size but it'll keep you warm.' He glanced down at her wet stockings. 'Take those off and hang them up to dry.' He prodded her into the bathroom and turned away to remove his own wet socks.

'I hope they dry,' she said with shaky humour. But she was conscious of a delicious exhilaration at being here this way with Paul.

'God, I hate this ruling against central heating!' He grimaced. 'Back home, oil is rationed, I gather, but there's enough to keep the house fairly warm during waking hours.'

He was talking compulsively, she thought, to make her feel at ease.

‘It’s good to be inside.’ In bare feet, Paul’s shirt lending welcome warmth, she gazed out the small window that looked out upon the street. ‘What a dreary day.’

‘I’ll put up a pot of tea,’ he said, ‘then we’ll make dinner.’ He was at the tiny two-burner gas range, reaching for the kettle. ‘Nothing fancy,’ he warned. ‘Dad and Doris keep me supplied with American salamis and cookies. And everybody in England keeps a supply of potatoes.’

They warmed themselves with strong Earl Grey tea, then began to prepare dinner. Together they peeled potatoes for boiling. When the potatoes were almost ready, Paul decreed, he’d make salami omelets. For now, the potatoes cooked gently on a gas burner.

‘The salami is great – it kills the lousy taste of the powdered eggs. And we’ll sauté the potatoes with some onion. Because I’m out of margarine,’ he conceded humorously.

Despite the chill in the tiny flat, the atmosphere was festive. Paul flipped on what he called the *radio* and which to Vera was the *wireless* and – courtesy of the BBC – the strains of a Brandenburg Concerto filled the room.

‘Your feet are like ice,’ Paul scolded as he reached down to touch one. ‘Let me get you a pair of my socks.’

‘Paul, no.’ She choked with laughter. She’d look ridiculous wearing a pair of Paul’s socks.

‘Vera, yes,’ he ordered. ‘I won’t have you catching cold.’ All at once the atmosphere was electric. ‘You’re very precious to me, you know.’ He reached for her hand, pulled her close. ‘I’ve never felt this way about anyone. I sit there in that classroom every day, and all I want to do is hold you in my arms. I walk with you in the street, and I want to hold you close.’

‘Paul, we shouldn’t,’ she said unsteadily. *Mama would be shocked.*

'Why not?' he challenged. 'All we truly have in this world is today. Vera, I love you so much –'

'I love you,' she whispered. Paul was right. How did they know they'd be alive tomorrow? She'd tried not to think about where Paul would be sent in a few short weeks. She never truly forgot that a bomb could fall from the sky and kill them any night.

His mouth was warm and sweet, then passionate on hers, his hands evoking feelings she'd regarded earlier with alarm. But how could this be wrong when they loved each other so deeply?

The chill in the tiny flat was forgotten as she moved with him. She thought not about tomorrow or next week or next year. Only about *now*.

Each day became doubly precious because once gone it could not be retrieved. She gave up her bed-sitter to move into Paul's flat because he was arranging for her to take it over when he must leave. He worried about her finances. She wasn't sure when she would acquire another tutoring or translation job. And he insisted they be married as soon as possible.

'You'll be the wife of an American soldier,' he explained. 'You'll receive an allotment cheque every month. I'll feel better knowing you have that security.'

They were married on a fog-drenched Sunday morning by an Army Air Force rabbi and spent their first night as husband and wife in a suite at the unscarred Ritz. They knew they might have to cram a lifetime into these short weeks. Vera understood she was not to question Paul about his secret assignment. She was sure he would write when he could. The assignment would be brief, he hoped. Then he would join the unit to which he had been assigned.

With reluctance they left the Ritz the following morning, yearning to prolong the pleasure of the night, and stopped at a Lyons Corner House for breakfast.

'Breakfast in London is always the worst meal of the day,' Paul said with wry humour. Vera was always touched by the way he insisted on carrying their trays himself. So often she saw women performing this chore for themselves and their men.

'I won't notice this morning,' Vera said, her smile dazzling. It was still unreal that she was Paul's wife – but she had the paper attesting to this in her purse. She wouldn't let herself think about how little time they had left together – for now.

'You'll love breakfast back home,' Paul mused as they settled down to eat. 'On weekends it's always pancakes with real maple syrup. And *real* coffee. Nobody in London knows how to make coffee.'

'Will your father and sister be upset that you've married somebody who's not an American?' she asked, anxious now. Paul had said they would wait until the war was over to tell his father and sister.

'They'll love you,' Paul promised. 'Dad's always been afraid I'd marry out of our faith. There are only two other Jewish families in Eastwood – and not a girl anywhere near my age among them. Doris married a few months ago – her husband was born and raised in Palestine, became a parachutist for the British military. He had a bad injury and was sent to New York on some diplomatic mission. He decided to stay there. That's where he met Doris. He's working for Dad now. If you listen to Dad, Wayne's the greatest thing since the invention of the wheel.' *But would Paul's father approve of her?*

The days were rushing past. Paul was convinced that soon there would be an Allied invasion of Europe – what he called 'the beginning of the end.' But Vera tried not to look beyond each day. With Paul she felt reborn. So many times she'd asked herself why she had survived when Mama and Papa and Ernst had died. But now she had a reason to live. She had Paul.

She tried not to show her fears as the last week of Paul's tutoring arrived. At his insistence, she had gone to the British diplomat who had acquired this assignment for her and was told that additional work as a translator would be available shortly. While London seemed safer now than at any time since the beginning of the war, she could never thrust aside the fear that one day the Nazis would invade London.

'I'm going to be so afraid while you're gone,' she confessed to Paul as she lay in his arms in their blacked-out flat on his last night in London. For the past week – in addition to their arduous sessions – Paul had been in conference with Colonel Brett and a team preparing him for other aspects of his assignment. 'I wish I had a gun to keep beneath my pillow,' she said with childish ferocity.

'Vera, you'll be safe. There'll never be a land invasion by the Nazis,' he soothed. 'We've reached the turning point in the war. The Allies will soon be on the attack in Western Europe, everybody's expecting that.'

'When?' she whispered.

'Baby, only the big wheels know when that'll come. But we're moving towards the end of the war.' She knew he was trying to be optimistic for her sake.

'I'm going to miss you so much.'

'I'll miss you, too,' he soothed.

When would she see Paul again? He'd warned her it could be months. '*When you hear that Paris has been liberated, then expect a letter from me soon.*'

They made love with a special urgency tonight – each conscious that there would be a long interval before they could be together this way again. Exhausted, they fell asleep in each other's arms, awoke to feel the stirring of fresh young passion.

The early morning was grey and cold. Paul insisted that Vera remain in bed while he made breakfast for them.

'Damn this lack of central heating,' he swore yet again as he brought scrambled eggs spiked with cheddar cheese to disguise their powdered taste, burnt-at-the-edge toast, and tall cups of tea to the tiny dining table. 'Now you can come,' he decreed.

The atmosphere was heavy with their anguish at imminent separation, though each strove to mask this.

'Now that I'm going to war again, it's sure to be over soon,' Paul drawled. 'And in Paris I'll buy you a giant bottle of perfume and one for Doris.' He hadn't said so in words, but she knew he would be dropped over occupied France. Though he'd never told her, she suspected his early morning training had to do with radio communications. 'And before we go home to Eastwood, I'll show you New York.' She heard the nostalgia in his voice. 'I'll take you up to the Columbia campus and show you where I lived for two years.'

'Paul, be careful,' she whispered. 'Remember, I'll be back here waiting for you –'

Vera didn't leave their flat for the next forty-eight hours – when her new job as translator would begin. She clung to the memory of Paul's presence here. The scent of his shaving cream – his ultimate wartime luxury here in London, he'd joshed – evoked tender memories of her standing by in the minuscule bathroom while he shaved. She was Paul's wife, and he was coming back to her.

On the new job she met a high-spirited London girl married to a Canadian Air Force sergeant. Almost immediately she and Iris were drawn together.

'Hank says his folks back home just can't understand

how we survive in the blackouts. And he's forever writing me to stay at home at night because God knows what can happen to a girl out there alone in a blackout.'

Iris had a brother fighting somewhere in Italy. Her widowed mother and sister-in-law lived in a small town in northern England. Iris had been working in London for three years.

Iris had married her Canadian sergeant early in the year. All she knew of his whereabouts now was that he was part of the aircrews that had been wreaking havoc on Germany. Mail arrived intermittently. Iris refused to allow herself to be afraid. Hank was coming home to her, and that was it.

Vera was grateful for Iris's presence in her life. Iris helped alleviate her towering loneliness. The British were wonderful, she thought recurrently. They'd been through so much, yet accepted it all with such calm.

She was touched when Iris insisted she come to her flat for dinner on the approaching New Year's Eve.

'And you'll sleep over,' Iris said firmly. 'It's taking your life in your hands to walk around in the blackout.' With Paul she'd never worried, Vera remembered wistfully – though most people were uneasy about the freakish accidents that kept occurring on nights when not even a sliver of moonlight lightened the streets.

The two girls were determined to make New Year's Eve a festive occasion. The moment they walked into the flat Iris flipped on the wireless, and music filled the room.

'I have a tin of baked beans to go with the sausage – such as it is.' She grimaced apologetically. 'Mostly flour and what else, let's just don't speculate. And I'll make a quick custard to go with our tea.'

'Let me help,' Vera said and paused to cover a yawn.

'You are the sleepiest one,' Iris scolded good-humouredly. 'Anybody would think you were pregnant –' She stopped dead as Vera gasped in sudden comprehension. 'Oh God, are you?'

'I lost track of time.' Vera was pale, her eyes a mixture of shock and glorious discovery. 'Iris, I may be.'

'That's wonderful!' Iris's smile was dazzling. 'I was dying to get pregnant before Hank's squadron was moved too far for him to get into London even for a day. But he was always so damn careful.'

'Paul was careful, too.' Alarm closed in about her. Would Paul be angry?

'They've got this crazy idea we're delicate little flowers,' Iris said, reading her mind. 'They worry about us, love. But you'll be fine. You see all the prams out on the streets again. The Nazis are too busy trying to save their own hides to drop bombs on us. And you're the wife of a fighting man – you'll get all the medical care you need. Vera, I think it's wonderful,' she repeated.

Later – on Iris's sofa beneath a mound of frayed blankets topped by her winter coat – Vera lay sleepless far into the night, enveloped in wonder that from the love she had shared with Paul had come this child within her. Tears of joy stung her eyes. Oh, she wished Paul could know! Where was he now? And all at once joy was joined by fear.

Please God, let Paul come home to them.

Chapter Five

Vera had known that Paul's absence from her life would be agonizing. It seemed doubly so now that she realized she was carrying their baby – and at the same time she found sweet solace in this new knowledge. Rumours persisted in the weeks and months ahead that the war could not last much longer . . . that there was to be an Allied invasion of Europe.

Vera was in the last weeks of her pregnancy – with not one word yet from Paul – when the news that Allied forces had landed on the coast of Normandy flashed around the world. It was D-Day – June 6, 1944. Early in the morning, Vera – like other London insomniacs – had heard the clamour of endless bombers taking off. Later she was to hear Edward R. Murrow describe this as 'the sound of a giant factory in the sky.' Later still, they were to learn that 11,000 planes had taken part in the first day of the invasion.

It was only a matter of weeks now before Paris would be liberated, Vera told herself with exhilaration. She would hear from Paul. But again – as at recurrent intervals during the past months – she asked herself if Paul were regretting their hasty marriage. Was he sorry he'd married her? Would he be upset about the baby? Would he feel he was too young to be tied down to a wife and child? She was impatient to hear from Paul – yet fearful.

Six days after D-Day, Hitler launched fresh vengeance on London.

'This wasn't supposed to happen!' Iris wailed to Vera. 'We're supposed to be winning the war!'

'Our planes will find their launching pads,' Vera said with a confidence she didn't feel. For the past six weeks she'd been working at home on translations. Iris was her conduit with the office. 'They'll destroy them.'

'I'm moving in with you till the baby's born,' Iris said firmly. 'You're not staying alone with all those things flying over our rooftops.'

The new buzz bombs became a way of life. A hundred a day fell over the city. Many Londoners declared these deadly robots harder to endure than the blitz. All at once, the British reserve seemed to disappear. Total strangers exchanged conversation about 'those pesky things making life miserable for us.' And with typical British calm and humour, they adapted. There were sirens punctuating the air day and night because radar detected their approach over the Channel. Independent warning systems were set up in public places, stores, large offices. The warning systems were geared to go off only when a bomb was almost overhead – to allow life to go on normally as long as possible.

Vera and Iris abandoned the cherished weekly visit to their neighbourhood restaurant because of its skylight and mirrors. Broken glass caused frequent injuries. Queuing up – a necessary part of life these days – was a time of anxiety for Vera, though most Londoners seemed to show a remarkable lack of unease.

'People are too nonchalant about the buzz bombs,' Vera said worriedly.

Only a handful of cinemas and theatres remained open, though the restaurants continued to serve the usual number of patrons.

'People want to eat,' Iris pointed out.

Like most Londoners – those who didn't go to the

shelters – Vera and Iris remained at home in the evenings. As the havoc continued, mothers and children were urged to leave the city. Churchill warned that conditions could become worse before they became better. Iris tried to persuade Vera to leave, but she refused.

'I'm not letting the *doodlebugs* drive me away,' Vera insisted, even while she was terrified for the baby's safety. 'I have to be here when Paul writes me.' She was terrified of the prospect of missing contact with him. And – again – she was tormented by nightmares, awakening in a cold sweat. Remembering *Kristallnacht*.

Late in July – with enemy raiders overhead – Vera gave birth after a lengthy labour to a daughter and named her Laurie Anne Kahn. At Iris's urging Lisl – her maternal grandmother's name – had been Americanized to Laurie. Anne had been her paternal grandmother's name.

'Isn't she beautiful?' Vera asked when Iris came into the hospital ward after seeing tiny Laurie, with her incredible mass of burnished gold hair and dainty features. 'Do you think Paul will love her?' Her voice was wistful. She still harboured fearful doubts that Paul might be overwhelmed by the new responsibility of fatherhood.

'He'll adore her,' Iris prophesied. 'I can just imagine his feelings when he gets the word.'

Again early in August Iris tried to persuade Vera to take Laurie and leave London. Most outlying areas were happy to receive evacuees.

'My head tells me to go,' Vera admitted, 'but my heart says *no*. I must be here when Paul writes me.' She refused to consider that he wouldn't – or couldn't.

Now British morale was lifted by rumours of dissension in Germany. On July 29, an attempt was made to assassinate Hitler. Word filtered through that many Germans were prepared to admit defeat. Still, the Nazi forces continued to fight doggedly.

As always, Vera worried about the Schmidts. Berlin had been under such intense bombing. *Were they all right*? And the Munches in Copenhagen? What was happening to them?

Vera and Iris were devoted listeners to the BBC reports of the fighting in France. Then at last – on August 25 – word came through that the suburbs of Paris had been liberated. The following day Allied troops entered the city. Paul had promised, '*You'll hear from me soon after the Nazis are driven out of Paris*.'

'Iris, I can't believe it! Paris is free!' Vera greeted Iris on her return from work on Saturday afternoon. Though Iris kept up her own apartment for the day that Hank would return, she continued to stay with Vera.

'Everybody is so excited!' Iris hugged Vera exuberantly.

But Vera sensed a wariness in Iris. Because she, too, worried about Paul's welfare. *Was he all right*? His special assignment was dangerous. And only after Paris was free was he to assume regular duties.

'How's my precious little love?' Without waiting for a reply, Iris sauntered into the bedroom, where Laurie lay in her crib. 'Oh, I woke her,' Iris reproached herself as a plaintive cry filled the air.

A week after the liberation of Paris – a week of painful waiting – Vera received her first letter from Paul. Her heart pounding, she gazed in wondrous excitement at the small, tight handwriting on the envelope. Paul's handwriting, Paul's APO number. *He was all right*. In tumultuous impatience she ripped open the envelope, began to read. He was fine, he insisted – though he admitted he'd experienced some difficult moments.

'*Everyone is sure the war in Europe will be over soon – but it can't be soon enough for me. I can't wait to hold you in my arms again, and we can begin to live normal lives*.'

Vera read and reread Paul's letter – segments cut out by a censor. He was safe. He still loved her. And now she must write and tell him about his very young daughter. Though it was difficult to come by, Iris had acquired – in anticipation of this moment – a roll of film, along with a borrowed camera. Too impatient to wait for the film to be developed, Vera wrote Paul the day she received his letter and promised that a snapshot of Laurie would follow soon. Yet her pleasure at hearing from him was invaded at intervals with fear of his reaction to fatherhood.

But the swift conclusion to the war in Europe that so many yearned to see eluded the Allied troops. Though American and British bombers were devastating German cities, the Allies still couldn't penetrate German borders by land.

How many more must die before it was over? Vera asked herself in recurrent terror.

Paul was grateful for thc small luxury of being billeted in a modest hotel in liberated Paris while he was to pursue a new post with an intelligence unit located in a nearby building. After witnessing the destruction in London, he was astonished by the well-being of Paris – saved by surrender.

He was shocked that Paris showed so few signs of having been a captive city. The woman appeared well-dressed – with none of the rationing limitations imposed on British and American women. The French textile industry had prospered, he learned. The French had devised television sets and transmitters. In an odd fashion, the French experience irked him.

He was distraught over the reports from London about the daily barrage of buzz bombs hitting the city – following a path across Kent, Sussex, and Surrey on their way to London. During the period between June 17 and the end of last month – August – 5,479 people were killed. Another 15,934 were injured, most of them women and children. He had tried – futilely – to have someone check on Vera in London. He admitted it was too much to ask in these chaotic times.

Arriving at his desk this morning, Paul hoped anxiously for word from Vera. So often in these last months he'd asked himself if he had made a terrible mistake in tearing off on a dangerous mission that meant leaving Vera – so young and vulnerable and scared – alone in London. He'd been so optimistic that this mission would be over in a matter of weeks rather than nine frustrating months. But he'd made the commitment before they even met. Now it was hard to realize there was a time she wasn't part of his life.

Paul glanced up with a surge of anticipation when a corporal appeared with a handful of mail.

'Come and get it,' the corporal called out ebulliently, and every man in the sprawling office area rose from his desk with a matching alacrity.

His pulse racing, Paul reached out for the pair of envelopes the corporal extended in his direction. He guessed the V-Mail – which arrived with such speed – would be from his father. The other was unmistakably Vera's handwriting. She was all right, he told himself with a surge of relief. Eagerly he ripped open the envelope, began to read.

'*My darling, it was so wonderful to receive your letter. I have news that will be a shock to you – but I hope a wonderful shock. We have a daughter who is seven weeks old today. Her name is Laurie Anne.*'

'Oh my God!' His head reeling Paul read on. 'Oh my God!'

'What? What?' The young major at the desk across

from his own – philosophical at not receiving mail this morning – swung around to face him.

'I have a kid – a daughter!' *And Vera went through it all alone.* 'When I left London, we didn't even know she was pregnant!' He tried to visualize this tiny miracle that was their daughter. Laurie Anne – Anne for his mother, he thought tenderly.

'Hey, put in for leave,' the major urged. 'With your background, you rate it.'

'I'll never get it.' Paul was sceptical, even while the prospect was exhilarating.

'Try,' the major ordered.

On September 8, 1944 the London blackout was lifted after 1,843 nights of darkness – but not for long. On that same night, the first of a series of blasts hit London. They were reported in official communiques as gas-main explosions, but Londoners quickly understood this was a censorship ploy. Hitler had unleashed a devastating new weapon. The terrifying aspect of this latest Nazi menace – arriving just as the doodlebugs had been eliminated by Allied destruction of their launching pads – was that they landed with no warning. They could be neither seen nor heard – until one hit with the force of a minor earthquake.

Vera emerged from her flat each day with trepidation – never knowing where one of these new rockets had landed since she had last been outdoors, what huge crater would meet her eyes. Knowing what was happening in London, Paul wrote and pleaded with her to leave the city.

'Remember, you have money in the bank to see you through in addition to your allotment cheques. I worry every minute about you and the baby.'

Paul wrote about trying through special channels to have her go to stay with his father in Eastwood, but the prospect of putting an ocean between Paul and herself was too alarming. While she cherished his eagerness to see them safe – and in her mind she knew this would be the prudent measure to take, she couldn't accept it. How could they know, she tried to reason, that the ship wouldn't be bombed on the way to the United States? And she clung to the conviction that since she had survived so much in her brief lifetime, she would survive this, too. Londoners called the new missiles *Bob Hopes* – 'You bob down and hope for the best.'

For weeks Londoners tried to convince themselves that the war was almost over, but the continued assault of what were now labelled V-2 bombs splintered that hope – despite the fact that American troops had crossed the border and entered Germany itself. Then, late in October, Vera opened the door to the flat – expecting to see Iris there with her usual remorseful explanation that she had forgotten her key.

'Baby! Oh, baby, how I've missed you!' Paul hovered in the doorway, his face luminous as he reached for her.

'Paul!' She gazed at him in a mixture of disbelief and wonder. 'You're really here!' She moved back to inspect his face as they swayed together.

'Just for a five-day leave,' he cautioned. 'Then it's back to my unit. Now, introduce me to my daughter –'

Vera stood beside the crib while Paul scooped up Laurie and held her in his arms. Tears blurred her eyes at the infinite tenderness she felt in him as he inspected Laurie's minute features.

'She looks just like you,' he decided, pleased with this discovery. 'The same gorgeous hair, the same blue eyes.'

'All babies have blue eyes until they're about three months,' Vera said, her own eyes lit with laughter. 'Will you disown her if her eyes turn out to be brown or green or grey?'

'Vera, there are no words to tell you how much I love her,' he said softly. 'I wrote Dad and Doris. I'm sure they're out of their minds with excitement.'

'They'll love her, too?' She needed this assurance. They would be Laurie's only family other than herself and Paul.

They started at the sound of the door to the flat opening.

'Vera, you forgot to lock the door,' Iris called out. 'You thought I'd forgot my key again –' She stopped dead at the tableau that met her eyes. 'Welcome home,' she told Paul with infinite warmth. They'd never met, Vera realized, but who else could he be? 'I'll pick up a few things and head for my flat.'

'He'll just be here for five days,' Vera explained, her head on Paul's shoulder, her eyes shining.

'Enjoy every minute of them,' Iris ordered, her smile sympathetic. 'I know when three's a crowd. Four,' she corrected herself. 'And may there be no Bob Hopes for the next five days.'

Chapter Six

Vera fought against despair as the war in Europe refused to come to a halt. In mid-December, Germany launched a savage offensive in the Ardennes Forest, soon labelled the Battle of the Bulge because of the shape of the battleground on an army map. The battle took a heavy toll on German forces – almost 100,000 casualties plus another 110,000 taken prisoners.

'This has to end soon, love.' Iris comforted Vera at regular intervals as Vera comforted her in other moments. 'Hank keeps writing that we're just around the corner to peace.'

But it wasn't until May 7, 1945, that Germany surrendered unconditionally to the Allies. The following day, the world learned that formal papers had been signed at General Eisenhower's headquarters at Rheims. Simultaneously – in London, Washington, and Moscow – Churchill, Truman, and Stalin announced on the radio that May 8, 1945, was V-E Day. The end of the war in Europe.

Vera knew nothing until Iris – leaving work in the sudden wild celebration that gripped London – came rushing into the flat. The wireless was off so as not to disturb Laurie, napping in her crib.

'Haven't you heard?' Iris grabbed Vera and spun her about the room. 'The war's over in Europe! It's over!'

'Iris, you're sure?' Vera veered between exultation and scepticism.

'I'm sure, I'm sure!' Iris was euphoric. 'Hank and Paul are coming home!' She released Vera and rushed to open a window. 'Listen to the crowds pouring out into the streets,' she ordered exuberantly.

Vera heard the sound of singing in the streets – groups and individuals, all caught up in the magic of the moment. The sounds of 'Roll Out the Barrel' suddenly erupted in the hallway and awakened Laurie.

Vera darted into the bedroom and scooped her up from the crib. 'Laurie, your Daddy's coming home!'

Caught up in the excitement of the occasion, Vera and Iris left the flat with Laurie – who, without comprehending, seemed to understand that this was a time of supreme celebration. The atmosphere in the crowded streets reflected the joy – the relief – that at last men and women in uniform would be coming home . . . those who had fought in the European theatre of war – the Allies still fought the Japanese in the Pacific, Vera forced herself to recognize. And underneath the joy, Vera was conscious of a poignant sadness, too – because so many were not alive to share in this day. The war had not been officially declared when Mama and Papa and Ernst died, Vera thought in painful recall – but they, too, were war casualties.

Vera waited impatiently for word from Paul. Five days later, he appeared at the door to the flat.

'I'm on a six-week furlough,' he announced ebulliently as he pulled her into his arms, then laughed at her bewildered stare.

'Furlough?' she asked.

'Honey, we'll be shipped out to the Pacific after furloughs back home. I went through all kinds of red tape to have my furlough here in London. I'll travel to the States with another unit.'

'You'll have to go to the Pacific?' She was cold with shock. 'Paul, you've had enough of fighting!'

'It won't last long over there,' he promised. 'A few weeks – maybe a few months.' *But in a few months – even in a day – he could be killed*, she thought in terror. 'Honey, we're almost out of the woods.'

The weeks of Paul's furlough flew past. He was enthralled with Laurie, sent a flood of snapshots home to his father and Doris. Vera revelled in the admiring smiles that Paul – now a major – garnered from passing Londoners when they took Laurie for outings in Kensington Gardens and Regent's Park. He glowed with pride when Vera showed him the white, asbestos-roofed temporary houses that 3,000 US Army soldiers – assigned by General Eisenhower – had built to give shelter to some of the families made homeless by bombs.

'Nobody could believe how fast they went up,' Vera told Paul. 'Each one has two bedrooms, a bath, and a living-dining-kitchenette area.'

'They look like igloos,' Paul said, chuckling. But his eyes showed his pleasure that Americans had made this possible.

Each night Vera and Paul closed the door to the bedroom when Laurie was asleep in her crib and made passionate love. It was as though, Vera thought as she lay in Paul's arms on the small, cramped sofa, they were trying to make up for the long, empty nights of separation. And afterwards they talked in muted tones far into the night.

'Dad's going to be upset that I don't want to go back for my engineering degree,' he confided sombrely. 'He figured I'd work as an engineer for a while, then come in and take over the business later.' He frowned in distaste. 'I don't want any part of dealing with guns.' He smiled wryly. 'I know – that's a weird thing for a soldier to say.

I could handle it because I knew this was a war that had to be fought. But guns kill.'

'Guns don't kill,' Vera objected gently. 'People kill.' Instantly she regretted this remark. She knew how Paul's mother had died. He'd never truly forgiven his father for that awful accident, she remembered compassionately.

'For four generations, the men in my family have been gun-smiths. My great-great-grandfather, great-grandfather, my grandfather, and my father. Dad looks upon guns with such reverence. He knows everything there is to know about them. To him a fine gun is a work of art. I don't share that feeling. To me a gun is an instrument of death.'

'Sssh,' Vera said gently. 'In the hands of our fighting men, they've saved lives.'

'The company did well in the First World War, but this time Dad was able to expand beyond his wildest dreams. In a few years, he's become a rich man. By Eastwood standards,' he amended. '*Because of the war.*'

'Paul, he performed a service for his country,' Vera said. 'You've told me how hard he's worked – and that was part of winning the war.' In a corner of her mind she recalled the traumatic moment in the fishing village near Copenhagen when a harbour policeman had threatened her escape to safety. Except for the guns in the hands of those two Resistance workers, she might be dead.

'Vera, I know now what I want to do with my life. It's not romantic and exciting, but it's what I want to do. I'll go back to college for a teaching degree. Hopefully go on to a PhD in education so I can teach at a college level.'

'If that's what you want, then do it.' She felt a fierce determination to see Paul pursue this new dream.

'We've fought two awful wars already in this century,' he said, a messianic glow in his eyes. 'If this world is to see lasting peace, we're going to have to educate the people. They have to learn to think for themselves . . . to be able to listen to a maniac like Hitler and understand his twisted mind.'

'You talk like my father.' Tears welled in her eyes. Papa had stayed in Berlin because he thought it was so important to be there to teach. Oh yes! She could understand what Paul was telling her.

'I won't make a lot of money,' he warned. 'But we'll be comfortable.'

'You'll be happy,' she said with conviction. '*We'll* be happy.'

'It'll be rough at first.' He squinted in contemplation. 'I'll go back to school under the GI Bill. We won't have much money.'

'I can work, too,' she said eagerly. 'At home. Tutoring or doing translations. I'll work.' Her smile was dazzling. 'We'll manage.'

In late July, Paul joined his assigned unit for the trip back to the States. Vera tried to convince herself that very soon she and Laurie would follow him. The US government was already making plans to transport GI brides and children to the United States to join their husbands when the war in the Pacific was over. Paul wrote that he was stationed in Texas. He expected to be transferred soon to the Pacific. But that was not to be.

On September 2, 1945 Japanese surrender ceremonies took place. The war was over. Impatient to have Vera and Laurie with him, Paul wrote that he was trying to get passage to England to bring his little family home without waiting for government help. Both he and Vera soon realized this was impossible. Every available ship had been commandeered to transport the American fighting men in Europe back to home ground. It would be months before this could be accomplished.

The Red Cross was organizing GI Brides Clubs because

over 66,000 brides of American servicemen were waiting to join their husbands. Vera signed up along with over 300 other young wives – most of them between 18 and 23 – in her area. Iris was preparing to go home to spend some time with her mother, brother, and sister-in-law before joining Hank in Canada.

'Mum thinks I'm out of my blinking mind to have married somebody from Canada.' Iris giggled infectiously. 'Can you imagine what she would be saying if I'd married an American?'

Vera knew that Britishers looked down on girls who married American fighting men. And some, Iris had guessed, were worried about their giving a bad impression of Great Britain to America. The general impression here was that only girls from the slums or 'Piccadilly commandos' were marrying GIs.

'On the other hand,' Iris drawled, 'do you think all those American girls who're looking for husbands are going to be happy about 66,000 British girls walking off with *their* men?'

Conscientiously Vera attended all the meetings held by her GI Brides Club. She listened with eagerness to all they were told about life in the United States. They were even taught to make coffee American style, she wrote Paul.

'Can you imagine?' a pretty 18-year-old whispered to Vera at one meeting. 'In the United States folks keep their houses heated to 70°. It must feel like being in the tropics!'

Vera and Iris talked about the courting between British brides and their servicemen husbands – often, she insisted, longer than that between American girls and servicemen.

'Hank and I didn't just jump into marriage,' Iris said. 'We went out together for five months. Of course, you and Paul jumped,' she kidded. 'But that's all right because you're perfect for each other.'

How would Paul's father and sister feel? Vera asked

herself with recurrent nervousness. Paul said they were pleased – but they wouldn't tell *him* if they weren't. He said his father kept snapshots of Laurie on his office desk and showed them off to everybody. She was glad that Paul was already back in school – though not at Columbia. He said it would be too expensive for them to live in New York. He was going to school in a city called Albany – where he could commute from Eastwood. She was a little uncomfortable at the prospect of their living with Paul's father for now – but as long as Paul was in school, it was the best thing to do.

'You know,' Iris mused, 'I think Canadian men are more like Americans than British. Hank just bowled me over. He was *nice* to me.'

'The girls at my Brides Club talked about that,' Vera remembered. 'They said American fellows made such a fuss over them – bringing them candy and flowers.' She giggled in recall. 'One of the girls was so impressed because her American boyfriend brought her nail polish.' Difficult to acquire in London. 'Paul took me to fancy restaurants – even before we were truly serious.' Yet, in a corner of her mind, she knew that Paul had been serious within days.

'Our boys take us for granted.' Iris nodded with conviction. 'They play the love-'em-and-leave-'em game as long as they can get away with it. American and Canadian men are the marrying kind. That's the way they were brought up,' she said with relish.

'I didn't go out with any men before Paul came along,' Vera said softly, 'but it wasn't long before I knew I wanted to spend the rest of my life with him.'

Vera tried to comfort Paul at the delay – the 'infernal red tape,' he called it – that kept the hordes of GI brides apart from their husbands. Still, both realized the frustrating slowness of transporting servicemen across the

Atlantic, even though every ship was packed beyond capacity. This, of course, took precedence over wives and children.

Finally, word came through early in the new year. Vera and Laurie would be aboard the first ship – the *Argentina* – that would carry GI brides to their husbands. She was eager to be with Paul, yet nervous at the prospect of beginning a new life on a strange continent. But Paul would be with her – so it would be all right. She wasn't running *away* this time – she was running *to* Paul.

Now Vera was caught up in the excitement of imminent departure. She went with Laurie to her assigned camp. Three such camps had been set up by the US government in England – and another in France. Here the GI brides and children were processed, given the necessary shots. Then on the appointed day, 456 brides and 170 babies – destined to be scattered across 45 states – were transported to Southampton to board the 20,600 ton *Argentina*, totally refitted to suit the needs of its passengers.

Standing on the deck in the bleak winter cold as the ship moved slowly out of the harbour, Vera joined the other very young wives in singing 'There'll Always Be An England.' She was conscious of a kind of bravura among them, a forerunner of the homesickness that would surely attack some before the *Argentina* completed its crossing.

'If we'd waited a week, we could have crossed on the *Queen Elizabeth*,' one starry-eyed bride bubbled. 'But I can't wait to be with my Joe!'

'In eight days you'll be with him,' Vera said blithely, yet she felt an unexpected apprehension as she jiggled Laurie in her arms. She was putting an ocean between herself and every place she'd ever known. She remembered stories she'd heard about Americans: 'They're always going on strike – they're noisy – always in a hurry – always drunk.' But Paul wasn't like that.

The unorthodox passengers of the *Argentina* were enthralled by what they found aboard. The crew included two army doctors, five army nurses, eight WACS to help care for the children, and many stewardesses and matrons. The sleeping quarters were admittedly small, 'but 4.6 times what was allotted to each soldier when the *Argentina* carried troops.' Sleeping accommodation – lower or upper bunks – was assigned without reference to the rank of spouses. There were cribs and playpens, special dishes for the babies, an abundance of toys.

'Did you ever see anything like this?' murmured one wide-eyed young mother. 'My little fella will be out of his mind with all of this!'

'And disposable nappies,' another effervesced.

'I know,' the other girl giggled. 'They figure on sixty nappies for each during the crossing. All of them going overboard when they're dirtied. But there's a laundry room for clothes.'

Meals this first day out brought expressions of amazement and delight. They gaped at platters of beef and chicken, bacon and eggs, even bowls piled high with oranges – all so scarce in England. Everyone was eager to shop in the canteen, which offered candy, lipsticks, even cigarette lighters. But by the third day, few passengers came to the dining saloon. Winds blowing up to 65 miles per hour were pounding the ship. The fog horn blared. Warnings to stay below came over the public address system at regular intervals. Vera was relieved that she was among the few who were not attacked by seasickness.

The weather continued unpleasant for much of the trip, though once some of the brides had overcome their seasickness they organized to present a show, dubbed *Argentina Antics*. There was a beauty contest for the babies. In calm weather, Vera joined those who enjoyed walks around the deck. And all the brides appreciated the services of the WACS.

'It's like a holiday,' the bride in the bunk above Vera's declared. 'Let's enjoy it. It won't be for long.'

For Vera, the shipboard days were both euphoric – weather permitting – and frustratingly slow. And rumours were circulating that because of the weather, the trip would probably extend to nine days. At unwary moments, Vera was assaulted by memories of the harried years behind. She wished wistfully that she could have gone to the synagogue in Berlin where her parents' and her brother's ashes had been buried. But they would be happy for her, she comforted herself. How they would have loved Paul and Laurie!

The rumours proved correct. The ship would arrive in New York in nine days rather than the estimated eight.

'My poor Bill will be hanging around the city for an extra day,' one girl mourned. 'He came all the way from Alabama to meet me.'

'You just hope he doesn't pick up some gorgeous chorus girl in New York,' another teased.

Except for their night clothes, Vera packed the night before they were to dock. She was on the deck with others in the raw, cold February dawn when the ship chugged into the iced-over harbour. Her heart pounded as the New York skyline came into view.

'That's the Statue of Liberty!' somebody cried out as the floodlit landmark became visible.

Soon the decks were mobbed with brides, ricocheted with the sound of excited conversations. At last the ship was at anchor. The gangplank was set in place. The Army band waiting at the pier broke into a rendition of 'The Star-Spangled Banner.' The joyous war-brides and their offspring began to disembark, some singing their new national anthem as they made their way down the gangplank. The day was grey and cold, but none paid heed to this. Their children were already American citizens, Vera remembered. In two years, the brides would acquire that status.

After physical examinations, brides and babies were transported across town, and in the cosy warmth of the Red Cross Chapter House they were at last greeted by their husbands.

'I've never seen you out of uniform,' Vera confided with wry amusement when she and Paul had exchanged kisses and Laurie had been tenderly greeted. 'Not ever!'

'You want to turn me in for another model?' he joshed.

'I never want to see you in uniform again,' she declared. 'No more wars! No more separations!'

'God, it's wonderful to have you both here!' His voice was fervent. 'I was too excited to sleep last night.'

'Me, too,' Vera confessed, her eyes clinging to Paul's face as though to reassure herself that she was really here with him. 'And I had this awful fear that we'd get off the ship and not be able to find you.'

'I've been here since yesterday,' he reminded with a chuckle.

'Walk,' Laurie said determinedly, squirming in Paul's arms. 'Wanna walk.'

'Tell me again,' he coaxed. 'Who am I?'

'My Daddy.' Her smile was angelic. 'My Daddy!'

'That's my baby,' Paul crooned and deposited her on her feet.

'Hands,' she ordered, all at once aware of the jostling crowd around them, and held up a hand to Paul and Vera.

'I can't believe we're here.' Joyous tears blurred Vera's vision as they made their way through the festive reunions on every side. 'It's been so long.'

'Dad and Doris are dying to meet you both,' Paul told

her. 'Would you be disappointed if we drove straight up to Eastwood instead of staying here in the city overnight?'

'Whatever you say.' Vera was euphoric. She was here in the United States – with Paul. *It wasn't a dream. It was real.*

'I'll bring you down to New York another time,' he promised. 'Let's go home now.'

Her smile was tremulous as her eyes held his. 'Let's go home.'

Chapter Seven

Paul lifted Laurie into his arms again so they could make better time in reaching the car.

'It's a long haul,' Paul warned Vera apologetically. 'About four hours' driving time. But we'll look for a diner soon and stop off to eat. No rationing, no shortages.' His eyes were teasing. 'Think you can handle fresh eggs, fresh milk, fresh fruit?'

'I'll make an effort.' Vera revelled in Paul's levity.

'You like ice cream, Laurie?' Paul asked gently.

Vera laughed at Laurie's bewildered stare.

'Paul, she's such a little girl. She's never had it.'

'We'll have to fix that.' Paul deposited an exuberant kiss on Laurie's cheek.

They settled themselves in the car – which Paul confided would be theirs as soon as new cars came off the line and his father had received delivery of the one on order. Now Paul drove across town towards the Westside Highway.

'That'll take us northward to the new twin-lane Henry Hudson Parkway,' Paul explained.

On Vera's lap, Laurie stared avidly at the passing landscape.

'I'm out of classes all this week and next,' Paul confided. 'It's the "winter break." The ship docked at the perfect time.'

Vera listened with rapt attention while Paul talked about his classes, about the provisions of the GI Bill to further the education of World War II veterans.

'This will be the best-educated generation in history,'

he predicted, grinning. 'With the government picking up the tab.'

'Papa would have been so impressed,' Vera said. She hesitated. 'Your father won't be upset that we're driving straight up to Eastwood? I mean, he wasn't expecting us until tomorrow.'

'Honey, he can't wait to see you two. But yeah, I should phone him when we stop off at the diner. He'll want to call Doris to be there with him to welcome you. And probably Wayne – that's Doris's husband – will be there, too. If I'd allow it, Dad would have hired a brass band.'

'You said Wayne is from Palestine,' Vera recalled, fighting against a tide of alarm at the prospect of meeting her in-laws. 'He fought with the Haganah.'

'That's right.'

All at once Paul seemed oddly withdrawn, Vera thought. Didn't he like Doris's husband?

'I think you'll be pleased with the house.' Instinct told her Paul was making a point of redirecting their conversation. 'It was built back in 1792 – when the country was just sixteen years old. But it's been enlarged and remodelled several times.' He took one hand from the wheel for a moment to caress one of hers. 'My great-grandfather bought it just before the Civil War. Then there were just two rooms downstairs and two upstairs – with a kitchen connected by a long ell. When Doris and I were little kids – and the house twice the original size, we found a secret panel in a second-floor ceiling. That's when the family discovered the house had been a stop on the Underground Railroad that took Southern slaves to Canada.'

'Tell me about the Civil War,' Vera prodded. She had acquired some knowledge about American history but was eager to know more.

Paul launched into a long monologue about the Civil

War, punctuated at intervals by questions from Vera. He segued into tales of earlier days. It was obvious he enjoyed retelling stories handed down in his family. Vera was mesmerized, too caught up in learning American history to note that they had left New York City behind them and were travelling over the rolling hills of Westchester County, gaunt and bare in midwinter. In contrast, Laurie was intrigued by the passing scenery – chortling at excited moments when she spied a dog or a horse or cow.

'Let's cut off here and look for a diner –' Paul interrupted his history lesson '– before Laurie falls asleep. I'll call Dad from there.'

In the sprawling living room of the charming – almost elegant – two-and-a-half-storey clapboard house that had served the Kahn family since 1859, Joel Kahn waited impatiently for his daughter to respond to his phone call. At 54 he was still a handsome man, his dark hair slightly tinged with grey, his manner quiet and almost courtly.

'Hello,' Doris's voice replied at the other end.

'Doris, I want you and Wayne to come over here.' Pleasurable excitement coloured his voice. 'Paul just called me from the road. He's on his way home from New York with Vera and Laurie. They decided not to stay overnight in the city. I want you to be here to welcome them. He said they should arrive in about two hours.'

'Perhaps I ought to fix dinner for them,' Doris began, her own voice vibrant with anticipation. 'It'll be –'

'No, they were having dinner down below,' Joel told her. 'We'll have cake and coffee ready for them. I'm sure Henrietta left something we can serve.' Henrietta was his long-time housekeeper and familiar with his habit of raiding the kitchen for pre-bedtime coffee and cake.

'It's still unreal to me –' she managed a bewildered laugh. '– that Paul has a wife and daughter.'

'We'll love them both,' Joel said with a show of conviction. He brushed aside the question that he knew entered the minds of other in-laws of GI brides. *Had Vera married Paul to get to the United States? The golden land*. 'Paul says Vera's very special. And he adores Laurie.' His first grandchild, he thought in a surge of sentiment. He knew that Doris yearned to have a child, but thus far it wasn't happening.

'I'll tear Wayne away from those reports he brought home from the office, and we'll drive right over. See you, Dad.'

Restless – too stimulated to settle down to read, though like Paul he was addicted to reading – Joel headed for the kitchen to make himself a cup of tea. It had been wonderful these last months – having Paul home. He had been proud of Paul's military service during the war years – but God, the nights he couldn't sleep for worrying!

With the same efficiency he used in running the factory, he poured exactly one cup of water into the kettle – to ensure speed. He switched the electric burner on *hi* and reached into an old-fashioned glass candy jar for a tea bag. The candy jar was a bit of whimsy introduced by his wife. All these years later, he still felt Anne's presence in the house – especially tonight. He had never remarried, though there had been women who'd pursued him. It wouldn't have been fair to marry again. His two kids would always take first place in his life.

The water boiled. He poured it over the tea bag, walked with cup and saucer back into the living room. He settled himself in his favourite armchair, glanced about at the eclectic collection of furniture – from comfortable to truly beautiful, acquired by four generations of Kahns. Would Paul's wife want to make changes? he asked himself uneasily. After all, for the next two years it would be her home, too. Until Paul had his degree and was teaching. Once Paul was working, they'd want a house of their own – like Doris and Wayne. He'd see that they got it.

It was strange how Paul always shied away from talk about the war. Wayne was almost compulsive in talking about his own experiences – bloodcurdling years with the Haganah from the time he was fourteen. Then the training by the British to parachute into enemy territory. He'd thought that would be a bond between Paul and Wayne, but Paul had ordered him to say nothing about his intelligence mission. Nor would Paul say any more than he'd already said in his letters about his years with the RAF. He'd come home, Joel comprehended, a confirmed pacifist.

He'd been astonished when Paul enlisted. They never talked about it, but sometimes he was sure Paul was unhappy about the family's involvement in the manufacture of firearms. As though it were somehow slimy. For an unwary moment he felt the sharp pain of recall. Though Paul's memory of his mother's death was clouded, Paul knew how she'd died.

Hell, he wasn't ashamed of the business! The Kahn factory had made a contribution in four wars! As three generations before him had been, he was proud of that. Sometimes he suspected Paul was uncomfortable, too, in the way their finances had escalated. He wasn't the only one who'd made a fortune in the war years, he told himself defensively. Not a colossal fortune like John D. Rockefeller or Henry Ford – but to the average small businessman, he was a huge success. Paul and Doris knew they'd never have to worry about money during their lifetimes.

Joel's face softened. Thank God for Wayne. If he couldn't have his son in the business, at least he had a son-in-law who had great respect for the Kahn Firearms Company, as it had become known in his father's lifetime. Wayne had astonished him by becoming an immediate asset. What he didn't know, he learned quickly – and he was a super salesman. During the war years, this had been an unnecessary talent. In peace time, the competition would be rough again. But that was now Wayne's department, he thought in relief. He himself loathed selling.

The phone rang. Joel put down his cup of tea and went to respond.

'Hello.'

'Dad, is the driveway clear?' Doris asked, faintly breathless. 'There was no snow when Paul went down to meet Vera and the baby.'

'The driveway's clear,' he soothed. 'Remember, I had to get home, too. Cal cleared it, as always.' Cal was their sometime handyman. 'Stop fussing and drive on over. You don't need to walk,' he joshed. 'We don't have to worry about gas rationing anymore.'

'This is a ten o'clock town,' Paul said humorously as they drove through the centre of Eastwood. Few people on the streets, shops closed, only a local tavern showing signs of life.

'It looks so pretty.' Vera gazed out at the one- and two-storey structures, the vintage church on Main Street, a filling station closed for the night – all snow-brushed, along with the ground on which they stood.

'Peaceful,' Paul said, almost with reverence. 'I loved my two years in New York, but I was always glad to come home on the school breaks.'

'How far to the house?' she asked, heart pounding now at the imminent confrontation with Paul's family.

'We make a left at the next corner. It's a mile up the hill. Laurie still asleep?'

'Once she's off, nothing wakes her,' Vera said with tender laughter. 'Nothing except the buzz bombs.'

The moonlight lent an eerie illumination to the snow-scape on both sides of the road. There was a quietness that was simultaneously beautiful and ominous. They drove past modest homes set close to the sidewalks; then the houses became far apart, larger and more impressive.

'Here we are.' Paul's voice was electric as he turned off the road into a circular driveway that led up to the brilliantly lit house that sat perhaps a hundred feet ahead. 'There's Doris's car.' He identified an old-model Chevvie that sat at one side. 'She and Wayne must be here.' Again, Vera sensed a hint of dislike in Paul for his brother-in-law.

Before Paul had drawn to a complete stop, Vera saw the front door open. A man and a young woman hurried out despite the icy cold of the night. In moments, Vera and Laurie – angelic though just awakened – were being warmly welcomed, drawn into the comfort of the foyer. The air was electric with the joyous excitement of the occasion. She needn't have worried, Vera told herself in relief and pleasure. Paul's family wanted Laurie and her here.

Vera stood with Paul's arm protectively about her while his father lifted Laurie from her feet and swept her up into the air while she chortled in approval.

'Vera, she's adorable,' Doris said, while Vera admired her tall, slender, dark-haired sister-in-law. So much prettier than the photo Paul had carried in his wallet. 'Dad's so proud of his first grandchild.'

Tears of elation glistened in Vera's eyes as she felt the sincerity of her father-in-law's show of love for Laurie. Paul's family was hers – and Laurie's, too. She felt reborn.

'Wayne's finally off the phone.' Doris's face lit up as a tall young man of about Paul's age – with a burnished tan, sand-coloured hair, and magnetic blue eyes strode down the hall.

Immediately Wayne welcomed Vera with a brotherly kiss, reached to take Laurie from his father-in-law. He would be the focus of attention in any gathering he joined, Vera thought in a corner of her mind. Tall and muscular – in grey slacks and a maroon turtleneck that emphasized his broad shoulders – he exuded an air of good-humoured rebellion. Paul said he'd been a member of the Haganah – the secret Jewish army in Palestine. She could envision him leading a furious counterattack against Arabs intent on a Jewish massacre. Why didn't Paul like him? Probably because he thought no man was good enough for his sister, she thought with indulgent humour.

Exhausted from her hectic day, Laurie began to yawn. Paul pantomimed to Vera to follow him. The room adjoining what was to be their own was now designated 'Laurie's nursery,' he explained. Doris hurried out to the kitchen to put up a bedtime bottle.

'Dad had a door cut through our room to the next one,' Paul indicated, Laurie's head on his shoulder. 'So she'll be practically with us.'

Their bedroom was a large, square room that would be drenched in sunlight in good weather, Vera guessed. The brass-framed bed sat in the centre. The dresser and chest of drawers, the night table, the lounge chair before the marble-faced fireplace were beautiful examples of an earlier period.

'What a beautiful rug!' Vera said, her eyes nostalgic as they rested on the rich, deep-toned Oriental at their feet. Much like the one she remembered from her childhood apartment in Berlin – and which had been sold because food on the table was more important than a fine rug.

Laurie was in her crib, in pyjamas, and already asleep

by the time Doris arrived with the night bottle. Leaving the nursery door open in the rare event that Laurie awoke, Vera went with Paul and Doris to the dining room on the lower floor. Already aromatic aromas were filtering through the house. She smiled, remembering Paul's promise of 'real coffee back home'.

Inevitably – over coffee and warmed cheese Danish – the conversation moved to the late war. Vera saw Paul's air of levity give way to an impatient frown a moment later, banished out of respect for his father and Wayne. He wanted so to put the war years behind him, Vera thought compassionately. She remembered what he'd said in those first hectic weeks together in London, about why he'd re-enlisted after his discharge from the RAF: '*I'm not sure I'm ready to go home yet. Back home, will people understand what we've been through over here? How can they understand? They haven't gone through it.*'

'Wayne was born in this country,' Joel told Vera.

'In Brooklyn,' Wayne filled in, grinning. 'We moved to Palestine when I was six. I was a little kid,' he reminisced while Doris listened, her face rapt. 'I remember when we first moved into the kibbutz. My mother loved it. My father and my sister and I hated it. We felt like celebrating when my mother decided two years later that we should go to live in Tel Aviv.'

'Tel Aviv couldn't have been a picnic, either, in those days,' Joel sympathized. Vera suspected he'd heard this many times.

'Tel Aviv was founded in 1909 with sixty families, but by the time we arrived there must have been 20,000 people there.' Wayne chuckled. 'At first I thought it was noisy and crowded and ungodly hot. Then we realized that parts of town were nice. Rows and rows of little houses, each with a tiny garden. Pepper trees and casuarina lined the streets – paved where we were to live. But there were areas that were a mess – half-finished, haphazardly set up. Not good.'

'But it was more comfortable than living in the kibbutz,' Doris prodded. She was madly in love with Wayne, Vera thought tenderly. Probably many girls were, she guessed and was all at once self-conscious. It wasn't wrong of her to admire Wayne – the way she'd admired American movie stars she and Iris had seen at London cinemas. 'You were glad to be there, weren't you.'

'Oh God, yes! We had our own apartment, our own bathroom – which a lot of apartments even in Tel Aviv didn't have,' he admitted. 'My parents wanted to become American-style capitalists. They opened a tiny shop in Tel Aviv. Even Beth and I helped out. Small as we were, we helped out.' Vera was aware of his intense scrutiny. Was he comparing his life in Palestine to hers in Berlin and Copenhagen? 'I'm glad they believed in their dream of a homeland in Palestine.' Now he was sombre. He turned to Vera. 'My parents and my sister were murdered by Arab terrorists.'

'My parents and my brother were murdered by SS men on *Kristallnacht*,' Vera whispered. For a moment it was as though they were alone in the room – two people sharing memories that the others could only imagine.

'Doris, are there any more of these Danish out in the kitchen?' Paul asked. 'You don't know how often I dreamt about American Danish when I was in Europe.'

Later – despite her exhaustion from the day's activities, the trauma of meeting Paul's family – Vera lay sleepless in Paul's arms, her head on his chest. Paul snored softly, an aura of contentment on his face. She had come home, Vera told herself. She felt reborn – as though nothing but good could ever happen to her again. For now she put aside her painfully learned knowledge that in this life tragedy may lie only seconds away.

Chapter Eight

Vera awoke this first morning in Eastwood with a sense of 'all's right with the world.' Morning sunlight filtered through the drapes, lay a ribbon of gold across the olive-tinted top blanket. Heat rattled in the radiators, lending an aura of comfort. Today, she thought with a flicker of humour, she relished the American habit of overheating houses.

Paul was asleep beside her, his face buried in his pillow. From habit she glanced at the clock on the night table, then remembered there was no need to check on the hour. Paul had no classes this week. The silence from the adjoining nursery told her Laurie, too, was still asleep.

Now she became aware of faint – oddly comforting – sounds on the floor below. That would be Dad, preparing to leave for the factory, she interpreted. She felt a shyness in calling her father-in-law *Dad*, but Paul had told her this was proper. Paul's father was so loving, she thought in a surge of gratitude.

Dad said that Henrietta came in every day at 1:00 PM and stayed until 7:30. She cleaned the house, made the beds, did the grocery shopping, and prepared and served dinner.

'She won't help with Laurie or even baby-sit,' he'd apologized. 'She can be ornery sometimes, but it's tough to get domestic help these days.'

She'd been startled that he could think she'd expect help with Laurie. *In London I took care of Laurie and the apartment and did translations at home.*

Doris had teased her father about not having more help in the house. 'Dad, you're just not comfortable at being rich,' she'd joshed. 'You've worked hard and have been very successful. Why should you have to make your own breakfast and wash breakfast and dinner dishes? You're a big wheel in this town now.'

Hereafter, Vera promised herself, she'd make breakfast each morning for Paul and Dad and herself. Laurie always slept till 8:00. By then Dad would be off to the factory and Paul heading for his first class – once the winter break was over. Dad had insisted – when she'd made a tentative offer to take over some household chores – that Henrietta took care of everything.

'You just worry about looking after Laurie,' he'd said. 'And you'll have to rustle up your own breakfast and lunch and Laurie's.' She'd laughed at his air of apology. 'Anything that isn't there that you'd like, you just tell Henrietta.'

In mid-morning Paul took her and Laurie on a tour of the town. She'd never lived in a small town before. All the buildings were so low, she marvelled. Nothing taller than two storeys. No signs here of war except for a small monument in a tiny park in the centre of town. A memorial to Eastwood residents who had died in the First World War. Paul said another was to be erected in memory of those who'd died in World War II. A marker in front of one of two churches in town indicated it had been founded in 1702. Everything seemed so peaceful. Even during the war it must have been like this.

'Oh, you haven't seen the supermarket,' Paul remembered when they were about to head back for the house. 'It's only been open six months, but people can't imagine how they ever got along without it.'

She was awed by the seemingly endless rows of food on display – such a contrast to London. She allowed

Paul to buy only one box of cookies because Laurie's consumption of sweets was strictly limited.

'I can't believe the way people buy,' she whispered, watching customers wheel shopping carts piled high with groceries to their waiting cars. She remembered the food shortages that were still rampant in Europe.

On Friday evening Doris and Wayne came to the house for dinner. It was the family ritual, Paul explained to Vera. The others gathered in the living room while she took Laurie upstairs and put her to bed. She was nervous that Laurie kept making excuses to keep her in attendance. Henrietta liked to serve at 7:00 PM sharp. By 7:30, she was heading out of the house to her ramshackle car. With Laurie at last making no more demands, Vera hurried downstairs. She smiled, remembering what Dad had said last night: '*The minute those automatic dishwashers they keep talking about come on the market, I'm buying one.*' He had been touched when she insisted she would do the dinner dishes until that time arrived.

Joel and Wayne were heatedly discussing the troubles in Palestine, where Jewish refugees were being denied admittance – and where Arabs were attacking Jewish communities. Paul listened in pain, wishing the other two would change to another subject. For Paul, the fighting was all too fresh.

'Where are the refugees supposed to go?' Wayne demanded. 'After what they've been through – the years in concentration camps – *how can they be turned away*?'

Perhaps Mama and Papa and Ernst had been lucky to have died rather than to have endured the horrors of concentration camps like Auschwitz and Bergen-Belsen.

'I saw what the Nazis did to those they captured!' Wayne's voice was mesmerizing. 'I jumped behind German lines – I saw!'

A pulse hammered at Paul's temple. Why must they

talk so much about the war? Vera fretted. It upset Paul so. Yet she felt herself drawn into Wayne's spell. She could visualize him in action – moving ahead fearlessly, intent on saving lives of Nazi victims.

'I'm puttin' dinner on the table,' Henrietta announced from the doorway in her brusque fashion. 'Eat while it's hot.'

Vera saw Doris's faint sigh of relief at the derailment of talk about the refugees. She suspected Doris worried that, despite his protestations that Eastwood was home now, Wayne might be drawn back into the conflict in Palestine.

Over dinner – as though sensing a need to introduce a lighter mood – Wayne regaled them with stories of his brief time in New York, where he'd lived on the Upper West Side with cousins.

'New York to me was insanity,' he confided ingratiatingly. 'So many people, the noise, that constant feeling of rush, rush, rush.' He chuckled. 'Remember, I was the kid who thought Tel Aviv was big and noisy.'

'You stick with me, Wayne,' Joel encouraged. 'Eastwood is a fine place to live. You learn the business, and one day you'll take over for me. When I retire to sit back and enjoy my grandchildren.' His eyes moved lovingly from Vera to Doris.

After dinner Doris joined Vera in the kitchen to do the dishes.

'Next week Paul's back at school,' Doris reminded. 'I'll give a small luncheon party, and you'll meet some of the girls. During the winter months, we're all inclined to hibernate. I went to school with them, from kindergarten through high school. Only a few of the girls in my class went on to college – and most of them are married now and settled down.' She paused in contemplation. 'Maybe I've changed in the years I was at school in New York.'

Vera recalled Doris had gone to Barnard and – after a year at home – to the Columbia School of Social Work. 'We just seem to have so little in common now.'

'Maybe we're what Paul calls oddballs.' Vera was sombre. 'I remember how it was on the ship coming over. Except that I was married to an ex-serviceman and had a child, I just didn't think like the others I knew on board ship.'

'But we have to try to fit in.' Doris was firm. 'This is our town – where we'll spend the rest of our lives. Maybe once Wayne and I have kids, it'll be different for me. But right now I want to talk about something besides what wax to use on the kitchen floor and who's easier to toilet train – boys or girls.'

'Women did so much during the war years. Not just in Europe – here in the United States, too, Paul said. Why are they satisfied to go back to the way everything was before the war?' Vera probed.

'Not all of them are,' Doris conceded while Vera stacked dishes in the sink. 'The smartest girl in my high school graduating class got married during the war. She couldn't wait for her husband to come home from Italy. Last month she left him – she's filing for a divorce. She spent three years in a responsible government position down in Washington, but he blew his stack when she wanted to open up a business here in town. There're more of us than you think.'

'Have you considered going to work?' Vera asked curiously. She doubted that Paul would be upset if she found some tutoring assignments – though she knew this was improbable here in Eastwood.

'Oh, Wayne would be furious.' Doris grimaced eloquently. 'It would be an affront to his manhood – as though he weren't able to provide for his wife.' She paused. 'I went for a masters in social work because it seemed the thing to do, but I really wanted to be a commercial artist. I don't have a big talent – but enough to make it in the commercial field. But that would mean living in a fair-sized city instead of Eastwood – and Wayne would hate it.'

'Back in London, girls just thought about getting married and having babies as fast as they could,' Vera remembered wryly.

'Damn it, Vera, don't they care what's happening in the world? They never even read a newspaper – or a magazine that deals with something besides "What Can You Do to Help Your Returning Veteran" or "How to Decorate Cupcakes for Halloween."'

'They just want to relax in this wonderful peace,' Vera alibied gently.

Still, there were many in the country who complained loudly – about the way prices were soaring, about the shortage of housing, about the strikes that afflicted the country. But to her, life had never seemed so wonderful. And Paul was happy. He was eager to be teaching. He'd already decided to go to summer school to hasten that time.

But he dreaded all the war talk that erupted when Wayne and his father were together.

As promised, Doris scheduled her luncheon party once Paul's classes resumed.

'You'll bring Laurie,' she told Vera. 'Nobody can get babysitters during school hours.' Doris had explained that – when available – local teenagers baby-sat for twenty-five cents an hour. 'The other girls will bring their kids, too. And don't dress. We'll all be in slacks and sweaters.'

Vera understood that Doris's party was an innovation in Eastwood. On the day of the party she waited with a glow of anticipation for Doris to drive over for Laurie and her. Laurie would be so happy to be with other little ones, she thought tenderly. These first two weeks in Eastwood, Laurie had seen no other children. Their neighbours on either side – each an acre away – were elderly couples. It wasn't like in London, Vera reminded herself, where she took Laurie to the park every day unless the weather was bad. She knew nobody here with children, but that was about to change.

Doris arrived in high spirits, hoisted Laurie into her arms.

'Oh, you're going to have a great time,' she crooned. 'You're going to make some new friends.'

'Let me get her into her snowsuit.' Vera reached for Laurie.

Again, snow threatened. The temperature was on a sharp, downward slide. With Laurie and Vera dressed for the outdoors, the three hurried from the house through the dank cold into the warmth of the car.

'Oh, the heat feels good,' Vera murmured gratefully.

While she drove, Doris explained that there would be four young wives and six little ones at the luncheon.

'I should say six and two-thirds,' Doris said humorously. 'Elaine is going into her seventh month. Two of the husbands work for Dad,' she added with an enigmatic smile.

Doris had shown her the house last week. She loved its spaciousness, its elegant grounds – impressive even in this drab weather. Doris said her father had given her and Wayne the down payment as a wedding present. What had Doris called it? A colonial cape, she remembered. The downstairs was furnished with beautiful antique reproductions, but only one of the four upstairs bedrooms had been furnished. 'But with the way Dad is giving Wayne raises, we should be able to furnish the upstairs real soon.'

'Doggie!' Laurie chirped. 'Doggie!' She leaned forward

in Vera's arms to wave to a wandering Irish setter.

Doris shot a swift glance at her watch as they walked from the car.

'I left the chicken roasting in the oven, and the salad's ready. I picked up dessert at the bakery this morning. The girls won't be here for at least fifteen minutes.'

All four guests arrived almost simultaneously. As Doris had said, everyone was in slacks and sweaters – slightly self-conscious at this unexpected socializing, candid in their curiosity about Doris's house. Vera suspected the others lived in more modest circumstances. None of them seemed intimidating, Vera realized with relief, struggling to absorb the introductions. Two of the girls had babies under a year – and one an infant plus toddler, the fourth a three-year-old plus a toddler who gave her doll to Laurie in an immediate gesture of friendship.

The living room ricocheted with high spirits – the little ones seeming to understand this was a festive occasion. Doris swept a mound of cushions onto the floor as a nesting place for the babies.

'I thought we'd have lunch off trays,' Doris said. 'So we can be comfortable with the kids.'

Everybody seemed to be enjoying the occasion, Vera told herself. She was aware of furtive inspections. She gathered from the candid remark of one of the girls that she was the only war bride in town. But they were friendly, she sensed with relief – no hostility on their part.

'How's Wayne?' the pretty blonde with Betty Grable legs asked at a break in the lively conversation. Her husband, Vera pinpointed, was an inspector at the factory.

'Oh, working like mad,' Doris said.

'Tell your old man to keep them all working hard,' the very pregnant redhead said good-humouredly. 'With another baby coming, Fred needs all the overtime he can get. The way prices keep going up, wow!'

'That is one handsome guy.' The blonde pantomimed her approval. 'If he weren't married to you and I weren't married to Lou, he could park his shoes under my bed anytime.'

Vera tensed. It disturbed her that she, too, felt drawn to Wayne in an unexpected fashion. Nothing had happened in her love for Paul, she told herself defensively. *He was her life*. But sometimes, when Wayne looked at her in that disconcerting way of his, she was conscious of feelings that were unnerving.

The girls talked briefly about their husbands – all of whom had seen active duty. Doris reminded them that Wayne had served under the British.

'He would have enlisted with the American forces after he came back to this country, but with the little vision he has in his right eye after the war injury, they said *no*.'

The conversation quickly settled into discussion of domestic matters. These girls might have grown up with Doris, but they'd moved far apart from her, Vera sensed. Their lives revolved in a tiny circle – around husband, babies, and house. There was a wall between them and Doris, Vera realized.

Vera was relieved when the first of the wives decided it was time to leave.

'David is a hellion if I don't put him down for his nap in time – and his father thinks he's on a starvation diet if I don't have a roast in the oven every night. You know – after all that Spam and army rations.'

'It'll be better once winter is behind us,' Doris consoled Vera when they were alone again. Neither of the toddlers' mothers had suggested getting together for playtime. 'Anyway, by then you'll have your driver's licence.'

'I have my library card now,' Vera said with an effort at lightness. 'Thank God for books.'

*

Early in April, Vera suspected she was pregnant again. Bursting to share this, yet wanting to be sure before she told Paul, she confided first to Doris, who had dropped by for an afternoon visit. The two women sat over coffee in the den while Laurie napped upstairs.

'You mean you haven't told Paul yet?' Doris was intrigued at being the first to know.

'I thought I'd wait another week – I could just be late.' But she was convinced she was pregnant again – and nervous that they were being irresponsible when Paul wasn't yet in a job. Their expenses were low – but so was Paul's allowance under the GI Bill. And he worked so hard, she thought lovingly – that long commute in all kinds of weather and the studying that spilled over into the weekends.

'Paul will be thrilled,' Doris predicted. 'And Dad will be popping the champagne.' She sighed now. 'I don't dare tell him Wayne doesn't want to have kids yet. I wish Wayne weren't always so damn careful.'

'Don't let on to Paul that you know,' Vera cautioned. 'I'll probably tell him tonight. And then we'll tell Dad.' And she'd write Iris, up in Nova Scotia. Iris was expecting in four months.

'We don't have any fancy obstetricians here in town, but Dr Evans – the local GP – is terrific. The hospital is small but decent.'

'Make Wayne change his mind,' Vera urged impulsively, 'so Laurie's brother or sister will have a playmate.'

She was an outsider in this town, Vera forced herself to recognize. Paul laughed and said you had to have lived in Eastwood for forty years before local people figured you belonged. Doris kept saying when the weather really warmed up and people started circulating more, there would be kids for Laurie to play with, she reminded herself – yet instinct warned her that not until *she* was accepted would Laurie have friends.

'I'm running down to New York weekend after next with Wayne.' Doris broke into her introspection. 'He's got some business deal going for Dad, so I figured it was a chance for me to visit with this friend from grad school. She's working for a social service agency down there. We'll drive down Saturday morning. Wayne has a one o'clock luncheon appointment with this man. I'll spend the afternoon with Sally, and we'll meet the two husbands for dinner. Wayne and I will drive back Sunday. I'm hoping to get a chance to see a play while we're there. I'm dying to see the Eugene O'Neill play, but I suspect Wayne will be more interested in a raunchy musical.' Her smile was indulgent.

What Wayne wanted Wayne would get, Vera suspected. Doris adored him. When his name had come up at the luncheon for the girls, they'd all reacted as though he were Clark Gable playing Rhett Butler, she thought self-consciously. But she was coming to dread the Friday-evening dinners at the house. Too often when she and Wayne were apart from the others for a moment or two, he gazed at her in the blatant way of a drunken soldier on leave in London. Wayne shouldn't look at anyone but Doris in that way. Nor should her heart begin to pound at such moments.

Vera revelled in Paul's delight – and his father's – that she was pregnant. But she was upset that Henrietta was showing impatience with Laurie – for no reason, she thought defiantly. Then on the Friday evening before Doris and Wayne were to leave for their New York visit, Henrietta announced while she was serving dinner that she wouldn't be back after tonight.

'I don't like working in a house overrun with kids,' she

said scathingly, her gaze focused on Vera for an instant. 'Mr Kahn, you get somebody else.'

'We love children in this house,' Joel said with deliberate calm, but Vera felt his rage. 'Yes, I think it's best that you leave.' He waited until Henrietta had finished serving, had left the house, and was headed for her car. 'That rotten bitch!' His voice soared in anger. 'I've only kept her on through these years because I figured she needed the job. With her disposition she'd have a rough time keeping one.'

'I can take over,' Vera said with determined confidence. 'I won't be as good a cook as Henrietta, but –'

'We'll hire another housekeeper,' Joel interrupted gently. 'I'll run an ad in the local newspaper and the one in Salem. Don't worry your head about it, Vera.'

'I'll ask around next week,' Doris promised. 'Maybe Betsy will know somebody.' Betsy was Doris's once-a-week cleaning woman.

'Laurie never caused Henrietta any trouble.' Vera was defensive now. 'I don't know why she was so upset.'

'She's a bitter, nasty woman,' Doris said. 'We always tried to close our eyes to that because during the war it was so impossible to get domestic help. They were all running to the war plants – or to the factory,' she teased her father. 'We'll find somebody. Maybe a live-in housekeeper,' she suggested. 'That way, if Paul and Vera want to go out in the evening, they'll have a built-in babysitter.' Joel offered babysitting services, but they all knew how often he was called back to the factory in the course of the evening or was involved with local civic organizations.

'Forget about it for now,' Joel ordered. 'You and Wayne have a great weekend in New York. But before you go, find a babysitter for tomorrow night. I'm taking Vera and Paul out to dinner and to a movie. We'll drive over to Saratoga.'

'Do you think it's all right to leave Laurie with a strange babysitter?' Vera was ambivalent. She'd never left Laurie with a sitter.

'Doris will find somebody who'll be fine,' he reassured her. 'This is Eastwood. We have great kids here.'

'I think it will be fun.' Vera exchanged a warm glance with Paul. This was the American way, she told herself. And she wished so much to be a real American.

Chapter Nine

A red velvet robe over her slip, Doris stood before her closet and debated about what to wear for the trip to New York. The morning was awash with sunlight, with the promise of a balmy spring day. From the bedroom window she saw the golden splash of forsythia that divided their property from their neighbours. Thank God, winter was behind them.

'Doris, you haven't started breakfast?' Wayne emerged from the bathroom – his perennially bronzed, muscular body wrapped in a towel. It was weird, Doris reproached herself, how she could get so aroused just looking at Wayne this way. 'I told you, we have to be on the road by eight.' His voice oozed impatience.

'I'm going right down to the kitchen. By the time you're dressed I'll have breakfast on the table,' she soothed.

'The house is beginning to look like a pigsty.' Scowling, he crossed to the chest of drawers that held his underwear and shirts while Doris gaped at him in shock. The house was immaculate. 'Bring Betsy in another day each week. And if she can't do a decent job, dump her and hire somebody else.'

'All right, Wayne.' Forcing a smile, she hurried from the bedroom, down the hall to the stairs. He didn't mean it, she told herself – about the house looking like a pigsty. He was just over-tired from the job. Even with the war over, he worked late three or four nights a week. It didn't matter that most of the country was back to the 40-hour work-week that went into law back in 1940, she thought with an effort at humour. Still, it unnerved her when Wayne was cranky this way.

By the time Wayne sat down at the breakfast table, Doris was sliding his eggs onto a plate. Toast and coffee were ready and his orange juice squeezed. Wayne was contemptuous of the new frozen orange juice that had just come onto the market.

She served Wayne, poured herself a cup of coffee, and sat down at the table with him, sitting on the edge of her chair.

'I'll just have coffee, then run upstairs and dress,' she placated when she saw his eyes move to the wall clock.

'If this deal goes through today, I'll be in for a big salary raise.' All at once his mood changed – a trait that was sometimes disconcerting. 'We might even be able to afford a housekeeper.'

Doris was startled. They didn't need a housekeeper. Maybe she'd ask Betsy if she could come in a second day during the week.

'Dad's always complained about how he hates selling.' She knew this was Wayne's first selling assignment – one that he had initiated.

'He never had to worry about selling for the past seven years,' Wayne scoffed indulgently. 'Business just poured in. But now the situation is different. We have to go out and push. And I just happen to have some important contacts.' His smile was dazzling. 'Hang out with me, kid, and you'll be rich without Daddy. You'll throw out the muskrat and replace it with mink.' She still occasionally wore the muskrat coat that had been Dad's twenty-first birthday present – mainly because it pleased her father.

'I know you'll do just great.' The earlier hurt vanished. It still amazed her that Wayne had brushed aside all those New York girls who'd chased after him to marry her.

'Move your butt, baby. I want to be in the car in half an hour.'

In twenty minutes Doris was hurrying down the stairs with the valise that held weekend necessities for Wayne and herself. She'd packed the black chiffon nightie that had been part of her trousseau. They'd spend tonight at the Essex House – where they'd spent their brief honeymoon almost two years ago. They'd have breakfast tomorrow in their room – with a view of Central Park, she promised herself in sweet nostalgia.

Wayne had brought out the car, was parked in front of the house.

'Okay, let's get cracking.' He took the valise from her, smacked her on the rump. 'I've got business to conduct.'

Every minute of their stay in the city was scheduled; Doris pinpointed them in her mind as she settled herself in the car. They'd check into the Essex House. Wayne would dash off for his luncheon appointment. She'd phone Sally and arrange to meet her in midtown. Sally was taking a half-day of annual leave. They'd have a long lunch, then grab a taxi up to the Metropolitan to see some exhibit Sally said was sensational. She and Wayne would have dinner with Sally and her husband, then – hopefully – they'd see a Broadway show. Tomorrow Wayne just wanted to lounge in their room, have breakfast sent up from room service, and read the *New York Times*. They'd head back for Eastwood in midafternoon.

'What does Sally's husband do?' Wayne asked.

'He teaches at NYU,' Doris told him. 'This is his second year.'

'Another one of those,' he derided good-humouredly. 'Like Paul. Satisfied to make do with little.'

'He and Sally are doing all right,' Doris said defensively. 'Sally has her social worker job, and Phil teaches. They earn a decent living between them.'

It wouldn't be that easy once Sally got pregnant and had to quit work, Doris acknowledged to herself. Still – despite all the cries about inflation – Sally said they'd manage. She and Phil were both anxious to start a family. *Why was Wayne so against that?* He drew a good salary. They were paying off their mortgage with no problems. Why shouldn't they have a baby?

Doris dozed much of the drive into the city. She awoke as they were heading across town to the Essex House.

'I can't wait to see Sally.' Doris glowed. 'It's been almost a year.'

'I'm meeting a man I haven't seen since 1942 – when I was being trained to parachute behind the German lines. He's come a long way since then.'

'Wayne, is this about selling arms to the Haganah?' Doris asked, simultaneously awed and unnerved by this prospect.

'That's illegal, Doris,' he reminded, an amused glint in his eyes. She'd heard many discussions between her father and Wayne about this ruling – which both abhorred. 'Don't ask questions.'

'Dad knows?' she asked after a moment.

'He knows.' Wayne's smile was enigmatic.

They arrived at the hotel and registered. Doris was exultant that they had been given a room on a high floor overlooking Central Park, where the first indications of spring were on display.

'You unpack for us,' Wayne instructed. 'I'll meet you back here by five.'

'That's going to be a long lunch,' she joshed.

'There's a big order at stake.'

In moments Doris was on the phone with Sally.

'There's a Longchamps right near the hotel. Let's have lunch there,' Sally said ebulliently and gave Doris directions.

In the red, yellow, and gold splendour of the Longchamps close to the Essex House, Doris and Sally talked exuberantly about their lives during the past year.

'I can't believe you're not involved in a job by now,' Sally scolded. 'You were so gung ho about social work at school.'

'There're no jobs in Eastwood,' Doris pointed out. 'Even if there were, Wayne would throw a fit.' She was always candid with Sally. 'I was thinking that maybe I could start a play group for pre-schoolers. Just a part-time deal –'

'Doris, we're living in a whole new world now. Women don't have to sit at home and clean the house and bake cookies.' She bristled at this vision. 'Look what women were doing during the war years! They worked in war plants. They drove trucks and ambulances. Some ferried planes. They served in the military. Now we're supposed to sit back and be second-class citizens? Phil's proud of me for having a career.'

'Wayne was brought up in a different culture.' Doris sought for an alibi. 'He –'

'Bullshit,' Sally interrupted. 'A lot of men don't realize the world's changing.' She sighed. 'A lot of women don't either. They think the war's over, and everything's going back to the way it was. But times are going to have to change. Too many women got a good look at the world outside the home, and they want to be part of it.'

'It'll take a long time,' Doris said wryly.

'Maybe. But we have to work at it.' Sally exuded determination.

'What about your job?' Doris asked. 'You're happy with it?'

'Happy and frustrated at the same time,' Sally conceded. 'Part of the time I feel as though I'm doing something useful. And then I run into a situation where I feel so damn helpless. Like the case that came in just this morning. She's a widow with a little girl just under two. Her husband was killed in service so she has his $10,000 GI insurance. Sure, she's got money to live on for a while. But she'd like to find a job so she can hold on to most of it – to make sure her little girl goes to college.' Sally's voice was rich with compassion. 'The only jobs she's ever held were doing housework – she says she wants better than that for Adele.'

'She's a good mother,' Doris said gently.

'But she can't go out to work because she has nowhere to leave her kid. Her mother has a full-time job. She came to us in the hopes that we might have some day-care programme. I explained that our waiting list was a mile long. It's so sad not to be able to help.'

Doris's mind clicked into action. 'Would she leave the city for a job? A sleep-in job?'

'Honey, I'm sure Fiona would love it. But what about Adele?'

'My sister-in-law has a little girl about the same age. Vera would adore having a playmate for Laurie. Part of the time Vera could watch both kids – and other times, Fiona. It could work out well for both of them. And Dad needs a housekeeper.'

Sally hesitated. 'Fiona is coloured –'

'What difference does that make? Does she have experience as a housekeeper?'

'Fiona's worked since she was fourteen. She earned her high school diploma at night school. She can clean, do laundry, and she's a good cook. And what she doesn't know, she's sharp enough to learn fast.'

'I'll call Dad tonight and talk to him.' This would be good for Dad, for Vera and Laurie – and for Fiona and her little girl. 'The house has gone through several additions through the years. There's a large room off the kitchen that used to be a playroom for Paul and me when we were little. Dad even put in a bathroom for us so we could shower there after we'd gone swimming in the summer. Fiona could have her own apartment.'

Both in high spirits after this plotting, they finished lunch, headed for the Metropolitan Museum for an afternoon of pleasurable browsing. At shortly before five, Doris returned to the Essex House. Wayne wasn't there yet. He'd be pleased that Sally had managed to acquire good seats for 'Annie Get Your Gun', she told herself. Everybody said Ethel Merman was marvellous.

She changed from the grey-wool slacks and matching sweater she'd worn into the city to the simply cut black-velvet cocktail dress that she'd bought at Lord & Taylor three years ago but seldom had occasion to wear. She'd brought along the double strand of good pearls that had been her mother's. She placed them about her throat – remembering with sweet nostalgia how as a little girl she'd been allowed to play 'dress-up' with them.

She glanced up with a welcoming smile at the sound of a key in the door. Wayne strode into the room. His face radiated triumph.

'The meeting went well,' she said in relief.

'Great,' he conceded. 'Your old man ought to be thrilled.'

'We should be leaving in about thirty minutes. Sally got tickets for "Annie Get Your Gun." We'll have an early dinner at Toots Shor's. Nice, hunh?'

'It beats hamburgers at the West End Bar,' Wayne said, then frowned as his eyes focused on her dress. 'Don't you have something a little more exciting than that? Black is for old ladies.'

'It's supposed to be very smart.' Crestfallen, she inspected her reflection in the mirror above the dresser.

'And those pearls,' he derided. 'They look like something from Woolworth's.' *Mom's pearls*? 'Oh well, I don't suppose you brought anything else?'

'No. I thought this was fine.' Her earlier exuberance evaporated. *Was* black for old ladies? Did Mom's pearls need a cleaning?

Her pleasure in the evening's festivities was shaky. Sally loved this dress. She remembered it, and the pearls. When they were back home, she'd drive over to Albany and buy a cocktail dress that didn't look so matronly, she promised herself. She'd take Vera with her. Vera had wonderful taste.

On Sunday evening Paul went directly upstairs after dinner to focus on studying. Vera remained in the living room with Joel to listen to the radio for a while, then joined Paul in their bedroom. Ever conscious of her own lack of a college education – so important to her university-professor father – Vera was making an effort to read everything assigned to Paul in his English Lit course. Now she curled up in the slipper chair beneath a well-placed reading lamp and concentrated on *The Great Gatsby*.

Caught up in the novel, Vera started at the sound of Joel's voice calling from down below.

'Vera, phone call for you,' he yelled from downstairs. 'It's Doris.'

'I'll get it, Dad.' She darted across to the bedroom extension, picked it up. She kept her voice low so as not to distract Paul. 'Hi, Doris, how was New York?'

'Did Dad tell you?' Doris effervesced.

'Tell me what?'

'That, if you approve, he's hiring this woman down in New York to come up as his live-in housekeeper. She has a little girl about Laurie's age, so it'll mean you'll probably be stuck with watching her some time during the course of the day – but I figured she would be a playmate for Laurie.'

'Of course I agree.' How wonderful for Laurie to have another little girl in the house! 'But tell me about it.'

Vera listened avidly to Doris's report, then left the phone to hurry downstairs to discuss this with Joel. She'd been so worried about Laurie's lack of playmates. Ten minutes later, he was on the phone with Doris. The job was Fiona Garrett's. He dismissed the thought of having her come up for an initial interview.

'If your friend Sally recommends her, I'm sure she'll be fine.'

Two days later Doris and Vera, along with Laurie, were at the tiny railroad station – flanked by beds of daffodils – to meet Fiona's train.

'The only thing that worries me a little,' Doris confessed while they waited for the New York train to arrive, 'is that they'll be the only coloured family in this town.'

'There're only three Jewish families in town,' Vera reminded her. 'That hasn't bothered you.'

Doris hesitated. 'There were occasional incidents,' she confessed. 'When I was in third grade and this punk kid yelled *Christ-killer* at me. Dad said it was just that he was ignorant and brought up badly.' She shrugged this away. 'The only time I was ever seriously conscious of any difference between me and the other kids when I was growing up was on Rosh Hashanah and Yom Kippur, when Paul and I stayed out of school and Dad went to Albany for synagogue services.' Unexpectedly she chuckled. 'Wow, was New York an eye-opener for me. There the entire public school system closed down for the High Holidays!'

Then the train was chugging into the station. Vera and Doris waited expectantly. Laurie was enthralled with a friendly calico cat that had appeared.

'Nice kitty. Nice kitty,' she crooned, patting the sleek fur.

Two men stepped down from the train. Then a slender coloured woman in her late twenties appeared. She glanced about, seeming faintly apprehensive, Vera thought in instant sympathy. She deposited her large valise on the ground and reached up for the toddler being handed to her by the conductor.

Doris moved forward with a welcoming smile.

'Fiona?' she asked and the woman nodded shyly. 'I'm Doris Solomon. My father asked me and my sister-in-law to meet you. The car's right over there.'

'Thank you.' Fiona bent to retrieve her valise.

'Let me take Adele,' Doris said, holding out her arms to the dubious little girl.

'Laurie, this is Adele,' Vera said, her smile indicating this was a special event. 'You're going to have a playmate.'

Now the two little girls exchanged warm smiles.

'Did you see the kitty?' Laurie asked ebulliently. 'Look!'

It was going to be fine, Vera told herself. Dad would have a full-time housekeeper, and Laurie would have a friend. She brushed aside incipient anxiety about Fiona's loneliness in a town where there was no other coloured family. That, too, would change, she reassured herself. Paul said towns like Eastwood would surely become integrated. 'It's part of the changing climate of the country.'

Chapter Ten

Vera was grateful for the presence of Fiona and Adele in the Kahn household. Fiona gentle and efficient, Adele a warm, affectionate playmate for Laurie. Only with their arrival did she admit to the depth of her loneliness in Eastwood – though she had denied this when Paul questioned her.

Both Paul and his father were absent from early morning until early evening. Two or three afternoons a week, Doris popped in for a brief visit. On Friday evenings Doris and Wayne came over for dinner. Weekends were a major study time for Paul. At rare intervals his father cajoled Paul into taking her out to the new drive-in movie outside of town. In pyjamas and with a light blanket tucked around her, Laurie slept blissfully on the back seat – oblivious to the film's soundtrack and the rush to the refreshment stands at the designated break. This was the extent of her socializing.

Before Fiona and Adele arrived, Doris had ordered a playpen, crib, and high chair from Sears for Adele. Together Vera and Fiona worked out a comfortable schedule. It was an arrangement devised in heaven, Vera declared. She insisted on preparing breakfast for the family – allowing Fiona time to deal with Adele's waking-up period. After breakfast, Vera settled the two little girls on the living room floor or in the playpen Joel had set up in the den for Laurie. The lower floor ricocheted with their high spirits. Vera contrived to watch Laurie and Adele and to read at the same time. Within weeks, it seemed to her that Fiona and Adele had always been there.

Vera's pregnancy was proceeding comfortably. Joel talked with enthusiasm about the 'little Hanukkah present' Vera and Paul were giving him. Vera was touched, too, by Doris's solicitude for her, sensing a fresh sense of anticipation in her sister-in-law. She waited for word from Doris that she, too, was expecting. It was a time of an exploding birth rate. The world was replenishing itself from the devastating losses during the war years. It was such a happy time, Vera thought in approval.

The one sombre note intruding on this was the period on each Friday evening when Wayne sounded forth with such rage about the happenings in Palestine – a rage that Joel, too, expressed. In June, the British government had rejected a plea by Palestinian Jews for the issuance of 100,000 immigration certificates – for which President Truman had given his approval. When this was denied, the Resistance Movement blew up bridges linking Palestine with neighbouring Arab states. On June 29 – Black Saturday – the British hit back, arresting members of the Jewish Agency, sent soldiers into dozens of Jewish settlements, arresting many. The Haganah was forced into hiding.

'The Haganah is not a terrorist organization,' Wayne explained while the family lingered at a Friday-evening dinner table, enjoying Fiona's superb pecan pie and robust coffee. As always in Wayne's presence, Vera felt uneasy. Didn't the others see the way he looked at her? Didn't they notice that while his kiss in greeting was casual, his hand at her waist was that of a lover? And he *knew* how she reacted to his silent overtures, she tormented herself. *This was crazy*. 'The Haganah is a self-defence force organized to protect Jewish communities from Arab extremists – and now,' he conceded, 'to help victims of the Holocaust to reach Palestine.'

'You told me that during the war the Haganah worked in close cooperation with the British military,' Doris reminded, her face luminous.

'Oh sure.' Wayne's eyes reflected a bittersweet recall. 'We blew up oil refineries in Tripoli to deprive Nazi planes stationed at Syrian bases of the fuel they needed to fly. We were involved in a stream of special missions for the British.'

'Paul flew with the RAF,' Joel said, though Wayne knew this. 'And then he joined up with the American forces. As if he hadn't seen enough.'

'I got turned down flat by the American army.' Wayne's smile was rueful. 'They didn't want a guy who'd lost most of the vision in his right eye.'

The words of the blonde at Doris's luncheon party darted across her mind: 'If he weren't married to you and I weren't married to Lou, he could park his shoes under my bed anytime.' The American army might turn him down. Many women wouldn't. If she weren't married to Paul and he weren't married to Doris, how would she react?

'Hell, you did enough,' Joel said quickly. 'I'm proud of my two boys.'

In early December, Vera gave birth to a second daughter, Tracy Anne. Paul was jubilant at being with Vera for this second birth – shocking the doctor with his insistence on being with her during the delivery. Tears of happiness blurred Vera's vision as she watched Paul hold his new daughter in his arms with an air of love and wonder at the miracle of life. Joel was so elated at having two grandchildren now that he immediately opened a bank account for each. A month later, Fiona shyly admitted she'd opened a bank account in Adele's name.

'I can't put much in it,' she admitted, 'but it'll grow. And she'll have a chunk of her Daddy's insurance money. I want Adele to be a teacher – like Mr Paul. That's a fine profession.'

Paul rejoiced in the knowledge that he would receive his degree in June. At his father's prodding, he'd applied early in the new year for a position at the local high school.

'Paul, so many women teachers are leaving to have babies,' Joel had pointed out. 'Get your application in there fast. And it won't do any harm that you're a Kahn. This family's done a lot for the town.'

Seven weeks before graduation, Paul received word that he would teach history at Eastwood High School in September. During the summer session he would already be working towards his master's.

'When I complete my master's, my salary goes up,' he told his father and Vera while they waited for Doris and Wayne to arrive for the usual Friday-night dinner. 'We won't have to keep sponging off you, Dad.'

'I can afford to pay for keeping up the house,' Joel said gruffly. He gazed from Paul to Vera. She saw the wistful question in his eyes. 'If you have extra money, throw it into the bank.' He cleared his throat in the way that telegraphed his anxiety. 'There's no rush for you to move into your own house. There's plenty of room here. I know you and Vera must look forward to having your own place –'

Vera exchanged a swift glance with Paul.

'Dad, we'll stay here as long as you want us.' Her voice was deep with love. 'You've been so good to us.'

'Then it's settled.' Joel's face was etched with relief. 'This is *our* home. When I go, the house will be yours. Another generation of Kahns will grow up within these walls. Paul, your mother would be so pleased.'

At a special session of the UN General Assembly, an international committee was appointed to go to Palestine to study the situation there. The British Mandate was scheduled to expire on May 14, 1948. The Higher Arab Committee – under the thumb of the Mufti's men – boycotted the study of the UN Special Committee on Palestine. There were ugly hints that the Arab world was considering armed intervention. Vera tried to convince Doris that Wayne would not walk out on his job with the company – growing in importance – to return to Israel to join up with the Haganah again.

'Vera, I'd die if anything happened to Wayne,' Doris told Vera in soaring alarm. 'Hasn't he been through enough for one man?'

'Wayne loves his job. He won't leave,' Vera said firmly.

'If I were pregnant, maybe he wouldn't want to leave me. *But nothing's happening*. At first, he thought we should wait to start a family – but that's all over. Now we both want to have a baby –'

'Wayne's ambitious,' Vera reminded. 'Dad's giving him more and more authority in the company. He won't run off to Palestine,' she insisted. Yet she remembered his fervour at the Friday-evening dinners. To Wayne this might be a challenge he couldn't resist. 'Oh, Dad's planning a surprise dinner party for the five of us after graduation.' She deliberately diverted the conversation. 'Tell Wayne not to let on to Paul, but keep that evening open.'

On schedule Paul began the summer session at the college. He was taking a full load since he was not to start teaching until September.

'Mom would have been so pleased that I'll be teaching history,' Paul said in tender recall on the evening of his first class. He and Vera sat in the pleasant twilight with the pungent scent of roses and honeysuckle permeating the air. The pesky mosquitos had not yet arrived. Laurie and Tracy were asleep in their room; their grandfather was attending one of endless civic meetings. They heard the faint hum of the radio in Fiona's tiny apartment – kept low so as not to awaken Adele. 'She was such a history buff.'

'She'd be proud of you, Paul.' Vera remembered the circumstances of his mother's death. How she and his father had been telling him about early pioneer days in the West. His father had brought down a pistol kept locked in the cabinet so they could act out a wagon trail scene, where pioneers were being attacked by unfriendly Indians. His father hadn't realized the pistol was loaded. One shot had killed his mother. 'And my father,' Vera continued whimsically, 'would be proud of a son-in-law who is a teacher.'

'Eventually I'll teach at university level,' Paul plotted. 'Maybe someday Laurie and Tracy will teach. We'll be a teaching family. Instead of a gunnery family.' Bitterness crept into his voice. Paul saw only the ugliness of guns, Vera thought unhappily. He didn't understand that guns – military weapons – were essential to holding the peace.

'Aren't the flowers coming up gorgeously?' Vera reached for Paul's hand. 'It was all that rain these past two days.'

'We'll sit out here another ten minutes and enjoy the scents,' he decreed. 'Then it's upstairs for me – time to crack the books.'

On this late July afternoon – with the temperature soaring to record heights – Paul was impatient to be in his car and driving away from steamy Albany. Somehow, the heat always seemed less oppressive in Eastwood. But the sooner he acquired his master's, the sooner his teaching salary would rise. He felt a compulsion to show his father that he could acquire financial stability without being part of the family business.

Finally the school day was over. With a sigh of relief, Paul headed for his car. The long commute in this weather would not be pleasant, he acknowledged – but at the house he'd collapse before a fan and swig down a tall glass of lemonade.

'Hey, Paul!' A student from his last class of the day was charging after him.

Paul turned to face him. 'In this weather you don't run,' he joshed. 'We're breaking records today.'

'Tell me about it.' David Meyerberg was grim. 'I can't get my car to move. You go to Eastwood, don't you?' His eyes were hopeful.

'You need a lift?'

'To Schuylerville,' David explained. 'My car's such a heap I want my own garage man to take care of it. Can you drop me off at Schuylerville?'

'Sure thing. I'll be glad for the company,' Paul told him. 'It's a real *schlep* to Eastwood.'

For a few miles they talked about the school programme, then about the way ex-GIs were flooding the campuses.

'We'll be the best-educated generation in history.' Paul repeated the popular platitude.

'It's costing me,' David said, his smile wry. 'I spent the war years in Palestine. No GI benefits for me. But I wasn't sitting on my butt.' All at once he was defensive. 'I fought with the British. I came back home right after the war because my father was in bad health and my mother needed me.'

'I spent almost three years with the RAF,' Paul acknowledged, startled by David's revelation. 'Then I switched over to American intelligence.' Usually he was reluctant to talk about those days, but he felt a special kinship to another American who had fought for a country other than his own. 'My brother-in-law was in Palestine, too. He put in a lot of time with the Haganah. Was that your deal?'

'We operated under a British commander but in close contact with the Haganah. A lot of us were Haganah members.'

'Wayne joined the Haganah when he was sixteen,' Paul recalled. 'He was born in Brooklyn, but his family moved to Palestine when he was six. He jumped behind the German lines to help bring out refugees. I gather they were working in conjunction with the British.' Paul was assaulted by recall of his own months behind the German lines. Wayne could talk about those times. He couldn't – except with Vera.

'Wayne? You're not talking about Wayne Solomon?'

'That's right.' Paul swung his gaze from the road for an instant. 'Do you know Wayne?' How weird, he thought – to meet somebody in Albany, New York, who might know Wayne from Palestine. 'Were you in the same unit?'

'Not exactly.' David seemed suddenly wary. 'But we had encounters at intervals.' He paused. The atmosphere laden now with unspoken recriminations. 'I was familiar with his activities.'

Paul hesitated. 'I get the feeling that you know more about Wayne than we do.'

'Look, I'm not sure you want to know –' David was uneasy.

'He's married to my sister. He works for my father. I want to know,' Paul insisted.

'God, I feel funny telling you this,' David admitted.

'Tell me.' Paul's hands were tense on the wheel. He'd never liked Wayne, never trusted him – but everybody else thought he was a super-hero.

'I gather Wayne was terrific in his early years with the

Haganah. He had nerves of steel – nothing fazed him. He was chosen to be trained for the parachute jumps. Oh, he did a lot of good behind the German lines – but then he went bad. He was making fantastic personal deals, piling up a bankroll for himself. To hell with the Haganah. He was caught in the act.'

'God, the crap he throws around!' Paul's throat tightened in rage. 'To listen to him, he was the hero of the Haganah.'

'He was lucky not to have been shot as a traitor – but we had more urgent problems at that time.' David was grim. 'The last I heard, he'd managed to slip out of Palestine and had headed for South America.'

'He landed in New York,' Paul picked up. 'He lived with cousins there while he took some courses at Columbia. That's where my sister met him.' But there'd been trouble with his cousins, Doris said. They'd expected him to come into their firm – and he'd left to move to Eastwood. Doris said they weren't on speaking terms now.

'Look, I hope I didn't do wrong in telling you.' David was troubled.

'I'm grateful,' Paul said. 'Now we'll know how to deal.'

Paul said nothing about David Meyerberg's revelation when he first arrived home. He played briefly with Laurie and Adele until both little girls were whisked off to be prepared for bed. He listened to the radio news with his father, discussed Truman's chances of winning the presidential election the following year. Since last November's off-year elections had swept so many Republicans into power, the polls were predicting that the tide had turned in their favour. Congresswoman Clare Boothe Luce had cheerfully declared that 'Truman is a gone goose.'

'Don't write off Truman,' Joel insisted. 'He's done much for a lot of people. He was the first to commission

Negro officers. He's gone to bat for the farmers, vetoed bills that were against labour. He tried to put through a major housing programme plus medical care for the elderly. Come election day, a lot of people will remember.'

Paul was relieved when Fiona came to tell them she was about to serve dinner. His father had a meeting with his veterans' group this evening. He'd have a chance to talk with Vera about Wayne. Later, he'd have to face his father with this.

Normally dinner was a relaxed time of day that he enjoyed. Tonight he was impatient for it to be over. He ate Fiona's delicious meal without tasting. *How could everybody be so fooled by Wayne?*

After dinner – with his father off to his meeting – Paul suggested to Vera that they take a stroll in the approaching dusk. The heat had receded. There was a comforting breeze outdoors.

'Tell Fiona. She'll listen out for the kids.'

Not until they were well away from the house – because he felt an obligation to keep this within the family – did he reveal what David Meyerberg had told him on the drive home.

'You believe Wayne's been lying all along?' Vera was visibly shaken.

'There's no reason for David to have dreamt this up. Dad's going to be so upset. And how are we going to tell Doris?'

'I don't think we can. I doubt that she'd even believe it, Paul. She adores him.'

'We must tell Dad. God knows what he could pull in the business.' Paul sighed. 'It seems wrong not to let Doris know the truth.'

'It would crush her,' Vera warned. 'If she believed it.'

'We'll put it up to Dad,' Paul decided after a moment. 'How can she spend the rest of her life in a lie?'

'She'll hate us for telling her – and she won't believe it.'

They returned to the house. Paul focused on studying. Vera made a show of trying to read, but Paul knew she was distraught about what he'd confided. *Was* David lying? What would be the purpose?

Paul and his father sat on the screen porch, and avidly discussed Jackie Robinson's performance as the first Negro baseball player in the National League. Vera rose from the glider, headed into the house for a pitcher of ice tea.

'I'm glad the Brooklyn Dodgers had the good sense to grab him,' Joel said with satisfaction. Vera recalled Paul's explaining to her that club owners were nervous about offending customers by bringing coloured players onto their teams. When Robinson was hired, the Cardinals had threatened a boycott. 'If I were a betting man, I'd put a bundle on Brooklyn's winning the pennant this year.'

From Paul's taut expression, she knew he was about to report his conversation with David to his father. When she returned with a tray laden with a pitcher and glasses, Paul leapt to his feet to take it from her. The atmosphere crackled with tension. Joel was gaping at Paul as though in shock.

'You believe that idiot?' Joel challenged, his face flushed.

'Why would he lie?' Paul countered.

'Wayne parachuted behind the lines to bring out Nazi victims. He put his life on the line time after time. You know about his war injury – he has almost no vision in his right eye. That man resents Wayne,' Joel scoffed. 'It happens all the time. Wayne's a war hero. He's a damn fine-looking man. That creep probably did nothing more than some pencil-pushing. He ought to be horsewhipped for lying like that! Don't say a word about this to Doris,' he ordered. 'It would break her heart.'

Chapter Eleven

Vera knew that Paul must respect his father's wishes regarding Wayne, but she feared it was creating a barrier between them. She felt disloyal to Paul in agreeing mentally with his father. Now she dreaded the Friday-evening dinners, when Wayne and Joel were inclined to dissect the volatile happenings in Palestine. Tonight, she vowed, she and Doris would focus much of the conversation on the opening of school on Monday morning. Paul was simultaneously excited and nervous about taking on his first classes.

Vera had enjoyed these past days. Paul was out of summer school and free to spend much time with her and the children. Out of his father's hearing, Paul acknowledged that he worried about Wayne's real background.

'Maybe I'm overly suspicious,' he conceded to Vera while they prepared to go downstairs on this Friday evening. Laurie and Tracy were asleep in their room. Tantalizing aromas drifted through the house. The heat wave that had imprisoned the town for days had let up. 'Dad could be right. Anyhow, I'll probably never run into David again. He's moving to Florida with his wife. They both hate the rough winters up here.'

'You don't really know this man,' Vera reminded gently. How could it be true, when Wayne was so obsessed by the volatile situation in Palestine? Doris was terrified that he'd run back to rejoin the Haganah, now illegal and underground. She paused at the sound of a car pulling up downstairs. 'That's Doris and Wayne.'

Despite Vera and Doris's efforts to steer the dinner conversation away from the tensions in Palestine, the five at the table were soon engrossed in the situation. On September 1, the UN Special Committee on Palestine had presented a recommendation that Palestine be divided into a Jewish state and an Arab state, with Jerusalem becoming an international city. Now it must be considered by the General Assembly.

'The Palestinian Arabs won't accept it,' Wayne predicted contemptuously. 'Hell, they could have had their own Arab state back in 1937 – and they turned it down flat. Why should we expect anything different today?'

'If the Jews get their own state – and I pray it happens – then half-a-dozen Arab countries will be poised to pounce.' Joel was pessimistic. 'Who's going to fight for them?'

'The Haganah,' Wayne pinpointed, a pulse hammering at his forehead. 'They're waiting for the day to show what they can do.'

'That can't be until the British Mandate goes off,' Doris reminded. 'You said that won't happen until May 1948. Wayne, let's not worry now.' She was struggling for calm.

Wayne's concern was so very real. How could she and Paul believe what David Meyerberg said? Vera taunted herself.

'Are you anxious about the first day of school?' Joel turned to Paul with a joshing smile.

'I'm a little nervous,' Paul admitted. 'And excited. This is what I want to do with my life.' Vera intercepted his fleeting, defensive glance at Wayne. To his father, he was thinking, teaching was pallid beside being a member of the Haganah.

'Doris, have you talked to the people at the church about setting up a nursery school group there?' Vera intervened.

'I have an appointment tomorrow morning.' Doris glowed. 'It'd be very small at first, of course. And just for three hours each morning.'

'Laurie and Adele would love it,' Vera said enthusiastically.

'Wayne doesn't.' All at once Doris's voice was reproachful. 'He thinks I'm out of my mind.'

'It'll work as long as you're willing to contribute your time.' Wayne was casual. 'But the minute they have to pay a salary, it'll fall apart. And how long will you be able to stay with it?'

There was a silent communication between Doris and Wayne that she and Paul and Dad were not supposed to understand, Vera thought. Wayne was saying that Doris would surely be pregnant soon and not available to run the day nursery. Oh, let it happen, Vera prayed. Doris would be so happy.

She was grateful for Doris's friendship, Vera thought, drawing away from the unexpectedly argumentative undertones of the dialogue between Doris and Wayne. More than friendship, she amended. Doris was the sister she'd never had. Now that Fiona was in the house, Doris would coax her out on small excursions. The two of them would drive to Cambridge or Greenwich or Schuylerville for lunch. They would drive to Saratoga or even Albany for a 'change of scenery,' as Doris would laughingly describe these outings.

She sensed that Doris's father, too, was aware of some dissension between Doris and Wayne of late. It seeped through in small ways – such as the faint recrimination on Doris's part that Wayne disparaged her efforts to start up the nursery group with one of the local churches. Doris and Wayne were both unhappy that she wasn't pregnant, of course. Once that happened, everything would be all right between them again. Yet Vera was ever conscious that Wayne – without the others being aware of this – was fighting to draw her into a traitorous situation. She was furious at herself for feeling attracted to him. *This was crazy.*

She forced herself back into the conversation. Paul was talking earnestly about the shortcomings in American education.

'I look at these kids, and I know we have to give them more to prepare them for the future. They're the leaders of tomorrow. If we allow ourselves to be caught up in another war, they're the ones who'll die.'

'Somewhere in this world, there'll always be fighting.' Wayne shrugged. 'It's human nature. That's why you're in the right business, Dad,' he joshed. 'There'll always be a need for guns.'

There was much apprehension in the Kahn household in the ensuing weeks as the General Assembly of the UN at Lake Success, New York, debated the Palestine problem. For Vera, Friday-evening dinners were an emotional battlefield. More than the others at the table, she acknowledged, she and Wayne knew the urgency afflicting Palestinian Jews, realized the impact of the decision on Holocaust victims yearning for a safe home. The crisis situation evoked a bond between them that she struggled to destroy.

On a blustery Saturday afternoon in late November – after putting Tracy down for a nap – Vera headed downstairs with Laurie. This was the one weekend in six when Fiona went with Adele to visit her mother in New York. Always on these occasions, Joel insisted on taking Vera and Paul out for Saturday-evening dinner. Cal's wife would come over to sit with Laurie and Tracy.

Arriving in the foyer, Vera was conscious of the excited voices of Paul and his father talking over the sound of the radio.

'Vera!' Joel greeted her with an air of triumph while Paul reached to scoop up Laurie. 'It's happened! The General Assembly voted this afternoon in favour of partition!'

'Oh, that's wonderful!' But to Vera it was a bittersweet victory. If this had happened in 1937 – when it was first proposed – the Jews in Germany would have fled there. *Mama and Papa and Ernst would still be alive.*

'We'll see a lot of trouble,' Paul warned. 'The Arabs are against it. They're talking already about war.'

'Let me call Wayne,' Joel said. 'He may not have heard the news.'

'Why don't you ask him and Doris to come over for dinner,' Vera suggested impulsively. Wayne could tell them what the Jews in Palestine would be up against. 'I can throw something together easily. I'll drive over to the butcher's for a roast and –'

'Great!' Joel beamed. 'This is a time for the family to be together.'

'It took Hitler to make us realize we were Jews,' Paul said with a touch of humour. He smiled at his father's glare of reproach. 'Oh, we knew in the general sense – and in big cities like New York, Jews were more aware of what was happening in Palestine all these years.' He reached for Vera's hand – knowing, she guessed, that her thoughts were with her parents and her brother today. 'I'll drive over with you to the butcher shop. Dad can practise up on his babysitting.'

'I know,' she jibed. 'You don't trust my driving.'

Three hours later, the three men sat at the dinner table while Vera and Doris brought in platters of food.

'Let's face it,' Wayne said bluntly. 'The Jews in Palestine are not entirely satisfied with the partition. But we'll accept it because it's a chance to live in peace. The Palestinian Arabs are going to riot. We *know* that.' Vera saw

Doris tense – she'd caught the 'we' that Wayne unconsciously used. 'Again, the Arabs have a chance to proclaim their own state and they're rejecting it. So what will happen? The other Arab countries will move in to grab as much of Palestine as they can manage.'

'What will happen to the Palestinian Arabs?' Vera asked.

'Those who've lived in what is to be the Jewish state will run,' he predicted. 'Oh, some will stay – the intelligent, thinking ones who're not eaten up by hatred. Most will run. They could have their own state,' he reminded. 'But they'll get lost now in the other Arabs' grab for land. We're not prepared for war, but we can be sure it's coming. The whole Arab League will be out for Jewish blood.'

It was a disquieting evening, yet Wayne spoke about the fighting spirit of the Palestinian Jews with an eloquence that was magnetic.

'They'll need money,' Joel said at last with fatalistic calm. 'And where better to look for it than from American Jews? If the homeland is to be established, it must be now.'

As usual on Monday morning, Wayne arrived at the factory a few moments past eight – emulating his father-in-law. But this morning he didn't settle himself at his desk to focus on the day's long-distance calls to be made. He went straight to Joel's office.

'Dad, let's talk,' he said, pausing at the entrance. A confident, determined figure in what was his daily uniform – expensive flannel slacks and one of the array of turtlenecks that Doris ordered for him regularly from Brooks Brothers in New York. Attire that established him as a rebel.

'Problems?' Joel glanced up in welcome.

'I see some tremendous business out there if we handle ourselves right.' He walked to a chair across from Joel's oversized desk, sat down. 'It's off beat,' he admitted, 'but it'll earn us a bundle and do a lot of good for the right people. I want to reach out to my contacts with the Haganah.' He chuckled. 'I'll run up a hell of a phone bill.'

'Sell them guns?' Joel was startled. 'Wayne, that's illegal.'

'We won't sell to the Haganah,' Wayne pinpointed. 'We'll find some small principality that we'll sell to. It's not our concern if they resell to somebody else. It won't happen right away. Lots of money will have to be raised before they can buy. You wouldn't believe how little they have! A few thousand rifles, some hand guns, machine guns. They have no tanks, no cannons. Against the heavy arms of the Arab nations. But we can help,' he pursued earnestly. 'We can put guns in the hands of the 45,000 men, women, and teenagers who make up the Haganah. Not right away,' he soothed. 'But it's time to lay the groundwork.'

'Wayne, it's illegal,' Joel repeated.

'It's illegal for Arabs to riot and kill Jews,' Wayne shot back. 'Riots are breaking out all over Palestine today. Jews are being killed for no reason other than that they're Jews. It's Hitler all over again!'

'I've never done anything against the law,' Joel stalled, but Wayne knew he was emotionally involved in the situation in Palestine.

'It was illegal for the American colonists to fight the British – but it was necessary. It's *necessary* for the Jews in Palestine to be armed. Egypt, Syria, Iraq, Saudi Arabia, Lebanon, Transjordan – they'll all be on the attack. We'll only be one supplier – but every one will count.'

'It's dangerous.' Joel was ambivalent.

'We'll be in the clear,' Wayne insisted, leaning forward zealously. 'I know how to handle this deal. Let me start laying the groundwork now.' His mind was rushing ahead. 'The British Mandate will be up on May 14, 1948. They'll withdraw. The Jewish state will be born. Between now and May 14, the Jewish defences have to be set up. We can be sure fundraising – in amounts you won't believe – is already in progress. I'll arrange meetings in London – say, sometime in March.'

'Will you be safe?' Joel was anxious. Wayne felt a rush of relief. The old boy was on his side now.

'Doris and I will fly to London for a second honeymoon,' he improvised. 'We'll go to Switzerland for another three days. Nobody will know that I'm conducting business.'

'I don't want anything to happen to you and Doris.' Joel was torn between the need to help, the realization that this was not a strictly legal transaction, and fear for the safety of Doris and Wayne.

'We're a young couple deprived of a honeymoon because of the war,' he said with deliberate calm. 'The business is doing well. You're giving us this as a belated wedding present. It'll work,' he said with conviction. 'No problems.'

Not until early in the new year – with Golda Meir on a frenzied fundraising tour in the United States and Palestinian Jews under violent attack by Palestinian Arabs and neighbouring Arab cohorts – did Wayne begin his campaign. Doris was enthralled when he announced her father was giving them a 'second honeymoon' in London in the spring. Guiltily she agreed that her nursery group could be postponed until the fall.

'And we'll pop over to Switzerland for three days – since everything is so close by plane,' Wayne told her. He exuded anticipation.

'We're going to fly to London?' She was simultaneously fascinated and alarmed at the prospect.

'Sweetheart, it's the only way to travel now,' he soothed. 'I'll make all the arrangements for transportation and hotels. You go for your passport. Oh, you'll want some new clothes. Drive down to New York for a day to shop. Take Vera with you,' he ordered. 'She has perfect taste. Let her choose.'

Later in January, Joel asked Vera if she would come into the office for an afternoon to serve as translator for correspondence Wayne was sending to Europe.

'Wayne is a real entrepreneur,' he said with pride. 'He sees whole new markets for us.'

'I'd love to help,' Vera said eagerly. 'I can type, too. If you can use me in the office for two or three hours each day, Fiona will look after the children.' This was a welcome adventure.

'You mean, come in on a regular basis?' Joel was startled by her offer.

'I have so much free time, Dad. I like to be busy.'

'Then Wayne will have a part-time, multi-lingual secretary,' Joel gloated. 'He will give you the letters in English. You can translate them into either French or German – whatever Wayne needs – then type them up for us. You'll go on salary,' he insisted and shook his head when she began to protest. 'You work, you're paid. I won't have it any other way.'

Now, each afternoon, Vera went into the factory. She looked forward to these brief excursions. A tiny office was assigned to her. Wayne gave her only two or three letters each day, but often revised them several times. It was clear he was serious about this new campaign.

Vera arrived at her usual time this Friday afternoon – the end of her second week on the job. Wayne was waiting in her office with two handwritten letters – already in the process of being revised.

'Hi,' he greeted her exuberantly. 'I want these two to go out today. No more revisions,' he promised with a chuckle while she slid out of her coat and hung it away. 'This may seem like chasing rainbows, but even one sale sets us up in a whole new arena.'

'I understand that,' Vera said softly.

'Oh, I have a special assignment for you today. I want you to write for reservations for Doris and me at a hotel in Geneva. Here's the address. The Geneva Intercontinental. Ask for a suite with a beautiful view. That's all part of the scene,' Wayne pursued. 'I must make people over there believe that Kahn is an important firm.' He leaned over her shoulder while she slid a letterhead into the typewriter, turned to read the first sales letter.

She was conscious of his hot breath on the back of her neck, the closeness of his firm, muscular body. Today, the door to the office was closed because he had said the noise from the factory floor was destroying his concentration. She was aware, too, that their father-in-law was in Albany on business.

'Wait,' Wayne ordered peremptorily. 'I want to change the second paragraph.' He reached to take the letter with one hand while the other fastened itself at her shoulder. A moment later it slid from her shoulder, under her arm, and to her breast.

'Wayne –' She stiffened in shock. 'Don't do that.'

'Why not?' he challenged, his mouth at her ear now. 'We've been fighting this since you arrived in Eastwood.'

'No!' She reached to remove his hand. Her heart was pounding. 'Wayne, stop it.'

'We were born to be together,' he said urgently and swung about to draw her to her feet. 'I dare you to deny that!'

'We can't do this,' she protested while he nuzzled against her. *What kind of magic did he hold over her?* 'It's wrong.'

'Who's to know?' he challenged, exuding triumph. 'We'll be discreet. Nobody will be hurt, but we'll grab a chunk of heaven for ourselves.'

'No,' she rejected, struggling to draw away. Assaulted by reproachful images of Paul and the children. Of Doris. 'I'm serious, Wayne,' she warned. 'You let me go or I'll scream.' Her eyes dared him to defy her. Wayne was too ambitious to gamble on losing this way of life. He wouldn't take a chance on her creating an ugly scene.

'I thought you were a ball of fire,' he taunted in rage. 'You're a scared little girl.' He bent to retrieve the letter that had fallen to the floor. 'Translate this and get it out airmail to Geneva.'

Vera sat immobile as Wayne stalked out of the office. She'd face no more such encounters with him, she calmed herself. But she didn't want to lose this small job with the company. Not even to Paul would she admit that she was increasingly restless in the pattern of her life. She needed these hours away from the house to use what skills she had to offer. If the company's foreign sales grew, she could move into a full-time job. It was a stimulating prospect. But she must be careful not to allow Wayne to interfere with that.

In the cosy dark warmth of their bedroom, Vera lay awake beside Paul, who was already half-asleep. This afternoon's confrontation with Wayne had left her shaken. It wasn't love that she felt for Wayne. What was the American word for it? She searched her brain, pulled out a sentence she had read in a woman's magazine. She was infatuated with him. *It had nothing to do with love.*

She moved closer to Paul, tossed a slender leg across

his, burrowed her face in the crook of his neck with a need to reassure herself that all was well in her marriage. Iris used to say that American men were faithful to their women – European men considered it their right to play on the side.

'Vera?' A faint surprised arousal in Paul's sleep-muffled voice.

'Oh, Paul, I love you so much,' she whispered.

'I love you, baby,' he murmured, his arms encircling her. Fully awake now. 'There's a poem by a much-loved British woman poet that begins with "How do I love thee? Let me count the ways." I love you, Vera, in every way a man can love –'

Chapter Twelve

Sitting in a corner of the living room sofa, Vera listened absorbedly while Paul and his father discussed the Soviet takeover of Czechoslovakia – just discussed in sombre detail on a radio forum.

'The world grows more insane every day,' Joel sighed. 'Last month Gandhi – a man of peace – dies at the hands of an assassin. Now Stalin has taken over a small, defenceless country. What'll he grab next?'

'Why has the world let the Communists do this?' Vera asked passionately, then paused, her eyes bright with comprehension. 'They're afraid of starting another world war –'

'Something like that,' Paul acknowledged.

'I'm not sure I'm happy that Doris and Wayne are going to London and Geneva in April.' All at once Joel appeared apprehensive.

'Dad, they'll be fine,' Paul soothed. 'We're not on the brink of war again.'

'Tell that to Stalin,' Jocl said grimly.

'Doris and I are going into New York Saturday week,' Vera reminded. It was unnerving to think about war again. *No more such talk*. 'To shop for clothes for her trip. You two will be on babysitting duty.'

'We'll survive it.' Paul chuckled.

'Oh, Fiona's going into the city, too,' Vera added.

'Let's live it up, Dad. Call in Cal's wife to stay with the kids while we go out to some fancy place for dinner. Vera and Doris probably won't get home until midnight.'

'Wayne will be on the loose, too,' Joel pointed out. 'We'll bring him along with us.'

Instinctively Vera glanced at Paul. The less he saw of Wayne, the happier he was, she thought ruefully – and was uncomfortable, remembering her ugly encounter with Wayne. He'd made no further physical overtures, yet at intervals she was conscious of his scrutiny. Sometimes mocking, other times amorous. And she was always fearful that others in the family would notice.

This Saturday morning was one of those rare March days when the promise of spring permeated the air, Vera thought with pleasure. Spring was her favourite season. She dressed in the bathroom so as not to awaken Paul. Laurie and Tracy, too, were asleep. They seemed to know, she thought tenderly, that Saturday was Daddy's day to sleep late. Later they'd sit before the television set their grandfather had just bought and watch cartoons. She glanced at her watch. It was a few minutes before seven. Doris would be here soon.

The downstairs quiet was broken only by Adele's effervescent chatter. She and Fiona were driving into New York with them. Fiona would visit her mother in Harlem, then meet them at the 116th Street subway stop at Columbia for the drive home. In a freshly pressed skirt and sweater, beguiling Adele sat at the breakfast table – small legs swinging back and forth in anticipation of a day with her much-loved grandmother.

'I'm just putting up pancakes.' Fiona smiled in high spirits. 'And the coffee's ready. Sit yourself at the table.'

They had just finished breakfast when Doris arrived.

'Fiona, nobody makes coffee like you,' Doris said, dropping into a chair at the table. 'May I have a cup before we leave?'

'You know you can,' Fiona said affectionately and reached for the percolator.

Traffic on the road was light this morning. Earlier than anticipated, Doris was turning off the highway and listening to Fiona's directions. Fiona's mother lived in the Harlem River Houses, the first large-scale Federally funded housing provided for low-income residents of Harlem.

'My mother was real lucky to get into the project,' Fiona said. 'There's room for only 574 families.'

The development was divided into three groups, Fiona explained. Her mother lived in one of the two buildings west of Seventh Avenue – arranged around a large rectangular plaza. The red-brick buildings consisted of four storeys and basement, with glass-enclosed stairshafts. Very simple, but pleasant, Vera decided.

'She's got electric refrigeration and steam heat. And there's a nursery school for working mothers,' Fiona added wistfully. 'But I wasn't allowed to move in with Mama. It would have been too many in that one apartment – her and my two sisters and two brothers and my older brother's wife. Even if I could have got on the list, it'd be five or ten years before I'd be up for an apartment.'

At Fiona's direction, Doris pulled up at the entrance to one of the buildings. Fiona and Adele emerged from the car with smiles of anticipation.

'Be sure to watch the time,' Doris cautioned.

'I know,' Fiona said lightheartedly. 'We'll be at the Columbia subway stop at six o'clock sharp.'

Vera was aware of Doris's odd silence as they drove away from the housing project. She seemed troubled.

'I always had a feeling of guilt the years I was at Barnard, then at Columbia grad school,' she said at last. 'There're maybe a dozen blocks between the campus and

Harlem – but they're worlds apart. I grew up in Eastwood, protected from so much. Even during the Depression years, I don't think I truly knew what it was like outside Eastwood. We read the newspapers and heard the radio – but Paul and I were so coddled by Dad. Then I went away to school – and so did Paul – and our eyes were opened.'

'Fiona's family sound like such good people,' Vera said. 'Her mother's always busy with some church activity.'

'When I was up at Columbia grad school, Sally and I used to go for long walks around Harlem. Once we went with some other students to the Apollo Theatre to see a show. The audiences there were mixed, but the performers and theatre staff were all Negro. And then we discovered the two synagogues for coloured Jews.'

'I didn't know there were coloured Jews.' Vera was astonished.

'The congregation on West 128th Street is mainly Ethiopian. Services are held in English and Hebrew. Oh, these are not the Falashas,' she began and laughed at Vera's bewildered stare. 'A few Falashas – also coloured Jews – live in New York, but they're a different group and don't mix with these. The Falashas claim to be descended from King Solomon and the Queen of Sheba. The Ethiopian Jews at the synagogue here trace their ancestry from Judah and Benjamin. I know,' she joshed. 'You're going to run for books to read up on all this.' Vera's thirst for knowledge was almost an obsession.

'I never knew any coloured people until I met coloured American soldiers in London.' Vera frowned in recall. The British couldn't understand the segregated armies. Paul had told her that after the war the situation was sure to change – and it had. 'I wonder sometimes if Fiona feels as though she's living in exile –'

'She goes to church every Sunday,' Doris reminded. 'I

don't think she socializes with any of the churchgoers, but she's welcomed there.'

'Adele and Laurie start kindergarten next September. I hope the children there don't see Adele as something – exotic. It doesn't mean anything to Laurie that Adele's skin is darker than hers – but I'm uneasy about other children,' Vera confessed.

'They'll see that Adele and Laurie are close friends. It'll be fine,' Doris insisted. 'Let's start our shopping at Altman's,' she effervesced. 'My favourite of all New York stores. And that means we can have lunch first at the Charleston Gardens. I'm famished.'

Vera was caught up in the excitement of Doris and Wayne's trip to Europe. She had briefed Doris on not-to-be-missed points of interest in London. For her, London would always be special. She was anxious to learn first-hand about conditions in London – which were said to be desperate, as in all of Europe.

On April 3, President Truman signed the Foreign Assistance Act of 1948 – already being called the Marshall Plan, for Secretary of State Marshall. Like many Americans, Paul and his father were jubilant.

'It's a wonderful effort on the part of this country,' Paul told Vera with pleasure. 'It'll help Great Britain and Europe get back on their feet. There'll be sufficient food, warm clothes, raw materials to rebuild factories and railroads. It's part of building a peaceful world.'

A few days later, Vera drove Doris and Wayne to the railroad station. From New York, they would fly to London on a TWA Constellation, remain there ten days, then fly to Geneva for another three days. Vera was enthralled at the thought of crossing the Atlantic in a matter of hours. She remembered her nine-day crossing with Laurie on the *Argentina*.

'I wouldn't dare tell Wayne,' Doris confessed as he brought their luggage out of the car, 'but I'm scared to death of flying.'

Doris fell in love with London. Their room at the famous Savoy Hotel was elegant. They dined in only the finest restaurants. Wayne was smug about the dollar exchange, hugely in their favour. They saw the Tower of London, Westminster Abbey, the British Museum, the Changing of the Guard at Buckingham Palace – all the landmarks sought out by tourists. Doris was awed by the magnificent art collections at the National Gallery and at the National Portrait Gallery behind it, though Wayne had little patience for her dalliance there.

At intervals their sightseeing was sidetracked so that Wayne could meet with what he called 'business contacts' that could mean possible orders for the Kahn factory in the future. On three evenings, they went to the theatre.

Because Joel had requested this, Wayne took Doris on a tour of London's East End – the equivalent, Joel had heard, of New York City's Lower East Side. They visited the Great Synagogue at Duke's Place.

The one disconcerting note, Doris admitted, was the feeling she sensed here in London that most Americans were boorish. The British were astounded at a standard of living that allowed so many Americans to travel abroad – too often, noisy Americans with undisciplined children. From a casual conversation with a pair of French tourists, she gathered that many Europeans were balking at the Americanization of their continent. They feared their own culture would be lost to that of America.

At the end of their ten days in London, Doris and Wayne flew to Geneva. On the late-afternoon taxi-ride from the airport, she was impressed by the city's air of immaculateness and serenity. She was delighted with their reservations at the elegant Hotel Richmond.

'Oh, Wayne, look at the view!' She stood awestruck at a window that looked out over dazzling blue Lake Geneva and across the lake to Mont Blanc in the French Alps. 'It makes me wish I had a canvas and paints right here.' For a few wistful moments she was catapulted back to those precious days at the Art Students League.

Wayne chuckled. 'Honey, it takes a master to do justice to something like that.'

'Wayne, not everybody is a master –' Should that relegate them to being only observers? she asked herself in silent defiance.

'Let's unpack and go down for a drink before dinner,' Wayne said. 'It'll be relaxing.'

Over a glass of white wine and later a superb dinner, Doris was conscious of an unfamiliar euphoria. Their coming on this trip was the best thing that could have happened to them, she decided. Wayne was in such a good mood. He'd been working too hard – that was why he'd kept tearing her down the way he had. He hadn't meant to be nasty. And *she* should have been more sympathetic.

As they prepared to retire for the night, Wayne talked ebulliently about the Swiss banking system.

'The Swiss have this terrific respect for money,' Wayne told her. Like himself, she thought involuntarily. 'They have the greatest banking system in the world. You wouldn't believe the amount of Jewish and German money that poured into Switzerland when Hitler started his rampage. And fortunes from royal families who've been thrown out of power.'

'What's so special about Swiss banks?' Doris asked curiously. 'I know they have that reputation –'

'They're the most solid in the world,' Wayne said with

gusto. 'And private. A Swiss bank assigns you an account number. Nobody in the world except you and one director of the bank knows that number – and he can't divulge it to another soul. You bank by number. Your name is never mentioned.'

Doris laughed. 'I don't know enough about business to understand why that's important.'

'You don't have to know.' He reached out to pull her close. 'You're looking beautiful tonight.' He nuzzled his face against hers. 'What's that perfume you're wearing?'

'Chanel No. 5,' she whispered. It had been an anniversary present from him.

'A great perfume but not right for you.' He made it a faint reproach. 'Try something else.'

'All right,' she promised, yearning to please him. 'I'll go shopping tomorrow.'

This would be a night when he was an eager, passionate lover, she told herself, exhilarated by the prospect. It wasn't always like that . . .

Doris awoke in the morning with an instant realization that she was alone in their suite. The slacks and jacket Wayne had dropped across a chair last night were gone. The scent of his after-shave lotion filtered into the bedroom. She pulled herself into a semi-sitting position, reached for the note propped against their travel clock.

'I've gone out for an early business appointment. Have breakfast and go shopping. Everybody will expect us to bring back clocks from Geneva. Use your American Express cheques. I'll be back at the hotel around noon.'

Doris fought down a wave of insecurity. It was ridiculous to feel this way because she would be on her own for a few hours. Many people spoke English here – and her college French was serviceable in a pinch. Not like

Vera's, she conceded – but she could manage to order breakfast, to shop for clocks for gifts back home.

She left the bed and crossed to the window. Lake Geneva lay before her – exquisite and serene. Beyond rose Mont Blanc, its peak wrapped in clouds. Now she noted the telephone book that lay open on the floor. She picked it up, saw the pencilled check mark beside the name of a bank. Why was Wayne going to a bank this morning? They could cash their American Express cheques here at the hotel.

Fiona had prepared a festive dinner to welcome Doris and Wayne home. Vera had decorated the living room and dining room with displays of golden forsythia. Now the family settled in the living room for more of Fiona's superb coffee. Paul was eagerly questioning Doris about London.

'Oh, I went to see the building where you and Vera lived in London,' Doris said conscientiously. 'I said *hello* for both of you.' And Vera glowed.

'Conditions will ease up with the Marshall Plan in effect now,' Paul surmised, and Vera nodded in agreement. 'It's time.'

'The British are so grateful,' Joel picked up. 'I read somewhere that Churchill called it "the most unsordid act in history" and that the London *Economist* wrote that it was "the most straight-forward generous thing that any country has ever done for others." I think most people realize that we're truly one world today.'

'Or should be,' Paul added, all at once sombre.

'How's the teaching?' Doris asked Paul.

'To me it's exciting,' Paul told her, his face brightening. 'I know, it seems mundane to others.' Vera intercepted his subconscious glance at Wayne. *Why must Paul apologize for teaching? It was important.* 'But I see an urgent need for better education in the years ahead. The future of the earth depends on that.' He paused, chuckled. 'Of course, not everybody agrees with my interpretation of how to achieve that. We had a special Parents Night last week. One mother was disturbed that I've set up my classroom in a non-traditional fashion. I like an informal arrangement – with chairs set up around tables. I try for a team effort, with teams competing. She shook her head and said, "Mr Kahn, I think you need a housekeeper here."'

'The kids love Paul,' Vera intervened defensively. She was proud that he was taking night classes towards his master's, would take additional classes during the summer session. 'Next week, he's taking a group to New York by charter bus to see "Kiss Me, Kate".'

'Have you been going into the office while Wayne's been away?' Doris asked. Only Doris knew how she welcomed the opportunity to be involved in activities outside the house. As Doris, too, yearned to be otherwise engaged. Why must women be satisfied being wives and mothers? *Some women wanted that plus more.*

'Dad's letting me take on some of the routine correspondence to relieve Gloria,' Vera told her. Gloria was Joel's longtime secretary. 'I love it.'

'Vera's sharp,' Joel said approvingly. 'She set up form letters that can be used with personalized figures. It saves a lot of work. She may be a kid in years,' he joshed, 'but she sure as hell has an old business head.' Now he glanced about at the others with an air of apology. 'You won't mind if I drag Wayne off to the den for business talk –'

'Did you take a lot of photos?' Vera asked Doris while Joel and Wayne secluded themselves in the den.

'I've got rolls of film to have developed,' Doris effervesced. 'That 35-millimetre camera Dad gave us never stopped working.'

Vera welcomed the arrival of spring. Still, Laurie and

Tracy had no playmate other than Adele. There were no others in their age range in the neighbourhood – but the three were a happy trio. Because of Doris, Vera acknowledged, Laurie had been invited to a birthday party next week. But Adele had not been included. Only to herself would she admit this was because Adele was their housekeeper's daughter – and coloured.

In September, Doris would open her small nursery group. Laurie and Adele would be part of it. And in another year, they'd both be in kindergarten. Their social lives would improve, Vera promised herself.

Because of Paul's role as a teacher, he and Vera were becoming involved in the social circle composed of local teachers. Most, Vera noted quickly, harboured thoughts far more conservative than Paul's. She was aware, too, of the undercurrent of politics that hardly meshed with Paul's own ambitions for the high school. Still, he was doing the work he loved.

In the weeks ahead, the table-talk at the Kahn household zigzagged between the happenings in Israel and in the Soviet Union. This was supposed to be a time of peace, Vera agonized along with Paul. The war was *over*. At the factory, Vera was conscious of the escalation of orders. Joel had scheduled a second shift again – the first since the end of World War II.

On May 14, 1948, the British Mandate in Palestine was lifted. At shortly past 4:00 AM on that afternoon, David Ben-Gurion announced the birth of the state of Israel. It was immediately recognized by the United States and tiny Guatemala. By the morning of May 15, the armies of Lebanon, Iraq, Syria, Transjordan and Egypt – with soldiers from Saudi Arabia fighting beside those of Egypt – had invaded the new state. The Arabs boasted they would crush Israel within ten days. But it soon became apparent that this was not to be.

At a Friday-evening family dinner in early June – after Laurie and Tracy had been put to bed – the three men were in noisy argument about conditions in Israel.

'Enough of this,' Vera interrupted with mock sternness. 'The dining room is becoming a war room in this house.'

'The Arabs won't be satisfied until they wipe Israel off the map,' Wayne shot back. 'Each time the Palestinians are offered their own state, they shriek *No!* They want all of Palestine to be Arab. They won't be happy as long as one Jew lives in Israel.'

'You said that the Israeli Jews didn't want the Palestinian Arabs to leave,' Vera pinpointed. 'You said Golda Meir pleaded with them to stay. The Haganah urged them not to leave. Why –'

'There was panic,' Wayne interrupted impatiently. 'They ran because they didn't want to appear traitorous to the Arab cause. Not millions left,' he emphasized, 'as the Arabs claimed. A little over a half a million became refugees because of the Arabs' determination to destroy Israel. They could have remained to live side by side with the Israeli Jews. In *peace*.'

'We must never forget that the Arabs invaded Israel.' Joel was grim. 'Nobody can expect Israel not to fight back. It needs help – not an arms embargo.' An embargo imposed even by the United States.

Was she right, Vera asked herself, in suspecting that in a small way the Kahn factory was helping to alleviate Israel's arms shortage? The letters she translated for Wayne were strangely cryptic. Was the company selling guns to Israel through secret channels?

'Everybody ready for dessert?' Fiona's cheery voice punctured the sombre mood about the table. 'I'm bringing in hot deep-dish apple pie and ice cream.'

Chapter Thirteen

A week later – with the Friday-evening dinner to be delayed because Joel and Wayne had a special meeting with clients at the factory – Vera allowed exuberant Laurie and her eager cohort Tracy to postpone bedtime by almost an hour.

'No more stalling,' she told them sternly at last, kissed each good night and headed downstairs to join Doris.

'I'm turning off the TV,' Doris said as Vera strolled into the living room. 'This business with the Soviet Union is too depressing.' Stalin had ordered a halt to rail traffic between Berlin and West Germany, stopped traffic on a highway bridge under the guise of making repairs.

'I'm worrying about all the violence and crime that's creeping into children's programmes.' Vera settled herself in a lounge chair across from Doris. 'I don't let Laurie and Tracy watch unless I'm with them – or Fiona is. I don't want them seeing all that gory junk that's being shown. Of course, there're some awfully good programmes, too.'

'You know what the producers say.' Doris grimaced. '"The programmes we're producing are no more violent than 'Jack the Giant-Killer'." But when Jackie Owens – all of three and a half – came in with two toy guns, I confiscated them right away. Dad says the number of toy companies making guns has exploded.' She paused. 'Sometimes I wish Dad were making toy guns instead of the real things.'

'I know Paul feels that way,' Vera said gently. Yet if the company were supplying guns to Israel, she could accept that. A tiny little country surrounded by hostile forces should be provided with the means of self-defence.

'I guess it's because of what happened to Mom. It was worse for Paul than for me. He was there.' She sighed. 'I cringe every time Wayne goes out hunting. I know – this is hunting country. The men up here hunt and they fish. But I remember Mom taking Paul and me to a game farm and the way we loved all the animals.'

The sounds in the hall told them Joel and Wayne had arrived.

'I'll tell Fiona she can serve dinner.' Vera rose from her chair. 'And call Paul.' He was in the den – correcting term papers.

Increasingly Vera dreaded these Friday-evening get-togethers. The atmosphere of conviviality seemed fragile, she thought. Everything was supposed to be so right with their world as opposed to what was happening in other areas. Yet there was an undercurrent of desperation when they were together that had nothing to do with the troubles in Israel and the Soviet Union.

Paul could not brush aside the sense that in his father's eyes he was a failure. What had happened to his RAF-hero son that he was content with his present ordinary life? Wayne filled that image now. At unexpected intervals, Doris appeared to be baiting Wayne into a battle, and her father was upset by this. She was ever-uncomfortable in Wayne's presence, Vera conceded – whether at the office or at the house.

At least she'd convinced Wayne she wanted no part of him. He concealed his anger, but she felt his resentment. He could not accept rejection. Thank God, he was unaware of the unsettling feelings he evoked in her at unwary moments – like tonight, when he talked so ferociously about the attacks on Israel. *How could she let herself feel this way?*

On June 24, Stalin imposed a blockade on West Berlin – based on his paranoia about the recovery of Germany. After much debate, the Western Allies voted against retaliation against the Soviet Union. Yet some serious action was required or West Berlin would be isolated. A major airlift to supply food and necessities to the two-and-a-half million people in West Berlin was launched.

'It won't work,' Wayne declared. 'The requirements are too high.'

'It has to work,' Joel reproached him. 'Those people have to be fed.'

Those who worried about the fate of the world watched and applauded the incredible efforts of American, British, and French fliers. Weeks became months and the airlift continued – now called *Operation Vittles.* Even coal was flown into the city to be rationed to its inhabitants. And Vera worried constantly about the Schmidts, who'd saved her from the Nazis. All her efforts to get through to them after the war had been futile. She corresponded three or four times a year with Margrethe and Herbert Munch. They were fine, thank God.

Word filtered back about the activities of a compassionate young lieutenant named Carl Halverson, who was parachuting bags of candy to Berlin youngsters on his route in and out of Tempelhof Airport in the American area – and the idea soon caught on among other fliers. At Christmas they began Operation Santa Claus, dropping thousands of tiny parachutes with toys and candy for the children of West Berlin – everything financed by the crews themselves.

At this same time, the UN was struggling to negotiate an armistice between Israel and the Arab states. Combat had not been continuous in these last months – there had been truces at intervals, which were soon broken. Despite its limited forces – with amazing determination and brilliant strategy – Israel had pushed first one and then another Arab state out of Israeli territory until at this time it was fighting only Egypt.

Vera knew Paul was upset that peace still did not prevail. He worried about the possibility of war in China. The Soviet Union appeared to be a growing threat. Greece was in the midst of civil war. Last year Truman had said, 'I believe that it must be the policy of the United States to support free peoples who are resisting attempted subjugation by armed minorities or outside pressures, and that American assistance should be primarily through economic and financial aid.' Meaning, no armed intervention.

Paul was troubled, too, by the plight of American Negroes – though President Truman was fighting for civil rights. He read William Faulkner's novel *Intruder in the Dust*, which pleaded for more time to bring about integration in the South.

'Doesn't the man understand that changes have to start now?' he said to Vera when she'd finished reading the popular Faulkner novel. 'You know what life would be like for Fiona and Adele if they were living in the South. We have to start making changes now!'

But most Americans, Vera thought, closed their eyes and ears to anything that disturbed their pleasant way of life. *Their* war was over. They were proud of their new houses and new cars – or plotted how to acquire these. They bowled and went to the movies and took endless photos of their little ones with the new Polaroid cameras that had just come out. Paul said they didn't want to know about pain and anguish and death that was outside their small, private worlds.

Would she ever be able to push aside the memory of *Kristallnacht* and live just for the present? Vera asked herself. Not even Paul knew the nightmares that disturbed her sleep at unexpected moments. He didn't know how she awoke cold and trembling, remembering the sounds in the hall on that November night in 1938 in Berlin – when Mama, Papa, and Ernst were dragged away from her forever. Her family. Her precious family.

Wayne flew to England again in February '49. On this second trip he travelled without Doris. It was admittedly a business trip.

'I couldn't go with Wayne this time,' Doris said as she drove with Vera to a Saturday benefit luncheon for the nursery group. 'I mean, I have to be here for the class.' She hesitated. 'I know it's ridiculous, but I hate seeing him go off alone for a whole week. You know how women chase after him. And he's so upset that I don't get pregnant.'

'Doris, why don't you see a doctor?' Vera suggested gently. 'There might be some simple little thing that could change the situation for you.' Wayne always made a fuss over Laurie and Tracy, she remembered – and each time Doris flinched because she felt she was failing him by not giving him a child.

'I'd be afraid of its getting all over town. You know Betty in Dr Evans' office. Dad calls her Eastwood's Walter Winchell.'

'Then go to a doctor down in New York,' Vera urged. 'Ask your friend Sally to recommend someone.'

'I'm scared,' Doris said after a moment. 'If the doctor says I can never have a child, then I'll be afraid that Wayne will leave me. I'd die if he did.'

'It could be his fault,' Vera said bluntly. 'Would you leave him if it were?'

'No.' Doris hesitated. 'All right, I'll talk to Sally.'

Three weeks later, when Wayne and her father were

in Boston for a gun show, Doris drove down to New York – ostensibly to spend the weekend with Sally and to see her seven-month-old son for the first time. Sally had made an appointment for Doris with her obstetrician. Vera waited anxiously for her return from New York.

Early Sunday afternoon Doris called.

'Can you run over for coffee?' Doris asked.

'Sure,' Vera said. 'Paul's playing with the kids.' Sunday was his special time with Laurie and Tracy. 'I'll drive right over.'

Doris was waiting for her in the French provincial living room of which Wayne was so proud.

'Hi.' Vera was breathless with anticipation, her eyes questioning.

'I've made fresh coffee.' Doris's smile seemed forced. 'I'll bring it in.'

'Let's have it in the kitchen.' Vera slipped out of her coat, dropped it on a chair. Don't rush Doris, she cautioned herself. Yet she was suddenly apprehensive.

Vera sat in one of the captain's chairs in the breakfast nook and waited for Doris to bring the percolator to the table.

'How's Sally?' she asked. She and Sally had never met, but Doris spoke often about her Manhattan friend.

'Dying to get back to work. But the baby's adorable.' Doris paused. 'The doctor gave me a thorough checkup. He says there's no reason why I shouldn't get pregnant. He – he suggested that Wayne have a checkup.'

'Will Wayne agree?' Instinct told Vera he would balk.

'I can't tell him.' Doris closed her eyes in anguish for a moment. 'Do you know what that would do to him? To discover it's his fault that I don't get pregnant?'

'Is it better to let him go on waiting for it to happen?' Vera reproached gently. But she knew Doris would say nothing of this to Wayne. 'Doris, you can adopt.'

Doris shook her head in vigorous rejection. 'Wayne would never agree to that. And I can't tell him the truth. If I tell him, I could lose him. I couldn't bear that, Vera. He's my life.'

Vera sighed in frustration. Wayne held Doris in a relentless bondage. That wasn't love – it was something evil. How could *she* have been so drawn to him? Now – at last – she felt free of that insane infatuation. Seeing what he did to Doris – all the sly put-downs – had accomplished this.

At Doris's encouragement – and with Joel's instant approval – Vera gave a small dinner party during the school spring vacation. The guests would consist solely of Paul's fellow teachers. But what began as a party for six mushroomed to twelve – an awesome number to Vera – because she had been fearful of hurt feelings among the uninvited. Now – dressing for the party – she felt the first flurry of nerves. She'd never entertained before.

Savoury aromas drifted through the house. Bless Fiona, Vera thought in gratitude. She'd insisted she would handle everything.

'You just make yourself beautiful for your guests,' Fiona had ordered. An outsider herself, Fiona was conscious of Vera's need to become accepted in Paul's hometown. Iris wrote that in the small town in Canada where she lived with her husband the situation was similar. 'First, I took away a man that belonged to a Canadian girl – and I hadn't lived here for a hundred years.'

'Paul, is this dress all right?' Vera turned to him with a need for reassurance.

'It's great.' His eyes swept over her full-skirted, turquoise silk dress. 'You look so gorgeous I'd insist you get right out of it if we didn't have guests coming.'

'Paul, we didn't forget anybody?' she asked in sudden panic.

'We can't invite everybody.' He reached to pull her close. 'I'm sure Martin Caine wouldn't have accepted if we'd asked him. He's still angry that I was hired when his girlfriend was still on the waiting list. He made cracks about Dad's throwing his weight around.'

'You deserved to be hired. You were a returning veteran.'

'Hey, that's what I love about you,' he joshed. 'You'll always vote for me.' He smacked her lightly on the rump. 'Okay, let's go downstairs and play host and hostess.'

Most of the talk at dinner revolved around the school and local politics. So many people in the country were isolated from what was happening in the world, Vera considered – more concerned with what affected their own lives. After dinner, Vera was astonished when the women gathered on one side of the living room and the men on the other.

The women talked about the latest in household appliances, whether it made sense to buy a television set when there were so few channels – though they were impressed that Truman's inauguration in January had been televised. The men argued about the best new car to buy and what baseball team would win the pennant the coming season. And both sexes were eager to own their own houses. Paul said it was natural in the aftermath of the war years for people to reach out for material things.

Paul was happy, wasn't he? For the moment she could block out the covert tensions between him and Wayne. Paul had a job he loved; he'd soon have his master's, and he adored the kids. He hadn't told his father yet, but he meant to put off going for his PhD for a while. He wanted to continue teaching at the high school level.

'These are formative years, Vera,' he'd said last night.

'And not all students go on to college. Yeah, I know,' he chuckled, reading her mind. 'Never before have so many high school graduates gone on to college – thanks to the GI Bill. But we shouldn't underestimate the value of vocational training. We should have respect for skills that don't require a college degree.'

Paul said that, once he wasn't caught up in the heavy commute to Albany, they'd drive down to New York once every two or three months for a weekend of theatre or ballet or museum-hopping. He was eager to see 'Death of a Salesman' and 'South Pacific'. Though she never admitted it aloud, he sensed she missed some of the advantages of city living. He always laughed and said it was a trade-off. You gave up some pleasures and acquired others. But she'd spent most of her life in exciting cities like Berlin and Copenhagen and London, she reminded herself. There were times when Eastwood seemed a wasteland.

In September, Laurie and Adele entered kindergarten. Each weekday morning, Vera walked the two little girls down to the spot where the school bus picked them up. Both were enthralled at being in kindergarten, were full of talk about what happened each day.

'You were worrying needlessly,' Paul scolded Vera gently at the end of Laurie and Adele's first week of kindergarten classes. 'The other little kids didn't notice that Adele's skin was a little darker than theirs. They haven't learned intolerance yet.'

'In Southern schools they would have noticed.' Vera's smile was rueful. Adele wouldn't have been allowed to attend classes with white children. 'But you're right, of course. Intolerance has to be taught.'

'Changes are coming,' Paul predicted. 'A lot of books about the evils of school segregation in the South are being published. Coloured soldiers who fought in the war want their children to go to school with white kids – and get a decent education.' He paused. 'I want to talk to Mr Kerrigan about setting up some after-school activities. All on a volunteer basis, of course. I'll bet Doris would be glad to contribute one afternoon to an art class. I'd like to work with a group on current events – what's happening in the world today. What do you think, Vera?'

'Paul, it's a wonderful idea!' Vera glowed.

'I may have a battle,' he warned. 'Kerrigan's set in his ways.' He chuckled reminiscently. 'Remember the fight when I wanted to set up my classroom with the cluster of tables? The only reason I got that through was because Dad offered to provide the tables. Kerrigan didn't want to tangle with the town's leading philanthropist.' Vera knew that at intervals the school system benefited from Joel's contributions – 'in memory of Anne Kahn.'

'Go for it, Paul,' Vera urged.

The next three weeks Paul fought to inaugurate a volunteer after-school programme at the high school. When he enlisted the help of the local small paper, Vera knew he'd win despite Kerrigan's opposition. Three dedicated faculty members in addition to himself agreed to serve. Doris was delighted to take on the art class on Wednesday afternoons.

'Mr Kerrigan delicately warned that nudity was not to be a subject,' Paul reported, grinning. 'Doris agreed.'

Every morning after seeing Laurie and Adele off to kindergarten, Vera drove Tracy to Doris's nursery group and often remained to help. The church provided free accommodation. Doris donated her services, and mothers were expected to serve as volunteers. But often the volunteers of the day were caught up in problems at home.

By the approach of the new year, Doris confessed that

she was having serious battles with Wayne about her determination to continue the nursery programme.

'He complains that I'm neglecting the house,' Doris said. 'I'm not. He tells me I'm not getting pregnant because I tire myself out. I tried to talk about our adopting – he screamed at me. Which was about what I'd expected. Most of the time he's so sweet,' she added hastily. 'I can't tell him the truth, Vera. I just can't.'

Vera knew that her father-in-law – like Paul – saw little of the tensions in Doris's marriage. Joel was spending interminable hours each day at the factory. He struggled to schedule the soaring orders that Wayne brought in. And now he was expanding the factory yet again and retooling to supply more sophisticated weaponry – a fact that, she knew, would upset Paul.

By midyear '50, Wayne had become a commuter between the United States and Europe, a fact that puzzled Paul.

'What's all this business Dad's doing in Europe?' he asked Vera on a lazy summer Sunday afternoon when they'd taken Laurie and Tracy on a picnic in the nearby woods. Now both little girls napped on blankets. 'And how did Wayne set it up?'

Vera shrugged. 'Wayne's always boasting about his "contacts."' As his translator and privy to his business correspondence, she continued to harbour suspicions she'd never verbalized.

'Do you think Wayne persuaded Dad to work out some kind of deal to sell guns to Israel?' Paul asked uneasily. Vera tensed. That was her suspicion – that the company was contriving to sell guns to foreign corporations that were reselling to Israel. She'd felt it disloyal to Joel to discuss this even with Paul. 'Vera, that's illegal.'

'I don't know,' Vera said after a moment of debate. She *didn't* know.

'Am I never to get away from instruments of war?' A pulse hammered at Paul's temple. 'Is the world intent on destroying itself? Maybe it was a mistake to come back to Eastwood. Perhaps we should have stayed in New York.'

'Paul, you don't mean that,' she reproached. 'You love the school. And your father would have been so unhappy if you hadn't come home.'

'Would he?' Paul countered. 'He has Wayne now. How can I measure up to that dazzling image?'

Chapter Fourteen

Vera was delighted when Doris invited her and Paul to spend two weeks at the cottage on Cape Cod that Wayne had rented for the month of August. They would go for the last two weeks, when Paul would have finished his stint of summer-school teaching and Wayne would be flying to Europe on a business trip.

'I'd be terribly lonely all by myself in the cottage,' Doris pointed out. 'I need you all there with me.'

'Oh, the girls will love it,' Vera bubbled. 'They've never seen the ocean.' Laurie had, in truth, seen the Atlantic when they'd crossed the ocean on the *Argentina* but had been too young to remember this. And Paul recalled with deep pleasure the times he'd spent with his college buddy at a beach house on Long Island.

'Next summer they'll have their own pool,' Doris reminded. In a burst of pride at his soaring commissions on the job, Wayne had bought an acre plot adjoining their own and was having a swimming pool installed. Now he talked about buying a new foreign car – the first in Eastwood. 'We'll have to teach Laurie and Tracy to swim.'

Vera was touched by Doris's devotion to her only nieces. Doris was resigned to never having children of her own, Vera realized. She'd admitted to one ugly encounter with Wayne when she'd suggested adopting. Now the matter was a closed subject. How tragic, Vera thought. Doris would be a wonderful mother.

Vera and Doris spent two hectic afternoons shopping

in Albany for beachwear. Frugal in memory of the war years, Vera had to be persuaded by Doris and Paul to buy clothes for herself. Doris had studied resort-wear in current issues of *Vogue* and *Harper's Bazaar*, daringly chose a black halter-neck swimsuit with midriff on display but countered this sophistication with the addition of an apricot romper-look suit.

'Black?' Vera protested, gazing at Doris in the halter-neck swimsuit.

'Wayne says today black is so sophisticated,' Doris said. 'I'm sure he'll love it.'

They bought bikini tops, shorts, shirts, slacks, and flat, comfortable beach shoes – aware of the warning that they should wear special all-over makeup to keep them from tanning or burning.

Vera was amused by the seriousness with which Laurie and Tracy tried on their new beachwear. Even at six and four they were very much 'girls,' she told Paul as Laurie and Tracy modelled their new attire for him.

On the first of August, Doris and Wayne left for the Cape. Two weeks later, Vera and Paul and the girls piled into Joel's new Cadillac convertible – which he'd insisted they take for their trip – and headed for Cape Cod. Vera had packed puzzles and other diversions for Laurie and Tracy. She'd gone to the library to research Cape Cod and spouted information to Paul while he drove.

'Did you know it was one of the first sections of this country to be settled?' she effervesced.

'I knew,' he said, grinning. 'But tell me more.'

'It still has houses dating back to the seventeenth century – but that's young to somebody like me,' she joshed. 'Remember when you took me out to St Albans – or was it St Michael's – outside of London and we had tea at a thirteenth-century house?'

Arriving on the Cape – en route to their specific

destination – they were intrigued by the ancient lighthouses and windmills, the sand dunes and salt marshes, the stretches of long, sandy beach. Then at last they approached Doris and Wayne's rented cottage – a charming white clapboard, yellow-trimmed, pitch-roofed little house with its own private strip of beach.

Vera was startled to learn – as Doris helped her unpack in the bedroom assigned to her and Paul – that Wayne was not scheduled to leave for another two days.

'He had to change his plans so he could meet with some buyer in New York before his flight to London,' Doris apologized. She was ever-unhappy at the covert hostility between Wayne and Paul and knew Vera and Paul had expected Wayne to have left already for London.

The two women went out on the deck of the beachfront cottage, dropped onto floral-cushioned chaises to watch Paul stroll with Laurie and Tracy to the water's edge – both little girls fascinated by their first glimpse of the ocean, a dazzling blue today. Inside the house, Wayne was involved in a long phone conversation. Why couldn't he have been gone? Vera fretted.

Three hours later – vowing they were not sleepy – Laurie and Tracy were drifting off before Vera had them into their pyjamas. They were exhausted from the long drive, the excitement of the day, she thought tenderly while she pulled a light blanket over each small frame. The night air was cool, the sound of the ocean lapping at the shore a soothing symphony. Vera tiptoed from the room, closed the door behind her.

Doris was bringing food to the dining table. The two men were absorbed in a news programme on television. More unpleasant news about the fighting in Korea, Vera noted. The first US ground troops had landed there the first of last month. Ten days ago, 62,000 reservists had been called up for active duty.

'Turn off the TV and come to the table,' Doris ordered while the programme moved on to the latest antics of Senator Joseph McCarthy. 'I can't bear that man!'

One area in which Paul and Wayne could talk without disagreement was about Senator McCarthy. Both men were too angered by their deep-seated dislike for the senator's politics to notice Doris's grim expression.

'All right, enough of politics tonight,' she intervened after a few minutes. 'Somebody's got to put a stop to that man soon.'

'Not as soon as we'd like,' Paul surmised. 'But what's happening with your nursery school group in the fall?' He knew Doris wanted to enlarge but was encountering financial difficulties.

Doris brightened. 'We're trying to open up a book shop in town, with the profits to go to the nursery school. I was talking to Dad about it last night. I didn't know he owned that little store on the corner of Main that just closed up. He said we can use it rent free.'

'This is not a book-shop town,' Wayne scoffed. 'You'll be wasting your time. You've lived in Eastwood all your life, Doris, and you still don't understand the people.' It seemed such a quiet, staid town, Vera thought, yet she often wondered about life behind the closed doors.

Earlier than she'd anticipated, they all retired for the night. It was the sea air, she thought sleepily, pulling the blanket over herself and Paul. He was already off, she observed with a surge of love and nuzzled close to his warmth. Poor Doris. Wayne was still taking potshots at her. That nasty crack about her black swimsuit – 'Anybody would think you'd just buried me. What possessed you to buy a black suit?'

In the morning Vera came awake slowly. She could hear the waves lapping at the shore. What a beautifully serene sound! Sunlight poured into the bedroom, filling her with a sense of well-being.

She turned on her side, discovered Paul was gone. Now she was conscious of the aroma of fresh coffee brewing in the kitchen. She heard Laurie and Tracy's voices. They were laughing at something Doris had just said. Paul must have gotten them up, she realized, and taken them outdoors so she could sleep. The girls sounded so happy, so delighted with the sight of the long stretch of beach and ocean, she thought with pleasure.

In record time, she showered and dressed, hurried out to the deck. Paul was nowhere to be seen. Doris and Wayne were playing ball on the sand with Laurie and Tracy while a joyous puppy of huge dimensions tried to join in.

'Paul drove to the bakery in town for fresh rolls for breakfast,' Doris called to her. 'We'll eat as soon as he gets back.'

The puppy abandoned his efforts to grab the ball. He was digging vigorously in the sand.

'Damn!' Wayne yelled, holding a hand to his left eye. 'The little bastard flipped sand in my face!'

Doris was instantly solicitous. 'Let's go inside. We have eye drops in the bathroom.'

'Come on, kids,' Vera called to Laurie and Tracy. 'Into the house. We'll have breakfast as soon as Daddy gets back.'

Vera sent Laurie into their bedroom for a puzzle – a favourite diversion – and Tracy trailed behind her. In the bathroom Wayne was cursing the puppy while Doris struggled to provide first aid. Perhaps Wayne ought to go to the hospital emergency room, Vera thought uneasily. He'd had a bad experience with an eye already. She hurried towards the bathroom to suggest this.

'Doris, you idiot!' Wayne yelled, a hand still cupped over his left eye. 'Eye drops aren't going to do it. There, the eye wash on the top shelf,' he said, pointing. 'In the blue bottle. Give that to me.'

Vera froze. Wayne's left eye – his *good* eye – was covered. But he could see the blue bottle of eyewash with his right eye . . . the eye that was supposed to have almost no vision. He'd said that had kept him out of the American army during the war. *He'd lied. Everything that David Meyerberg had told Paul must be true.*

She turned away, headed back for the kitchen. She forced herself to consider the situation with utmost fairness. Was it possible Wayne had known the eyewash was on the top shelf – that he hadn't needed to see it? She doubted that. She'd watch, she told herself with grim determination. Wayne would slip up again. Not until then would she tell Paul. But in her head she was convinced Wayne was a fraud.

With Wayne gone, Vera found the days at the cottage delightful. A teenager from a neighbouring cottage called to offer her services as a babysitter. Laurie and Tracy were enthusiastic about her presence. Vera hired her immediately. Now the three adults were free for sightseeing around the area. On two evenings they went to the nearby summer theatre.

On the Thursday before the Labor Day weekend, Vera and Paul headed home with the girls. That evening Wayne was scheduled to arrive at the Cape. They left the cottage midmorning, stopped at a roadside diner for lunch. After lunch Laurie and Tracy fell asleep on the back seat of the car. Vera debated with herself, remembering her earlier determination not to tell Paul about the incident with Wayne's eye until she had more substantial information. But her need to share won out. In a rush of words she reported what had happened.

'I've never trusted Wayne since that talk with David,'

Paul admitted. 'But we don't have positive proof. He may have known the eyewash was on the top shelf.'

'I'm sure he saw it, Paul. He's been lying all along! But, yes, we need more proof.' Vera sighed, fighting frustration. 'At least, we're on the alert now. We'll watch.'

'And if we know for sure?' Paul's hand tightened on the wheel. 'What do we tell Doris? That her husband is a fraud? That everything he's told us about his life is probably untrue? She'll never believe it. And you know how Dad feels about him.'

'But Dad isn't blinded with love,' Vera pinpointed. 'If we show him positive proof, he'll believe. David told you Wayne was a step ahead of a charge of treason.'

'Wayne's a winner business-wise.' Paul was troubled. 'Dad's forever boasting about the soaring sales figures at the company – mostly due to Wayne.'

'David said he was thrown out of the Haganah for crooked deals,' Vera shot back. 'How do we know what he's doing to Dad's business?'

'We can't argue with the sales he brings in,' Paul said reluctantly.

'Whom is he selling to?' Vera countered. 'I have this crazy feeling he's selling to Israel.' She saw the glint in Paul's eyes. So, he, too, harboured the same suspicions. 'But would they deal with him, knowing what he is?' At intervals this question haunted her.

'Honey, in Israel's position, they'll buy from anybody who delivers,' Paul surmised. 'I know – it's illegal. And in normal circumstances Dad would be the last person to do anything illegal. But Israel's in a desperate situation. This embargo on arms to them is insane.'

'Then all we can do is watch for proof and build up a case. I worry about Dad's being so deeply involved with somebody whose background is as questionable as Wayne's.'

'I worry about Doris,' Paul said after a moment. 'She's living a life built on lies.'

Vera spent the first few days back in Eastwood in shopping for clothes for Laurie's entrance into first grade – '*Real* school, Mommie!' Fiona accompanied her on two such excursions so that Adele, too, could be properly prepared.

'Fiona's so eager for everything to be right for Adele,' Vera confided affectionately to Paul on a warm evening when they went for a stroll. 'She won't spend on herself, but Adele must have the best she can manage.'

'How's Doris doing with plans for the book shop?' Paul asked.

'She hopes to open by October 1. You're enlisted along with Dad to help with carpentry.'

'Wayne's too busy dreaming up big deals?' Paul drawled.

'Something like that, I gather. You don't mind, do you?' Vera smiled, confident that Paul would be willing to help. 'I promised to work in the shop one afternoon a week.'

'Sure, I'll help. This town needs a book shop – even one that'll be open only afternoons and Saturdays.' He hesitated. 'Ted Mills told me he's having trouble about one of the books he's ordered for his senior English class. The school board told Kerrigan that they want to be sure no Commie authors are included. Censorship hits Eastwood,' he said ruefully, 'but Ted's fighting. The whole damn situation's got out of hand.'

'I remember in Berlin when books written by Jews were burned. I was nine years old, but I understood what a terrible thing it was to burn books.'

'That won't happen here,' Paul said quickly, but Vera knew about the Red-baiting that was infecting the nation and was afraid.

Vera enjoyed Paul's pleasure in setting up his lesson

plans for the new term. This was the most impressionable age, he reiterated regularly – when students moved into their teens. But she shared his rage when early in the school year a parent appeared to denounce his bringing his pacifist leanings into his after-school group.

'She lambasted me for being unpatriotic at a time when American boys are being shipped to Korea to fight against Communism,' Paul reported. 'Not that most people seem to realize there's a shooting war going on over there.'

'What are you going to do?' Vera asked.

'I'm not tailoring my group – or my classes – to suit one parent,' Paul told her. 'I think if we're going to have peace in this world, we have to make these kids understand its value. Our civilization is becoming so complex we're going to have to retailor our schools to meet the challenge – but principals like Kerrigan fight change. Anyhow, I haven't had any flak from Kerrigan so far.' But he was worried, Vera suspected.

At the factory, Vera was ever watchful for some move where Wayne would betray himself – and frustrated that this wasn't happening. Doris tried opening the book shop on schedule, but she was running into staffing problems.

'When women offer to help, why do they change their minds two days later?' she wailed. 'All these ego problems that pop up. Linda called up mad as hell because the *Herald* gave Sonia credit for suggesting we give part of the profits for the first month to the library to buy new books. Wayne tells me I'm stupid to think it's ever different. But we can't afford to pay salaries.'

'Paul said he'll give some time on Saturdays,' Vera consoled. 'And once Gloria gets back to the office, I can help.' Joel's secretary was recovering from a broken ankle, and Vera had been drafted for full-time duties at the office until she returned. At intervals she felt guilty that she wasn't there when Laurie and Tracy came home from school and nursery group. But Fiona was wonderful with the children. They loved her.

Everybody thought teaching was such an easy job, Vera mused. Short hours, much vacation time. They forgot about the time for setting up lesson plans, for correcting papers and tests. And Paul was giving after-school time to work with students who were having problems keeping up. Paul said that many people didn't understand the special problems of handling teenage students struggling through the most difficult of all ages. Still, he loved his work. That made it all worthwhile.

Paul was in a job he loved. They loved each other deeply. They both adored the children. Living in the family house and with Fiona taking over much of the household responsibilities, she should be extremely happy, Vera told herself. Why did she so often feel a strange restlessness? As though she ought to be doing more with her life.

In mid-September, Doris ran into complications regarding the projected book shop. Two women who'd pledged financial support withdrew their offer. The husband of one suddenly rejected her participation, and the husband of the other made a counter suggestion. 'My husband says we should open a thrift shop. That way we just collect merchandise without having to pay for it. We won't run up bills.'

Wayne brushed off Doris's hints that he should help the nursery group's effort to raise funds. He was annoyed at her involvement. It was her father who made a substantial donation – 'in memory of your mother.' Now Doris pushed ahead with the opening. In mid-October – only two weeks behind schedule – the small cluster devoted to the nursery triumphantly opened the book shop. The local newspaper – which appeared every Wednesday afternoon

– carried a glowing report of Eastwood's first book shop.

Books became a primary topic of conversation in Eastwood three weeks later. A parent descended on the high school principal's office in rage because Ted Mills had included on his senior English class's reading list a title by Theodore Dreiser.

'The man's a Commie!' she shrieked indignantly. 'I read all about it in a newspaper. We don't want our children reading a book by some dirty Red!'

Mr Kerrigan agreed to look into the matter immediately. By nightfall, the word had ricocheted around town – building to the conclusion that Ted Mills himself must be defiled by Communist thinking. Paul was indignant that Kerrigan had approached Ted about the novel.

'The Dreiser book the stupid woman's complaining about is *An American Tragedy*. It's a classic! Dreiser's no Communist. What the hell is going on in this country these days?' he railed. At regular intervals in the past year, one book or another had been banned by a school board or a library. But to see it happen in Eastwood was unnerving to Vera and Paul.

Vera was uneasy when the local paper reported on the incident of the book-banning in the high school without taking a stand one way or the other. With painful frequency, the memory of book-burnings in Berlin jogged across her mind. Another mother explored the shelves of the tiny public library, discovered the Dreiser book – admittedly seldom checked out, and demanded its removal.

'Ted's had to take it off his reading list,' Paul reported to Vera and his father at dinner two nights later. 'It was an order from Kerrigan's office. He could lose his job if he refused. I can't believe we're seeing something like this here in Eastwood!' He grunted in exasperation.

'Can't Ted fight back?' Vera asked.

Paul hesitated. 'We're talking about writing an article under both our names and taking it to the *Eastwood Herald*. He'll be over later to work on it with me.'

'That might be a mistake,' Joel said, visibly disturbed. 'This is a conservative town.'

'This is beyond conservative!' Paul shot back. 'This whole craziness has to be stopped!'

Late that night – both too upset to sleep – Paul and Vera discussed the situation. Paul admitted he wasn't sure that the newspaper would run the article he and Ted had laboured over earlier.

'Why don't we ask Doris to order a dozen titles of the book and show just that in the window of the shop? That'll make a statement.' Vera glowed in anticipation. 'It can be our contribution. We can afford it, can't we?'

'We can afford it,' Paul agreed tenderly, 'and we'll do it. Tell Doris to make it a rush order.'

The following evening – alone with Vera at dinner because it was Joel's night at the Lions Club – Paul reported that the newspaper had refused to run his and Ted's article. 'They complain it's too controversial.'

A week later – because of vigorous efforts on Doris's part – twenty copies of *An American Tragedy* arrived at the bookstore. That evening Doris commandeered Vera and Paul to help change the window display. By the following evening, the whole town was talking about the book shop's window display.

'Doris says she'll have to pull it soon because she's getting too much flak from other members of the nursery group. But she'll hold out as long as she can.'

In midevening Ted Mills arrived at the house.

'You won't believe what's happening,' he chortled when Vera opened the front door. 'Where's Paul?'

'Right here,' Paul called from the entrance to the living room. 'What's up?'

'I just had a phone call from one of my seniors. A half dozen of them are pooling their spending money to go over to the book shop after school tomorrow to buy two copies of *An American Tragedy*.'

'It would be an American tragedy if some of our kids didn't understand what's happening in this country. Ted, as teachers we must be doing something right.'

Minutes later Joel arrived from his Lions Club meeting. Vera went out to the kitchen to prepare coffee for the four of them. When she returned, the men were discussing the jail sentences meted out to The Hollywood Ten and how The Kellogg Company had dropped its sponsorship of Irene Wicker, the 'Singing Lady' – much loved by Laurie and Tracy and millions of other young children. *Red Channels* continued its nefarious name-calling.

'I'm not sure Doris is smart in thumbing her nose at those people who're nervous about that book,' Joel said sombrely.

'Dad, not everybody in town feels that way,' Paul said. 'A few creeps –'

'The display at the book shop was my suggestion,' Vera told her father-in-law. 'How can people in a country like this sanction the name-calling that's going on? People's careers – their lives – are being wrecked by gossip.'

'Vera, you don't understand.' Joel seemed to be searching for words. 'This is a very small town. Sometimes it's wiser to flow with the tide than to try to buck it. This kind of thing won't go on. It'll peter out soon.'

'People have to begin to take a stand.' Paul leaned forward earnestly. 'We have to –'

'Paul, we have to live here! We're part of this town. We don't want to create enemies.' Joel was pale now. He didn't want to lose his place in all his local organizations, Vera thought. He was afraid of becoming an outsider.

'Not everybody feels the way those parents do about

banning the book,' Paul reiterated. 'Some of our high school students are ready to fight it. We have to let them know it's right to fight against what's wrong.'

'The more fuss you make about this, the more important you make it seem,' Joel said impatiently. 'Just let it fade away.'

Vera was shaken. How could something like this be happening in the United States? Not just here in Eastwood, but in towns and cities all over the country. Was there a place in the world that was safe for decent human beings? She'd been frightened in Berlin, in Copenhagen, in London. *It wasn't supposed to be this way in America.*

Chapter Fifteen

Along with Paul, Vera worried that the war in Korea would escalate into World War III. Too often for comfort these evenings, she listened while Paul and his father debated the situation.

'It could be out of control so fast,' Paul argued. 'If Russia or China intervenes, it could become catastrophic.'

Side by side with American troops were soldiers from England, Australia, New Zealand, Thailand, and Turkey. General MacArthur was promising to 'have the boys home by Christmas.' Paul rejected this, refusing to accept his father's conviction that this was a 'tempest in a tea-pot.' And now there was posturing by Chou En-lai in China. Chou En-lai vowed to drive 'American aggressors' out of Asia and went on to notify the world that the Chinese People's Republic would fight beside the North Koreans if the UN forces crossed the 38th Parallel.

Vera was grateful for Paul's pacifism. If he'd joined the reserve, he could be fighting in yet another war. A pall hung over Hanukkah and Christmas this year. Chinese Communist troops were unofficially fighting on the side of North Korea. No chance now that American troops would be home for Christmas. And casualty figures were appalling.

Paul was concerned, too, that – except for a handful of students – the high school body of Eastwood High seemed disinterested in the fighting in Korea, in any of the problems that racked the world.

'They're more interested in what's new on the jukeboxes and when's the new Doris Day picture coming to town than what's happening in Korea and how do we stop this Joe McCarthy guy.'

By February of the new year, Vera was outraged that people had 'lost interest in the war in Korea.' The newspapers complained that few people bothered to read the news reports.

'Here at home we have a booming economy,' Paul derided. 'Everybody's concerned about making a lot of money, buying a new refrigerator or television or dishwasher. Don't they understand American boys are dying every day in Korea? Is this the way it's going to be forever? *Why can't we learn to live in peace*?'

Vera was astonished when Joel asked her if she'd like to come into the office on a regular basis. Gloria was back; but at the end of each week, he'd asked, '*Are you clear for next week*?'

'You're more than a secretary,' Joel said with candid respect. 'You make a great sounding board for me. You've got a great instinct for business.'

'I'd love to be permanent,' she said instantly.

But once her permanent status was announced, Vera sensed that Wayne was annoyed by this. Was he afraid she'd discover something he didn't want Joel to know? Or was she being paranoid?

She couldn't erase from her mind the encounter at the beach when she'd been convinced Wayne had lied about having no vision in his right eye. And the regular flow of letters she translated into German and French were strangely phrased – almost as though in some secret code. If Paul's friend at school could be trusted – and instinct told her he could – then Wayne had been thrown out of the Haganah for crooked deals. Let her watch to see what she could learn. *If Wayne were cheating Dad, let them know.*

New houses were going up in Eastwood. New shops appeared. New people were taking up residence in town. To the family's astonishment, Wayne invested in a small liquor store.

'It's the way to go. I would have thought by now you'd own half the stores in this town,' he jibed at his father-in-law at a Friday-evening dinner. 'With a little effort, you could be one of the richest men in the state.'

'Wayne, we're doing great at the factory.' Joel chuckled. 'How many Cadillacs can I drive? I don't need a swimming pool – you've got one. I don't need a mansion. Though maybe Vera would like to chuck out the furniture and redo the house.' He shot her another indulgent smile. 'We can afford that right now.'

'I love the house the way it is,' Vera said quietly, loathing Wayne's arrogance. His greed. To many of the girls and women in town he was Eastwood's younger version of Clark Gable, but to her he was an atomic bomb that could explode at any time. Thank God, she could look at Wayne now and see him for what he was.

On a rainy Saturday morning Vera sat reading in her favourite lounge chair in the living room while the three little girls sprawled on the floor and concentrated on the latest puzzles provided by Doris. When the phone rang, she rose to answer.

'I've got it, Fiona,' she called, reaching for the receiver.

The caller was Laurie's classmate, Serena Robinson. Vera knew of the family, though they'd never met. Serena's father was an attorney with an impressive practice in Manchester, Vermont, roughly twenty miles across the state line. Divorced from his wife, he lived in the most luxurious house in Eastwood, with a housekeeper to raise seven-year-old Serena and her four-year-old brother Lance.

'It's for you, Laurie,' Vera said. 'Serena Robinson.'

'For me?' Laurie scrambled to her feet in a flurry of excitement. Phone calls were a rarity in her young life. She darted across the room to take the receiver from her mother. 'Hi, Serena.'

After a few moment's conversation, Laurie put down the phone. 'Mommie, can I go spend the day with Serena at her house?'

'Let me talk to Serena's mother,' Vera stipulated, then rephrased this. 'Let me talk to their housekeeper.'

The housekeeper explained that with the weather expected to be rainy all day she'd offered to let Serena invite a friend over.

'They can watch television and play Serena's records. I'll make them a nice lunch and give them ice cream and cookies in the afternoon,' the housekeeper said good-humouredly. 'And I'll keep an eye on them, of course.'

'Can I go?' Laurie asked eagerly when her mother hung up the phone.

'Oh, I think we can handle that.' Vera was suffused with love. 'Go upstairs and get your raincoat. I'll drive you to the Robinsons.'

All at once Laurie seemed puzzled.

'Mommie, is Adele supposed to come with me?' Adele was in their class, too.

'I don't think so, darling.' Vera contrived a casual air. She suspected that Serena's father – who was considered a blatant snob in local eyes – was not inclined to invite the daughter of a domestic into his home. At school it was accepted that Laurie and Adele were 'best friends,' lived in the same house. But there was a social division that was sure to exclude Adele from occasions where Laurie would be welcomed. How did you explain that to an almost-seven-year-old? 'Adele and Tracy will play together,' she soothed.

'Okay, I'll go get my raincoat.'

On the floor of the Robinsons' spacious living room, Laurie and Serena sat enthralled, listening to a recording of 'Peter and the Wolf,' which included narration along with the music. Serena's little brother listened from the archway that led into the hall, where an electrician laboured to repair a ceiling fixture.

'Let's hear it again,' Serena said when the last words of the narrator and the final strains of the Prokofiev score faded away. She reached to return the needle to the beginning of the LP.

'I gotta go back to the shop for something,' the electrician called to the two little girls. 'You tell Mrs Hall I'll be back in twenty minutes.'

'Sure,' Serena said, 'I'll tell her.'

Lance opened the hall closet door to pull out his latest truck, which Serena said he was allowed to play with in the hall but not in the carpeted living room. Moments later, Mrs Hall looked in on the children.

'Are you ready for chocolate cake and ice cream yet?' she asked, her eyes teasing.

'Yeah!' the three youngsters yelled in unison.

'The man fixing the lights said he'd be back in twenty minutes,' Serena told Mrs Hall. 'He had to go back to his shop for something.'

The two little girls focused again on listening to 'Peter and the Wolf,' though they knew every word of the narration by now. This was the mostest fun she'd ever had, Laurie thought, giddy with the pleasure of Serena's company plus the diversion of 'Peter and the Wolf' and the imminent arrival of chocolate cake and ice cream.

'Lance, what do you think you're doing?' Serena shrieked in sudden outrage. 'Come down from there this minute!' While they'd been listening to the record, Lance had climbed up on the ladder, which he'd pulled to the closet door, and was gingerly descending now. '*What have you got*?'

Lance waited until he was at the bottom rung of the ladder to reply. He swung about with a dazzling grin.

'Let's play cowboys and Indians!' he said exuberantly, holding out a revolver. 'I'll be a cowboy. Bang, bang!'

'You give that to me!' Serena scrambled to her feet and charged towards Lance. 'You know Daddy said we're never, never supposed to go in that closet!'

'I wanna play,' Lance howled. 'I'm Hopalong Cassidy!'

'You're a bad boy!' Serena reached to take the gun from him. He tried to move away without relinquishing it. 'Give me the gun!'

All at once a shot rang out. Laurie gaped in terror as Serena – still clutching the gun – fell to the floor.

'Serena!' Laurie screamed. 'Serena!' She rushed to hover above Serena, lying inert on the floor while blood began to stain the front of her pretty dress. 'Mrs Hall!' she screamed, her eyes fastened to the widening stain of red across Serena's chest. 'Mrs Hall, come quick!' She was vaguely aware that Lance was crying uncontrollably.

'Was that a car backfiring?' Mrs Hall arrived at the archway to the living room – tray of cake and ice cream in her hands. Her eyes took in the tableau. 'Oh, no! No!' The tray fell from her hands. She collapsed unconscious to the floor.

For a moment Laurie froze, then with an intuitive knowledge that action was urgent darted to the phone, dialled. Her heart pounding, she waited anxiously for someone to answer.

'Hello.' Her mother's voice greeted her.

'Mommie, come quick!' Laurie pleaded. 'Serena's been shot and Mrs Hall fainted. I don't know what to do!'

'I'll be right there, darling. Just hold on.' Pale and

shaken, Vera put down the phone. 'Paul,' she called to him in the den. 'Bring the car out of the garage. We have to go to Serena's house. Something awful has happened.' Barely aware of his anxious reply, she rushed into the hall and towards the kitchen. Fiona was there, allowing Tracy and Adele to help with baking cookies – a rainy day diversion for the little girls. 'Fiona, call the hospital,' she gasped. 'Tell them to send an ambulance to the Robinson house. Serena's been shot!'

Vera heard the car emerge from the garage. Without stopping for a coat, she hurried outdoors and moments later joined Paul on the front seat of the car.

'Laurie just said that Serena's been shot and that Mrs Hall had fainted.' Her voice was raspy with alarm. 'Fiona's calling for an ambulance.'

'What the hell happened? Where was the housekeeper?' Paul's concern revealed itself in an air of rage. Vera knew he had plunged into the past, when another such incident had taken his mother's life.

'I didn't take time to ask. My poor baby,' Vera moaned. 'To be alone at a time like this!' Only a few months older than Paul had been when his mother was killed, she thought.

Paul drove with unprecedented speed. In the distance they heard the sound of the ambulance siren. Few such emergencies arose in a small town such as Eastwood, Vera thought. The local ambulance responded quickly.

Before Paul had pulled to a full stop, Vera thrust open the door and hurried to the stairs that led to the Robinsons' Georgian mansion.

'Laurie,' she called out, striding into the foyer.

'In the living room, Mommie.' Laurie's frightened young voice guided her. She could hear someone being violently ill in the rear of the house. Instinctively she knew this was the housekeeper.

In the living room Vera saw Laurie leaning over the prone body of Serena. With a towel already crimson with blood, Laurie was trying to staunch the wound. Without reaching for Serena's wrist, Vera knew she was dead.

'Darling, the ambulance is here.' She heard the shrill siren become a whisper as the ambulance drew up before the house. 'You can let go now.' Gently she pried Laurie's small fingers away from the blood-soaked towel, lifted her to her feet.

'What happened?' Paul demanded. '*Laurie, what happened*?' He ignored Vera's pantomimed plea to avoid questions.

'Lance went up on the ladder and brought down the gun. Serena tried to take it away from him. It went off – and she fell down. Mommie, will she die?' Laurie's eyes begged for reassurance.

'Here comes the doctor now.' How could she tell Laurie that Serena was dead? 'Paul, try to call Serena's father,' she began and froze. Paul had dropped into a chair, his face in his hands.

'Oh, my God,' he said. 'Oh, my God!'

The doctor on ambulance duty rushed into the room, followed by an attendant. For the next few moments Vera was involved in explaining the situation. Then she became aware of a child crying inconsolably. Lance had taken refuge in the hall closet. While Serena was being taken to the ambulance, an unsteady Mrs Hall stumbled down the hall and into the living room. She forced herself to take charge of Lance, drawing him out of the closet and into her arms.

'I'll call Mr Robinson at his office,' Mrs Hall stammered. 'I was only out of the room for a few minutes. I went to bring the children cake and ice cream.'

'Will you be all right?' Vera asked, clutching Laurie's

hand in hers. Paul sat motionless in the chair, his head still in his hands.

'Yes, I'll be all right,' Mrs Hall stammered. 'I can't believe this happened. I was only gone a few minutes. Sssh,' she whispered to Lance, whose arms clung about her neck. 'You're all right now. Nobody's going to blame you.'

Why had Mr Robinson kept a loaded gun in that closet? Vera asked herself in anger. How many children had to die before people realized that was criminal?

'I'd like to take Laurie home now,' she told Mrs Hall. 'If you're sure you're all right.'

'As all right as I can be,' Mrs Hall said in anguish. 'I just fell apart when I saw what happened. Thank God, Laurie knew to call you.'

'Paul, let's go home.' Vera dropped a hand on his shoulder. He was reliving those awful moments when his mother had been shot, she understood. 'Paul –'

He lifted his face – etched with pain – to hers.

'Yes, let's go home.'

Only in the car – in the comfort of her mother's arms – did Laurie begin to cry.

'Serena's going to be all right, isn't she? I didn't know what to do. She didn't open her eyes. She kept on bleeding.'

'We'll talk to the doctor at the hospital later,' she hedged. 'You were wonderful, Laurie. You did everything right.' Oh, yes, for a little girl not quite seven, Laurie had been wonderful.

Paul drove the short distance home in silence. His tense grip on the wheel, his pallor, the set of his jaw told Vera he was caught up in recall of his mother's shooting. Laurie sobbed softly in her arms, exhausted by the harrowing experience at the Robinson house.

How could Serena's father have left a loaded gun on

a closet shelf? Vera asked herself with recurrent fury. There were no guns in their own house – none since Anne Kahn's death. The huge cabinet that contained guns collected by four generations of Kahns had been moved to the factory, were on display there as fine examples of Kahn craftsmanship.

Paul had told her how he had refused to set foot in the living room for months after the shooting. That was when his father had added the den. He loved his father dearly, yet deep in his heart Paul had never forgiven him for his mother's death. Now it was all fresh in his mind again.

Fiona rushed onto the porch as the car drove up before the house. Her face anxious, she watched Paul take Laurie into his arms and walk up the stairs, Vera at his side.

'Tracy and Adele are watching television,' she said, her eyes full of questions. Mutely Vera shook her head. 'Let me put Laurie down for a nap. There's a pot of fresh coffee on the stove.'

While Paul walked trance-like into the living room, Vera headed for the kitchen. Coffee in tow, she joined him there a few minutes later. She sat beside him on the sofa, deposited the coffee tray on the table. What could she say to ease his pain?

'Vera, I walked into that room and my mind exploded.' He began to tremble.

'That was natural,' she said gently.

'Vera, you don't understand.' He closed his eyes, shook his head in a gesture of incredulity. 'All of a sudden I remembered. What I'd shut out of my mind all those years ago leapt into place before my eyes. Dad didn't kill Mom. *I* did.'

'Paul, no,' she rejected. 'Your father told me what happened. It was a tragic accident that –'

'I held the gun.' He was ominously calm. '*I can see it right this minute*. I ran over to the cabinet, took this gun that my grandfather had especially prized, and I pointed it at my mother. I pulled the trigger, and there was this awful noise. Then she fell to the floor. She died instantly.'

'You're fantasizing, Paul,' Vera insisted. 'We know what happened.'

He shook his head – again and again.

'I know what happened. I remember.'

'We'll talk about it when Dad comes home,' Vera soothed. 'You're letting what happened to Serena confuse your memory.'

'Dad won't be able to deny it. I must have been so terrified that I blocked it out all these years. *Dad didn't kill Mom. I did.*'

Two hours later, Joel arrived home from the factory. He was ashen when Paul haltingly told him what had occurred at the Robinson house.

'How awful.' He was shaken. 'To happen again in this town.'

'Dad, I was holding the gun that killed Mom. Not you,' Paul said.

'No,' Joel shot back, unnerved by this accusation. 'I shot your mother.'

'I remember, Dad – as clear as though it were yesterday. Why did you take the blame all these years? And don't deny it. I know.'

'It seemed too much for a six-year-old boy to carry on his shoulders,' Joel said after a moment. 'I never wanted you to have to deal with that. And it wasn't your fault. It was a tragic error. The guns in the cabinet were never loaded. My father – who was so proud of that particular revolver – had taken it out to show to a business associate in town for the day. They went out behind the house for target practice with it. A phone call summoned them inside. Papa put the gun away without removing the bullets. It was a terrible, terrible accident that I'm sure brought on his fatal heart attack a few weeks later. It wasn't your fault, Paul,' he reiterated.

'You loved me enough to take the blame.' Paul's voice was a shaken whisper.

'Of course I love you that much,' Joel said gruffly. 'You're my son.'

Vera felt tears well in her eyes. The barrier between Paul and his father had crumbled. But how would Paul deal with the knowledge that *he* had held the revolver that had killed his mother?

Chapter Sixteen

Vera knew that the Robinson tragedy would evoke recall in Eastwood of the similar tragedy in the Kahn family twenty-four years ago. She worried that Paul would insist on retracting the original story of what had happened. She was relieved that her father-in-law was adamant when Paul brought this up the evening after Serena's funeral.

'It serves no purpose,' he rejected. 'It would only reflect badly on your grandfather – that he could leave a loaded gun where a child could reach it. Enough already about this.'

Later – privately – Joel promised Vera that no reprise of the earlier tragedy would appear in the local newspaper.

'The *Eastwood Herald* knows not to drag it up again. I carry some weight in this town. Now's the time to use it.'

The town was, of course, shocked and horrified by Serena's death. With his small son, Mr Robinson moved immediately from Eastwood. The Robinson house was placed on the real estate market. Visitors to town were shown the site as though, Paul said indignantly, it were a tourist attraction.

Vera worried about both Paul and Laurie in the months ahead. She knew Paul's inner battle to accept his own part in his mother's death – and his guilt at blaming his father all these years. She was anxious about Laurie's recurring nightmares, the blend of shock and rage that had eradicated her young exuberance. Thank God for

Adele's presence in the house, she told herself at grateful intervals. Laurie clung to Adele.

At intervals she'd worried that Fiona would tire of her 'life in exile,' as Paul sympathetically referred to it, and return to New York. It couldn't be easy for her to be the one coloured woman in Eastwood. Far more difficult than being one of three Jewish families in town, she conceded. Most of the time they were assimilated into the Eastwood population. At the turn of the century, Paul's grandfather had been the mayor of the town for several terms.

But she knew that Fiona was concerned that even at her tender years Adele's social life was limited. Yet, she comforted herself, Adele was not conscious of this. Not yet. She'd been so relieved, Vera thought, when Fiona confided after her last visit home that she was happy to be able to keep Adele out of a city housing project.

'I'm not sure why it's happening, but the city projects are becoming awful places. Nothing ever gets repaired. The elevators don't work half the time – and when they do, some people use them for toilets. And kids just roam around – inside and out – with nobody looking after them. That's not the way it was supposed to be. I don't want to bring up Adele in a place like that.'

Three months after Serena's death, when Joel was preparing to leave for a gun show in New York City, Vera came face to face with Laurie's rage. The family was at dinner. Joel was talking with pride about the magnificent workmanship of an antique revolver he'd been invited to display at the show.

'I hate guns!' Laurie shrieked. 'They're bad! They kill people! I hate you for making them!' she told her grandfather while Tracy gaped in disbelief. To Tracy their grandfather was the source of unbounded love, support in parent-daughter battles, and gifts.

'Laurie!' Vera was pale with shock. 'Apologize to

Grandpa this minute.' She turned to him. 'Laurie didn't mean that, Dad.' But Laurie was already running from the dining room.

'She's still hurting,' Paul said gently. 'It'll take time to pass.'

All at once Vera understood the reproachful glances in Laurie's eyes each morning at breakfast. Dad and Paul had breakfast earlier – Dad to be the first at the factory in the morning and Paul to be in his classroom early. Breakfast with Laurie and Tracy was a special time for her – but now she understood Laurie's oddly reproachful glances each morning. Laurie resented her going in to work in an office associated with guns, just as she resented her grandfather's being in the business of manufacturing guns.

'Vera, it'll fade away in time,' Paul comforted when she confided her fears to him. 'Poor baby, she's so young to have been put through such an ordeal.' One he, too, had survived.

'She's still angry with me and Dad because of the factory. In her eyes we make guns – and guns kill. She doesn't understand that guns help to keep peace in the world, that they protect against criminals. It's not guns that kill but the people who use them.' She realized she was quoting Joel. 'Paul, there's this wall between Laurie and me now. I can't get through to her.' She felt so helpless. And Dad was so hurt. What was happening to their beautiful family? And for an agonizing few moments, her mind bolted back through the years to the devastating night when her family in Berlin had been taken from her. And now she felt as though she were losing her precious Laurie.

'We'll be going to the Cape soon with Doris,' Paul intruded on her recall. 'You know how Laurie loves the beach. She'll put all this behind her.' *Would she?*

Over the sultry July 4th weekend Tracy came down with chicken pox, and a few days later both Laurie and Adele were displaying the familiar symptoms. Again, Dr Evans came to the house.

'Now you remember not to scratch,' he told Laurie with mock ferociousness, 'or you'll have to take the most evil-smelling medicine.' He turned to Vera. 'You know the routine,' he said good humouredly. 'Call me if her fever goes up – but it won't, young lady,' he told Laurie, 'because you're going to do whatever Mommie tells you.' He lingered briefly, then left to look in on Adele.

'Mommie, it itches,' Laurie complained when they were alone. 'When will it stop?'

'I'll put the lotion on, and then it'll feel better,' Vera soothed and reached for the bottle and a swab of cotton.

'Mommie, I love you,' Laurie said a few moments later when Vera had applied ample lotion. 'I love you so much.'

'And I love you, darling.' She reached to draw her small daughter into her arms. Was Laurie over her anger about the factory? Maybe Paul was right when he said she was just imagining it now.

Dad was pleased with her latest suggestions for speeding up the work, she thought with satisfaction. For over a month she'd had her own small office – and a title: Assistant to the President. And a salary raise that had impressed Paul. She knew Wayne resented her growing involvement in the business. She ignored his snide remarks – made behind their father-in-law's back. Was Wayne afraid she'd find out something he didn't want her – or Dad – to know?

Moments after Vera heard Dr Evans' car drive away, Fiona came to Laurie's bedroom.

'It's confirmed,' Fiona said, chuckling. 'Adele's got chicken pox.'

'What a surprise!' Vera joshed.

'That Dr Evans is so sweet.' Fiona seemed simultaneously grateful and self-conscious. 'You know, he wouldn't let me pay him? He said he had to come here anyway to see Laurie, so why should he charge me?'

'The town's lucky to have a doctor like him.' Vera nodded in respect.

'Mommie, I'm thirsty,' Laurie said. 'Can I have some orange juice?'

August arrived. Vera looked forward to two weeks on the Cape with Doris – to coincide with Fiona's vacation time. Again, they'd avoid being there with Wayne, who was off on some business jaunt in South America. Paul was philosophical about their not being able to trip up Wayne. She harboured a continuing frustration over this. But then, she rationalized, Paul was wrapped up in his battles at school regarding book censorship. Ted had agreed to withdraw *An American Tragedy* from his reading list on the grounds that it was too 'sophisticated' for high school seniors but won out on the book's remaining on the library shelves. A clique of parents assiduously followed the advice of McCarthyite groups and demanded the removal from reading lists and library shelves of book after book.

'Most people are decent,' Paul said with an optimism Vera found difficult to share. Some were decent, she conceded – remembering the Schmidts in Berlin, the Munches in Copenhagen, and those who had helped her escape from Denmark. 'A small group of nasty, noisy people are always the troublemakers. This can't go on much longer.'

By early in the new year, Vera had convinced herself that Laurie was her effervescent self again. She and Adele were caught up in a good-humoured competition over grades – the two brightest in their class, their teacher had confided. Paul admitted to some trying periods, but he accepted the fact that he had unwittingly held the gun that killed his mother. '*Damn it, Vera, people who own guns have to realize they have a tremendous responsibility. There should be some kind of legislation to establish that.*' Still, at disconcerting moments she felt as though she and her father-in-law were defiled in the eyes of Laurie and Paul by their involvement in the firearms industry.

Did Paul expect his father to throw aside a flourishing, four-generations-old business? she asked herself in defiant moments. His father was proud of the contribution the family had made through four wars and now, in a small way, in the Korean War. She tried to block out of her mind the possible – probable, she conceded – sale of arms to Israel, where the tiny country was ever-battling to strengthen its forces because Egypt vowed to see its extermination and candidly prepared for war.

She respected Paul's dedication to peace. She shared that dream, she told herself. Along with him, she worried about possible Soviet aggression, about the rumoured development of more weapons of destruction. But the Kahn factory made handguns, rifles – only small weaponry. They sold to sporting goods stores, gun clubs, governments. *What was evil about that*?

Wayne was spending much of his time 'on the road,' as he preferred to call it. Joel confided to Vera that he was worried about the state of Doris and Wayne's marriage.

'Do you think he's spending more time away because Doris seems to be picking fights when they're together? Or is she picking fights because he's away so much?' Joel sighed. 'I wish she'd get pregnant – then she'd have a baby to occupy her time.' Vera forced herself not to point out that Doris was not beset by idle time. Sure, she had a housekeeper now because Wayne considered that enhanced his image as a successful businessman, but she spent long hours at the nursery group and the book shop. They constituted a full-time job.

'It's something they'll have to work out for themselves,' Vera said after a tortured moment. Doris was a sweet, wonderful woman. Why couldn't Dad – and Paul – see what Wayne was doing to her? Should *she* bring it out into the open? Yet each time she considered this, she backed away. Dad and Paul didn't understand what Wayne was doing to Doris, and Doris herself would deny it. And she was under oath to say nothing to anyone about Wayne's inability to father a child. 'Doris would love to adopt,' she said – and reached out for help on this. 'Maybe if you could – could kind of hint to Wayne about their adopting, he might agree. Doris tried, but Wayne just gets angry.' *Doris could have a baby. Why couldn't she tell Wayne the truth?*

'I'll try,' Joel said, yet instinct told Vera that he wouldn't. Why did men always think it was the woman's fault if she didn't get pregnant?

It seemed to Vera that time was racing past. Still, the fighting continued in Korea and McCarthyism raged on. In October 1952, the British made their first atomic bomb test in Australia. The following month, the United States exploded a hydrogen bomb – the most destructive weapon in history – at Eniwetok Atoll in the Pacific. Paul agonized over both events. Wayne derided this reaction.

'Look, the only way to guarantee peace in the world is to let the bastards know we've got what it takes to blow them off the face of the earth.'

With a new year rolling in, business at the Kahn factory continued excellent, though Wayne focused mainly on international sales. Then, at Joel's suggestion – and after serious prodding – Vera agreed to take on the task of approaching new American accounts.

'Joel, you're off your rocker!' Vera heard Wayne's

explosion when he discovered this. 'What the hell does Vera know about selling? And in a man's field at that!'

'Wayne, calm down,' Joel soothed. 'You don't have time for that. You're after bigger game. And you know how I hate selling. She's young and enthusiastic and, let's face it, she's got one great advantage over me: She's young and beautiful. The buyers – all men – will like her.'

'Watch it, Joel,' Wayne warned. He'd long ago dropped the more affectionate 'Dad' to use his father-in-law's given name. To him, Vera guessed, that put them on an equal footing. 'Don't let her screw up some big deal for you.'

Joel admitted that her first assignment was a rough one.

'For several years we did business with the three Gregory Winston sporting goods shops. Then, just as they began this tremendous expansion about four years ago, we lost the account. Wayne couldn't get through to them. I understood they were getting impossible discounts from somebody else. Anyway, this is a test run for you,' he said good-humouredly. 'If you don't land an order, don't cry about it. Just go on to the next candidate.'

In an odd fashion, Vera analysed, she enjoyed the challenge of selling. Still, she was a nervous wreck, she confided to Paul as they prepared for bed on the night before her first trip to an account in New York City.

'Honey, you don't have to do this.' Paul was solicitous. 'Dad'll understand –'

'I have to do it,' she insisted. 'I have to prove to myself that I can do it. It's kind of an accomplishment.'

'Hey, you keep this up,' he teased, 'you'll be making more money than me.'

She settled herself in bed and watched while Paul did

his nightly push-ups. 'I hope I don't get lost in the city.'

'You?' Paul chuckled. 'A girl who escaped from Berlin, then from Copenhagen?'

'I've only been in New York three times since I arrived,' she reminded. A year ago – with Fiona and Joel watching over the girls – they'd gone into New York for the weekend. They'd stayed at the St Moritz, gone to the theatre to see Tennessee Williams' latest play, 'The Rose Tattoo'. On Sunday, before they headed back for Eastwood, Paul had taken her to the Columbia campus. They'd gone to the West End Bar across from the campus for an early dinner. And a few weeks ago they'd gone to New York to see Laurence Olivier and Vivien Leigh in 'Anthony and Cleopatra'. 'But I don't have far to go,' she said with a fresh burst of confidence. 'From Grand Central to the Winston Stores office on Madison Avenue. And the weather's fine.'

Early next morning – crisp, cold, but sunlit – Joel drove her to the Albany railroad station. 'We'll make better time in the car than the train from Saratoga to Albany with all the backing up they do.' After her luncheon appointment with Gregory Winston, she would take an afternoon train to Albany, where Paul would pick her up. Paul had given her his copy of the new Hemingway novel, *The Old Man and the Sea.* Settled in her seat on the train, she opened the short novel – which Paul had claimed that she would finish before the train pulled into Grand Central.

The book lay open but unread on her lap as the train chugged southward. Her thoughts dwelt on Doris. Perfectly suited to working with the young children in the nursery group, she was developing such insecurities, Vera fretted. Even at the book shop Doris was doubting her ability to order what was saleable; she constantly questioned the other volunteers. Wayne was doing that to her – with what Dad thought were affectionate witticisms. Paul worried that she seemed depressed so often.

Lately Wayne had taken Doris with him on some of his whirlwind trips to Europe, even to Rio between Christmas and New Year's. He made such a fuss about her shopping in New York – at Saks and Altman's – for a beautiful wardrobe. But that was for his own pride, Vera thought in bitter candour. Wayne Solomon's wife must wear the most expensive clothes – a testament to his success.

Every woman in Eastwood seemed to admire the mink coat Wayne had given Doris on their last anniversary. Didn't they remember – didn't Wayne remember – that Doris had finally come out and admitted she loathed furs? 'They belong on the animals that grew them – not on women.'

Because she'd slept little the night before, Vera began to doze. She woke up when the train passed through the 125th Street station – and recalled what Doris had told her about the poverty of Harlem. Fiona had escaped that, she thought tenderly – so determined to give Adele the best she could manage. Yet at times she suspected Fiona felt that she lived in exile.

Vera was conscious of a flurry of excitement when she walked from the train and up through the splendour of Grand Central Station. She glanced about at the other women, hurrying to their own destinations. Was she dressed smartly? It was important to appear successful when she met Gregory Winston. Her black coat was cut in the new princess line with the belt high at the back, as decreed by Christian Dior. Her grey suit was a copy of a Dior of last year – ultra feminine, the jacket cut on the cross and with raglan sleeves. She'd spent far more on the suit and the coat than she'd ever intended – but

Paul, who had been with her, had insisted on both purchases. Now she was glad he had.

Walking across 42nd Street to Madison Avenue, she felt herself caught up in the electric atmosphere of midtown Manhattan – in such contrast to the streets of Eastwood. Her earlier insecurity evaporated. When the receptionist at the Winston offices inspected her suit with candid admiration, she was conscious of a surge of fresh confidence.

From almost her first few moments with Gregory Winston – a slender, grey-haired man in his late fifties – she sensed he had agreed to see her out of curiosity. Over luncheon in an elegant French restaurant off Madison Avenue, she realized he had revised his initial impression that she meant to use her femininity to snare an order. She talked about Laurie and Tracy, and he brought out snapshots of his young granddaughter.

'I'll be blunt,' he said when she began a low-keyed sales pitch. 'I was annoyed when Kahn sent that arrogant young salesman to call on me. My impression was that he didn't really want our account. Maybe we weren't big enough for him.' His smile was wry. 'That was in '48. We had three stores then. Now we have twenty-three.' He paused. 'And the prices he quoted were exorbitant. Up till then, your prices had been competitive and the service excellent.'

'Mr Kahn would have been furious if he'd known,' Vera apologized. 'That's not the way he operates his company.' *What had been wrong with Wayne*?

Now they settled down to frank dickering. Winston was buying for twenty-three stores. Vera knew he would want special volume discounts. She relished the game, wound up with a large order at prices above Joel's bottom line. She knew her father-in-law would be delighted. But Gregory Winston's last words – spoken in jest – ricocheted in her brain: 'Maybe he just didn't want to sell in the United States. He talked about having no problems with his price list in Europe.'

On the train ride to Albany, she dissected the situation. Winston had been talking about four years ago. Had Wayne been trying to divert most of their production to Israel? Even now, the arms embargo on Israel remained in effect. Did Wayne have some scam going on overseas? Was she being paranoid? Believing what David Meyerberg had told Paul, she doubted that Wayne harboured any loyalty towards Israel – other than what profits it could mean for him.

Paul was waiting at the Albany station for her.

'I could have taken the train up to Saratoga,' she said tenderly when they were settled in the car. 'You wouldn't have had this long *schlep*.'

'This way you'll be home by the time Laurie and Tracy are ready for bed,' he reminded. 'They're eager to hear all about your trip to New York.'

'Oh, Paul, I forgot to pick up presents for them!'

'Presents are in the car,' he soothed. 'I figured you'd be all excited about your lunch meeting and then you'd be rushing for the train. I picked up two puzzles.'

Now she talked about her meeting with Gregory Winston and her suspicions about Wayne.

'You figure Wayne may have dreamt up a way to skim off the top?' Paul asked.

'It's a gut feeling,' she admitted. 'But I don't know how he could do it.'

'If there's a way, Wayne would find it,' Paul said. 'You're there in the office every day. Start watching the correspondence. I mean, all of it – not just the translations you do for Wayne.' The translating was a small part of her duties these days. She managed the small office staff, was the liaison with the warehouse division, sought for ways to increase factory efficiency. And now she would be pursuing new accounts – via phone or personal approach where practical. 'Somewhere in the correspondence we'll find the answers.'

Vera made a point now of checking on all correspondence that dealt with Wayne's activities with the company. His major accounts were out of the country – what he boasted was an untapped market for American small-arms companies. She studied the bills of lading for the destination of shipments. They all appeared routine: sporting goods stores and rifle and pistol clubs. His volume was heavy, she conceded – and he connived on occasion to make sure shipments went out to his accounts ahead of hers when there was an inventory problem. He seethed each time their father-in-law mentioned a new account she'd brought in, she sensed – though he was too canny to allow this to be obvious.

She was impatient that she could make no real deductions about possible clandestine operations on Wayne's part. The European accounts were steady, ordering regularly.

'It's not going to happen overnight,' Paul soothed, 'but one day Wayne will slip up. That is, if he is pulling something crooked on Dad.'

'Paul, we know he is!' Vera sighed in frustration.

Early in the summer Wayne announced at a Friday-evening dinner that he was buying the Robinson house. Doris dropped her eyes to her plate. It was clear she had opposed this.

'It must have cost a bundle,' Joel said in shock while Paul stared in disbelief. It was commonly assumed that the house – Eastwood's showplace – would be sold to an outsider, someone who was unaware of the tragedy it had witnessed. How could Wayne consider living in that house? Vera asked herself – knowing that the others at the table shared her revulsion at his action. *How could he be so insensitive*?

'I got it at a steal,' Wayne boasted. 'And with real estate prices rising the way they are, we'll sell our house at a substantial profit. Oh sure, we'll have to carry a huge mortgage,' he conceded, 'but it's a terrific investment. We'll close in sixty days.'

'Have you approached the bank yet about a mortgage?' Joel seemed uneasy. 'With a house like that, they'll want a big down payment and –'

'Robinson is giving me the mortgage himself,' Wayne broke in. 'No sweat there. He just wants the property off his back.'

On Saturday afternoons, Vera and Paul alternated helping out at the book shop. The following afternoon was Vera's turn. Paul would take Laurie and Tracy – along with Adele – on a trip to a nearby game farm. Vera was anxious for some time alone with Doris – which she hadn't been able to manage last night. Instinctively she knew that Doris wasn't happy about the new house.

'Vera, I didn't know a thing about the Robinson house,' she confessed moments after Vera walked into the shop. 'Wouldn't you think Wayne would have consulted me?'

'And now it's too late.' Vera tried to be calm. That house was full of terrible memories. How could Wayne expect Doris to be happy there? But he didn't care about her happiness. 'Has he signed the contract?'

Doris nodded. 'Oh, he's playing this great scene about how it was his big surprise for my birthday,' she said bitterly. 'I'll hate living there.' Now Doris forced a welcoming smile – their first customer of the day had walked into the shop.

News in Eastwood always circulated with telegraphic speed. Still, Vera was startled when Olivia Ames – a veteran local real estate broker – came into the shop to buy a children's book as a birthday gift and proceeded to scold Doris for ignoring her to buy a house direct from the seller.

'Mr Robinson gave me the listing the day after that poor little girl died,' she rattled on. 'Of course, it wasn't exclusive – Sally Rice and Bill Edmonds have it, too – but to go right over our heads and approach Mr Robinson direct? We were all so hurt.'

'I'm sorry,' Doris stammered. 'I didn't know a thing about it. Wayne bought it as a birthday surprise for me.'

'That huge house for just the two of you?' Olivia clucked sweetly, but Vera saw the malicious glint in her eyes. 'It just cries out for a big family.'

'Do you suppose we'll ever be able to persuade Laurie to come to the house?' Doris asked when she and Vera were alone again.

'It'll be a while,' Vera admitted. 'We won't even drive by if Laurie is with us.'

'I don't know why Wayne lied about the mortgage,' Doris said and Vera stared in surprise. 'I shouldn't be saying this, of course. I told you how Wayne won't let me go into his office at the house. The maid's not even allowed to go in there to clean. But he left the window open when he drove into Albany this morning on some business appointment. Remember that sudden downpour earlier? I had to go in and shut the windows. There was this file on his desk – and I opened it. The contract for the house was in it. Vera, he's paying *cash*.'

Vera's mind was in instant turmoil. Where had Wayne come up with that kind of cash? Was it money he'd sneaked out of Israel? Or was it from some scam he was pulling on Dad?

'He's not earning commissions in that category from the factory.' Vera was blunt. 'He might have smuggled a big bankroll out of Israel and kept it for something special,' she acknowledged.

'Vera, he left Israel ten years ago!' All at once Doris was distraught. 'Everybody in New York thought he was penniless. He was living in a tiny room in his cousin's apartment. Could he have been lying all this time?'

'Maybe he borrowed it from one of his "connections."' Wayne dropped hints at regular intervals about wealthy, important connections. But why would anybody loan him such a huge chunk of money – unless he was providing some urgent service? *Such as illegal arms.*

'Vera, don't say anything about this to anybody,' Doris pleaded. 'Not even to Paul. I just can't believe that Wayne would keep something like this from me. He was making remarks how we'd have to watch our spending because he'd taken on such a big mortgage –'

'I won't say a word,' Vera promised. 'Maybe Wayne will come up with some reasonable explanation.'

'He lied to me. That's what hurt worst of all.'

She mustn't tell Paul, Vera warned herself. She'd made a promise. But it would be so hard not to tell him. Somehow, she must break through this dark, secret cloud that surrounded Wayne. Yet even as she considered it, she felt an overwhelming sadness. Whatever was discovered, instinct told her, would be devastating to Doris. It could present a ghastly legal entanglement for Dad.

Chapter Seventeen

Vera felt an overwhelming sense of relief when late in July the Korean armistice was signed – though President Eisenhower told the country that 'we have won an armistice on a single battleground, not peace in the world.' She knew how the fighting in Korea had troubled Paul. She, too, had worried about the unnecessary deaths caused by the war, but for Paul the Korean War had resurrected his anguish over the deaths his RAF bomber squad had caused in World War II.

'*My mind tells me that the fight against Hitler was necessary – but I'll forever be haunted by the lives we took each time we dropped a bomb over enemy territory. Civilians had to have died in those attacks.*' At regular intervals Vera wondered if the Schmidts had survived the war – if they were all right. Every year at Christmas she heard from the Munches in Copenhagen and Iris in Canada.

Vera's relief that the Korean War was over was short lived because the following month – when again she and Paul and the girls were at the Cape Cod cottage with Doris – news flashed around the world that on August 12, the Soviet Union had exploded a hydrogen bomb. After Laurie and Tracy had been put to bed that evening, the other three sat before the television set and listened to a recap of the news about the bomb. After a few minutes Paul leapt to his feet and strode across to the TV to switch off the news programme.

'God, are we out to destroy ourselves?' He grunted in frustration.

'The Soviets are not about to use the bomb,' Vera soothed. 'It's their way of saying, "Don't mess with us."'

'There'll be peace in this world when not one gun, not one weapon of war can be had,' he warned.

'That'll never happen,' Doris predicted.

Vera intercepted the guarded exchange between Paul and Doris. Meaning, she interpreted, that their father manufactured guns – a source of distress to both.

'We're not involved in the armaments race,' Vera said defensively, for a moment erasing from her mind her conviction that Kahn Firearms was supplying arms to Israel. 'We make handguns and rifles.'

'Vera, who do you think went in to do the final cleanup in the battles in the Pacific?' Paul demanded and she winced at his caustic tone. 'The riflemen!' *But that had been a necessary war.*

'I know Wayne's making a fortune selling handguns and rifles,' Doris said, her face taut with rejection. 'But I live with this awful guilt that what he sells is taking lives.'

Did Laurie still resent her working at the factory? Vera asked herself, ever troubled by this possibility. Laurie hated fireworks because they reminded her of guns. She'd refused to go to the Fourth of July fireworks display in town. Dad had taken Tracy down to see it.

'I hate when hunting season opens,' Paul said sombrely.

'Over and over again, I ask myself how Wayne acquired the money to buy the house outright –' Doris stopped dead, startled by this admission to Paul. 'He paid cash,' she told Paul. 'And I keep asking myself, where did he get the money? Does it have something to do with guns?'

'I didn't know that.' He turned to Vera in shock. 'You're familiar with the business. Could he have earned enough commissions to buy a showplace like the Robinson house? For cash?'

'No way. Unless,' she made an effort to remove the

stricken expression on Doris's face, 'unless he's been secretly saving since the day he went to work for Dad.'

'How could he save the way we live?' Doris countered. 'Buying the Jaguar, taking over the liquor store, making me hire Millicent as soon as we moved into the new house.' Millicent was their full-time housekeeper. 'Spending a fortune on his clothes. Wayne can't buy around here,' she mocked. 'He has to run down to New York to some fancy tailor. He shops in Brooks Brothers on Madison Avenue, orders shirts from London.'

'What did he tell you?' Paul probed.

'He didn't tell me,' Doris flared. 'I found out by accident. He doesn't tell me anything.'

For the first time, Vera thought, Paul was beginning to understand that Doris was unhappy in her marriage, that Wayne might be less than the ideal husband she'd once proclaimed.

'Where's Wayne on this trip?' Paul asked, clearly troubled.

'Somewhere in Central America.' Doris shrugged, turned to Vera. 'You'd know more about that than I.'

'Wayne's gone to line up some huge game and fishing club in El Salvador, and then he's heading for Guatemala,' Vera reported. 'He's –'

'I shouldn't have said what I did,' Doris broke in, distraught now. 'Wayne was brought up in another culture. He doesn't understand American women. He means well. He works so hard.' Her eyes pleaded with Paul, then Vera, to dismiss her earlier confidence. 'Forget it, please.'

'Sure.' Paul managed a smile. 'Is there any more of that strawberry shortcake we had for dinner?'

'I'll get it.' Doris rose to her feet in an aura of relief that the conversation had been diverted. 'And I'll put up a fresh pot of coffee.'

Later, in the privacy of their bedroom, Vera and Paul discussed Doris's revelations in whispers.

'Maybe I'm way off the track,' Paul said, 'but I have this strong suspicion that Wayne may be selling to revolutionary groups.'

'Dad would be furious!' Vera broke in. Dad wouldn't consider Israel a revolutionary group. 'You know he –'

'Dad wouldn't be aware of it,' Paul told her. 'But you said Wayne was headed for El Salvador and Guatemala. Remember the outbreaks in El Salvador and Guatemala in the past few years? As for his European trips,' Paul pursued grimly, 'there's trouble all the way from Lithuania through the Balkans and the Ukraine. The market for illegal arms is huge.'

'How can Wayne manage to sell to those groups?' Vera shook her head in bewilderment.

'They set up phoney rifle clubs or some such deal,' Paul surmised. 'I'm damn sure Wayne's aware of what's happening. He doesn't care as long as he's bringing in heavy sales. But you said yourself, his commissions wouldn't add up to enough cash to buy the Robinson house.'

'Maybe he's collecting something on the side.' Vera was grim. 'A lot on the side – to keep his mouth shut.'

'Dad would keep silent if he thought the guns were going to Israel, because Israel's still fighting so desperately to survive. But he won't be silent if Wayne's selling to guerrilla groups.' Paul sighed. 'Any way you look at it, Doris is going to be hurt.'

Vera and Paul struggled to unearth proof that Wayne was involved in clandestine arms deals, came up with nothing. True, Wayne's letters – and despite her elevated position in the company, Vera still served as his translator – sounded odd, as though they could be coded. But he had been raised in another culture, Vera reasoned. Sometimes his English was stilted. Yet both she and Paul sensed something unsavoury in Wayne's business deals.

'Keep watching,' Paul urged Vera. 'We'll hit pay dirt yet.' Both knew not to approach Joel without concrete proof.

Shortly after the first of the year, Vera returned from lunch at the nearby café – the Blue Lantern – that was her daily destination to overhear Wayne in an argumentative conversation.

'Listen to me,' he said menacingly and Vera froze at attention beyond his line of vision. 'And I'm not going to say it again. This is my last offer for the store. Who in this God-forsaken town is going to buy out the fixtures at that price and pay the outrageous rent you're asking? Who's going to take over a business that couldn't keep Joe Leslie in cigarette money these past two years?' Vera remembered that Joe Leslie – who'd run the only sporting goods store in town for the past twenty-eight years – had recently died of lung cancer. 'You have my price – and it's good only for the next forty-eight hours. After that, I'm out of it.'

Vera hurried to her office. She was disappointed not to have overheard some incriminating revelation. But her mind focused on the efforts of Joe Leslie's landlord to sell the store fixtures and rent the premises. Suddenly decisive, she left her office and strode to that of her father-in-law. He glanced up with a warm smile.

'Got a minute?' she asked.

'For you, anytime,' he said affectionately.

She told Joel in a burst of words that she thought it would be a profitable deal for the company to take over Joe Leslie's business.

'His major sales were handguns and rifles – and we'll show a large profit selling at the retail price. It'll be a simple matter to fill in with sporting goods and attire,' she finished breathlessly. And she'd enjoy beating Wayne to the punch, she admitted to herself without a trace of guilt.

'Aha! The entrepreneur in you comes out,' Joel joshed. 'Okay, run with it.'

'Just like that?' Vera was taken aback by her immediate success.

'Honey, I realized from your first week in the office that you're the smartest woman I know. You make the deal, set it up the way you feel it should be. Hire your staff. You supervise, but I want you here with me,' he pinpointed. 'I need that bright little head of yours.'

As she'd anticipated, Vera was the object of Wayne's rage when he discovered the company was taking over the sporting goods store at her suggestion. He stalked into her office and slammed the door behind him.

'You knew – how I can't figure out – that I was after that store!' he hissed at her. 'You think you're so damn smart. You think you can wind Joel around your little finger.' At the moment Joel was at the monthly Lions Club luncheon.

'You've told Dad half-a-dozen times that he ought to be buying up businesses around town, that he could become one of the richest men in the state.' She refused to be ruffled. 'The store seemed a natural for us.'

'You're a smart-ass,' he snapped, yet she sensed he was oddly aroused by her. 'Pity you've got that stupid puritan streak.' His eyes swept over her for a moment in naked passion. 'Together, we could make it right to the top of the heap. Rich and powerful.' But passion was quickly replaced by fury. 'Don't get in my way again, baby – because you might be sorry.' He spun around and strode from her office.

Vera sat motionless, digesting what he had said. She'd ruffled his feathers, she mocked herself. But she wasn't afraid of his threats. Yet she found it impossible to dismiss the encounter from her mind for the rest of the working day.

At the house she focused her attention on Laurie and Tracy, who were both clamouring to talk about their school day. Why was she letting Wayne upset her? she rebuked herself in a corner of her mind while she managed to appear totally absorbed in what Laurie and Tracy were reporting in their exuberant fashion. There was nothing for her to fear in Wayne's threats. *Was there?*

Now she felt a new urgency in unmasking Wayne's covert activities. She dissected his letters – which she translated into German or French – in a desperate determination to locate clues. She checked the books to confirm her conviction that Wayne's income could not have allowed him to buy the Robinson house. And all the while she focused on setting up the newly formed Kahn Sporting Goods Shop – a diversion she found challenging.

Vera was grateful that the school's spring holidays arrived just as she was preparing to go into New York in her new role as buyer for the shop. Paul decided to accompany her on the two-day trip.

'Live it up for a couple of days,' Joel ordered. 'Fiona and I will take care of the kids – and Doris will love the chance to play surrogate mommie.'

On a deliciously springlike April morning – with promises to Laurie and Tracy to return home bearing gifts – Vera and Paul climbed into the car and headed towards New York. They'd spend the night at the Essex House – in a room facing the park, Paul had reported in high spirits. This afternoon and tomorrow morning Vera would visit manufacturers' showrooms. She and Paul would have a hasty lunch and catch a Broadway matinée.

They'd have an early dinner at Lindy's – close to the theatre – then drive home.

'I feel as though I'm playing truant,' Vera told Paul. 'And it's such fun.'

'Don't say that to any of my kids at school,' he joked. But Vera knew he was proud of the attendance records in his classes. That was a plus, she comforted herself, in Paul's latest battle with Mr Kerrigan. Why couldn't Kerrigan understand that Paul was fighting to bring something fresh and important into the Eastwood school system?

'I wish I'd taken a course somewhere about buying,' Vera confessed. 'I'm going into this whole scene blind.'

'You've got great taste,' Paul insisted. 'And you said yourself that the main thrust of the shop is hunting and fishing equipment – and Dad's taking care of that.'

Vera chuckled reminiscently. 'Wayne's still fuming about the shop. He thought he had the deal all tied up – on his terms.'

'He's doing well with the liquor store, I gather from what Dad says. But Wayne won't be happy until he owns this whole town. His fiefdom,' Paul drawled.

'We're receiving re-orders from both El Salvador and Guatemala.' Vera was serious now. 'I can't believe we're shipping that many handguns and rifles for sporting use.'

'How are they gotten out of the country?' Paul was curious. 'Aren't there governmental rules?'

'There's no federal legislation against shipping what's known as "sporting arms,"' Vera said. 'And the shipments to Israel go by way of other countries.' Because the United States still maintained an embargo on weapons to Israel. 'What Wayne labels a *distribution centre*. I suspect Dad worries about that – he's so very ethical in everything else.'

'I hate our involvement in selling guns even for sporting activities. Yet I understand how he feels about Israel – and that bugs me, Vera. How can I condone being part of war in one instance and reject it in others?' He sighed, his hands clutching the wheel. 'When, Vera – when will the world learn to live without killing?'

In Manhattan, Vera and Paul checked into the hotel, had lunch sent up from room service in deference to Vera's tight schedule. While they ate, Paul gave Vera directions to her afternoon's destination – situated happily in the same area.

'Sure you don't want me to go with you?' he probed.

'Absolutely not,' she assured him. 'I know the streets and avenues I'm heading for – you said yourself, New York cabbies are great.' And she knew he was eager to spend the afternoon at the United Nations.

Driving back to Eastwood the following evening, Vera congratulated herself on a successful business trip. And both she and Paul had enjoyed the non-business hours. The shop was the beginning of a new era, she'd told herself in soaring pleasure.

Early in May, Doris enlisted Vera's help in arranging a rummage sale to benefit her nursery group.

'We can have it in the grounds of the church,' Doris said. 'If it rains, we'll schedule it for the following week. But we do need money for more materials. The group is being so well received, Vera.' She radiated enthusiasm. So often Doris seemed steeped in despair, Vera thought compassionately. At least, she was finding satisfaction in her nursery group.

'I hear great things,' Vera said gently.

'I've got so much stuff stashed away in the basement to dig out for the rummage sale.' Doris sighed. 'I can't get into any of my clothes from last summer.' She tried for a chuckle. 'During the winter it's dismal so much of the time, I head to the refrigerator too often. No, you don't know,' she said before Vera could respond. 'You're one of those people who never gains an ounce.'

'I'll look around, too,' Vera promised. 'I'm sure there're a lot of things Tracy's outgrown that are still good.'

'Neither of us is on duty at the book shop tomorrow,' Doris remembered. Their Saturday off. 'Will you have time to run over and help me sort things out? I don't want to bring over things that are too beat up.'

'Sure.' When they'd first met, she'd admired Doris's self-confidence. Wayne had destroyed that through the years. 'Paul's taking the three girls to see the litter of pups at the MacDonald house in the morning.' Adele was included in most activities involving Laurie and Tracy. 'I'll run over after breakfast.'

'Millicent's off on Saturdays and Wayne's driving over to Manchester for an early golf date with some big wheel over there.' Her smile was ironic. 'You know how Wayne loves to collect "important contacts." Why don't you have breakfast with me? Or at least, coffee,' she amended – aware that Saturday-morning breakfast was a special occasion for Vera and Paul and the kids.

'I'll come over for coffee,' Vera promised.

On Saturday morning, the two women lingered in the charming, sunlit breakfast room over coffee. The scent of the first summer flowers drifted in through the open windows. A deceptive serenity permeated the house. Vera sensed that Doris was upset but determined to mask this. At last Doris confessed to her annoyance. Once again, Wayne had taken the house on the Cape for the month of August.

'He must have booked it weeks ago,' Doris said. 'You know summer rentals are grabbed up early in the year. Sure, it's beautiful up there, but I'm lonely as hell until you and Paul come out with the kids. You will come out again?' she asked, suddenly anxious.

'We love being on the Cape with you,' Vera told her. 'But won't Wayne be there with you the first two weeks?'

'Supposedly he's there.' Doris played with a corner of the tablecloth. 'But I hardly see him. He's either playing golf with someone or heading into New York for two or three days. I don't know anybody there. I don't mix well with strangers.' She gestured apologetically. Doris didn't mix well with strangers since Wayne had destroyed her ego, Vera thought with fresh rage.

'Maybe I can arrange to take three weeks off this summer. Paul will be teaching summer school still, but I could come out with the kids,' she offered on impulse. 'One week alone won't be bad, will it?' But she'd dread that extra week in the house with Wayne, Vera admitted to herself.

'You'd hate it,' Doris said bluntly, 'and Wayne would hate it. But thanks for the try. Now let's go down into the basement and see what I can dig up for the rummage sale.'

In the basement Doris brought out cartons of stored clothing, pulled out garment after garment amid sighs of regret.

'I must have gained twelve or fourteen pounds over the winter. I know I can't get into anything from last summer.' Doris groaned. 'How did I let it happen?'

'You don't look that much heavier,' Vera consoled, yet in a corner of her mind she remembered at one point becoming aware of this. 'You'll take it off during the summer,' she said with conviction. 'Save the best things for next year.'

'I'll start a diet tomorrow,' Doris decided. 'But I won't be wearing any of these this summer.'

'What about those magazines?' Vera pointed to several piles. 'They won't bring much, but it'll add up.'

'Sure, they can all go,' Doris agreed. 'I don't know why I've hung on to them.'

'You have two or three years of *Ladies Home Journals*,' Vera noticed. 'Let me take a few home to Fiona. She collects recipes.'

'Take all you want.' Doris glanced around. 'There're some shopping bags over there. I'll get one for you.'

Vera flipped through the *Ladies Home Journals*, checked the contents of a few for interesting recipes, made her selection.

'They've been lying around for a while. Let me find a dust cloth.' Doris handed her a shopping bag and turned to yet another carton.

Vera glanced curiously at a magazine atop another pile. Nothing familiar. Magazines that Wayne read, she surmised, scanning the title. *Male Adventure. Espionage and Violence.* Oddball publications with small circulations. She skimmed the table of contents of a couple of them. African safaris, daring espionage. Yes, that would appeal to Wayne. Without knowing why, she slid one issue between the copies of *Ladies Home Journal* she was taking home to Fiona.

Vera returned home in time for lunch with Paul and the girls. Fiona – off to some church fair now with Adele – had left a tuna-noodle casserole warming in the oven. Laurie and Tracy were euphoric over their visit with the pups, though they knew they couldn't have a dog of their own because their father was allergic to both cats and dogs.

After lunch Vera and Paul settled on the screen porch at the rear of the house while Laurie and Tracy sprawled on the swing-chair, each involved in the latest book given to them by Doris.

'Wouldn't you say this is the idyllic vision of a small town Saturday afternoon in May?' Paul teased. 'If we can forget the troubles of the world –' Vera knew he was concerned particularly about the fighting in Vietnam. Just three weeks ago, the US Air Force had flown a French battalion there to help Vietnam fight against Communist forces in North Vietnam.

'Let's forget for today,' Vera encouraged lightheartedly. 'Oh, I picked up some weird magazine in Doris's basement. It's on the table here with the magazines I brought home for Fiona.' She leaned forward to ferret out the unfamiliar publication. 'Have you ever heard of it?'

'No,' Paul conceded, flipping through the pages. 'One of those deals designed to appeal to men fascinated by espionage and violence,' he assumed.

Suddenly Paul's eyes seemed riveted to a page. Curious about what had captured his interest, Vera read over his shoulder. Columns of personal ads, she thought.

'Paul, what is it?' She sensed a sudden electric excitement in him.

'You said this came from Doris's basement?'

'That's right. There was a pile of them, going back at least two years, I think. Why?'

'Read this item here.' He pointed to a small listing in the personal column which gave a box number at the magazine's New York office for replies. 'It's carefully worded, of course – but I'd lay odds it's being run to contact revolutionary groups looking to buy arms!'

'You're guessing that Wayne is running ads in *Espionage and Violence* to attract business?' Possibly this ad.

'It's going to be rough to track down,' he warned, 'but yes, I'd swear Wayne is selling arms to illegal organizations – and he's using phoney pistol and rifle clubs as a front. The problem is – how the hell do we prove it?'

Chapter Eighteen

Vera and Paul were impatient to acquire current editions of *Espionage and Violence*. The one Vera had ferreted from the basement was six months old. On Sunday morning, the two of them searched magazine racks in Eastwood and in nearby towns – coming up with nothing.

'Maybe we'll find a store in Saratoga that carries it,' Paul decided. 'Let's give it a whirl.'

A search of every possible outlet in Saratoga was futile. Paul resolved to drive to Albany the following afternoon. But en route to Eastwood they stopped at a soda fountain at the edge of Schuylerville. While they settled themselves at a small marble-topped table for two and waited to be served, Vera glanced about the long, narrow store.

'Paul, they have magazines in the back.'

'I'll look.' He rose to his feet, strode towards the magazine racks. Vera saw his face light up. He held up a magazine in triumph. 'This is it!'

The same ad that they had seen in the earlier issue appeared here. The same ambiguous wording. It probably ran every month, she surmised.

'I think we're in business,' Paul said with quiet satisfaction.

'How do we prove Wayne's running the ad?' If he were. 'The magazine won't tell us.'

'There's this old Columbia buddy of mine who went on to law school,' Paul told her. 'He was brilliant but eccentric, most students thought. He carried on about how he wouldn't be corrupted by large corporations. He cherished his independence. He has a small office in Manhattan – with small billings.' Paul chuckled reminiscently. 'Frank said 85% of lawyers are crooks. Actually he wants to be a mystery writer. Anyhow, he has a collection of offbeat friends – actors and singers and writers on the fringe. He'll hire somebody for us who's hungry for a fast fifty dollars.'

'You mean, once we know Wayne's going to be in New York for the day, Frank will hire somebody to tail him? No,' she corrected herself, 'to be at the magazine's address and watch to see if Wayne goes to their office.' Her mind was on high alert. 'I have some snapshots of Wayne and Doris. I'll have a negative made, then an enlargement. Paul, it could work!'

Paul spoke to Frank, who was sure he could have somebody available. Vera sent an enlargement of the snapshot of Wayne and Doris by special delivery. Now the waiting period began. Ten days later, Vera learned that Wayne was scheduled for a trip to New York at the end of the week. Paul alerted Frank.

'We could be all wrong,' he cautioned Vera, fearful of disappointment.

'Paul, we can't afford not to follow through!'

On the day Wayne drove into Manhattan, Vera jumped every time her office phone rang. Ostensibly Wayne was calling on an old account that was adding two new stores on Long Island. She was convinced the magazine was his major destination.

There were no calls from Frank during the day. When she arrived at the house, Paul indicated by a shake of his head that he had heard nothing. He was sprawled on the floor with Laurie and Tracy while the two little girls concentrated on the 500-piece puzzle they'd been working on for the past two days. Vera sensed his disappointment matched her own.

As usual, Joel arrived home an hour after Vera. Fiona ordered the family to the dinner table. Near the conclusion of dinner the phone rang. Paul rose to his feet.

'I'll get it.'

Joel listened with grandfatherly interest to Laurie's avid report of a class trip to the state capitol at Albany while Vera struggled to conceal her anxiety about the phone call. *Was it Frank*?

Fiona glanced into the room, noted that forks and knives were now idle. Moments later she appeared with dessert.

'Ooh, strawberry shortcake!' Tracy glowed.

'Is it somebody's birthday?' Joel kidded.

'I saw these beautiful strawberries in the store this morning, and I figured everybody here loves strawberry shortcake,' Fiona said good-humouredly. 'But no seconds,' she warned Laurie and Tracy. 'That's a lot of whipped cream.'

Paul hurried into the dining room. He managed a victory signal – unseen by the others – for Vera. They hadn't been wrong, Vera guessed with jubilation. Whatever insanity Wayne had brought upon the company was about to be aired.

After dinner Laurie and Tracy went upstairs to their bedroom to focus on homework. Joel left for one of his endless civic meetings. Vera and Paul settled themselves in a corner of the living room.

'Paul, what happened?' Vera demanded impatiently when Fiona was out of the room.

'Frank's spy nailed him,' Paul said. 'He followed Wayne right up to the magazine's office. He hung around the floor for twenty minutes until Wayne came out. He wanted to make sure he had the right guy. It was Wayne.'

'We have to tell Dad,' Vera said quietly.

'When he comes home from his meeting.'

In the den – the door shut lest Laurie or Tracy should wander downstairs and overhear what was being said – Joel gaped in shock as Paul finished his report on Wayne's covert activities. It was legal – in most instances – to sell to gun clubs in foreign countries. It was a different matter to smuggle guns to illegal organizations.

'Reading between the lines of the ads, we know Wayne's using phoney gun clubs as a front,' Paul wound up.

'I've been used all these years!' Joel's face was drained of colour. 'All that crap about his being an Israeli hero – it was like that friend of yours said! How could this go on right under my eyes?' He turned to Vera. 'You translated his correspondence. Didn't that tell you anything?'

'I translated the letters he wanted us to see,' Vera pointed out. 'But somewhere along the line he must have a secret file.' She hesitated. 'And he had to have worked out some deal where he was paid additional money separately.'

'A lot of money,' Paul said. He turned to his father. 'Wayne paid cash for the Robinson house. No mortgage.'

'This has to be reported to the FBI.' Joel was shaken. 'I won't allow Kahn Firearms to be part of that kind of operation. But oh God, how will Doris take this?'

'Before you do that, Dad, we need more information.' Caution crept into Vera's voice. 'What have we got to tell them? That we suspect Wayne is running an ad in that creepy magazine and using it for illegal arms sales? We've got invoices indicating sales to gun clubs – it appears legitimate. Wayne just might wiggle out of this.'

'We can't let that happen!' Paul's eyes shone with determination. 'We need to make contact through that ad – have concrete evidence of what Wayne's pulling.'

'We can't do that ourselves.' Vera's mind was charging ahead. 'But I may have an angle. Remember I told you about the wonderful family in Copenhagen who helped me escape?' she asked Joel. He nodded. 'Mr Munch is a diplomat with contacts in several countries. Let me write him, explain the situation. He may be in a position to help us track down Wayne's operation, make a direct contact through that box number.'

'It's worth a try,' Joel agreed.

The following day Vera sent an impassioned letter to Herbert Munch. He was at present assigned to an embassy in the Balkans. The three geared themselves to wait for a reply, but with gratifying speed a letter arrived from Munch. He was already making contact through the box number in *Espionage and Violence.*

'Your man will assume an American agent of my so-called guerilla organization put me in touch with his ad. There is much unrest here. He will be confident he's snared a revolutionary group prepared to pay high for weapons.'

Vera was relieved that Wayne was spending little time in the office, that he missed two Friday-night family dinners in a row. His absence lessened the strain of keeping up the pretence that they knew nothing of his covert activities. Then Joel reported that Wayne was fighting with him about their need to produce more sophisticated guns and rifles. He complained the company would lose out to competition.

'Damn him!' Paul blazed. 'He lives on blood money!'

Vera flinched, exchanged a guilty glance with Joel. Both knew that Paul hated their own involvement with weapons of death. But guns were weapons of peace, too, she thought defiantly. Why else had the framers of the Constitution added the Second Amendment – the right to bear arms?

The time was approaching for Wayne and Doris's annual visit to the Cape. Vera was anxious to see the situation with Wayne brought out into the open even though she dreaded Doris's reaction. She knew this was a terrible trial for her father-in-law. And he feared, too, that by exposing Wayne he himself would be found guilty of illegal arms-trading. But it was something he had to do.

Then, with startling swiftness, the proof they sought about Wayne came through from Herbert Munch. The seasoned diplomat had used his contacts to flush out Wayne's operation. A letter had gone out to Wayne's box number at the magazine. He had replied, then negotiated by trans-Atlantic telephone. Munch's letter was explicit.

'He explains how the would-be arms-buyer sets up a dummy pistol-and-rifle club, which orders from Kahn Firearms Company. But before the Kahn company ships, the purchaser makes a substantial deposit into a numbered Swiss bank account. Then the routine shipment goes through. It all appears legitimate. When the orders arrive, they're rerouted to their illicit destinations.'

Through his private sources Munch had discovered that Wayne had sold not only to Israel through the years, but also to Egypt and other enemies of the young nation. He sold wherever revolutionaries were eager to buy.

Simultaneously triumphant and uneasy – not knowing how Joel and the company would fare in this situation, Vera summoned Paul and Joel into the den after dinner and presented them with the communication from Munch.

Joel read and reread Munch's letter plus the incriminating data.

'All right,' he said at last. 'I'm calling Wayne to get over here right now. But first,' he specified, 'let me call my lawyer. And Doris.' The book shop was open one evening a week. Tonight Doris was one of two volunteers on duty there.

Twenty minutes later – while the other three sat in the den with coffee, Fiona went to respond to the doorbell.

'They're in the den, Mr Solomon,' they heard Fiona tell Wayne. 'Would you like me to bring you some coffee?'

'No,' he said tersely.

Vera tensed at the sound of his heavy footsteps striding down the hall. He stalked into the den.

'I hope this is important, Joel,' he said. 'You interrupted me in the middle of my dinner.'

'It's important.' Joel's face telegraphed his rage. 'You have thirty-six hours to get out of the country.' He paused as Wayne stared blankly. 'That's when I'm going to the FBI to tell them I've discovered my international sales manager is selling to illegal organizations.'

'What the hell are you talking about?' Wayne's gaze swept from Joel to Vera, settled on her. 'What kind of craziness did you throw at him?' he challenged. 'You've been after my hide for years!'

'We know about your ads in *Espionage and Violence.*' Vera contrived to sound cool, almost impersonal. 'We know that you've sold to Egypt and other countries hostile to Israel. And to guerrillas in the Balkans and in El Salvador and Guatemala. We –'

'Joel knew about Israel.' Wayne swaggered, feeling himself in safe territory now. He turned to Joel. 'Look, you knew I was selling guns to Israel. What the hell are you bitching about now?'

'To Israel and its enemies,' Joel lashed back. 'And to any group of thugs out to destroy a democratic government supported by its people. We know about the funds paid into your numbered bank account in Geneva. Only because of Doris I'm giving you notice, Wayne. You have thirty-six hours before I go to the FBI.'

'You'll go to jail,' Wayne yelled. 'How do you think Doris will like that?'

'I'll take my chances. But before you leave, you'll sign two papers. My lawyer and a notary are standing by. First, you sign over the house to Doris. Then you sign papers agreeing to a divorce. Then pack your bags and run, Wayne. And be grateful you have a head start.'

'Doris will go with me.' Wayne's eyes exuded confidence. 'She won't believe this shit!'

'She'll believe,' Paul said quietly and walked to the door and pulled it wide. 'Doris, please come in now.'

Wayne stared wildly at Doris. 'Tell them you're going with me,' he ordered. 'We'll live like royalty in Switzerland. We'll –'

'Not Switzerland,' Paul interrupted. 'The Swiss police know now that you're an illicit arms-merchant. You'll be stopped and seized at Customs.'

'We'll go to Israel. Doris, I'm a hero there!' He started at the sound of a car pulling up out front.

'That's my attorney and the notary,' Joel told him. 'You'll sign the papers and leave.'

'Doris, tell him you don't want to divorce me,' Wayne demanded. 'Tell him that –'

'I'm not going with you, Wayne.' Doris was pale but determined. 'I'm free at last.'

The days ahead were tumultuous and nerve-wracking for the family, Vera took over the management of the factory while Joel appeared before committees in Washington DC. Doris accompanied him to supply whatever information she could about Wayne's activities – no doubt in her mind, Vera realized, that Wayne was forever out of her life.

Paul was fearful of punishment that might be meted out to his father.

'Dad's always been so ethical,' he reminded Vera as they sat on the screened porch late on a hot June evening.

'Only where Israel was concerned did he ever do something against regulations. And he was right,' he added defiantly. 'How could he not do whatever he could to help Israel?'

'He brought the whole situation to the FBI,' Vera pointed out. 'From the way Wayne set up the operation – Wayne's Swiss bank account – they must understand that Dad was unaware of the other deals. I'm sure that –' She paused at the shrill intervention of the phone.

'I'll get it!' Paul leapt to his feet and hurried into the house, Vera at his heels. They'd been waiting for a call from Washington all evening.

The caller was Joel. Vera clung to Paul, strained to hear what Joel was saying.

'It's all right,' Joel said jubilantly. 'I've got to pay a stiff fine, but they're letting me off the hook. They know I had nothing to do with what Wayne engineered. Our sales figures will take a steep drop – but we did all right before. We'll do all right again. Thank God, this madness is over.'

But in Paul's eyes the madness wasn't over, Vera thought involuntarily. The madness was the family's being in the business of manufacturing guns. She'd asked herself – over and over again – if Laurie resented her being part of the family business, knowing in her heart that Laurie raged inwardly over this. In prescient moments she envisioned – with soaring anguish – a time when Paul and Laurie would align themselves against her and her father-in-law.

They mustn't become a family divided.

Chapter Nineteen

Vera was anxious about Doris's reaction to Wayne's departure from her life. She knew there would be ups and downs in the course of the next few months. Despite Doris's outside activities, she had considered her main role in life to be that of Wayne's wife. She'd felt guilty that she harboured other ambitions – voiced only in secrecy to Vera. Maybe now, Vera thought, Doris would take up her painting again.

Word ricocheted around Eastwood about Doris's pending divorce – and Wayne's exit from the business. The situation shocked the town, but nobody dared ask questions. Along with Vera and Paul, Joel agonized over the possibility that word of the Washington hearings would leak out.

The former Robinson house now belonged to Doris. Joel had immediately suggested that Doris come home to take up residence in the guest room and list the house with the real estate brokers, but she dismissed this.

'I'll stay in the house,' she told the family a week later. 'I want to divide it into two apartments. One for myself and one to rent out. That'll provide me with a fair income.' It was clear that Doris meant to be independent.

'A great idea.' Joel was eager to be supportive.

'Maybe you'd like to work afternoons in the company shop,' Vera suggested. Doris was accustomed to living well – the extra income would be helpful. Only her mornings were involved in the nursery group. 'Not right away,'

Vera amended hastily, 'but once you've handled all the business of converting the house.' No one doubted that Doris could acquire a loan to cover the construction costs. 'And after you're back from the Cape.'

Doris was startled. 'I hadn't thought about going there.'

'Of course, you'll go.' Paul exchanged a swift glance with Vera. A change of scenery would be good for Doris. 'It's been paid for – why not utilize it?'

'The girls and I will come out with you,' Vera said. 'Paul can come out for the last two weeks. You can manage without me for the month of August, can't you, Dad?' she appealed to Joel.

'Any problems that come up either in the factory or the store you can deal with on the phone.' He nodded in agreement, but Vera saw the concern in his eyes. The three of them – Dad, Paul, and herself – were apprehensive about Doris's emotional state. They knew her control was precarious. 'And I'll come out for the Labor Day weekend,' he resolved.

In the course of the month on the Cape, Vera – on the phone at least once a day with her father-in-law on business – was conscious of Doris's mood swings. There were days when her spirits were high, others when she admitted to Vera that she was unnerved about the future. Despite Vera's efforts to prod her into painting again, Doris resisted. Too early, Vera cautioned herself. But it would be wonderful therapy, she thought impatiently.

Because she knew that Vera limited the sweets Laurie and Tracy were allowed, Doris indulged in her emotionally driven craving for candy bars in the privacy of her room – but her added weight was a giveaway. Still, Doris was determined to get her life back on track, Vera comforted herself.

In September – with most of the work on the house completed and a rental already arranged – Doris went to spend a week with Sally, now living in Westchester County.

'Oh God, I'm glad to see you,' Sally welcomed her with obvious pleasure. 'I think Phil and I must have been out of our minds to move up here.'

'The house is beautiful.' Doris glanced about in admiration while they sat over lunch in the attractive dining area.

'For me, it's a beautiful prison.' Sally's eyes telegraphed her disillusionment. 'I'm dying to get back to work. And Phil has that lousy commute into New York.' She sighed. 'But he's convinced it's great for the children. Conditions in the city have become so bad. The crime rate is unbelievable.'

'It's not just New York.' Doris was sombre, recalling an article she'd read just the previous week. 'The crime in every major city in the country – even in some of the smaller cities – is shocking. And New York isn't the worst.'

But in New York, statistics told its residents, a serious offence was committed in the area every two minutes – and the Police Commissioner predicted the figures were on the rise. She remembered how Fiona worried that there were insufficient patrolmen on duty in her mother's area of East Harlem – where she'd moved last year from her earlier housing project. 'And the way the kids are behaving scares me. They're acting real wild.'

'You don't worry about the crime rate in Eastwood, I'll bet.' Sally's smile was wry.

'The worst crime we see,' Doris admitted, chuckling, 'is when some woman calls up to complain that a teenager is using her bushes for a urinal. Or somebody steals an antique plough from a front yard and then pretends they thought the owner wouldn't mind.'

'You enjoyed your trip,' Vera decided when Doris

returned. 'It was good for you to get away.' They never discussed Wayne, though Vera knew that despite Doris's determination to erase him from her mind she was concerned for his welfare. For ten years Wayne had been the focal point of her life. The last years had been punishing for her, yet Vera suspected there were moments when – remembering the happy periods – Doris wished painfully for his presence. In dividing the house into apartments, she'd made a point of delegating the bedroom she'd shared with Wayne to the rental apartment. She filled the evenings when she was not at the family house with local activities. But it would be a long time, Vera thought compassionately, before she erased Wayne from her heart.

Joel admitted to gratitude that Wayne had vanished. 'The bastard will land on his feet – wherever he is. But thank God, he's out of our lives.' But Vera knew he worried about Doris's future.

Now Joel and Vera were wrestling with the situation at the factory. Sales had taken a deep slump, which both had anticipated with foreign deals no longer coming in to the company. In addition to being apprehensive about the company's financial situation, Joel worried about keeping his employees on the payroll. This was a recurrent topic of discussion. At the approach of Thanksgiving – with Christmas and its attendant expenses not far behind – Joel expressed his anxiety at the dinner table.

'This town expects me to keep our people working. We cut back, they suffer. They *depend* on me.' He seemed drained, Vera thought sympathetically, but she understood his sense of responsibility to the town.

'Shouldn't we consider cutting back on hours?' Vera tried for a calm approach. They could afford to operate in the red for a time – but not indefinitely. 'No layoffs,' she emphasized. 'Put everybody on a four-day week –

and explain why we're doing this. Dad, they realize sales have dropped way off.'

'But with Christmas coming up?' Joel sighed. 'You know how big the Christmas season is here in town.'

'Let it be a little smaller,' Paul said, 'but everybody will have some income.'

'They won't be happy. We haven't cut back on hours since the Depression.' Joel paused in thought. 'But, yes, we'll cut back to a four-day week, stagger the hours – but no layoffs.' He seemed faintly relieved.

Joel cut back on his own salary and Vera's, made this known to the employees. Still, Vera was conscious of a depressing atmosphere in the factory. Now she made a tremendous effort to acquire new accounts – ever aware that the firm was under constant scrutiny by the government because of Wayne's activities.

Though a large number of local residents were feeling the pinch because of the shortened hours at the factory, the town soon wore its usual air of holiday festivity. Immediately after Thanksgiving, red and green lights were strung at intervals across Main Street. Christmas trees appeared before each shop. After dark, most houses were bright with Christmas lights.

The new year brought a burst of prosperity to most of the country – along with an easing of the Cold War due to Eisenhower's proposal that the United States and Russia share aerial inspections and military blueprints. There was a building-boom in cities. Housing construction soared. Sales of big-ticket items such as TVs and major appliances kept cash registers ringing in the stores and factories working. The one troubling note was the situation in the Far East. Hoping to combat Communism there, the United States was giving financial aid to South Vietnam, Cambodia, and Laos.

Paul was at first elated, then wary when Kerrigan announced that he would retire as principal at the end of the school year.

'Kerrigan is terribly behind the times,' Paul said to Vera when the word came through. 'But a couple of the board members are pressing for very progressive education. I can't go along with the super-permissiveness that's growing popular. I mean, this business of no grades – just *satisfactory* or *unsatisfactory*. Maybe it's easier on the kids' egos,' he acknowledged, 'but it does nothing for education.'

'It was dreamt up by lazy teachers,' Vera decided, laughing lightly. 'Think how much easier paper-grading becomes.'

'Progressive education started out fine.' Paul was serious now. 'It was meant to provide an imaginative kid with a chance to develop as an individual. But now, intellectual achievement is taking a back seat to the development of social skills,' he drawled sarcastically. 'What happens when these students go to college? The colleges insist – rightly – on specific courses. They don't want to hear about *progressive education*.'

Fighting for an increase in business, Vera was disturbed when she realized that the orders coming into Kahn Firearms were often from the South. On an unseasonably hot night in early June, she and Paul sat on the screen porch and discussed this situation.

'It's almost unbelievable,' Vera said sombrely, 'but statistics show the sale of small arms all over the South have gone up almost 400%. And the feeling is that it's due to the decision on segregated schools.'

'You're damn right.' Paul was grim. 'All the Washington DC schools were integrated immediately, and some Southern states have seen partial integration – but none in the Deep South. It scares me – the thought of all those handguns on the loose down there. And just anybody can buy a gun.'

'This will blow over.' Vera forced a smile. *Why had she mentioned guns?*

'There'll be hell to pay before we see school integration in the Deep South,' Paul predicted. 'And putting guns into the hands of racist Southerners guarantees explosive situations.'

Vera forced herself to be silent. How would Paul react when he learned – once the mechanics were worked out – that the company was considering going into the mail-order business? Mostly sporting goods, Vera thought defensively – but yes, they'd be selling guns, too . . . if Dad went along with her persuasion for the company to move into mail order. In a small way, at first . . . selling in a tri-state area. But mail order, she was trying to convince her father-in-law, was the wave of the future.

She remembered what Paul had said just yesterday about de Tocqueville. 'He predicted – maybe a hundred years ago – that the day would come when Negroes would rise up and demand the same rights as whites.' She remembered, too, how Dad had said Jews were especially sympathetic towards the coloured people because they knew what it was to be persecuted.

At uncomfortable intervals she asked herself how to cope with Paul's continuing unhappiness that his father and his wife were involved in the manufacture of guns. She tried so hard not to talk business in the house, but it was inevitable that this happened; and each time, Paul flinched. But that couldn't come between them – ever. Not with the love they shared, even after eleven years of marriage. Could it?

How would she handle it if Paul asked her to leave the company?

*

Vera tried to comfort Paul when the school year opened with a new principal – Roland Ames – in place. A man who was the total opposite of Kerrigan.

'Couldn't they have chosen somebody somewhere in the middle?' Paul asked three weeks later as he and Vera settled themselves in bed for the night. 'This guy is so *progressive* he scares the hell out of me. I suggested that I might take a group of our kids to Washington DC next month. And you know what the bastard said? "That's counter-productive, Paul. Take them to the local dairy or perhaps your father's factory. Let them touch reality,"' he mimicked distastefully. 'Can you see me taking a class to a gun factory?'

'Did Tracy tell you she was going to be Cinderella in the class play?' Vera was impatient to divert the conversation. 'I promised to be there, of course.' Her face grew tender. 'She said, "I won't be scared if you'll be there, Mommie."'

'I wish I could come, too.' Paul was apologetic.

'Darling, she understands that you can't take time off from school.'

He paused a moment. 'I didn't meant to yell at Tracy this morning the way I did. But I couldn't believe it when she asked Dad to teach her to shoot.'

'It's because she heard the little Bradley boy bragging about how good he was at target practice with his father,' Vera soothed.

'I don't want her learning to shoot.' Paul was suddenly tense.

'I'll talk to Dad about it,' she promised. This was hunting country. Most little boys learned to shoot. 'He'll make up some excuse.'

She moved her head to Paul's shoulder, thrust a leg across his. She knew the surest way to divert him. It was wonderful, she thought, the way he responded – as though this were still the first year of their marriage. Alone in bed they lived in a special Eden, isolated from the rest of the world.

Nothing must ever come between Paul and her. Doris was learning to survive without Wayne. He'd been a hurtful husband. Paul was so *good*. She could never survive without Paul.

During school vacation in the spring of '56 – when Vera and Paul were taking Laurie and Tracy for a much-anticipated week in Bermuda – Fiona decided to go with Adele to visit her mother in New York for four days.

'Mama just spoils Adele rotten,' Fiona said in high spirits while Vera waited with her for the train to pull into the Saratoga station. 'But she insists that's a grandma's privilege.'

'Adele's so bright and sweet she'll survive the spoiling,' Vera said affectionately. 'Just enjoy your vacation.'

Moments later, the train chugged into view. Fiona and Adele climbed aboard. Vera drove back to Eastwood for her final day at the office before their trip to Bermuda. Paul needed the relaxation, she thought. Pressure at the school was horrendous these days. She knew, too – with recurrent attacks of guilt – that Paul was upset that the company was taking the first move into the mail-order field. With a sporting goods catalogue, they would be selling hunting rifles by mail.

'Don't you realize what this means, Vera?' He'd stared at her in disbelief when she'd briefed him on this new business angle. 'Any lunatic can buy a gun!'

'These are hunting rifles,' she'd pointed out uneasily. 'We'll have a sporting goods catalogue. Rifles are standard items.' While neither she nor Paul wanted any part of hunting, it was a tradition in many parts of the country.

For the first time in their marriage, she felt that Paul

was truly angry with her. As with every couple, they'd had minor tiffs – but this was an unnerving hostility. That evening, she remembered with recurrent anxiety, she had hoped to reconcile in bed. But when she had reached out to Paul, he'd pretended to be asleep. In the morning he had been his normal self, yet she couldn't wash from her mind the memory of those moments when she'd felt a wall rise up between them.

Today, the hours at the office raced past. In the morning they would be en route to Bermuda – Laurie and Tracy enthralled by the prospect of flying. She had been dubious about their taking such an expensive vacation. It was Paul and Dad who had insisted. Would she ever be able to relax totally about money after the fearful years in Berlin?

The week in Bermuda was an oasis of lazy days and relaxing evenings. Their room looked down on the turquoise ocean and pink sand. Too soon they were boarding a plane for the flight to New York. There they collected the car for the drive to Eastwood.

While Laurie and Tracy slept on the rear seat of the car, Paul talked to Vera – her head on his shoulder – about the laws being passed in some Southern states that allowed them to bypass the Supreme Court ruling on school desegregation.

'What they're doing is subsidizing all-white private schools,' Paul said in frustration. 'There's going to be blood shed down there.' He was remembering, Vera thought guiltily, how the sale of handguns in the Deep South had escalated since the Brown vs. Board of Education decision. He knew that some of those guns had been supplied by their company.

'I suspect that a lot of Southerners realize they have a moral responsibility to desegregate in every area,' Vera said softly. 'And this isn't pre-World War II Germany;

Americans are free to speak their minds.' Not every German was a Nazi, but the ones who were out of sympathy were frightened into silence.

'I wish more would speak up,' Paul said bluntly. 'Before more people die. Like that young kid, Emmett Till, in Greenwood, Mississippi.'

When they turned into the driveway – golden with forsythia now, they saw that the entire lower floor of the house was lit. Doris's car was parked far down the circular driveway.

'We've got a welcoming party,' Paul said affectionately. 'I'll bet Fiona's been cooking up a storm.' Fiona and Adele had returned three days ago, Vera remembered. Laurie and Tracy had picked out presents for each.

Before they were out of the car, Joel and Doris appeared on the porch.

'You had a wonderful time,' Joel decided after an exchange of kisses. 'You all look refreshed.'

'It was heavenly,' Vera told him. 'Just what we needed.'

'I can go back to school tomorrow without flinching,' Paul said in high spirits. 'I've got the strength to deal with all the problems.'

'We figured right about when you'd arrive,' Doris said. 'The roast is just ready to come out of the oven.'

'And are we starving! I'll wait until after dinner to bring in our luggage,' Paul decided. 'The kids fell asleep midway, so we didn't bother to stop even for a snack.'

There was something spurious about their conviviality, Vera sensed in a sudden surge of alarm while Doris and Joel plied Laurie and Tracy with questions about Bermuda.

'But Paul said you were all starving,' Doris remembered with an over-bright smile. 'Let me go out to the kitchen and turn off the roast.'

'Where's Adele?' Laurie asked. 'I want to tell her I brought her a present.'

'She's still down in New York,' Doris said, strangely evasive. 'Vera, come out to the kitchen with me.' Her eyes pleaded for compliance.

Her heart pounding, Vera followed Doris down the hall and into the kitchen.

'Doris, what's wrong? Where are Adele and Fiona?'

'Dad and I thought Fiona had decided to stay in New York a couple of days longer. I didn't want to tell you in front of the kids.' Doris's voice broke. 'Fiona was struck by a hit-and-run driver near her mother's apartment building. One of her sisters called this morning. After her funeral.'

Chapter Twenty

Early on Sunday morning – dank and cold with the threat of snow in the air – Vera and Paul headed for New York. Last night they'd talked by phone with Fiona's mother, grieving but resigned. Adele had been asleep.

'It'll be warm in a few minutes,' Paul soothed, switching on the car heater. He paused a moment. 'The kids are awfully upset.'

'Fiona and Adele have been part of their lives ever since they can remember. Adele's like their sister. I just wish Fiona's mother would let her stay with us.' It was as though they'd lost a member of the family, Vera thought disconsolately.

'Her mind's made up,' Paul said gently. 'Let's focus on persuading her to allow Adele to stay with us until the end of the school year.' In a crisis Paul was always practical. 'Changing schools now – upset as she must be – would be traumatic.'

Last night she'd told Fiona's mother – Mary Lou – that they'd be happy to raise Adele, Vera fretted. In a few years Adele would be going off to college – hopefully to Hunter, as Fiona had wished. 'It's real kind of you, Miss Vera.' Born and raised in South Carolina, she was part of the old Southern tradition in many ways. They were Miss Vera and Mr Paul to her. 'But it wouldn't be right for Adele. She needs to grow up among her own folks, to know who she is. I always worried about Fiona and Adele living up there. It was like being in a foreign country.'

'It's good for Adele that Fiona has a large family. All those aunts and uncles.' Paul punctured the leaden silence that engulfed them for painful minutes. 'Three sisters and two brothers?'

'That's right. Two of her sisters still live at home with their kids.' No husbands, she recalled. Five daughters between them, from teenage pregnancies. *Three generations of women*, Fiona had confided in a bitter moment, *And no hope for none of them*. 'Gladys, the youngest, has a civil service job. She's in her own apartment. And the older brother, Henry, and his wife have their own place, too. He has a good job with Con Ed. They haven't seen Tyrone – the other brother – in years.' It had always upset Fiona that two of her sisters were on welfare – with no sign of getting off. She could understand that her mother had been unable to work for the past two years because of her arthritis, but she was ashamed that these two sisters made no effort to find jobs.

'I hope they catch the bastard who ran down Fiona.' Paul exuded fresh rage. 'Why should a fine woman like that have to die?'

On the long drive into Manhattan, Vera and Paul talked in bittersweet recollection of the years that Fiona and Adele had been part of their lives.

'Remember last year when we decided to buy the encyclopedia for the kids?' Tears stung Vera's eyes. 'I told Fiona that Adele could use the books whenever she liked, but Fiona insisted she'd buy a set for Adele. She said, "I always wished I had more time at school. Adele's smart. She'll finish high school. Maybe she'll even get into Hunter College. She wants to be a school teacher like Mr Paul. That's my dream for her." '

'Tracy's upset, yes – but Laurie's desolate,' Vera told Paul when they stopped at a diner for lunch.

She knew the weeks ahead would be difficult. Laurie

was so sure they'd convince Adele's grandmother to allow her to stay with them. Neither she nor Paul felt much hope that this could be accomplished. At least, she prayed in silence, let Adele come back with them to finish out the school year.

'It's always weird for me to come back to the Columbia area,' Paul said wryly an hour later when he turned off the highway and headed for the project where Fiona's mother lived – a dozen blocks north of the Columbia campus. 'That was another lifetime.' One hand left the wheel to reach for hers. 'Before I found you.'

They parked at the project, went in search of Mary Lou's building. Subconsciously Vera reached for Paul's hand. The atmosphere reeked of poverty and decay. Clusters of children and teenagers roamed about the area, noisy in their exchanges. At intervals they spied a neatly dressed family, their attire mute evidence that they were returning from church services. Fiona's mother – like Fiona herself – was very devout, submerged in various church activities. She could hear Fiona's voice now: '*It's the church that gives Mama and me the strength to carry on.*' She and Paul had not even been here for Fiona's funeral, Vera thought in anguish.

The moment she and Paul walked into the neat, modest living room of the apartment, Vera spied Adele slumped in a chair by a living room window – staring out but seeing nothing, she suspected. At the sound of their voices in conversation with her grandmother, Adele straightened up, ran in a desperate race for the comfort of Vera's arms.

'We just found out, Adele,' Vera whispered, tears falling unheeded down her cheeks. 'You have to be brave, darling.'

'Can I go home with you?' Adele pleaded, her dark eyes searching Vera's.

'We're trying to convince your grandmother to let you come with us,' Vera told her.

'Adele, you go out to the kitchen and you tell Edna to make a pot of coffee,' her grandmother instructed. 'Tell her Fiona's folks are here.'

'Yes'm,' Adele said, trained by her mother to be scrupulously polite. But her eyes turned to Vera in supplication before she left the room.

'Adele, you help Edna,' her grandmother added. 'Fix up a plate of cookies real pretty and put out the nice paper napkins.'

Vera understood Mary Lou was providing them a few moments together without Adele's presence.

'We love Adele,' Vera said earnestly. 'We'd be happy to keep her with us until she's ready to go away to college.'

'We talked about that, Miss Vera.' Mary Lou was polite but firm. 'Adele has to know her own folks. It was all right when she was little, but she'll be thirteen next year. Everything changes then. She has to know what her life is going to be like when she grows up. Fiona always talked about how wonderful you were to her and Adele,' Mary Lou said gratefully, 'but she worried a lot about when Adele got a little older and – and began to want to go out with boys.' Her eyes were eloquent. 'I'll raise her the best I know how.'

'Let her come home with us to finish out the school year,' Paul said gently. 'It would be a terrible experience to throw her into a strange school just at this time. It'll be easier for her in familiar surroundings.'

'Please,' Vera pleaded. 'Fiona would have liked that.'

Before they prepared to leave for Eastwood – with Adele – Paul explained to Mary Lou that Adele would receive Social Security cheques from her mother's benefits while she attended school. Mary Lou was bewildered.

'I know most people think it's a joke for employers to pay Social Security for domestic help, but my father realized it was important,' Paul told her. In truth, his father had paid both employer and employee's share.

'I know it's no joke,' Mary Lou told them. 'If the folks I worked for all these years had paid it – and me, too,' she added conscientiously, 'then I'd be getting Social Security instead of being on welfare. But we figured that meant we'd have to be paying taxes, too – and we saw little enough as it was.' She managed a shaky smile. 'But my daughter Gladys works for the government, and one day she'll get a pension – and Henry pays Social Security, and he'll get benefits some day.'

In Eastwood, Adele was welcomed with silent but obvious sympathy. Vera had arranged for Tracy to be promoted to a room of her own – the former guest room. Adele would share with Laurie – as Laurie had wished. It was a sad homecoming for Adele, Vera thought, but at least, she was surrounded by familiar faces.

Vera didn't want to think about the end of the school year – when Adele would have to go to live in the project with her grandmother.

Vera was upset when the junior high school decided to have a prom at the end of the school year. What she had been struggling to face – bearing out that Adele's grandmother was more honest than herself in seeing the problems of early dating – became glaring reality. She overheard a pair of mothers making acid remarks at a PTA meeting about interracial dating.

At the present there were only three coloured students in the entire Eastwood school system. Two were in junior high. Those mothers were fearful their *white* sons might be exposed to Adele on a social basis. How could she allow Adele to face a situation where she might be terribly hurt? Sweet, bright, pretty Adele – so vulnerable at this time.

While Laurie said nothing about a date for the prom, Vera knew she was already anxious about being asked.

'I hate this whole business of junior high school kids going to proms,' Paul said bluntly. 'It's a pressure parents are dumping on them. We don't see it in the cities. It started as a suburban deal. Now they're pushing it in the small towns. "Teach them social skills at an early age,"' he mimicked. 'Is it any wonder we're seeing so many teenage marriages?'

'I heard Tracy ask Laurie why she hadn't tried out for cheerleader.' Vera was sombre. 'Tracy told her that cheerleaders always have dates. But up until now – with the prom coming up – Laurie didn't think about dating. She was happy being with Adele. And thank God, she never brought up the dating question,' Vera said defiantly. 'I don't want to see our twelve-year-old daughter behaving as if she were eighteen.'

'If she gets a date for the prom, she'll take it for granted she can go,' Paul warned. 'Unless – ' He hesitated. 'Unless Adele has no date. Then Laurie won't date. And considering the general feelings about interracial dating,' he said ruefully, 'I think we can rest easy.'

But as the prom date grew closer, Vera determined to sidestep the issue. So she was an old-fashioned mother. She didn't want Laurie – or Tracy – going out on dates with boys at their ages. It was absurd.

Vera plotted for a moment to speak alone with Laurie. Together she and Paul had decided to take the two girls, along with Tracy, into New York the night of the junior prom. They'd have a pre-theatre dinner, then go to the theatre to see 'Silk Stockings', the hit musical by Cole Porter. But Laurie was outraged when she talked about going to New York that night.

'You mean, miss the junior prom?' She stared at her mother in disbelief.

'It's a wonderful musical.' Vera struggled to sound persuasive.

'Mom, everybody's going to the prom!' Laurie gazed at her mother with naked hostility.

'Laurie, you love Adele, don't you?' This was a moment when honesty was the only weapon.

'Sure.' Laurie was baffled by the question.

'Well, we – we live in a strange world.' She was groping for words. 'If Adele goes to the prom, I'm afraid she'll be very hurt.' Still, Laurie appeared baffled. 'You know about the trouble with school integration down South.' The grown-ups in this household spoke openly in front of the girls about the Supreme Court ruling and the reaction in the Southern states. They knew about the ugly demonstrations that appeared at regular intervals. It was more important for them to know what was happening in their world, she and Paul had long ago decided, than to 'build social skills.' Laurie and Tracy's school might ignore the integration crisis, thinking families would not. 'It's in the newspapers and on television all the time.'

'We don't have segregated schools here,' Laurie said, growing impatient with this discussion.

'No,' Vera conceded, 'but we have people who don't realize that the colour of somebody's skin shouldn't be important. Laurie, if Adele goes to that prom, she's going to be terribly hurt.' Her eyes pleaded with Laurie to understand what she was trying to say.

All at once comprehension overtook Laurie. She was shaken. She was bright and compassionate, Vera told herself with gratitude. *She understood.*

'Okay,' Laurie said after a moment. 'So we'll go to New York the night of the prom.'

*

Today had been humid and enervating, but now at dusk a breeze brought welcome relief. In the bedroom next to Laurie's Tracy listened to the latest Pat Boone record their grandfather had added to their collection. Both girls were Pat Boone fans. In the bedroom she'd shared with Adele these last weeks, Laurie sat at the edge of her bed while Adele packed. It was going to be terrible without Adele here, she thought in recurrent rebellion. Why hadn't Mom persuaded Adele's grandmother to let her stay with them? She hadn't tried hard enough. All Mom cared about was being at the factory. *Selling guns.*

'Your father said we could put my encyclopedia in two cartons and put them in the trunk of the car,' Adele remembered.

'Sure.' Laurie struggled to sound matter-of-fact. Didn't they understand how awful it would be for Adele? She would have to share a room with her grandmother and a little cousin. A tiny room with bunk beds. Mom should have made Adele's grandmother understand Adele should stay here. 'Mom said I could drive down to New York with you.' Mrs O'Reilly – who came in every morning and stayed until she'd served dinner – would be with Tracy. Grandpa had decided not to have sleep-in help now. Mom and Daddy took turns making breakfast. Mrs O'Reilly came in at eleven.

'You'll write me?' Adele's eyes were wistful.

'You know I will. Every week,' Laurie promised. 'And Mom's going to ask your grandmother to let you come here for two weeks before school opens.' New York was miserable in the summer, she'd heard Daddy say. 'We'll always be best friends,' she said with sudden urgency. 'Forever and ever.'

'Forever and ever,' Adele said solemnly.

Long after they had turned off the lights and settled themselves in their beds, Laurie and Adele talked in whispers. It wasn't fair for Adele's grandmother to make her live in New York, Laurie told herself over and over again. Grown-ups could be so mean.

In the morning Laurie and Adele awoke before the scheduled time, both desolate at the imminent separation. It wasn't fair, Laurie railed yet again, for Adele's mother to be killed that way and for her grandmother to make her go live in New York. Best friends should grow up together. *Why did God let this happen*?

By eight o'clock, Laurie and Adele were settled in the car while Laurie's father brought out Adele's luggage and the cartons with the encyclopedia. Mom gave Adele a box of fancy stationery and a sheet of stamps, Laurie remembered. Adele would write Mom once in a while, Laurie told herself triumphantly, but she'd write *her* every week. She and Adele were *best friends*.

Mom said they'd have breakfast at a diner on the highway. She and Adele could order whatever they wanted. But it would be so awful driving home, she mourned, without Adele.

Early in August – after much persuasion – Vera was able to convince Mary Lou to let Adele come to visit for two weeks. She would be in New York for a business meeting, would remain overnight in the city, pick up Adele the following day. Laurie and Tracy could drive down with her, both thrilled by the prospect of a trip to the city. Midmorning of the second day in the city, Vera checked out of the hotel with the girls, went with them to collect the car, and drove uptown. Her heart ached for Adele when they approached the housing project, so different from what Adele had known most of her life. Fiona had run away from this, wanting better for her bright, sweet child.

In the hot August sunlight children roamed the

grounds, the older screeching orders to the younger. A toddler lay asleep on the ground beside a tree. Inside the building the air was fetid in the oppressive heat. The elevator reeked of urine. Not from pets, Vera guessed; animals were not permitted in the project.

Mary Lou greeted them with warmth. Adele – her face radiant – rushed to exchange exuberant hugs with Laurie, then with Tracy and Vera.

'Edna, you bring out that pitcher of ice tea I just made and some glasses,' Mary Lou ordered her eldest daughter, crouched before the TV set along with her sister, both seemingly mesmerized by the programme.

'Yeah, sure.' Reluctantly, Edna rose to her feet, her eyes following the screen as she ambled towards the kitchen with a perfunctory smile for their visitors.

Vera was touched by the relief she sensed in Adele at the prospect of leaving the project apartment behind her for two weeks. She'd been here only since the close of school, Vera thought, but Adele had matured far beyond her age in that time. But she was a strong little girl, Vera thought tenderly. A survivor.

Driving back to Eastwood – Vera pondered the odd division between Mary Lou's children. Like Fiona, Gladys and Henry were bright and determined to improve their lot in life. Edna and Lottie – and she suspected the same could be said of the long-missing Tyrone – had left school early and were semi-literate, devoid of any ambition. A cross for Mary Lou to bear, Vera thought in sympathy.

She was betting that Adele would pull herself above the project existence, but it would be a long, difficult road. And she was conscious of a lingering suspicion that Laurie held *her* responsible for Adele's having to live in the squalor of the Harlem housing project – just as Laurie had never let go of her anger that her mother and grandfather were involved in the business of manufacturing guns.

How was she to make Laurie understand that she had tried desperately to have Adele remain with them? How did she make Laurie understand that guns were weapons of peace as well as death? Without weapons how would Israel survive? How could the Allies have stopped the madness of Hitler?

Chapter Twenty-one

The blanket of snow that surrounded the house on this New Year's Eve lent a spurious air of serenity. But moving about the spacious kitchen while she prepared dinner – because Mrs O'Reilly was off today and tomorrow – Vera was remembering the crises inflicted on the world during the last twelve months. The riots in Poland, Nasser's seizure of the Suez Canal – with British and French troops bombing Egyptian airfields in retaliation and Israel capturing the whole Gaza Strip and the Sinai Peninsula in less than 100 hours. The Soviet invasion of Hungary, Tunisia's fight for independence from France, Sudan's battle for freedom. Paul couldn't just listen to the TV news and sympathize. He suffered for the killed and the maimed.

She smiled tenderly at the sound of Laurie's voice – in intense telephone conversation with Adele – drifting down the stairs. Because this was New Year's Eve, Laurie had been permitted to phone Adele down in New York. They still wrote each other every week.

In the living room, Tracy and Dad argued high-spiritedly about a chess move. Paul was engrossed in a book. Vera was grateful that Tracy had become so enamoured of chess sessions with her grandfather. There were moments when she feared Tracy felt shut out from the closeness she had shared earlier with Laurie.

'Hi.' Doris strolled into the kitchen, puncturing her introspection. 'I finally found a place that was still open and had vanilla ice cream. You know, Dad, hot apple pie *has* to be topped with vanilla ice cream.'

'Oh, great!'

'I'll have just a smidgeon,' Doris said wistfully. 'I've got to drop twenty pounds.'

'The turkey should be ready in about twenty minutes,' Vera decided, thrusting a fork into one burnished thigh.

They'd had the usual party at the office. Each year they expected to be on the way home by one or two, and always the party dragged on until four. She'd rushed home to put up the turkey – a tradition in the Kahn household at New Year's as well as Thanksgiving. Paul and the girls, of course, had been on school vacation since before Christmas.

Paul was wonderful about spending time with them, but she could never quite brush aside the suspicion that Laurie resented *her* working. She was always there for special events at school, she reminded herself defensively. She went on school outings for both Laurie and Tracy's classes two or three times a year. Yet she knew that to her daughters she wasn't 'like other mothers.' She'd overheard a brief discussion between the two girls once. '*Why can't Mom be like Gail's mother*?' Laurie had complained. Gail's mother was there every afternoon when they came home from school, made fancy cookies, and loved working in her garden. Tracy had said, '*Mom's the nicest mother in the whole world.*'

Vera's mind charged back to the Friday night three weeks ago when she'd come home from a particularly difficult day at the office. After dinner she and Paul and Tracy had settled themselves in the living room. Laurie was away at her first 'pyjama party.' Dad had gone to a Chamber of Commerce meeting. Paul focused on correcting exams, Tracy did homework, and she studied the layout for their spring catalogue. At Tracy's bedtime, she went upstairs with her, ran her bath, and prepared to go downstairs for another hour's work on the catalogue.

And then Tracy had thrust her into troubling self-examination.

'Mom, stay with me while I bathe,' she'd pleaded wistfully.

'Darling, I have this catalogue copy to work on,' she'd begun.

'Can't you do it here?' Tracy asked. 'Put down the toilet lid and sit there. I won't talk. I'd just like us to be here together.'

'The work can wait for later,' Vera had said instantly. How could she put work ahead of her precious baby? 'Tell me what happened at school today.'

She *wasn't* 'the nicest mother in the whole world,' she reproached herself. Tracy and Laurie – *family* – must come before the business. She wasn't some frantic, single mother struggling to survive, who had no choice. If something happened and she couldn't work, the family would manage.

'I hope the dressing is good.' Doris broke into her introspection. This year the dressing had been Doris's project.

'I'm sure it is.'

Together she and Doris brought dinner to the table. She knew that Doris's thoughts on holidays such as this reached out to earlier such occasions when Wayne had been with her. Doris frequently confided her relief that she was a free woman now, yet she also conceded there were still dark moments when she remembered the early *good* years. *'When I loved a man who didn't exist.'*

'Everybody to the table.' Doris summoned the others. 'You'll finish your chess game later,' she told her father and Tracy. 'Paul, yell upstairs to Laurie to come down to dinner.'

Joel sat at the head of the table and concentrated on carving the turkey, amid kibitzing from Paul and Tracy.

'I know,' he drawled good-humouredly, 'every turkey should come equipped with four legs. But this is a big bird – four can share two.'

'How's Adele?' Vera asked Laurie.

'Okay.' Laurie shrugged. 'Except she hates living in that noisy, crowded apartment and hates her new school.' Without meeting her mother's eyes, she extended her plate to her grandfather for a helping of turkey.

Vera tensed. Laurie was still angry with her for not persuading Mary Lou to allow Adele to live with them. But Adele's grandmother was a wise woman. She knew it wouldn't be good for Adele to live up here, one of three coloured children in town.

'How's Adele doing in school?' Vera asked and berated herself for pursuing this. She knew Laurie didn't want to talk about Adele.

'Adele's smart. She's doing fine.' Laurie turned away. 'Aunt Doris, could I have some dressing?'

Vera saw the sympathetic glance Paul beamed in her direction. He didn't want to admit it, but he knew there was friction between Laurie and her.

For a while the table conversation was lighthearted; but as so often happened in this family, a more serious tone soon took over. Paul and Joel began to rehash the events of the past twelve months. She didn't want to think about those things, Vera told herself in simmering impatience. *What was she to do about this wall between Laurie and herself?*

'Look, Nasser grabbed the Suez Canal so that the whole world would recognize him as the supreme Moslem power,' Joel scoffed. 'But the real objective was to destroy Israel. That would clinch it for him. But it still pisses me –' He stopped short, grinned. 'Laurie, Tracy, you didn't hear me say that. It tees me off,' he amended, 'that the UN insisted that Israel withdraw from the Gaza Strip and the

Sinai. It just means more fighting in the years ahead. We'll see –'

'Dad, we're almost at the beginning of the new year,' Doris interrupted. 'No more war talk. Let's feel festive.'

'There wouldn't be war if people didn't make guns,' Laurie said, a defiant glint in her eyes.

'Laurie, don't start up with that again,' her grandfather scolded lightly, but Vera sensed his irritation. 'As long as there's a world, there'll be guns. Without guns there can be no peace.'

'Paul, what's happening with your plans to take a busload of kids down to Washington this spring?' Doris asked in an effort, Vera understood, to rechannel the conversation. 'You'll make sure to go during the cherry blossom season?'

'Cherry blossom season, yes,' Paul said. 'But I need another few committed for the trip before I can finalize arrangements. A trip to New York to be in the studio audience for a TV performance by Elvis Presley would generate a lot more excitement.' He gestured his frustration.

'I'd love to see Elvis Presley!' Tracy was enthralled at the prospect.

'What's for dessert?' Joel asked Vera. To him, Elvis Presley was still 'Elvis the Pelvis,' pushed into fame by his hips rather than his voice.

'Hot apple pie and vanilla ice cream,' Vera told him. 'We have to start the new year off right.'

But she was starting the new year with painful anxiety about her relationship with Laurie. Paul kept telling her it was just the beginning of the crazy adolescent period. In a few months they'd be the parents of a teenager. Everybody said that rebellion and protest were part of becoming an adolescent, that this was always a tough period in parents' lives.

Vera's thoughts hurtled back through the years to the time when she had been thirteen – a period when no child, whatever age, questioned a parent's authority. Sometimes she was taken aback when Laurie or Tracy answered a decree with *Why? I don't think that's fair.* Paul said it was the result of the weakening of the educational system. Teenagers were coddled in school – and expected the same at home.

At thirteen, Vera mused in poignant recall, family had been the focus of her life. And then she'd lost her family. The pain had never totally disappeared. And now she was terrified by this breach between Laurie and herself.

Later, as she and Paul prepared for bed, she confessed her fears to him.

'We'll get through this,' he consoled. 'Most parents do.'

'I listen to teenagers today, and I don't believe what I hear sometimes.' Vera turned down the bedclothes and slid beneath. She hadn't been a normal teenager, she conceded. She'd been grateful to be alive, to have a home. 'I heard this sixteen-year-old in line behind me at the supermarket on Saturday. He was complaining because his parents wouldn't let him have his own car. "What's the matter with them? They've got good credit. They can get a car loan." Today's kids – today's people,' she amended, 'have lost all sight of saving for tomorrow. They expect the good times to go on forever.' Even now, with their income so healthy, she saw to it that they saved.

'I work with these kids.' Paul was grim. 'I can't stand what we're doing to them. It's adults who're doing it,' he went on before she could intervene. 'We treat them like royalty, give them every conceivable goodie.'

'So it's natural that they take this for granted – and then demand more.' Vera flinched in comprehension.

'Our whole educational system is going to backfire, Vera.' Paul shook his head. 'We worry so much about

Russia and their grasp at new technology. Hell, Russian kids go to school six hours a day, six days a week. Their kids are *required* to take ten years of math, four years of chemistry, six of biology, five of physics. At Eastwood High, we're not even *offering* physics or chemistry! I'd guess their high school graduates have a stronger background in science and math than a lot of our college grads.'

Vera recalled conversation at the dinner table. 'Laurie says Adele hates her school.'

'Of course she does,' Paul said gently. 'Eastwood schools are full of shortcomings, God knows – but Harlem schools are in far worse shape. But Adele is very bright. She'll dig in her heels and get herself a decent education despite that. She's a determined little girl with her goal always in mind. She'll have to fight for her education, but she'll get it.'

'I worry about Laurie. I worry all the time. She blames me for Adele's not being here. How do I make her understand that we did everything we could to keep Adele with us?'

'You can't.' Paul slid under the covers, reached to draw her into the comfort of his arms. 'It's something she's going to have to arrive at herself.'

'It's so awful,' Vera whispered, 'knowing Laurie thinks badly of me . . . when I love her so much.'

'It's part of being a parent. The rough comes with the good. Laurie's a lot like you, baby.' His voice was gentle. 'You're both so intense about what you think is right and wrong. You're both –'

'Everything I do is wrong in Laurie's eyes,' Vera broke in with painful urgency. 'She hates the business. She hates my working. She hates me for not fighting Adele's grandmother more forcefully.'

'That's for now,' Paul comforted. 'She'll –'

'You hate the business, too.' Vera searched his eyes in the soft light of the night-table lamp. 'You resent my working there.'

'I don't resent it,' he said after a moment. 'I just wish Dad would move into the mail-order business – without selling hunting rifles – and forget the rest. I want our kids to grow up in a peaceful world, a world without guns. Look at England – even their cops don't carry guns.'

'Look at Israel and Switzerland,' Vera countered. 'Almost everybody owns a gun. It makes Israel's survival possible, and Switzerland is the most peaceful nation in the world – and has the least crime.' She paused. 'Sometimes Laurie makes snide remarks to Dad about the business. It hurts him.'

'Dad understands she doesn't mean to do that,' Paul soothed.

'And what's wrong about my working?' she demanded with fresh defiance. 'I don't neglect the girls because I work. What law says I have to stay at home and cook and clean and wax floors? I heard a couple of men at the factory making cracks about *working wives*. To them we're neurotic women with ants in our pants who can't stay home and be real wives and mothers.'

'I don't feel that way,' Paul insisted. 'Dad always says what a major asset you are to the business. I just wish it were another kind of business –'

'For generations your family has made guns and rifles,' Vera said tiredly. 'Dad's proud of his contribution to this country. He feels he's helping to keep the peace.' But Paul was writing letters to the editors of newspapers around the state urging them to promote control of handguns. To a lot of people in town he was an oddball. That was upsetting to Dad, with his obsession to be loved by everyone in Eastwood.

'Baby, relax,' Paul soothed, drawing her face to his.

He knew the best way in the world to make her relax, she thought tenderly, and closed her eyes while his mouth reached for hers and he slid one hand within the neckline of her nightie. Thank God for this, she told herself, already responding to his ardour. Together in bed they could push aside – for a little while – all their doubts and fears. It had been this way when bombs rained over London. It would be this way until death separated them.

She had to believe that.

Chapter Twenty-two

As the months went by, Vera watched for signs that Laurie was forgiving her for Adele's absence in their lives. Only in early spring – when Laurie came down with a bad case of flu – did she feel that Laurie loved her as before. She stayed away from the factory for a whole work-week – something other working mothers might not have the privilege of doing, she admitted to herself – and spent most of her waking hours at Laurie's bedside.

'Mommie, I love you,' Laurie whispered as Vera washed her face and brushed her hair after a bout of nausea.

'I love you, too, darling.' Vera clung to this brief moment. She had not totally lost Laurie. *Mommie, I love you* was sweet solace on those trying occasions when her young daughter seemed to regard her as a mortal enemy – as when she'd refused to allow her to wear lipstick before she was fifteen and insisted on going shopping with her to buy her first bras. Laurie was simultaneously enthralled and embarrassed by the obvious need for this purchase.

'Vera, don't get so upset,' Paul pleaded. 'We've entered a new era. We're parents of a teenager.'

She and Paul socialized mainly with his fellow teachers, some of whom were also dealing with the adolescent phenomenon. At a barbecue at one couple's house at the close of the school year, the subject monopolized the conversation.

'Monica thinks we're millionaires,' their hostess

declared in frustration. 'I tell her that her father is a teacher, not a TV star. I don't want to tell you what she put us through with her senior prom. I know it happens in suburbia, but here in Eastwood?'

'They see television,' a mother of early teenagers picked up. 'They see Hollywood movies. Our world revolves around teenagers. But I told my kids bluntly, if I catch them smoking, they're grounded for a month. I don't care how they carry on.'

'If my kid tells me one more time – when I tell her she can't do something – that Gerry's parents say it's okay, I'll probably wring her neck,' one father contributed grimly. 'They're getting too much too soon.'

By mid-July, Laurie was already impatient for Adele's arrival for two weeks in Eastwood. Adele was fun – she made her laugh. The first two weeks of school vacation had been terrific. She'd slept till noon, spent the afternoon at the pool, listened to her records all evening. Now she was bored. The kids here at home were so *immature* – a word she used frequently these days. Donna and Gail would spend hours just playing around with lipsticks and eye shadow. Or talking about boys. Boys were so silly.

Donna was still moping because she didn't make the drum majorette squad. Her mother had promised her a whole collection of Bobby Darin records if she did. Gail and Donna thought she was a real nerd because she was excited about being on the math team. Dad and Grandpa thought it was terrific. Mom made a big fuss about it – but she didn't really care. She was only interested in sales figures at the factory or how well the shop was doing and how the catalogue mailing list was growing.

She had been the only girl in the after-school Current Events group, then five more had come in because it looked like what Gail called 'a dating zoo.' But none of the boys in the Current Events group were on the football or basketball team, so the other girls dropped out. Was there something wrong with her because she liked math and current events?

On the day Adele was to arrive, Laurie was awake at 7:00 AM even though Adele's train wasn't due for hours. Adele's grandmother worried that nobody would be at the Saratoga train station to meet her. If she and Mom weren't there on time, her grandmother would *never* let Adele come up again.

Laurie felt queasy at the thought that she and Mom might not be there when Adele's train pulled into the station. For the first time since school vacation began, Laurie was at the breakfast table.

'We have to be in Saratoga to pick up Adele,' she reminded her mother anxiously as she sat at the breakfast table.

'We'll be there, Laurie.' Her mother smiled and poured her a glass of orange juice. 'Come over to the factory at eleven and we'll head for Saratoga. We'll stop off somewhere for lunch on the way home.'

'Walk to the factory?' Laurie's eyes widened. 'Daddy won't be here to drive me. He'll be at summer school.' She turned to her father for confirmation.

'It's a ten-minute walk,' he told her and chuckled at her blank stare. 'Laurie, you've got two healthy feet.'

She intercepted the amused exchange between her mother and father. Mom or Daddy always drove her where she needed to go. Was this some kind of strike? Everybody knew parents drove you wherever you had to go. She couldn't wait till she was old enough to get her driver's licence.

Laurie was relieved that they were at the Saratoga station half an hour before Adele's train was to arrive. She'd forgotten, Laurie conceded, that Mom was always early everywhere. They sat down in the all-but-deserted waiting room – hot and sticky today. Her blouse was damp with perspiration, clung to her back. With no real interest, she accepted a segment of the newspaper her mother handed her and scanned the front page.

Mom said Daddy would drive her and Adele out to the Eastwood pool for a swim when he came home from summer school. Adele would like that. She just hoped Daddy wouldn't say something awful about their bathing suits – the way Gail's father had at her church picnic. 'Gail, what's that you're almost wearing?'

Adele's train arrived on schedule. They exchanged exuberant embraces, settled in the car. They discussed the merits of hamburger over pizza, decided on hamburgers and Cokes. 'After lunch, we'll stop for frozen custard,' her mother promised.

The world seemed beautiful as she and Adele sat together after lunch on the back seat of the car and made enthusiastic inroads on cones piled high with chocolate frozen custard. In ecstatic pantomime they discussed the bras each wore now as a symbol of having attained the exalted status of teenager.

Laurie knew it was going to be terrific to spend two weeks with Adele. They laughed a lot, but they could be serious, too. Every night they watched the TV news with Mom and Dad. There was a lot of talk about the trouble breaking out in the Deep South over school integration. Laurie was incensed when Adele remarked that going to school in Harlem was like going to a segregated school.

'But that's not even in the South,' Laurie exploded.

'I know.' Adele shrugged. 'But that's the way it is.'

Laurie listened sombrely while her father – clearly sympathetic – questioned Adele about her school.

'When I grow up and graduate from college, I'll get a

job teaching in my school,' Adele said with calm conviction. 'I want to help make it better.'

Too soon it was time for Adele to return to her grandmother's apartment – *where Edna and Lottie sit and watch soap operas all day*. Laurie watched wistfully while Adele's train pulled out of the station, slowly disappeared from view. It was as if a special part of her life were being snatched away again, she thought. Adele belonged in this family.

'Laurie, we have to go back home now,' her mother said softly.

Along with many Americans, Vera and Paul were upset by the violence that continued to explode in the Deep South over school integration. In September, the family clung to the TV screen every night to see the latest developments in the efforts in Little Rock, Arkansas, to enroll nine brave young Negro students in the Little Rock high school.

'It'll take time, but we'll see integrated schools in the next few years.' Joel was philosophical. On occasion, Vera thought, Dad's determined optimism was trying. 'It'll happen.'

'It's the law!' Laurie blazed. 'Why doesn't it happen now? What's the matter with people?'

Vera watched helplessly while sibling hostility soared between Laurie and Tracy. Tracy felt left out of Laurie's orbit now, she realized in anguish. While Laurie had developed no intense friendship with other girls at school, she made it clear she considered Tracy a 'baby' compared to her newly achieved adolescent status.

'It's normal at her age,' Paul comforted, and Doris backed him up.

On the October night when news spread around the world that the Soviet Union had launched a space satellite called Sputnik 1, Vera made no effort to prod Laurie and Tracy to their bedrooms to start their homework. She and Paul and the girls – along with Joel – were spellbound by the report on TV evening news.

'That's the first step in space travel,' Joel marvelled. 'They've got a space satellite!'

'And we've got egg on our faces,' Paul said bluntly. 'The United States is supposed to be the Great Innovator. How can we be when we're turning out half the number of engineers and scientists than the Russians?'

A month later, the Soviet Union launched its second satellite – Sputnik 2. For once Laurie and Tracy united in their outrage. An Eskimo dog had been sent into space aboard the second satellite.

'That's awful!' Laurie shrieked. 'How can they send up that poor little dog?'

'He'll be scared to death,' Tracy mourned. 'He'll be awful sick!'

Shortly after this Tracy announced to her parents that she intended to be a vet. A few months earlier, she'd vowed to be a rock star, Vera remembered. There would be a dozen other choices, she guessed indulgently, before Tracy found her niche in life. Just let her find some profession that would make her happy, she prayed. She and Paul wouldn't push either of the girls in any direction.

But ten days later, Vera and Paul were shocked when Tracy confided that she honestly didn't know what she wanted to be when she grew up but added one stipulation.

'I just know it has to be something that'll make me rich.'

'Why?' Vera demanded, aghast. What had she and Paul done to make Tracy believe that money was all-important?

'Money buys things. I want to live like a movie star,' Tracy said blissfully. 'Like Natalie Wood and Robert

Wagner. And Tuesday Weld. Did you know that Tuesday Weld owns six cars? One of them is a Mercedes.' *Tracy had never even seen a Mercedes.*

'Where do you find this weird information?' Paul exchanged a bewildered glance with Vera.

'My movie magazines,' Tracy explained. 'They tell you everything. I adore them.'

'And she's not even twelve?' Paul turned accusingly to Vera. '*You let her read movie magazines*?'

'Paul, all the girls do.' Vera was startled by the hostility in his voice.

'And God, do they use that as a force.' Paul was grim. 'Why can't we say, "We don't care what so-and-so's parents let them do. You do what *we* say."?'

'We save it for important matters,' Vera decided after a moment. 'The ones that bring out that wail we all know.' She tried for humour. '"Mom, you, just don't understand!"'

Vera and Paul both worried at the tendency in this decade for girls to marry very young. She had been young, of course, Vera acknowledged – but she and Paul had been living in traumatic times. She couldn't become accustomed to today's high school marriages. Thank God, she thought, Laurie wasn't caught up in the junior high 'going steady' scene. Laurie considered it 'nerdy.' But one of her classmates was already talking about her wedding.

'What's their rush?' Vera wailed. 'Fewer girls are going to college these days than before the war. Wouldn't you think it'd be the other way round?'

With shocking swiftness, it seemed to Vera, they were facing another New Year's Eve. It worried her that Paul felt that he was accomplishing so little at the school. She worried about Doris, who proclaimed herself happy with her new life style but was eating herself into obesity. Dad worried that the country was heading for a serious recession. Was there ever a time when you could just sit back and enjoy being alive?

Dad had been right about a recession, Vera conceded in March of the new year, when unemployment soared to over five million. But he was proud that they were avoiding layoffs at the factory. *We survived the Depression. We can sit this out.* Despite the recession, Vera was expanding their catalogue business. She switched a crew from the factory to the catalogue mailing room.

It was a year of upheavals around the world. After rioting by French settlers in Algeria, France had seized power. King Faisal II of Iraq was assassinated and the country proclaimed a republic. In Hungary, former President Imre Nagy was executed following a secret trial. In Venezuela, Perez Jimenez was overthrown.

Their own lives, Vera mused while she and Doris prepared New Year's Eve dinner, had changed not at all – except that Tracy was almost as tall as she now and Laurie had bypassed her by two inches. Dad was shrugging aside good-humoured taunts of his friends that he could retire. 'So I can apply for Social Security. Then what? Retire to Florida and die of boredom?'

Paul would have loved teaching if he could have instituted some of his ideas for change in the Eastwood school system. While the big city soaring crime rate was not reflected in towns like Eastwood, he warned that the ripple would spread to include them. 'With our slipshod education, what else can we expect? We're losing the education battle!'

As did many Americans, Vera and Paul rejoiced when on the first day of 1959 Fidel Castro and his followers drove the repressive dictator, Batista, out of Cuba. On January 3, Alaska became the 49th state. 'Wow, the flagmakers must be happy!' Tracy chortled. By the end of the month, Paul was agonizing over his approaching birthday.

'Vera, I'll be thirty-eight years old. What have I accomplished in my life?' It wasn't enough, she knew, to remind him that each year he had a core of students who were devoted to him. He wanted to soar, she thought with a rush of compassion, but this happened for only the fortunate few.

At a Friday-evening dinner Vera was ambivalent when Joel announced that for Laurie's fifteenth birthday he was offering a student trip to Paris during school vacation.

'I have to tell you now,' he explained, 'because all reservations must be made by March 15. Do you think you'd like it?'

'Oh, Grandpa, it'd be cool!' She turned warily to her mother. 'I can go, can't I?'

She turned to Paul. He nodded in agreement. 'Of course you can go. It'll be a wonderful experience for you.' She'd be a nervous wreck while Laurie was away, Vera warned herself. Laurie had never been away for longer than overnight. It was scary to envision an ocean between them.

'It doesn't mean Adele can't come here for two weeks?' All at once Laurie was wary.

'Of course Adele will come to us as usual,' Vera reassured her – ever touched by the two girls' devotion to each other.

'It won't all be fun,' Joel teased. 'You'll have French classes every morning. And don't you look so downcast, Tracy. I've got a birthday surprise for you, too. Months early, of course.' Tracy's birthday was in early December. 'What about a student bus tour to the Grand Canyon?'

'Cool,' Tracy echoed and automatically cast an inquiring glance at her mother.

'Dad, you're spoiling them rotten,' Vera scolded goodhumouredly. 'They'll have a wonderful time.'

‘I didn’t tell you and Paul,’ he apologized and grinned. ‘I was scared you’d spill it before I was sure there were openings. And with both kids away, what are you two planning?’

‘We’ll think of something,’ Vera said, her eyes meeting Paul’s. It would be like a second honeymoon – just the two of them. They’d never had a real honeymoon, she corrected herself. The nearest thing to that was Paul’s furlough in London at V-E Day – but all the time the spectre of his being shipped to the Pacific had hung over them.

In due time they were seeing Laurie and her group off at Idlewild Airport in New York, and two days later they were down in New York again to see Tracy – struggling to appear confident about the imminent separation – off with her group on a tour bus. She’d be all right, wouldn’t she? Vera asked herself in yet another flurry of unease.

She and Paul would spend three nights in New York – seeing as many plays as they could manage – then drive up to an inn at the end of Long Island for ten days. Both had a special fondness for Manhattan, they readily acknowledged – yet they were always happy to be back in the serenity of Eastwood after a trip to the city.

They were triumphant at managing to see three evening performances and one matinee before heading far out on Long Island for a charming inn at Montauk that Doris’s friend Sally had recommended. On a brilliantly sunny morning they checked out of their hotel, went to the garage to pick up their car, and drove out of Manhattan en route to Gurney’s Inn.

‘Do you think the kids are having a good time?’ Vera asked, her head on Paul’s shoulder.

‘They’re having a ball,’ he surmised. ‘No need to worry about Laurie’s plane arriving safely,’ he reminded. ‘You checked with the tour office and the airline office. And

Tracy called from their first stop and told Dad she'd made friends already.'

'I won't think about them again until we're back in Eastwood,' she promised lightly.

'Don't you feel about twenty years younger? Fancy free with no kids around?'

'Let's do this every year,' she said, feeling a rare serenity.

They were charmed by their room at Gurney's Inn, which nestled on a knoll overlooking the Atlantic. The seemingly endless stretch of beach a pristine white, the ocean a dazzling blue beneath a sunlit sky. Without bothering to unpack, they left their room and hurried down to walk at the water's edge.

That evening – lying in Paul's arms – Vera told herself they must learn not to lose themselves entirely in parenthood. They were not just Laurie and Tracy's mother and father, they were Vera and Paul, too. Now they made a point of being two carefree people in love with their surroundings and each other. They explored the quaint little town, visited the lighthouse, walked barefoot along the water's edge. And every night they made passionate love. Even after almost sixteen years of marriage, their feelings for each other hadn't changed.

Only on the night before they were to return to Eastwood did Paul allow himself to become serious. They sprawled on chaises on their deck and held hands while Paul confessed to his anxieties about the coming school year.

'Nobody's coming out and saying it aloud, but everybody's sure Ames is suffering from lung cancer. You know he's always been a chain smoker. Ted says the board is secretly discussing a new principal.'

'You deserve the promotion,' Vera said quickly. But was Paul too innovative, too independent in his thinking to win over the board? There was a clique in town who would want to see him running the high school – but did they have the clout to make it happen? 'Paul, fight for it!'

'Sometimes I think I should have gone on for my PhD, tried for a college post. Here I am, staring at forty and –'

'You're not staring at forty,' she contradicted. Again, with the age! 'You'll be thirty-nine on your next birthday. And that isn't ancient.'

'I want to be principal,' he said with savage intensity. 'I see so much that the school needs to make our students competitive. Too few go on to college as it is. And those few that go are not making it into top schools.'

'What can we do to help your chances?' Her eyes searched his. Oh, he deserved this promotion! She knew that some teachers – and some faculty wives – cultivated members of the Board of Education in hopes of winning favours. In their culture, wives were supposed to help their husbands move up in their chosen fields. Doris's friend Sally had given up her cherished social worker job to become a suburban housewife when her husband moved from teaching to business administration. 'They've moved three times in the past six years. Sally says they're a team, it's her job to entertain couples who can help Phil in his career. She admits she hates it, but that's the scene these days.' She'd done nothing to help Paul's career.

'I guess it's your connections with board members that make a difference.' Paul echoed her thoughts. 'Ted says they may bring in somebody from the outside.'

'Dad has connections,' Vera reminded him. 'He's into everything in town.' Waves of guilt rolled over her. She loved her job. Dad gave her such leeway. Look how he was letting her build up the mail-order catalogue – even though it was a tremendous gamble. But Paul kept running into roadblocks at every turn. 'Talk to Dad,' she urged. 'You know he'll do anything he can to help you.'

'Sure, Dad knows everybody – and everybody likes him.' Paul's smile was ironic. 'But they figure no matter what they do, good-natured Joel Kahn will remain their friend. Don't count on Dad to wield any influence.'

'You deserve to move up to principal. What changes have been brought about at the school in the last twelve years have been because of your efforts. You started the after-school programme,' Vera tallied. 'Without you, it never would have happened. You inaugurated the –'

'Vera, that's not what will propel me into the principal's job.' Paul broke in with rare bitterness. 'And if I don't land it, I know I'm at a dead end. I'll keep on teaching until they put me out to pasture, but I'll never have a chance to make a real contribution to the field. I wanted to make Eastwood High a model school, to demonstrate what public education in this country can and should be. *I wanted to make a difference.*'

She hadn't been the kind of wife that could help make that happen, Vera reproached herself. She'd failed her husband and she'd failed her older daughter. What could she do to make amends at this late date?

It was a terrifying challenge.

Chapter Twenty-three

Vera and Paul waited for official news that Roland Ames would resign as principal. It was clear to everyone that his health was deteriorating. He was irascible when approached with routine school problems, Paul told Vera.

'Not just with me,' Paul pointed out. 'To his camp-followers as well. But the board is being tight-lipped. Not a word is coming through. God knows, Dad has tried to dig up inside information from his cronies. Nothing!' he said in exasperation.

A week before the Christmas holidays, the board of directors announced Ames's retirement. At the same time, his successor – an out-of-towner – was announced.

'The man has a decent background,' Paul reported to Vera and his father at dinner that evening. 'He also happens to be the brother-in-law of a board member.'

'Who?' Joel demanded, a pulse hammering at his temple.

'Steve Jackson,' Paul said wearily.

'The bastard!' Joel exploded. 'I played chess with Steve last week. He knows how much I wanted that spot for you! You deserve it!'

'I'm not traditional enough for some people in this town,' Paul said and shrugged. 'And I'm not the only one disappointed. *C'est la vie.*'

Vera knew the depth of his hurt. She yearned to ease that pain. Perhaps this was the time for him to consider going back to school to work towards a PhD. He'd originally wanted to teach at college level. With a PhD that would be possible. She recoiled from the implications. It would mean moving away from Eastwood – an unnerving prospect. But Paul immediately dismissed her proposal.

'Vera, I'm too old, too set in my ways to go back to school. God, I could be fifty before I pinned down the damn degree. What college would take me on?' he challenged derisively.

'You have such innovative ideas,' she pressed. 'You have something special to offer the educational system. Paul, try writing for some of the educational publications.' She clutched at this new thought. 'Put your ideas into words. Start with one article. Write it. Send it out.' She glowed with enthusiasm.

'I'm not sure I could –' But Vera saw the first inner excitement stirring in him as he spoke.

'Try,' she prodded.

'I'll give it a whirl,' he said after a moment. 'But don't expect miracles.'

At their customary New Year's Eve dinner – to welcome in the new decade – Paul and his father spoke heatedly about the coming presidential election.

'It's time for a change,' Joel predicted, 'but I'll lay any odds it'll be a close race.'

'There's a freshness in the wind,' Paul said with an air of approval. 'I feel something new in the kids going off to college next fall. We've heard a lot about the apathy of this generation, but I don't believe it anymore. These will be the *war-babies*, and they're asking questions. They're not old enough to vote yet, of course –'

'And they're complaining about that,' Vera broke in. 'You hear more and more about 18-year-olds demanding the right to vote.'

'Yeah, why do we have to wait until we're twenty-one?' Laurie demanded. 'We can get married, but we can't vote.'

'This won't be a silent generation.' Paul chuckled. 'I hear questions from some of my seniors that make that clear.'

'You're hearing from your daughters,' Tracy said grimly.

Paul's prediction was borne out in the spring. On February 1, four young Negro students went into a Woolworth store in Greensboro, North Carolina, and sat down at a lunch counter – long off-limits to other than whites – and ordered coffee. In the succeeding days they returned, always with additional Negro students. They were polite, calm, ignoring taunts of angry whites. And then the movement took off. At Yale the following month, 300 divinity students marched through downtown New Haven in support. Three days later, 400 students from Harvard, Brandeis, Boston U, and MIT simultaneously picketed a dozen Woolworth stores in Greater Boston.

Many evenings Vera and Paul – along with Laurie and Tracy – sat glued to the TV screen watching the latest demonstration being televised. Laurie wrote letters almost every other day to Adele about what was happening in the fight for integration, and Adele returned with matching fervour. Adele was graphic about life in a Harlem project – which she loathed. '*It's scary – the gang-fights all the time, the killings* – but when I'm a teacher, I'll come back here and help to make it better.'

Tracy, too, was caught up in the excitement of fighting for integration.

'Mom, do you think it would be making a statement,' Tracy asked while the family watched the latest TV news on student demonstrations, 'if I dated Jeremy Wilkins?' Jeremy was the sole young Negro boy in the Eastwood school system.

'I don't think so,' Vera said, fighting back laughter. 'Darling, Jeremy is nine years old.'

Tracy nodded sagely. 'Yeah. I guess it would be like cradle-snatching.'

Doris launched a Women for Stevenson group as Democrats began to take sides on presidential candidates, though Joel was frank in his conviction that Stevenson wouldn't win the nomination. Paul and Vera, too, were active in support of Stevenson – with Laurie and Tracy delegated to distribute circulars.

'Will he pass a law for gun control?' Laurie asked.

Then all at once family focus zeroed in on Laurie's approaching sixteenth birthday in late July. Vera was relieved when Doris offered to take on the task of arranging for the sweet sixteen party. The party, Vera hoped, would make up for Laurie's disappointment that this summer Adele wouldn't be coming to Eastwood for two weeks as she and Adele had planned. Adele's grandmother had arranged for her to be a mother's helper on Fire Island for the entire summer.

'Don't let the party become a Hollywood spectacular,' Vera warned Doris affectionately.

She had been unnerved, she confided to Doris, when the mother of one of Laurie's classmates told her that arriving at sixteen was the time when Laurie's generation considered it time to 'go all the way.'

'Laurie isn't even going steady,' Vera pointed out in shock. 'And I'll bet anything most of the girls who're bragging about "going all the way" don't. At that age they talk a lot.'

But she knew that another classmate had mysteriously gone to 'live with her grandmother' for a few months – which translated to worried mothers that she was pregnant. And Vera's mind charged back through the years to Berlin, when Frau Schmidt had shipped her daughter Alice to live with her grandmother because she feared for Alice's safety in Hitler's Germany. It was a whole different world today – with new anxieties replacing the old.

Tracy viewed the party preparations with impatience. 'You'd think Laurie was being crowned queen of England,' Tracy said distastefully. 'I'm glad she doesn't want me to come. Anyhow,' she confided, 'I've got a date that night with David.' Tracy had never 'gone out on a date' thus far. There were co-ed parties at one house or another – and David Marcus's name peppered Tracy's conversation. 'We're going for hamburgers and Cokes at The Oasis. Oh, it's all right,' she added. 'David's Mom will drive us there, and then she'll drive us home.'

David and his parents had lived in Eastwood just over a year, Vera recalled. His father was a lawyer with a client list that ranged from Saratoga to Manchester, Vermont. His mother had instantly become involved in local clubs. She made a point, the rumour circulated around town, of entertaining her husband's clients from neighbouring communities at lavish dinner parties.

Vera knew that her father-in-law was pleased that another Jewish family had moved into town, though David's being Jewish had nothing to do with Tracy's liking him. She knew, also, that Joel worried that Laurie – dating now – was seeing boys not of her faith. There were no Jewish boys of Laurie's age in Eastwood, Vera thought uneasily. It was a problem that she and Paul discussed at sombre moments. Her mind shot back to a conversation they'd had just last night with Joel.

'Look, we live in a crazy world,' Joel had said. 'It's better to marry within your own faith. Catholic parents want their children to marry Catholic. Jewish parents live in dread of their kids marrying non-Jews. Protestants feel the same about their faith. It's just one of those things that make life less complicated.'

But Laurie wouldn't be marrying for years, Vera comforted herself. She was so eager to go off to college. She vowed to make either Barnard or NYU. She wanted desperately to live in New York, Vera thought with simmering trepidation. Paul had made it sound so exciting. But New York was a heady place for a girl who had grown up in a tiny town in upstate New York. She didn't want to think about Laurie being away at college. She'd miss her so much. She'd worry every minute.

The plans for Laurie's party escalated to such proportions that Paul was nervous about the costs.

'Vera, we have to have an orchestra?' He lifted an eyebrow in dismay.

'It's just a trio to play for dancing,' Vera explained. 'And Doris is paying for it. It's her birthday gift.'

Vera was relieved when Laurie's sweet sixteen party was over, pleased that it had been such a success. And she was intrigued by a new glow about Doris these days. She suspected it had something to do with Phil Richman, the pianist who'd been part of the group at Laurie's sweet sixteen.

When Phil wasn't playing the piano, he managed a small shop in Manchester – where he'd moved just a few months ago. After the party Doris had drafted him to come in to play for a special Evening with Books at the book shop. He had taken her to a community theatre production in Saratoga. Now she was dieting with frantic determination.

'You think there's something between Doris and that fellow from Manchester?' Joel asked hopefully.

'Don't let on you're even thinking that,' Vera urged. 'But yes, I think they're very attracted to each other.'

During the next month, Vera noted with pleasure, Doris and Phil were seeing much of each other, though Doris admitted to much uncertainty about the situation.

'We're both skittish,' she confessed to Vera. 'Both divorced – you get the picture. But I wish he wouldn't keep on about our going swimming. I look awful in a swimsuit. Why is it so hard to lose weight?'

Paul hurried to the school cafeteria to meet Ted for lunch. He'd asked Ted to go over the article he was submitting – after two rejections – to a third educational publication. One rejection had been tepid. The second admired the article but suggested he was moving too fast. Still, Paul was buoyed by the continuing complaints by leading intellectuals that American education was sadly lacking.

Paul spied Ted at a table for two in the corner of the cafeteria reserved for teachers. He waved, indicated he'd join the line at the food tables. Several minutes later he seated himself opposite Ted.

'I think it's great,' Ted said without preliminaries. 'You don't waste words. You get right down to the heart of the problem.'

'So why am I having such trouble finding an editor who agrees?' Paul challenged.

'Look, it takes time,' Ted soothed. 'Type up a fresh copy. Send it out again.'

'That's what Vera said.' Paul managed a lopsided smile. 'Maybe you two are prejudiced.'

'If you were *Dr* Paul Kahn you'd have less trouble being published.' Ted was unabashedly cynical. 'With a PhD you're a savant.' He hesitated. 'Are you still arguing with our learned principal about setting up special after-school tutoring for students who have borderline chances at a Regents' diploma?' In New York State, to acquire this status diploma it was necessary to pass the Regents' exam.

'He came flat out and said *no dice*.' All at once Paul felt drained. 'It didn't matter that I could round up teachers who were willing to contribute the extra hours. "You're trying to coddle dumb fucks," was his way of putting it.'

Paul regarded Ted with recurrent curiosity. Ted was single, with no romantic attachments, dedicated to teaching, but able to turn off that dedication after hours. He seemed content with his music collection, his books, his pair of Siamese cats. Ted didn't make huge demands of himself, perhaps that was the secret to his contentment.

But Paul wanted to do more than pass through life. He wanted to make some contribution, something that said he'd paid his dues for being in this world. God, he admired those kids at the campuses who were demonstrating for integration in the South. They realized something was terribly wrong in this country, and they were going out to fight for change. Why couldn't he do something to improve education here in his own town? If enough teachers arose and demanded change, it would happen.

At dinner that evening Laurie read a segment of her most recent letter from Adele. Paul listened with recurrent frustration.

'A lot of kids cut classes. You wouldn't believe how many. Still, the classes are so big there's hardly room for the chairs that have to be brought in. A fight broke out in my English class yesterday, and two guys were cut up. There was blood all over the place. If I weren't determined to be a schoolteacher, I'd go to medical school.'

'Adele is sure to teach one day,' Paul told Laurie. 'She'll be a fine teacher.'

'I think maybe I'll go to medical school,' Laurie said, her tone over-casual.

'Hear, hear!' Joel chortled, aglow with approval. 'My granddaughter, the doctor.'

'Of course, medical school is awful expensive,' Laurie conceded. Her eyes reflected sudden doubts.

Before Paul could reply – taunted by guilt that teaching was a low-paying profession, his father rushed to reassure Laurie.

'You want to go to medical school, you'll go,' Joel said with conviction. 'This family can afford it. Just make sure you cram a lot of science into your high school schedule between now and graduation.'

Paul's mind shot back through the years to the traumatic day when he and Vera had arrived at the Robinson house to find tiny Laurie leaning over Serena's body and trying to stop the flow of blood from the bullet wound in her chest with a towel. Perhaps that was the day when the thought of becoming a doctor took root in her mind. Instinct told him this was not a passing fad – like Tracy's catapulting from one avowed career to another.

He knew, too, what was reverberating through Vera's thoughts. Would Laurie come home – after college, medical school, and internship – to practise in Eastwood? He knew Vera's obsession to keep the family together. It was unnerving today, the way so many children found no future in their home towns and ran off to live in a large city, which seemed to offer so much.

Like Americans throughout the country, the Kahn family gathered before the television screen on the eve of the presidential election. Almost everybody expected it would be a very close election. By 10:30 PM Kennedy was projected the winner, but Vera and Paul remained before the TV set until past midnight. By that time, Kennedy's popular-vote margin was dwindling.

'He'll win,' Paul predicted to Vera. 'Let's go to bed.'

Americans awoke in the morning to learn that Kennedy had, indeed, been elected president – by a margin of less than two-thirds of one per cent of the popular vote.

Vera's thoughts focused now on the approaching Thanksgiving holiday. Laurie would still be around for the long weekend. And by Thanksgiving Vera was convinced Doris and Phil were serious about each other.

She'd invited him to Thanksgiving dinner. Joel was euphoric despite Doris's warning that she and Phil merely enjoyed going to the movies together and having dinner. 'His divorce was an awful experience. He just needs a sympathetic ear.'

At Thanksgiving breakfast Vera and Paul were alone. She knew Paul was upset that Tracy and her grandfather had gone off to the nearby quarry for target practice. He hated guns almost as much as Laurie. Tracy had become a crack shot under her grandfather's tutelage. 'She's got a better eye than I do,' Joel bragged. But Tracy never went hunting, Vera reminded herself conscientiously. It was just that she enjoyed 'hitting the bullseye every time.' Laurie would sleep until noon, Vera surmised.

'Dad's all excited because Doris is bringing Phil to dinner,' Paul said when Vera poured him a second cup of coffee. 'He's dying to know more about him but scared to ask questions.'

'Doris said his wife married him because she thought he was going to be rich and famous. When that didn't happen, she was furious. He hung around the music business after college, had a song in an Off-Broadway musical. It was picked up by a record company but never went anywhere. He said he finally realized that he had a small talent – not big enough to make it professionally.'

'The way Doris felt about her art,' Paul said gently. 'But she never really gave herself a chance. I kept telling her that it's not enough to have talent, you have to have the discipline to use that talent. But of course, once she met Wayne, she lost all confidence in herself.'

'She feels very comfortable with Phil. She's even started painting again. And she loves to hear him play. They're good for each other, Paul.'

'You're such a matchmaker,' he teased, but his eyes were tender. He glanced at the wall clock. 'I know you have to cook Thanksgiving dinner and Doris is coming over to help you –' She recognized the ardour in his eyes.

'I won't put the turkey into the oven for another hour and a half, and Doris won't be here for two.' How wonderful, she thought in rising passion, that she and Paul could still feel this way about each other. 'I haven't even made up our bed yet.'

'We'll do it together,' he promised. 'Later . . .'

'It seemed the right thing to do to invite Phil to dinner,' Doris said self-consciously while the family waited for him to arrive. 'I mean, he was going to be alone on Thanksgiving. He has no family except some distant cousins down in Texas.'

'Of course it was,' Joel agreed expansively, with a furtive wink at Vera.

'Let me get back to the kitchen,' Vera decided. 'The turkey may need basting.' She paused. 'Laurie and Tracy, come give me a hand.' Let Phil not be overwhelmed by a huge welcoming committee.

With savoury aromas floating through the house, Vera kept the two girls occupied until she knew from the lively hum of voices in the foyer that Phil was being welcomed. Everything must be right for Doris and Phil today, she told herself.

'All right, everything's under control,' she announced. 'We'll serve dinner in twenty minutes.'

The house reverberated with festive spirits. Joel was reminiscing colourfully about earlier Thanksgivings – when Paul and Doris were little. Then Vera ordered everybody to the table. As always at this time, she thought what a wonderful holiday the early colonists in New England had established for the future country.

After dinner the girls helped clear the table. Everything had gone well, Vera thought with pleasure. This was their first occasion to exchange more than a few words with Phil. He was charming, warm, and gentle, Vera decided. Something Doris needed in a man after the tortuous years with Wayne. He'd won Dad over completely by sitting down at the piano before dinner and playing a medley of Gershwin tunes.

'He's cute,' Tracy told Doris. 'I mean, for somebody that's old.'

When Vera and Doris joined the men in the living room – Laurie and Tracy remaining to stack the dishwasher – they found the other three focused on a special TV news report.

'More trouble down in Peru,' Paul said. 'Revolutionaries killed three Americans.'

'There's been so much trouble down there these past few years,' Vera began. 'First, it was –'

'Ssh,' Joel ordered and leaned forward as a fresh bulletin was handed to the newscaster.

'The names of the three Americans have been released. They're Lloyd Crane of Los Angeles, California; Fred Mitchell of New York City, and Wayne Solomon of New York City and Tel Aviv, Israel.'

'Oh my God!' Doris was ashen. 'Wayne dead? I don't believe it.' Her voice soared in hysteria. 'I don't believe it!'

Chapter Twenty-four

Exhausted from the trauma of the day, Vera settled into one corner of the living room sofa she shared with her father-in-law. Laurie and Tracy – both shaken by the news of Wayne's murder – had retreated to their bedrooms. At last succumbing to the sedative Vera had forced upon her, Doris was asleep in the guest room. Compassionate and yearning to be helpful, Phil had finally gone home. Paul was out in the kitchen preparing a fresh pot of coffee, the family crutch in time of crisis.

'I didn't expect Doris to be so distraught,' Joel admitted. 'Can't she remember what the bastard did to her?'

'She's remembering the first years – when Wayne was her knight in shining armour,' Vera said softly. 'It's wonderful, though, the way Phil's come forward to help.'

It was Phil who'd leapt into action. Already he'd made preliminary arrangements for Wayne's burial, once the body would be released by Peruvian officials. He'd been on long, involved phone calls, first with Washington, DC, then with the American Embassy in Lima – determined to track down the proper parties. Doris had remembered how Wayne had deliberately cut himself off from his only relatives, the cousins in New York. It would be up to his ex-wife to see that his body was laid to final rest. Phil understood, Vera thought with tender gratitude, that if he were to have a place in Doris's life, then he must help her through this period.

'In the early years we all thought Wayne was wonderful.' Joel winced in retrospect. 'How could we have been so stupid?'

'It's over, Dad,' Paul reproached, striding into the living room with a tray laden with tall cups of strong, black coffee. 'It was a shock to Doris, but she'll snap back.'

'How does Phil feel about this?' Joel turned from Paul to Vera.

'Dad, he understands,' Vera soothed.

'He's a good man. I hope Doris realizes that.' Now Joel seemed less tense. 'Ask him over for dinner tomorrow night. Let Doris see how he's handling everything.'

'He's flying down to Washington tomorrow,' she reminded him. He was acting as the family representative.

'I'll blame Wayne if this breaks up the closeness between Doris and Phil,' Joel flared. 'Why did this have to happen just now?'

For the next few days Doris seemed to live in a daze, yet Vera sensed that she was very conscious of Phil's efforts. Phil tracked down Wayne's cousins in New York, persuaded them to follow through on a burial in a Queens cemetery – once they understood all expenses would be borne by Doris.

'I don't want to go to the funeral,' Doris confessed forlornly to Vera.

'You don't have to go,' Vera insisted. 'You've been divorced from Wayne for years.'

'I just can't go,' Doris whispered. 'It'll bring back so much I've tried to forget.'

Early in the new year, Phil coaxed Doris to go away with him for a three-day weekend.

'I didn't tell Dad I'm going with Phil. I know he'd be upset,' Doris confided to Vera in a late-night phone call. 'I said I was going with one of the women from the nursery school.' Her smile was wry. 'Even at my age he'd worry about my reputation.'

Vera broke into laughter.

'Doris, we're living in a new era. College girls go off for weekends with their boyfriends.' But her voice was sympathetic. For their generation it was not routine for an unmarried man and woman to spend a weekend together. Of course, she'd lived with Paul before they were married. But that had been wartime – a special swatch of time.

'I've never come out and told you,' Doris said, colour flooding her face, 'but we've slept together three times. And Vera,' she whispered, 'it was wonderful.'

'It's time,' Vera approved. 'You two are perfect for each other.'

'I've warned him not to rush me. I don't even know how long this'll last –'

'Enjoy,' Vera ordered affectionately. 'Is it a secret? Where you're going?'

'I thought we'd go out to Montauk. You and Paul liked it so much.'

'It'll be off-season,' Vera warned. 'There'll probably be very few people around.'

'Perfect. We'll have the beach to ourselves. We'll dress warmly and walk and walk and walk. I've always had a secret love affair with the ocean.' She paused. 'Remember the Cape?'

'It was beautiful,' Vera recalled. But by then Doris's marriage had been a shambles.

'And now I have a secret lover.' All at once Doris was whimsical. 'Are people talking about us?'

'Of course they are,' Vera joshed. 'You know this town. If you talked three minutes to some man in the supermarket, they'd be gossiping.'

'I'm driving over to Albany tomorrow afternoon and

shop for a gorgeous nightie and negligeé,' Doris said in good-humoured defiance. 'It's crazy! I feel like a kid again.'

On a grey, cold Friday afternoon Doris and Phil drove in his eight-year-old Plymouth into the town of Montauk. They stopped to ask one of the few pedestrians on what they assumed was the main business street for directions to Gurney's Inn.

'We may have picked a bad weekend.' Phil was apprehensive as they turned onto the road flanking the ocean. 'The weather's ghastly.'

'I don't care,' Doris rejoined. 'I have the landlubber's love for the ocean. Vera promised we'll be right on the water, with miles of beach to walk. That's all I ask. Oh, and some good food,' she conceded.

Almost immediately Doris felt herself riding on a cloud of serenity. It was clear that this was off-season. Despite the damp cold, the greyness that enveloped the ocean and beach, she and Phil left their unit without bothering to unpack. Hand in hand they walked along the clean, white sand. Not another human was in sight, only clusters of seagulls here and there.

At last – cold and exhausted, yet exhilarated – they returned to their ocean-facing unit.

'Tomorrow will be nicer,' Phil promised. 'I've put in a special order.'

'This is fine,' she insisted. 'I feel so at peace here.'

'Okay.' He laughed. 'I'll cancel the order.'

Except for them and two solitary diners, the dining room was deserted at this early hour. Dinner was a gourmet feast. They lingered in relaxation, then returned to their unit with an unspoken pact to retire unusually early. This would be the first time they'd spend an entire night together, Doris thought in pleasurable anticipation as she dawdled in a warm tub and Phil watched a TV news programme.

She suppressed a giggle. Would Phil laugh when she emerged from the bathroom in a flannel nightie? She hadn't packed the sheer black nightie and peignoir she'd shopped for this weekend. He'd warned her the nights would be cool with the ocean no more than seventy feet from the door to their unit.

He didn't laugh, she thought exultantly when she walked into the room in her demure, flower-sprigged nightgown.

'You look like a little girl,' he murmured, reaching for her. 'A beautiful, vulnerable little girl – and I can't wait to take advantage of you . . .'

Vera sat frozen at her office phone – the catalogue copy spread across her desk forgotten.

'Paul, what do you mean – Tracy's been suspended from classes for a week! Why?'

'I just got called into Franklin's office,' he repeated tiredly. The new principal whom he had come to loathe. What had appeared to be a decent background had revealed itself as ultra-conservative. 'Tracy was caught smoking in the girls' gym – with two others. Normally Franklin would have expelled them. You know what a tough disciplinarian he is. But one of the other two was Steve Jackson's granddaughter.' Steve Jackson, Vera recalled, was the principal's brother-in-law. 'He's letting them off with a week's suspension.'

'What got into Tracy?' Vera was shaken. She wasn't part of the small, rebellious clique in the high school. She was competitive about grades – that was what was important to her. 'I can't believe she'd want to smoke.'

'Vera, let's play this cool,' Paul said. 'Let's don't get all excited and yell.'

'I don't yell,' she began and paused. 'Not often.' Sometimes – under stress – she could be emotional, she conceded guiltily.

'Maybe this is her reaction to the excitement over Laurie's sweet sixteen party.' But Paul was upset, too, Vera realized.

'That was months ago,' she protested.

'We'll talk to her tonight. We'll make her understand we're disappointed in her.'

'Nobody in the family smokes.' Vera's voice rose in pitch. She remembered the girls' saying 'Mom, don't yell' – but she wasn't yelling, she thought defensively. She couldn't talk on an even level when she felt deeply about something. It wasn't yelling. 'She's heard us talk about how dangerous it is to smoke.'

'This is rebellion.' Paul was blunt. 'And it's hardly uncommon. We'll have to ground her for a week. Then comes the spring break. By the time she gets back to classes, the incident will have cooled down.'

Vera told herself that they'd make Tracy understand she must abide by rules. There was a tacit agreement not to discuss the subject until after dinner, when Dad was scheduled for a town meeting. Vera suspected that Tracy was more upset about her grandfather's learning of her being caught smoking than about her parents' learning of it. There was an endearing special closeness between Tracy and her grandfather.

Not until Laurie had gone up to her room to study and Joel was off to his meeting did Vera and Paul confront her.

'I don't know why they make such a fuss about students' smoking,' Tracy flared. 'Teachers smoke. Lots of them.' She focused on her father. 'Aren't you always complaining how you can't even go into the teachers' lounge because it's so full of smoke?'

'That doesn't mean you should smoke,' Paul said with a calmness Vera knew he didn't feel. 'It's a terrible habit. It –'

'It kills people,' Vera broke in. 'Smoking causes lung cancer, among other things!'

'Nobody really knows that.' Colour touched Tracy's sculptured cheekbones.

'The scientists know,' Vera shot back. 'Smoking kills!'

'And aside from that,' Paul pursued, 'you know it's against the rules for students to smoke.'

'I think it's a kooky rule. If teachers can smoke, why can't students?'

'School rules are made to be observed, Tracy. You'll be grounded for the week of your suspension. We won't talk about it again. Don't let it happen again.' Paul reached for the newspaper on the nearby coffee table. 'Let's see what craziness is happening around the world now.'

Tracy hesitated, turned to her mother.

'Can I call David? Grounding doesn't mean I can't make calls, does it?'

'You may call David,' Vera agreed. 'But don't tie up the phone all night.'

'David has his own phone.' Tracy was faintly defiant. But she leapt to her feet in an aura of relief. The dreaded confrontation was over.

'I think we handled that okay,' Paul said when he and Vera were alone again.

'I'll bet Tracy doesn't even like to smoke.' Vera shook her head in bewilderment. 'What makes it a magic deal to teenagers?'

'It's *cool*,' Paul said ruefully, borrowing Tracy's current favourite bit of slang. 'It makes them feel sophisticated. From what I hear, more than half the kids at the high school smoke. It's a definite problem. Tracy just happened to get caught. Some parents are making rules – their kids can't smoke until they're sixteen. And the fourteen-year-old wants to know, what difference does two years make?'

'I can see why they rebel – when teachers and parents smoke,' Vera admitted.

'We've had a couple of parents come in and ask why we can't set up a special area and a special time for students to smoke,' Paul said. 'For once I agreed with Franklin. No smoking on school grounds. When will people face up to the fact that tobacco is a killer?'

'When we were teenagers, we didn't behave like today's kids.' Exasperation blended with frustration in Vera's voice. 'Why are these kids so different?'

'Because they live in a totally different world from our generation,' Paul said slowly. 'We grew up in the Depression and moved into World War II. They don't know such things. Sure, they've heard us talk about them – *but they don't know*. They don't understand what it is to do without. Except for ghetto kids and the rural poor,' Paul amended. 'But I'm talking average middle-class kids. Parents – and we're no different – want to give their kids everything they possibly can. And the kids assume it's coming to them. Every now and then Dad gets pissed and says that kids today have no respect for their elders. We haven't taught them to have respect. But basically, Vera, they're good kids. They think. They ask questions. I have respect for the students who're fighting for civil rights. Who want to make things better. It's the young who make changes in the world – and God knows, there are changes that need to be made.'

Stifling a series of yawns as she unlocked the door, Doris wished that this was not her Saturday to volunteer at the book shop. She was so sleepy today. And tonight she was having dinner with Phil and going to the movies. Afterwards he'd take her home – and they'd make love. Why was it accepted that Saturday night was the night to have sex? she asked herself querulously. It was as though 90% of couples – married or otherwise – put a mental note on their calendars that Saturday night was sex night.

Phil was being so good, she acknowledged with a rush of tenderness, after that last scene when she'd threatened not to see him again if he persisted in all that talk about their getting married. She loved him, she told herself – yet she shied away from making a permanent commitment. The years with Wayne had left a mark on her. *She was afraid to make the marriage commitment again.*

It was really silly for them to open the shop at 10:00 AM on Saturdays, she thought. Nobody showed up before noon. She hung away her coat and settled down to read the new Steinbeck, *The Winter of Our Discontent.*

She was so involved with the novel that she started when Vera walked into the shop.

'You're early,' Doris said.

'Go on and read your book,' Vera urged. 'I left the house early. Everybody was asleep except me, and I was suddenly restless. I figured you'd be in the mood for company. Shall I put up the tea kettle?'

'Yeah, maybe that'll wake me up.' Doris laid aside her book. 'Anyhow, we're getting off early today. Stella and Rae are coming in at one o'clock to relieve us. I said, loud and clear, that the two of us are being put upon.'

'In any volunteer group, there're the ones who do most of the work and the ones who talk about doing it.' Vera chuckled. 'Dad's forever bitching about that.'

'And I suppose Paul is still moaning and groaning about being so close to his fortieth birthday.' Doris chuckled.

'I remember his holding my hand in sympathy when I got there two years ago.'

'Why is forty supposed to be such a landmark?' Vera challenged. 'Did you feel any different when you hit forty?'

'No.' She reconsidered. 'Just a little pre-menopausal. Another landmark I won't appreciate.'

'I think it's how you face it,' Vera decided after a moment.

'I may be facing it early.' Doris sighed. 'Some women do, you know. It doesn't have to happen between forty-five and fifty. I think I may be hitting it already. I haven't had a period in six weeks. Isn't that the first indication? When you start missing periods?'

'Either that – or you're pregnant.' Vera's matter-of-factness startled Doris.

'Vera, that's ridiculous!'

'Is it? You and Phil aren't just holding hands these days.'

'But at my age?' *Could she be pregnant*? Her mind was assaulted by a medley of emotions. 'No, you're way off base, Vera.' But her heart was pounding. After all those years of marriage? But it was Wayne who hadn't been able to have children.

'You're sleepy all the time, I gather,' Vera picked up. She'd been complaining about sleepiness for the last two weeks, Doris remembered. 'You're late. And I'll bet you and Phil haven't always been careful.'

'At our age it didn't seem important.' Phil said his wife had refused to have children – it would ruin her figure.

'Go see Dr Evans,' Vera ordered.

'Vera, I couldn't!' She recoiled from the situation. 'He'd be shocked.'

'Darling, this is 1961,' Vera reproached. 'But all right, make an appointment with that new woman obstetrician who just opened offices in Albany if you feel self-conscious about this. I'll go with you.'

'I'm not pregnant,' Doris said with fresh insistence. 'But yes, I'll make an appointment with her, and you are going with me. Oh, I feel so silly,' she wailed. 'So I'm a little late and a little sleepy. She'll laugh like hell at me.'

How weird! Wayne was dead – and she might be pregnant. It would be like getting another chance at life . . .

Chapter Twenty-five

Vera sat in a lounge chair in Dr Langdon's reception room and flipped through the pages of *Newsweek* without seeing. Two early-twenties women in advanced pregnancy sprawled awkwardly on the sofa across the room and discussed their weight gains in the past month. Doris had been in the doctor's examining room for what seemed an interminable period, Vera thought. Doris *was* pregnant, wasn't she? During the last couple of days – nervous at waiting for her appointment – Doris had become morbid.

'Maybe I'm not pregnant. Maybe there's something terribly wrong with me in that area. Or maybe –' she'd reached for a less melodramatic note '– maybe it's just early menopause.'

The door to the inner office opened. Vera sat upright. Doris was emerging. She seemed in a trance. Vera's heart began to pound. She watched while Doris paused at the receptionist's desk.

'I'd like an appointment a month from now,' Doris told the receptionist.

Doris was pregnant. Vera felt herself encased in tenderness, her mind darting back through the years to her own two pregnancies. What a cherished period in a woman's life, she thought poignantly.

Doris accepted a card from the receptionist, slid it into her purse. She turned to Vera, her smile simultaneously euphoric and fearful. She didn't speak until they were out of Dr Langdon's office.

'Either I get married or leave town,' she said with an

effort at humour that was overshadowed by a sense of awe. 'Vera, after all these years I'm pregnant!'

'Dad will be out of his mind,' Vera said softly.

'What about Phil?' Doris countered. 'He wanted to marry me when I was a divorcée – an unpregnant divorcée.'

'He'll be thrilled,' Vera predicted. 'Remember, he was married to a woman who refused to have children.'

'Maybe he thinks we're too old to have kids.' Her anxiety lent harshness to her voice. 'We've never discussed it.'

'Tell him tonight,' Vera ordered. 'And apply for your marriage licence tomorrow. So you'll have a slightly premature baby,' she joshed. 'Nobody will care.'

'I'm a little scared,' Doris admitted when they'd settled themselves into the car. 'Having a baby at forty-two isn't the best time.'

'Millions of women have children in their forties. You're a normal, healthy woman.' Unexpectedly Vera chuckled. 'Oh God, we're going to have three very startled males on our hands: Phil, Dad, and Paul.'

Doris was relieved that the restaurant was lightly populated this early in the dinner hour. She'd chosen their favourite place, had asked for a secluded table. Phil had sounded excited when she'd called and said she'd like to have dinner with him this evening – not their customary evening. *We need to talk about something.* She suspected he thought she was ready to talk about marriage. At the same time, she'd detected an undercurrent of alarm in his voice. Could she be telling him it was time to end their affair?

She wouldn't want to think he was marrying her because she was pregnant, she told herself defensively. She had to be sure Phil wanted this baby. If not, she thought defiantly, she'd move away from Eastwood, have the baby anyhow.

Tenderness surged through her. She'd waited so long for this to happen – sure it never would. Involuntarily a hand moved to rest on her pelvis. Their baby was growing within her. Already she envisioned herself holding her newborn in her arms. A small miracle had entered her life.

She glanced up with an incandescent smile when Phil approached their table. His eyes were questioning. Hopeful. Would he be pleased when he heard her news – or would he feel the timing was all wrong? Her smile evaporated. Her throat tightened in fresh alarm.

He seated himself across the table from her, managed small talk as their waiter approached. They made their usual gay production of ordering – as though each such meeting were very special.

'You're looking beautiful tonight,' he said, his eyes making love to her. 'As always.'

'Phil, I'm pregnant,' she said and glanced hastily about in fear she might have been overheard.

'Did I hear you right?' His voice was hushed. 'Say it again.'

'I'm pregnant,' she whispered, simultaneously exhilarated and defiant and awed.

'Then you'll have to marry me.' His face radiated joy. 'You have to make an honest man of me.'

'You're not upset?' She reached out for reassurance.

'Doris, I feel so humble. What have I done to be given such happiness? I've always wanted a family. I won't only be acquiring a wife – I'm getting a son or daughter in the bargain.'

'You're not upset?' she pressed.

'This is the happiest moment of my life.' His hand reached out for hers. 'Tomorrow we go to the courthouse for our marriage licence. I was afraid this day would never happen,' he confessed. 'But I kept hoping.'

A week later, Doris and Phil were married by a rabbi under an improvised *chuppah* according to Jewish tradition in the living room of the Kahn house. It was already understood that Phil would leave his job in Manchester and take over management of the company shop in Eastwood. With his sixty-ninth birthday approaching, Joel hinted at possible retirement – though the family knew not to take him seriously. Still, he made it clear that he felt a certain security in having a son-in-law with a business background, someone who could join Vera in running the family business when he did retire.

Joel was ecstatic at the marriage and the prospect of becoming a grandfather for the third time. 'With a little luck, a grandson. Not that I won't love a third granddaughter just as much.'

In the ensuing months, the whole family became wrapped up in Doris's pregnancy. Laurie and Tracy had already established themselves as future babysitters. Joel revelled in having Phil sit down at the piano – his late wife's joy and the piano where Doris had practised as a very young music student – to play the show tunes of years past that were his favourites.

This was such a happy period in their lives, Vera thought in a tidal wave of sentiment as the family gathered in the comfortably air-conditioned living room on an August evening to hear Phil play the score from *Gypsy*. At intervals she sensed a wistfulness in him that he'd never fulfilled his dream, yet most of the time he seemed to be philosophical about the limitations of his talents.

Phil's dreams, she suspected, would be transferred to his child. Wasn't that a familiar pattern? And Doris was painting again – not with the thought of a professional career but with a need to express herself in the medium closest to her heart. After selling two articles – admittedly to obscure publications – Paul was running into rejections with his latest effort.

Paul was ahead of his time, Vera thought tenderly, and the Eastwood high school was in the grip of an ultra-conservative group. He was in a constant state of frustration. Despite that, Paul was the favourite teacher in the high school. Both Tracy and Laurie – going into her senior year now – attested to that with pride.

'Laurie, what do you hear these days from Adele?' Doris's voice brought her back to the moment.

'She expects to go to Hunter,' Laurie said. 'Her grades are great.'

'Adele knows we'll help her through college if she needs it,' Vera began. 'We'll –'

'She's okay,' Laurie interrupted. 'She wants to handle it on her own – the way her mother would have liked it.' She sighed blissfully. 'It'll be terrific – both of us in New York. Adele will be at Hunter, and I'll be at Barnard.' She held up crossed fingers. 'Freshmen at Barnard have to live in the dorms, I think – but after that, we figure on taking an apartment together. It won't cost any more than a dorm,' she added defensively. 'Adele says we can get a studio on the Upper West Side real cheap.'

'God, it makes me feel old,' Paul said wryly. 'I remember my days at Columbia and roaming about the Upper West Side. It's probably changed a lot.'

Laurie couldn't wait to get away from Eastwood, Vera thought with anguish. They were all so impatient to be on their own. Laurie had grown up so *protected*. Would she be homesick? Would she be lonely in a huge city like New York? But she was determined to go to a college in Manhattan. She wanted to get away from the sight of the family business, Vera tormented herself. She never gave up hating their manufacturing guns.

Paul said that kids today were spoiled. They were the centre of the universe. Her mind hurtled back to her own young years. But you wanted better for your children than what you'd had. An easier, more satisfying life. And Paul admitted, too, that this generation of teenagers were a new breed. They cared about what was happening to others. They were willing to fight for what they believed was right.

Next year this time, Laurie would be preparing to go away to school – and two years later, Tracy would be a freshman. How strange – how frightening – it would seem to come home from the office each day and know that Laurie wouldn't be there. And two years later, neither she nor Tracy would be at home except on holidays and summer vacations. The house would seem so empty.

A sense of panic invaded her. She'd be losing her family – first Laurie, then Tracy. Her mind shot back to *Kristallnacht* in Berlin. She'd lost Mama, Papa, and Ernst. A family belonged together – but her daughters were moving away from her. Not just physically, she taunted herself. To Laurie she was the enemy. And sometimes she suspected Tracy felt that way, too.

On the last Saturday in August, Doris went into labour. Just past midnight, she gave birth to a son, Frederick Neal. The family was euphoric. At last, Vera thought, Doris had come into her own. What she had believed would be forever denied her had come to pass. At odd moments in the years ahead she would be sad that her dreams of becoming a serious artist had never developed, but she would have Phil and her son to fill her life. Dreams came true for a chosen few.

The new school year brought frustrating problems for Paul. At a time when he was fighting for programme enrichments, the school board had to deal with budget cuts. Laurie had taken her college boards and – like millions of high school seniors across the nation – was alternately optimistic and depressed about the outcome, which would not be known for months.

Already Tracy, ever-anxious to be in step with Laurie, was caught up in plans for college. She and David vowed to attend the same school. 'A co-ed school,' Tracy had announced. 'Of course, Laurie will have all of those Columbia boys when she goes to Barnard – but it's not the same as having them in classes.'

Vera had long disapproved of the 'going steady' scene for early teenagers, yet she acknowledged that David brought something special into Tracy's life. *She* had a boyfriend, whereas Laurie avoided any commitments. It was as though she and Paul had acquired a foster son, Vera thought with gentle amusement at intervals. David was constantly underfoot.

She felt a blend of compassion and affection for David. He seemed hungry for approval, love. His father was becoming involved in state politics. Many evenings and weekends, David would have been alone or under the eye of the sleep-in housekeeper, except for Tracy's family. On occasion he and Tracy baby-sat for tiny Neal – who, Vera knew, would never lack for love.

'David's parents are so busy campaigning, they have no time for their son,' Vera fumed to Paul at the end of a weekend when David had spent most of his waking hours at the Kahn house. 'What's the matter with them?'

'Ambition,' Paul said distastefully. 'Ambition and greed.'

Night after night Vera listened sombrely while Paul and his father argued about crises around the world – civil rights demonstrations here at home, the Berlin Wall erected by the East Germans, the handful of American soldiers training the South Vietnamese in guerrilla warfare, instability in Latin America. She'd been so convinced that after World War II the world would learn to live in peace. Would that day ever happen?

At the approach of Christmas, Laurie received a letter from Adele. Her grandmother was in precarious health now but vowing to be at Adele's high school graduation. Reading between the lines, Laurie suspected that Adele would be allowed to visit during the Christmas school vacation if an invitation were extended.

'Mom, let me invite Adele to come up to us for the holidays,' Laurie pleaded.

'Will she want to leave her grandmother at Christmas?' Vera questioned. She sensed that this might be the last Christmas Adele would spend with her grandmother.

'Read her letter,' Laurie ordered. 'I think her grandmother wants her to come to us.'

'Phone and ask her,' Vera said when she'd scanned the letter. 'Adele is always welcome here.' Perhaps, Vera thought, her grandmother wanted Adele to be close to this family when she was gone rather than her own dysfunctional family. She'd always been loving and wise.

'They don't have a phone anymore,' Laurie reported. 'Adele said the money for the phone came out of her bank account, but the others were running up the bill so high her grandmother had it taken out.'

'Write Adele and take the letter over to the post office,' Vera instructed. How much of the money Fiona had saved for Adele still remained? she asked herself anxiously. Tuition at Hunter was free, but Adele would need money to live on while she was in college.

Adele arrived two days before Christmas. Vera was touched by her gratitude that blended with a philosophical sadness. She knew her grandmother was dying but was dealing with this imminent loss. How mature for seventeen, Vera thought.

She was outraged when Adele confessed that much of her funds had been diverted to the needs of her welfare-raised cousins.

'Grandma had to do it,' Adele explained without censure. But a glint in her eyes told Vera that the cousins would not intrude on her life in the future. 'She was trying to keep Tyrone out of jail. He showed up after being away for years. It worked for a while.' Adele shrugged. 'But he was just no good.'

Adele was determined to earn her degree and go on to teach in a ghetto school.

'Nothing's going to change for those kids until they get a decent education,' she said with conviction, and Paul nodded in agreement.

'That and family support,' Vera stipulated. Education was fine, she conceded. But along with that, ghetto kids – and all others – needed parents who were concerned about them, took responsibility for them. She was ever-upset by the flagrant lack of responsibility on the part of David's mother and father. You brought a child into the world, you had obligations to that child.

On New Year's Day, Vera stood with Paul on the porch and watched while Laurie and Adele joined Joel in his car for the drive to the Saratoga railroad station.

'There go two kids with their heads on straight,' Paul said with satisfaction. 'They know where they're headed in this world.'

Unexpected tears filled Vera's eyes. She was remembering her brother. Ernst, too, had hoped to become a doctor. Instead, he'd died in a concentration camp in Hitler's Germany. She was sure that could never happen to Laurie – yet she still grew anxious when she heard about the activities of the Ku Klux Klan and the newly organized ultra-conservative John Birch Society, which labelled FDR, Truman, and Eisenhower Communists.

'You're getting chilled out here.' Paul dropped an arm about her shoulders. 'Let's go inside and have a tall mug of hot apple cider.'

Waiting while Paul did his magic with two mugs of apple cider – cinnamon sticks plus a dollop of rum – Vera worried yet again about Laurie's going to school in New York. It would be a culture shock after growing up in a tiny town like Eastwood. Would Laurie be able to cope?

Paul said she was obsessive about keeping the girls close. Of course, children must have lives of their own – but they mustn't grow away from family. Nothing in this world was as precious . . .

Chapter Twenty-six

Vera frowned at her inability to hear the heated conversation in the living room as she rinsed the dinner dishes and handed them piece by piece to Tracy to stack in the dishwasher. The kitchen was cosy, windows steamed over on this bitterly cold February evening. Doris had gone upstairs to check on Neal, asleep in the crib set up for him in the guest room.

Vera suspected that Paul was arguing with his father and Phil about the presence of American troops in South Vietnam. He dreaded the possibility that once again – only nine years after the end of the war in Korea – Americans might die in battle. He was unnerved by President Kennedy's statement a few days ago that American troops in South Vietnam were to fire if fired upon, 'to protect themselves.'

'I don't know why Laurie always gets off without helping with the dishes,' Tracy complained with an air of martyrdom.

'We only do dishes ourselves on Friday and Saturday evenings,' Vera reminded her. Five nights a week the chore was handled by Irene, the latest in a line of housekeepers. 'And loading them in the dishwasher isn't exactly doing the dishes.' It was growing increasingly difficult to keep domestic help, Vera thought with recurrent frustration, and recalled the pleasant era when Fiona had filled this spot in their lives. 'When I was your age, we didn't have automatic dishwashers.'

'But why does Laurie run off every Friday night and I get stuck?' Tracy challenged.

'Laurie has to go to her debating group four Friday evenings – that's not every Friday night,' Vera pointed out. When did kids outgrow sibling rivalry – or did they ever? 'All right.' She capitulated at Tracy's melodramatic sigh. 'Leave the others and go on over to David's.' David's parents had recently built a showplace of a house just across the road, where they entertained at frequent intervals. The Kahns were not part of their social circle. Few local residents were.

'David and I just have a study date,' Tracy said virtuously, but her smile was dazzling.

'His parents are home?' Vera asked with obvious expectation of a positive reply.

'If they're not, the housekeeper is.' Tracy was already charging towards the door. 'I know. Be home by eleven,' she tossed over her shoulder before the familiar warning was voiced. 'The other kids stay out till midnight on weekends.' But it was a routine gripe that Vera ignored.

A few moments later Doris joined her in the kitchen, pitched in to help.

'Neal asleep?' Vera asked.

'All curled up like a puppy.' Doris exuded maternal love. 'Sometimes when he's asleep, I have to reach out and touch him to make sure he's breathing. I'm so happy sometimes I'm scared.'

'Enjoy him,' Vera said, remembering her own feelings when Laurie was born. 'This is such a precious time.' In a few months Laurie would graduate from high school and in September go off to college. It was absurd to feel she was losing her little girl. They grew up, and you had to learn to let go.

'Sometimes I walk into the nursery in the evening – you know, to make sure he hasn't thrown off the covers or to see if he's dry – and there's Phil, just standing by the crib looking down at him.'

'Ask the guys if they want more coffee,' Vera said.

'When do they not want a second cup after dinner?' Doris chuckled. 'But I warned Phil – no second helpings of dessert. He has to watch his waistline, in a few years he'll have to play catch with his son.'

When Vera and Doris joined the men in the living room with a tray of coffee, they found them arguing loudly – ignoring the TV newscast. Exchanging a glance of mock dismay with Doris, Vera walked to flip off the set.

'I don't care what Kennedy says.' Paul's face was flushed. 'When he tells American soldiers in South Vietnam – supposedly there as advisors – that they're to fire back if they're fired upon, that makes them combat troops.'

'Paul, we have 200 men in Vietnam,' Joel scolded. 'You're making a *tzimmes* out of nothing.'

'Better we should worry about the recession,' Phil said wryly. Vera knew Phil was uncomfortable at talk of war – self-conscious that a punctured eardrum had exempted him from the draft during World War II. 'We thought the unemployment problem was over late last year; now we have a relapse. That's –'

'Things will improve soon,' Joel interrupted defensively. 'We're keeping our heads above water.'

'You're keeping people working whom you don't need,' Phil said gently. 'You can handle that, but a lot of businesses can't or won't.'

'Do they expect us to move into another war to bring on prosperity?' Paul challenged.

'We're not going to see another war,' Joel soothed. 'Communism isn't the wave of the future.'

'What do you think about the Philadelphia Warriors moving to San Francisco?' Phil intervened.

'When will Laurie know if she's accepted at Barnard?' Joel grinned, knowing Phil was sidetracking them from sombre discussion.

'April, I believe,' Vera said.

With Laurie away from home, the gap between them could only widen, she agonized. Why couldn't she come out and talk to Laurie about this? God knows, she'd tried – but Laurie always cut her off.

'Mom, aren't you dressed yet?' In a white evening gown – chosen by the girl graduates of Eastwood High as official attire – Laurie hovered in the doorway of the master bedroom. Her stare was reproachful. 'I have to be in the auditorium in twenty minutes!'

'I'll be downstairs in five minutes,' Vera soothed, reaching for the flowered-print dress that lay across the bed. 'You look lovely, darling.'

'I hope I remember my speech.' Laurie was class valedictorian. 'I don't know why I'm so excited. It's only high school graduation.'

'It's an important occasion, Laurie.' Vera's voice was muffled as she pulled the folds of her dress over her head.

'I'll get my flowers out of the refrigerator and wait in the car,' Laurie decided. 'I don't know why we couldn't have carried red roses instead of mixed flowers. They're so much more sophisticated.' Laurie's favourite new word.

Paul came into the room, beaming as Laurie darted past him. 'Dad said I should ask you if this tie is okay,' he told Vera. 'He's as nervous as a bridegroom. His granddaughter, the class valedictorian.'

'The tie's fine. Where's Tracy?' She reached for a brush to smooth her tousled hair.

'On the phone with David. Where else?' But his eyes were sombre.

'You don't look very festive for the father of the sweet

girl-graduate,' Vera teased, reaching for a quick hug.

'I worry about these kids.' Paul sighed. 'So few of the graduating class are going on to college. Three of the boys are going into the army because it's that or work part-time at the supermarket – if they're lucky.'

'Dad said several have applied for jobs with us, but with the recession we're not hiring.' Vera, too, was sombre now. It was disturbing that there was so little future for the young people in Eastwood. 'People are laying off – not hiring.'

'I hope Laurie realizes how lucky she is – Dad coming across with that student tour of London as a graduation present.' His eyes were nostalgic. 'You and I never saw a London that wasn't wracked by bombs. Our kids have so much, Vera,' he said with sudden intensity. 'I wish we could make them understand how fortunate they are. Not to take things for granted.'

'Mom! Dad!' Laurie's voice called from below. 'I'll get killed if I'm late!'

Vera knew it was absurd, but she sat in her seat in the auditorium and fought back tears while they listened to Laurie make her speech. She wasn't the sentimental sort, she scolded herself – but she glanced across the row of seats and saw that Doris, too, was misty-eyed. Dad was bursting with pride. As though conscious of the emotions that tugged at her, Paul reached for her hand.

In such a little while, Laurie would be going off to college. Vera closed her eyes, envisioning Laurie boarding the train at the Saratoga railroad station. Laurie would turn around to wave goodbye to them – and then she would be lost to their view.

All at once Vera was assaulted by devastating memories. She was hovering in the darkened foyer of the Schmidt house in Berlin, her heart pounding in terror. She heard the noisy clamour as Nazi storm troopers herded Mama and Papa and Ernst down the stairs from their apartment. *She never saw Mama or Papa or Ernst again.*

Vera fought against panic. Laurie was just going to college. She wasn't being dragged to a concentration camp. Laurie would be home for Thanksgiving. What was this madness that attacked her?

Laurie put aside her textbook, reached for her purse, and hurried from the dorm. She was meeting Adele at the West End Bar for a hamburger, then they were heading down to the Village and that coffeehouse her roommate had been bragging about being so cool. She had had to learn her way around the subway system on her own. After four weeks at Barnard she was still nervous about taking subways. But she was here in New York – on her own. Only now and then did it seem scary. College wasn't like high school at all. She wished Adele were her roommate instead of Dodie – but next year, with any luck, she and Adele would have their own pad off-campus.

Her skirt wasn't too short, was it? Dodie said hemlines were going up, up, up. Dodie really wanted to be a fashion designer, but her parents insisted she focus on something more practical, so she was an English major. 'Something to do with publishing' was the vague way Dodie put it.

She waited outside the West End in the final heat wave of the year. Then she saw Adele striding towards her with an air of agitation.

'Hi,' Adele said breathlessly. 'I'm starving. Also, I'm pissed.' Adele's language had become more colourful in her years away from Eastwood. 'Courtesy of the project,' she attributed this. She prodded Laurie towards the entrance. 'Let's get inside and cool off.'

Adele wasn't living in the project anymore. When her

grandmother died in July, she'd moved right out of the overcrowded apartment – where Edna's 14-year-old daughter and Lottie's 15-year-old had added to that state by giving birth to daughters of their own. Now she lived in a furnished studio on West 88th Street. She'd explained to Laurie that she had to watch her money to make sure she'd be able to go full-time to school, but her new part-time job at a bookstore across from the Columbia campus would help.

'What are you pissed about?' Laurie probed when they were seated in the restaurant. 'The job is lousy?'

'No, it's okay,' Adele said. 'It's what happened out on the campus at Mississippi U,' Adele said tensely.

The efforts to enrol Air Force veteran James Meredith at Ole Miss had been viewed by most Americans with horror. Rioting had erupted. A bulldozer had been seized and used to push past the line of state marshals there to protect Meredith and see him registered. Molotov cocktails made from soda bottles had been hurled, bricks and broken benches thrown. Then the 82nd Airborne had been brought on campus to quell the rioting – in the course of which two men had been killed, one a French journalist and the other a spectator. Injuries were high before Meredith was at last registered at the university.

Laurie grimaced in pain. 'I think it's awful.'

'My instinct is to forget about school and get involved in civil rights. But I'm not going to do it,' she added swiftly as Laurie gasped in shock. 'Mom meant for me to go to college – and I mean for me to become a teacher. I won't let anything get in the way of that. I look at Mom's two sisters – and their bunch of kids – and it's scary. The last week before their welfare cheques come in, they're looking at an almost-empty refrigerator. And they don't see anything better in the future. That's the worst of it.'

'But you said your mother's other sister and one brother are doing great,' Laurie reminded.

'They had the strength to fight their way out.' Adele's face was luminous. 'Like me. But I want to go back in there and fight to help the kids who don't have the strength on their own. They don't have a chance without a real education, Laurie.'

'I think maybe we have to be realistic, too,' Laurie said slowly. But Adele mustn't take this the wrong way. 'Not everybody can be a schoolteacher or a business executive or a doctor. You said your mother's sister has a civil-service job and your younger uncle is a supervisor for Con Ed. Maybe the others aren't capable of that. Maybe they should focus on jobs they can handle. Dad says this country desperately needs good vocational high schools to train workers in the crafts. And we need to show respect for craftsmen, Dad says. They're an important part of our daily lives.'

'But all those people in the projects look at television,' Adele said impatiently. 'They see people living so well, and they can't understand why *they* can't live like that. Why do you think Edna and Lottie sit there and watch TV all day long and half the evening? They're living vicariously. They turn off the TV, and they're smacked in the face by reality.' Adele's smile blended compassion with exasperation. 'They'd go without food on the table if they needed money to have their TV repaired. That's their drug, Laurie.'

Now Adele told Laurie about the storefront that a group of young doctors were trying to set up as a free clinic in Harlem.

'They can just be open for four hours a day in the beginning, but it'll be a help,' Adele said with an air of exhilaration. 'I said I'd come in as a volunteer if they need me.'

'Me, too,' Laurie said, churning with enthusiasm. 'I'll do whatever I can. It'll be terrific experience for me.'

'Let's finish eating and run downtown,' Adele said. 'I want to see this coffeehouse you keep yakking about.'

In the weeks ahead, Laurie found herself absorbed in her new life style. She'd been intimidated by the city in her first days at school, but she was soon caught up in its electric excitement. And going to college wasn't like high school. Here she mingled with students who all had high SAT scores, came from comfortable homes, all anticipated fine futures.

As generations before her, she sat up till dawn in heated conversation with other students, exchanging a variety of ideas. *New* ideas, she thought with pleasure. About a new kind of world where people cared about one another, tried to make things right. There was something new in the air these days – and she was part of it.

Then, with surprising suddenness, the Thanksgiving holidays approached. Laurie had expected Adele to go home with her to Eastwood for the long weekend.

'I'll be working over the holidays,' Adele explained. 'Filling in for someone who's taking time off. I can use the extra money.' She hesitated. 'I know – I make a lot of nasty cracks about my family and the project; but if Grandma were alive, I'd be there for Thanksgiving. Gladys and Henry and his wife and kids will be there. I'm pissed at my aunts and uncles and cousins in the project – I hate the way they live. But I *understand* what's happened to them. I think I should be with them for Thanksgiving – even though they figure they don't have much to be thankful for.'

'Okay,' Laurie said softly. 'But we'll miss you.'

Chapter Twenty-seven

The first weeks of the new year – 1963 – brought mixed responses from Americans. Republicans lamented that President Kennedy had sent a budget to Congress that was the largest in history, with a deficit of $11.9 billion forecast. Democrats applauded his programme of federal aid to combat mental illness and mental retardation. And older Americans – including Joel – applauded his proposed Medicare bill, which would provide medical-hospital insurance for those over 65. Laurie spoke enthusiastically about his programme for a Youth Conservation Corps and a domestic Peace Corps.

The situation between the United States and Russia remained difficult. On January 31, the Soviets broke off informal nuclear-test-ban talks with the United States. On February 12, at a 17-nation UN Disarmament Committee in Geneva, the Soviets called for elimination of foreign missile and nuclear submarine bases – but nine days later, Cuban-based Russian jets fired rockets at a disabled American shrimp boat adrift in international waters, roughly 60 nautical miles north of Cuba. Then on March 16, the US made a formal protest to the Soviets when two Soviet reconnaissance planes were seen flying over Alaska.

Each bellicose incident sent chills through Vera. Her frightening childhood in Nazi Germany, the uneasy time in Copenhagen, and living in London under Nazi attack were ever-close to the surface of her consciousness. But the expanding business occupied much of her thinking – and always she focused on the activities of Laurie and Tracy.

She had enjoyed every moment of Laurie's presence at home during the spring break from Barnard. But now – sitting with Laurie and Paul in the living room on this last evening before Laurie's return to the campus – she listened in shock to her older daughter's report on summer plans.

'You're not coming home for the summer?' Disbelieving, she repeated Laurie's pronouncement, familiar fears welling in her. 'What on earth will you be doing? Summer school?' She clutched at this possibility.

'I'll be home for a few days,' Laurie amended. 'Then Adele and I will join this group that's going down to Alabama and Georgia to work on voter registration.' She smiled determinedly. 'You know, to make blacks realize that it's urgent that they vote. We want to make sure they go to the polls in the fall elections.'

'The Democratic party will approve,' Paul joshed. Vera caught the silent message he was sending her: *Don't make a fuss about this*. 'Kennedy needed the black vote to win in 1960, and he'll need it again in 1964 to hang on to the White House.'

'I'll come home for a week before school opens.' Laurie's voice was conciliatory. 'I won't be going into the dorm next year,' she added with the super-casualness that said she hoped not to make waves with this announcement. 'I'll share Adele's studio as we've always planned for my sophomore year. With luck we might even find a one-bedroom apartment at the same rent. Living with Adele won't cost any more than my room and board on campus.'

'I'm sure we can handle that.' Vera exchanged a swift glance with Paul. She mustn't make a big deal of this –

though the prospect of Laurie's living off-campus was strangely unnerving.

Tracy burst into the room with an exuberant grin. 'Hey, guess what? David's mother just came back from London – and she brought him these sensational records by the Beatles. It's a group that all the kids in London think is just sensational,' she explained at their blank stares. 'David's loaning them to me for a whole week!'

'There won't be any peace and quiet in the house for a week,' Laurie predicted. She was relieved, Vera suspected, for this diversion. 'Is David still running around with his hair as long as yours?'

'What's wrong with that?' Tracy challenged. 'College guys are letting their hair grow, too. Carla's brother Robert was home from Boston U. His hair is just as long as David's.'

'You're taking an early train tomorrow,' Vera reminded Laurie. 'Let's get to bed at a decent hour.' Already she felt a sense of loss. Each time Laurie returned to school, she fought against panic. It was as though *Kristallnacht* hovered over her again. It was absurd, she tried to convince herself, to feel this way. Laurie wasn't going to the gas chambers. She was going to a fine school.

'I'll go to bed as soon as Grandpa gets home from his meeting,' Laurie promised. 'So I can say goodbye to him.'

'He'll be up to see you off,' Paul told her. In the last year, Joel had begun to shorten his hours at the factory. He didn't go into the office until ten. 'At 70, I'm becoming a union man – a forty-hour week and just occasionally some overtime.'

'I'm hungry,' Tracy announced. 'Is there any more of that turkey from dinner?'

'Don't you ever stop eating?' Laurie grunted in distaste.

'Hey, I'm a growing girl.' Tracy giggled. 'But I can still fit into that Mary Quant dress that's so-so short on you.'

'I was considering leaving it for you,' Laurie acknowledged. At this point she was two inches taller than Tracy and her mother. 'But what have you got to trade?'

'My newest Peter, Paul and Mary?' Tracy bargained.

'Deal,' Laurie agreed.

'Mercenary characters, aren't they?' Paul drawled to Vera. 'But I'm hungry, too. Let's see what's in the fridge.'

A pall hung over the Kahn living room on this early May evening. Paul and Joel sat hunched on the sofa before the television set, mesmerized by the latest reports on the grim situation in Birmingham. Vera walked into the room, gave a mug of coffee to each of the men, and settled in a lounge chair with a mug for herself.

'What's happening?' she asked when Paul moved forward to mute the commercial, struggling to conceal her inner turmoil. It was so illogical, she taunted herself, to feel threatened because of something that was happening hundreds of miles away. 'Any new developments?'

'He's been summing up what's occurred these past days,' Paul told her. The black children of Birmingham had been enlisted in the crusade for desegregation. Minister-led children – boys in immaculate white shirts and girls in neatly ironed dresses – had marched from the Sixteenth Street Baptist Church to downtown Birmingham singing 'We Shall Overcome.' Almost a thousand of them had been arrested on the orders of the avowed segregationist police chief, Bull Connors.

The next morning other black children and teenagers had marched, and Bull Connors ordered fire hoses turned on them. Day after day, the marches continued – but Connors had grown desperate. Today – at the height of his fury – he had added a new terror and ordered snarling German Shepherds unleashed to attack the marchers, all of this visible to horrified TV viewers.

The events of these past days catapulted Vera into the past – into *Kristallnacht* and her final fear-laden days in Copenhagen. What happened there couldn't happen here, her mind told her – but she saw the terror in the faces of those innocent black children, and she remembered her terror.

'I can't believe what we saw on TV!' Joel's voice reflected the recrimination of millions of Americans. 'Where did he get the nerve to let loose his snarling dogs on those kids? That finishes him!'

'And Laurie talks about going down to Alabama this summer to help with voter registration?' Vera was shaken. 'How can we let her do this?'

'Vera, we can't stop her,' Paul cautioned, but she felt his compassion. And she knew that he, too, missed Laurie. 'She's not a child anymore.'

'We have to let them go,' Joel said gently. *But these weren't normal times. Terrible things were happening.* 'I remember how I felt when Doris went off to school, then Paul. At first I hated to come home to the empty house – but then I adjusted. It was a new phase of my life.' His smile was reminiscent. 'That's when I became so busy with my evening groups. You and Paul have each other,' he reminded her. 'I was alone. You two will be fine. You'll even learn to enjoy the new freedom. It's only natural, Vera,' he added at her stare of shock.

The sharp ring of the phone was jarring. Paul reached for the receiver.

'Hello.' His face lighted. He turned to Vera. 'It's Laurie. She's watching the TV news.' He returned to Laurie. 'Sure, we're watching. It's unbelievable.'

Bringing Adele with her, Laurie came home for four days at the close of school. Again, Vera was conscious of Adele's maturity beyond her years. She felt some relief about the projected voter-registration effort. There would be seven in their group – in addition to Laurie and Adele, two students from Columbia, two from NYU, and one from Fordham.

Their first evening in Eastwood, Laurie and Adele talked with exhilarating enthusiasm about the work that lay ahead.

'We're just one small group that's going out,' Adele explained. 'But it's a movement that's going to grow. Blacks have to learn the importance of political power – and how to use it.'

The term *blacks* seemed harsh to Vera's ears – but it was part of the changing times, she told herself. You didn't say *coloured* or *Negro* these days. Fiona would have been proud of Adele. But in herself, pride threatened to be overcome by fear.

Later – while Vera and Paul prepared for bed – they discussed Laurie's summer project.

'Some of these kids today surprise me,' Paul said quietly. 'I know, the general opinion is that college students are all involved with their personal lives, their hopes for success and security. But if you look around, you see something new. You see those who understand the world must change – and are determined to do something about it.'

'I'm afraid for them.' Vera was sombre. 'I don't want our kids to be part of the violence we knew.' She as a Jew fleeing Nazi persecution, Paul fighting in World War II.

'It won't be like that,' Paul comforted. 'This isn't wartime.'

'But Laurie's going down to Alabama – and I remember what just happened in Birmingham.' She reached out a hand to Paul as he slid into bed beside her. 'I can't help but be afraid.' And each time Laurie left home, she fought against panic – an insidious fear that she was losing a child. That her family was disintegrating.

Vera was grateful that Laurie phoned home every Sunday night. She was anxious because of the violence that was erupting again. White extremists had bombed the Gaston Motel in Birmingham where Martin Luther King had proclaimed a 'great victory' on the part of the black movement. The home of King's brother had been bombed. There was rioting not only in Birmingham but in dozens of other cities and towns.

Laurie remained enthusiastic about their project, talked already about how next summer's effort must be larger and stronger. Tracy – along with David – was on a student tour of Canada for the month of July. These little *vacations from parenthood* – as Paul labelled them – were always oddly refreshing, Vera realized with a flicker of guilt.

She was startled when in mid-August Doris talked about going down to Washington, DC, to be part of the March on Washington that was being planned by black leaders.

'Didn't you read that article in the special July 29 issue of *Newsweek*?' Doris probed. 'This is a time of peaceful revolution.' *Peaceful, when every time you picked up a newspaper or watched the TV news there was fresh violence*? 'Phil feels we should be part of it. Anyhow, he's taking his vacation that week – and maybe Neal will be too young to remember, but I'd like to think he was part of such an important march. Why don't you and Paul come with us?'

'I don't think so,' Vera hedged. From what the newspapers said, there would be a huge crowd from all over the country. Probably a hundred thousand people. The prospect of a crowd of that dimension repelled her. 'It must be an eight-hour drive, Doris –'

'I know.' Doris refused to be disturbed. 'And Washington in August is hot as hell, I hear. But Phil says that thirty years from now we'll be proud that we were part of the march.'

At the usual Friday-evening dinner at the Kahn house – on the night when Tracy returned from her student tour of Canada – Doris brought up the question of the planned March on Washington.

'You're going, Doris?' Tracy – who along with Laurie had dropped the more formal 'Aunt Doris' years earlier – was enthralled.

'I wouldn't miss it. And when I talked with Laurie last night, I promised to fill her in on every detail.' Doris hesitated, turned to Vera with an apology. 'I forgot to mention that Laurie called me last night. She was mourning that she and Adele wouldn't be able to be part of the march. But she's glad family will be there.' *Why hadn't she discussed it with her mother*? Vera tormented herself. *Always that wrenching gap between them.*

'I don't think it's a great idea,' Joel said bluntly. 'It could turn into something ugly. You'll have thousands of angry black radicals chomping at the bit. But I know you're stubborn. At least, leave Neal with me. Don't expose him to what could become an ugly scene.'

'It's not going to be ugly,' Paul soothed. 'The leaders won't let it be. The whole purpose is to make Congress conscious of the need for a major civil rights bill.'

'I want to go, too,' Tracy pleaded. Vera was startled. Since when was Tracy involved in civil rights? 'Can David and I go with you?' Her eyes moved from Doris to Phil. 'David's parents are away in the Greek Islands. His housekeeper won't mind.'

'If your mother and father say it's okay,' Doris stipulated.

'Say it's okay, Mom!' Tracy's smile was electric. 'I know Dad won't mind.'

Vera was unnerved. Did the girls think *she* was less understanding than Paul? It was a disconcerting supposition.

Paul turned to Vera. 'Why don't we go, too? It should be an inspiring experience.'

'How can I leave the office?' she stammered.

'You can take a day off,' Paul insisted.

She didn't want to go! Had he forgotten how she hated crowds?

'Washington is going to be a madhouse,' Joel protested. 'Watch the march on television. Don't go looking for trouble!'

For a moment Doris seemed torn.

'We'll leave Neal with you, Dad.' She rejected her father's anxiety. 'There won't be any trouble. This will be a peaceful demonstration.'

'How many times have we heard that this summer?' Joel retaliated apprehensively. 'There've been over 700 riots in 186 towns and cities. And you're talking about a hundred thousand people showing up for this march!' A vein pounded in his forehead. 'You'll be exposing yourself to all kinds of cranks and crackpots!'

'We'll be all right, Dad.' Paul was firm. *He meant for them to go, too*! Vera thought with astonishment. *Couldn't he consider her feelings on this*? 'And we won't try to drive back the same night.' He turned to Doris and Phil for agreement. 'We'll stay over at a motel somewhere between Washington and New York, then drive home the following morning.'

'Good deal,' Phil approved.

Long after Paul had fallen asleep, Vera lay awake and restless. Life was moving too fast for her. She worried so about Laurie being down in Alabama in such troubled times. She understood – as did most Americans – that blacks must have the rights of whites. She'd recognized that when she met the first coloured soldiers in London. But she was terrified of the violence that was part of the change. These days, the past was too much with her.

Paul and Phil took charge of the plans for the Washington trip – with Joel continuing to be vocal in his opposition. Vera forced herself to remain silent about her own apprehension. Busloads of people – black and white – would be coming in from all parts of the country. It would be a *peaceful* demonstration, she kept reassuring herself – even while she recoiled from being part of such a huge gathering.

Doris had never been away from Neal overnight, but reiterated constantly that he would be asleep when they left on Tuesday evening and would be fine with his grandfather. 'He won't miss me a bit. We'll be back before lunch on Thursday.'

After a very early dinner on Tuesday evening – with Neal happy to remain with his grandfather – the six of them settled themselves in Doris's station wagon for the first segment of the trip to Washington. They'd stop at a motel in New Jersey tonight, leave early in the morning for their ultimate destination. Ceremonies were scheduled to begin at 11:00 AM.

As Tracy had predicted, David's housekeeper had given permission for him to join them. He was almost a family member now, Vera thought with wry amusement. Then amusement was replaced by troubling questions that she usually managed to dismiss. David and Tracy were almost seventeen. How close was that relationship? *How could a parent know*?

Some of the stories that circulated about teenagers

today were unnerving – especially their casualness about sex. All right, she had slept with Paul when she was only eighteen – before they were married – but they'd lived in such a traumatic world. In some ways today's kids seemed so much more immature than they had been, so much more protected.

She'd been upset – was it two or three years ago? – when Tracy had been caught smoking in school. Now Paul said the staff was unnerved to discover marijuana being smoked in the high school. 'You think it's just happening in big cities, but the kids here are getting it, too. They don't want to believe it can damage their health. They just want to get high.'

'What are you reading, Tracy?' Doris asked, puncturing Vera's introspection. Sometimes, Vera thought, Tracy and David acted like a long-married couple. Tracy was reading a magazine and David had his face buried in a book.

'*Playboy*,' Tracy said calmly. 'Do you know they pay a fortune to the girls who pose naked for the magazine?'

'You're not posing naked for anybody,' Paul said bluntly.

'My boobs are too small,' Tracy said and giggled because David glared at her candour. 'Well, they are.'

Vera remembered hearing a pair of mothers complaining that it was ridiculous the way the makers of Barbie dolls were giving Barbie realistic breasts. But in real life, the kids were growing up so fast, she fretted, and wondered yet again about Laurie's social life at college and down in Alabama. How did you know what they were doing? She recalled a remark of Fiona's not long before she died. '*We got a good idea what goes on in the minds of the kids in the ghetto – with fourteen and fifteen-year-olds getting themselves pregnant and thinking nothing of it.*'

'Phil, take a look at that list of motels,' Paul instructed. 'We never did decide just where we're going to stop. Maybe we should call ahead for reservations.'

Not until they were deep into New Jersey and Tracy and David both fast asleep did they pull into a Howard Johnson, where they divided by sex into two units. Early in the morning – with another three hours of driving ahead of them – they headed south. Already the weather was steamy. Approaching Washington, DC, they were frustrated by the tremendous traffic jam. Cars, trucks, passenger-loaded buses were pouring into the city.

With much difficulty, they found a parking area, then began the long trek to the Mall. On the car radio they'd heard that only a small number of people were turning out for the march. '*Around twenty-five thousand are assembling at this hour*,' a radio newscaster had reported at eight-thirty. '*A hundred thousand had been expected*.'

'Wow, this is a mob!' Tracy chortled as they moved along with the hordes around them, everyone in high spirits.

'That newscaster was way off,' Phil said. 'What will you bet they'll hit the 100,000 mark by the time the ceremonies start?'

When they arrived at the Mall, they encountered wall-to-wall people. Wherever their eyes could reach, there were people. Perhaps a fourth of them were whites, Vera surmised. All ages and from every state of the Union, she judged, listening to the accents around her. In truth, she realized, the black leaders would not lead the march. The crowd that had been waiting since early morning had fallen into place, filling the Mall from the Washington Monument to the Lincoln Memorial. Despite the oppressive heat, the blazing sun, the delay in the ceremonies, the mood was upbeat.

'Laurie and Adele should be here,' Doris said sentimentally as they waited for the ceremonies to begin.

'They couldn't take the time off,' Vera commented. Despite her phobia about crowds, she was glad she had come here today. 'They have a job to do, Doris.'

Then at one o'clock Camellia William began to sing 'The Star-Spangled Banner.'

'Marian Anderson was supposed to sing,' Paul whispered in Vera's ear, an arm protectively about her waist. 'But I heard somebody say her plane still hasn't arrived.'

Even before the first speech, Vera knew she would forever remember this spectacle. She forgot her exhaustion as she listened to the speakers – though by three o'clock some of the crowd had begun to drift away because of the excruciating heat. Then Mahalia Jackson rose to sing, and the drifters returned as her magnificent voice soared with 'I've Been 'Buked and I've Been Scorned.' After this, A. Philip Randolph came forward to introduce the final speaker of the evening, Dr Martin Luther King, Jr.

The assemblage listened as though mesmerized to Dr King's speech – and when he concluded with his *I have a dream* sequence, Vera could no longer see him because tears blurred her vision. After he spoke, there was a long moment of awed silence – and then the thunderous response of 250,000 people.

At Vera's suggestion, her small group didn't rush from the Mall. They allowed the crowd around them to disperse. She was too caught up in the events of the afternoon to want to hurry from the scene. It was an afternoon she would forever remember.

'Glad we came?' Paul asked gently.

'Oh yes,' she conceded.

But she suspected that all would not be as peaceful as today in the weeks and months and years ahead. And she worried still about Laurie and Adele, down in what they called 'enemy territory,' fighting to encourage blacks to go to the polls and vote.

Please God, she prayed, let them be safe.

Chapter Twenty-eight

Laurie and Adele arrived for a four-day stay in Eastwood before heading for New York and their respective schools – and to track down a one-bedroom apartment they would share. Eager to see as much of Laurie as possible, Vera took time off from the factory – though she was always within telephone reach if problems arose. Joel was candid in admitting that the bulk of responsibility for running the business rested in her capable hands.

Exhausted from their summer activities – but exhilarated by the results, Laurie and Adele slept till noon each day, lounged around the house in candid delight at this inactivity.

'It was a terrific summer, Mom,' Laurie confided while she and Adele relaxed with Vera over tall glasses of ice tea in the torpid heat of the late afternoon. 'We felt we were doing something useful.'

'There'll be a lot more of us going down next season,' Adele predicted, and Laurie nodded vigorously.

Vera understood now why Laurie had rejected Doris's impulsive offer to throw a 'welcome home' party for her. In the course of a year, Laurie had moved far away from the others in her graduating class. They existed now in different worlds. Two of the girls were studying to be nurses, one had completed a year-long business course and worked as a secretary in Saratoga. Several had married – two of whom were pregnant. Two worked part-time at the local supermarket.

Of the boys, only one had gone on to college. One had

joined the Peace Corps. Two had enlisted in the army – one was among the 16,000 Americans JFK had sent to Vietnam.

Vietnam was becoming what Joel called 'a dirty word' among a small number of draft-age young men, though most Americans considered it the right thing to do, to fight for 'the free peoples of Vietnam.' Weren't the North Vietnamese Communists trying to take over democratic South Vietnam? Joel was upset when he overheard David make a disparaging remark about this country's presence in that tiny strip of land that before 1954 had been part of French Indochina.

Tracy was exuberant in her status as a high school senior, though in constant doubt about where to attend college.

'Talk to Laurie when she comes home for Thanksgiving,' Vera urged.

'I don't want to go to the same school as Laurie,' Tracy said instantly.

'I know that,' Vera soothed. Tracy had hated having teachers recognize her as *Laurie's little sister*. They were both top students, though Tracy never seemed to realize that. 'But Laurie might have some inside information on other colleges. From talking with other students. Discuss it with her.'

'David is acting like such a jerk.' Tracy sighed. 'He keeps telling his parents he wants to take a year off before he goes to college because he doesn't know yet what he wants to do with his life.' Vera tensed in alarm. 'I keep telling him that's crazy. For once his parents are right.'

'He doesn't have to make a decision just yet,' Vera pointed out gently. 'He doesn't have to declare his major until the end of his sophomore year.'

'But his parents have their minds all made up.' Tracy's

tone was scathing. 'He'll be either a pre-law or pre-med student, they keep telling him. Maybe David doesn't know yet what he wants to be – but he knows he *doesn't* want to be a doctor or a lawyer.'

'He doesn't have to make his decision yet,' Vera reiterated. 'Nor do you.' Her voice softened. 'Just make up your mind where you want to go, and take it from there.'

'I think I'd like to go to a state college. Maybe Albany.' She was struggling to sound casual. 'You know – where I can come home for a lot of weekends. David's grades may not be the greatest – not that he isn't smart, he just doesn't study unless it's something that interests him – but they're high enough to get him into SUNY.' The State University of New York.

'You'll go wherever you like – provided, of course, you're accepted.' But Vera was happy that Tracy preferred a school close enough for some weekends at home.

'I'll work on David. I've already told him there's no chance we're going to join the Peace Corps. What good would we be? We don't have any skills. Besides,' Tracy said realistically, 'we're underage.'

Vera was ever-conscious of the tiny but increasingly vocal peace movement. Voracious newspaper and magazine reader that he was, Paul kept her up to date on what was happening. Like Paul, she yearned to see a world at peace – but the peace movement, she feared, would only enhance Laurie's hostility towards the family business. Laurie couldn't understand that keeping the peace was one of the responsibilities of guns. She remembered Joel's oft-repeated observation: 'Switzerland is the most peaceful country in the world – but every home is armed. Israel remains in existence only because every household owns a gun.'

Now – just a week before Laurie was due home from

college for the Thanksgiving weekend – Joel was fascinated by the reports coming through on the new M-16 Colt rifle. To Joel, it was a work of art.

'Some army guy has said it's one of the reasons the Viet Cong are being wiped out so easily,' Joel said with satisfaction. 'The M-16 is lighter and smaller than the M-14. It's perfect for guerrilla warfare.'

'Don't talk about that when Laurie comes home next week,' Paul warned his father. 'When I spoke with her on the phone last Sunday night, she sounded so upset about the situation in Vietnam.' He paused. 'Not without reason.'

Vera remembered that last month the White House had issued a statement that American aid to South Vietnam would continue, that the administration anticipated the war might be won by the end of 1965. But how many Americans – as well as Vietnamese – would die by then?

Thanksgiving was the American holiday she most loved, Vera thought. It was a time of families coming together. This year there would be eight at the dinner table. Though she rarely indulged herself by taking time off from the factory during the work-week, this pre-Thanksgiving Friday she plotted a long lunch hour. She would drive to Saratoga to buy a new tablecloth for the occasion. The local shop was limited in choice.

On impulse she phoned Doris at the nursery group, explained her errand.

'Come with me,' she coaxed. 'I'll pick you up about ten past twelve, when the kids have been dismissed.'

'Sounds great,' Doris effervesced. 'I'll leave Neal with Mrs Ambrose. She's always glad for extra hours.' Mrs Ambrose was her part-time housekeeper/babysitter. 'But let's stop off somewhere along the road for a hamburger and coffee. This gorgeous, crisp weather makes me famished by noon.'

On schedule Vera picked up Doris. They decided to stop at a popular eatery several miles out of Eastwood on the road to Saratoga.

'I feel like I'm playing hookey,' Doris confessed in high spirits when they'd settled down at a table with their hamburgers and tall mugs of steaming coffee. 'For once everything's going well with the nursery group and the book shop volunteers. Do you know how wild I get when somebody calls up at 7:40 AM to say, "Doris, I'm so sorry, but something's come up and I just can't make it this morning."?'

'I've heard about it a few times.' But Vera was sympathetic.

All at once Doris was sombre. 'Sometimes I wonder if Phil resents my running off five mornings a week at eight o'clock when he doesn't have to leave for the shop until nine-thirty. I stack the breakfast dishes and tell him to leave them for me – but he always rinses them and throws them into the dishwasher. And he's been so good about helping with Neal.'

'Neal's his kid, too.' Vera frowned remembering her secretary's battles with a husband who resented her going out to work – even when it was his wife's job that was paying the mortgage on their new house. 'Men today help out with the kids and the house. At least, some of them,' she amended.

'I'm not neglecting Phil or Neal by running the nursery group,' Doris said defensively. 'I'd be climbing the walls if I didn't have something besides the house to occupy my time.'

'Is Phil complaining?' Vera challenged, knowing this was unlikely.

'No.' Doris's smile was wry. 'But I hear about other husbands who *do* complain.' She paused. 'I remember Wayne.'

'That was another life,' Vera said gently. 'Phil is the most adoring husband I know. You can't do anything wrong in his eyes.'

'He's so sweet. I just wish he could have done something with his music. I always feel this underlying sadness in him because he could never make it in the music field. Most of the time it's under wraps, but I know it's there.'

'Paul's upset about our school-budget situation. He says it's insane to cut back at a time when school registration is increasing, but everybody balks at raising school taxes.'

'As long as we're going to be in the department stores, I'll look for a sweater for Phil. I'm so glad he insisted I keep a separate checking account for myself – you know, from the rental income for the apartment. This way I can spend as much as I like on a present for him without feeling guilty about wrecking the family budget.'

They shopped with an eye on their watches, left Saratoga on schedule. At a few minutes before three, Vera dropped off Doris at her house and headed for the factory. Walking through the entrance, she realized instantly that something momentous had occurred. The receptionist was not at her desk. There was a strange quiet in the normally noisy building.

Vera rushed down the narrow hall that led to the cluster of offices. All were deserted. Now she became aware of the sound of a radio on the silent factory floor. She opened the door that led to what Joel called the *heart* of the business. Four deep, the workers encircled the supervisor's desk.

'Vera, you haven't heard –' Joel's shaken voice greeted her. 'President Kennedy has been shot!'

From Friday through Monday, when JFK was laid to rest in Arlington National Cemetery, the country gave itself over to grief. Americans clung to their television sets, following every step in this national tragedy. It was an unreal period, Vera thought as the family sat down to dinner on Monday evening.

'What has happened to this country?' Joel asked – half in rage, half in sorrow. 'What – who – was behind this assassination?'

'All it takes is one madman,' Paul said tensely. 'I doubt that we'll ever know if it was more than that.'

'It's a warning that this country has gone off track.' Vera closed her eyes for an instant, remembering Nazi Germany. Remembering her terror on *Kristallnacht*.

'This has been such an awful year. All the riots, the murder of Medger Evers, this business in Vietnam –' Paul's voice intruded on her ugly reverie.

'It wasn't all awful.' Tracy's light young voice was earnest. 'What happened in Washington in August was beautiful. Mom, you said you'd remember it for the rest of your life.'

'Let's pray that we've reached rock-bottom,' Joel said. 'What in our lifetime can ever hit us the way this has?'

Laurie and Adele left their recently acquired one-bedroom apartment in the West 80s early on Thanksgiving morning.

'I wish you were going home with me,' Laurie said wistfully.

'Yeah, it would be fun. But I know Grandma would want me to be with the family on Thanksgiving. She was always big on Thanksgiving and Christmas. I'm not taking any money with me, though,' she said with mild defiance. 'Last time, one of the kids took off with my wallet. They all swore they didn't, but I had it when I went into the apartment and it was gone when I got ready to leave. Why can't they understand that's not the way to live?' Her voice soared in a blend of anger and frustration.

'It'll take more than you and me to figure that one out.' Laurie checked her watch. 'I'd better grab a cab to Grand Central. I don't want to miss the train, and it'll probably be mobbed today.'

'Don't eat too much turkey,' Adele teased. 'I know it beats our tuna-noodle casserole or hamburgers.'

'I'll try to get some studying in –' Laurie abandoned herself to an extravagant yawn. 'We sat up yakking so late last night.'

'Don't sleep past your station,' Adele warned. 'Your father will be there waiting for you.'

'Yeah, Mom's probably been up since six to start on the pumpkin pie – and Doris will bring the homemade cranberry sauce and a pecan pie because that's what Grandpa prefers to pumpkin. But it's kind of hard to think about celebrating Thanksgiving Day when President Kennedy has just been assassinated.'

Fighting off sleepiness, Laurie utilized the travelling time for study. She was pleasantly surprised when she at last put aside her book to realize the train was pulling into the Saratoga station. Peering through her window, she spied her grandfather's car in the parking area. Then she saw her father and grandfather, waiting with eager smiles. Her initial sense of pleasure at seeing them was almost obliterated by a sudden involuntary surge of anger.

JFK had been assassinated by a mail order rifle. Had it been made by Grandpa's company? How could he and Mom be so proud that the company was thriving? *They were selling instruments of death. Dad never said so*, she thought rebelliously as she headed down the aisle with her valise, *but he must hate having his father and his wife selling guns and rifles. He was a pacifist, for God's sake.*

'Let me take your valise.' Her grandfather reached to relieve her of this, then extended a hand to help her down.

'Oh, you look beautiful, baby.' He kissed her with tender pride.

'It seems so long since we've seen you, Laurie.' Her father kissed her warmly. 'Welcome home.'

At the house Vera inspected the turkey. Another forty minutes and it would be ready to come out of the oven. Doris had taken Neal upstairs to change him into fresh clothes because he'd spilled his 'taste' of cranberry sauce over his shirt. In her bedroom Tracy was listening to her new Beatles record. Rock 'n' roll filtered through the house. *Were all teenagers hard of hearing*? Vera asked herself in mild frustration. *Why must Tracy play her records so loud*?

She heard the car coming up the driveway. Her face luminous with anticipation, she hurried from the kitchen down the hall to the front door. Oh, it was good to have her precious baby home!

It seemed to Vera that Laurie had barely arrived when she was driving her to the railroad station to catch a train back to New York. But in roughly four weeks, Laurie would be home again, she consoled herself.

With the arrival of the new year, the family was caught up in Tracy's college plans. She'd finally decided that, yes, she would go to State at Albany. With obvious reluctance, David had agreed to go there, also.

'His parents were livid when he kept talking about taking a year off,' Tracy reported. 'They still think he's going to be pre-law or pre-med, but he's only going to school to make sure he's got draft-deferment. He's not afraid of fighting. It's that the war seems so pointless.'

Vera and Paul knew David's parents only well enough to exchange greetings when they met on the street. Vera was outraged by their lack of interest in their son's activities except where this reflected on themselves. But she was admittedly shaken when word leaked out that his parents had grounded him for a month when they caught the unmistakable scent of marijuana seeping from beneath his bedroom door. Tracy was immediately grilled.

'He was just testing.' Tracy was nonchalant. *Was Tracy, too, smoking marijuana?* Vera asked herself in alarm. 'You know, experimenting. It was no big deal.'

'It is a big deal.' Vera fought for calm. Paul had warned her to be *cool* about this. 'We have no way of knowing yet what damage it causes. We –'

'Mom, it's no different from smoking a cigarette or guzzling Scotch or taking tranquillizers.' Tracy's tone was that of one talking to someone considerably younger. 'It just provides a *lift*. You know.'

'I don't know.' Vera was grim. 'Nobody in this house smokes.' She remembered Tracy's one experiment in that area. 'We don't drink except for an occasional glass of wine.'

'David's parents serve cocktails before every dinner party. His father always has a drink with his dinner. More than *a* drink,' she emphasized. 'So he smoked a joint.' Her ire was becoming obvious. 'It was rotten of them to ground him for a month. He wasn't doing anything different from what they were doing!'

'It isn't a good thing for him to smoke marijuana – or anything else.' Vera was struggling to sound matter-of-fact.

'Some of the kids at school smoke every chance they get.' Tracy sounded simultaneously defensive and rebellious. *Kids needed to know they faced limits*, Vera told herself. *Was the school aware they had this problem with marijuana – and God only knows what else?*

Later – in the privacy of their bedroom – Vera and Paul discussed the situation while they prepared for bed.

'We know there's a small group of kids – very small –

involved in smoking pot,' Paul acknowledged, rinsing his toothbrush, sliding it into place beside Vera's. 'But it's not widespread,' he insisted, walking back into the bedroom. 'I just hope to God none of the kids are into hard drugs.'

'Is the school doing anything about this?' Vera turned down the bedcovers, settled herself on her side of the bed.

'Not much,' he admitted, pausing at his night table to wind up the clock. 'I've read somewhere that back in 1900, statistics showed that 1% of our population was addicted to morphine, opium, cocaine, or heroin. By the early 1940s, marijuana was the fashionable drug. But what the kids are picking up,' Paul continued with a fresh intensity, 'is that the law is moving in on the use of marijuana, but Congress does nothing to stop the sale and advertising of cigarettes – which we *know* cause cancer. There are no figures on death from smoking marijuana. How do we rationalize that to them?'

'I was listening to that song Tracy likes so much,' Vera said reflectively. 'You know – the Bob Dylan song – "Blowin' in the Wind." It tells us what a lot of kids are thinking these days. They're impatient and disillusioned and angry because we're not delivering the kind of world they expect.'

'I love that song,' Paul said. 'I love the kids for what they want to see happen in this world.' In a familiar pattern he began to pace about the room. 'Not smoking pot. The good things. A civil rights bill with teeth. The kind of freedom the Founding Fathers visualized for this country. A world at peace.'

'We can't solve those problems tonight,' Vera said softly. 'Stop pacing and come to bed.' Her smile was a loving invitation.

One thing in their life never changed – and for that Vera was grateful. The world might fall apart, but for a little while they could forget the horrors around them in each other's arms. Tomorrow, she told herself, she would worry about drugs in their high school. But even as Paul reached for her in the cosy comfort beneath the blankets, she was remembering Tracy's reaction to smoking pot.

'Mom, it's no different from smoking a cigarette or guzzling Scotch or taking tranquillizers.'

One question plagued her in the weeks and months ahead. Was Tracy smoking pot?

Chapter Twenty-nine

The family was caught up now in Tracy's imminent graduation from high school. Vera was uneasy when her father-in-law announced that he was giving Tracy her own car as a graduation present.

'It'll be easier for her to drive home on weekends if she has a car.' *Laurie wouldn't feel slighted, would she*? Vera asked herself uneasily. *No*, she told herself almost immediately – *Dad had given her that trip to London.* Paul scolded her for being phobic about the girls being treated equally.

Perhaps it was a hangover from her own youth – when every possession was hard-earned, Vera mused – that she worried that material things came so easily to her own children.

'Hey, it's a whole new generation,' Doris said when Vera expressed her fears. 'The middle class and up never had it so good. The poor still have to fight for even the tiniest luxuries. And I don't mean just the inner-city poor. We have it right here in Eastwood. Don't think of the poor as just those on welfare. Phil says that both the Democrats and the Republicans will probably make poverty a big issue in this year's presidential campaign.'

Vera was pleased that Laurie would be home for three weeks before heading down to Georgia and Alabama again on a voter-registration drive. Adele would be going south with her – first coming to Eastwood for a week in June. Tracy pretended to be casual about it, but Vera knew she was delighted that Laurie and Adele would be in Eastwood for her graduation exercises. Following in Laurie's tracks, Tracy was class valedictorian. '*Thank God*,' Vera told Doris. '*There'd be no living with her if she hadn't been chosen*.'

This summer Tracy and David were both signed up to go on a student tour of Israel. Vera had chosen their destination out of a sense of guilt that her daughters were being raised with little religious teaching. They knew all the major holidays, observed by the family. They knew the history of the Jewish people. They knew about her own escape from the Nazis and about their father's war experiences. But there was no synagogue closer than Albany, so this was a good time for Tracy to get in closer touch with her heritage. David was allowed to go along with the group, Vera surmised scornfully, because he would be out of his parents' hair for a month.

Late in June, Laurie left for New York to join her dedicated group for the drive down to Georgia. She was convinced that at this point voter-registration was more urgent than antisegregation demonstrations. Political power was out there for the black *and* the white poor – *if they'd just learn how to use it.*

A week later Vera and Paul drove Tracy and David to JFK for their flight to Israel. In December of last year, Idlewild had been renamed in honour of the assassinated president.

'I feel like such a traitor,' Tracy mourned for a moment, 'leaving my car all alone for a whole month.'

'I'll talk to it every day,' Paul joked.

'Ten days after we get back, I have to register for the draft,' David said grimly. He would be eighteen. 'That's the pits.'

'You kids eat decently while you're in Israel,' Vera ordered. 'Don't try to live on junk food.'

'You're talking to the snack-food generation,' Paul

warned her and turned to the other two. 'Eat something beside hamburgers, peanut butter with marshmallow stuff, and popsicles.'

Finally the group's flight was announced ready for boarding. In a burst of exuberance, the cluster of high-spirited teenagers joined the other waiting passengers. Vera and Paul made their way out of the airport terminal and sought out their car.

'It feels so strange, knowing the kids are heading across the ocean.' Vera reached for Paul's hand. 'And Laurie's already down in south Georgia.'

'I want to see a big smile,' Paul ordered, squeezing her hand. 'We're about to begin our latest honeymoon.'

They would spend tonight at a motel close to the airport, then drive west on Long Island to the oceanfront cottage at Montauk that they'd rented for a week. A glorious week of lying on the cottage deck and gazing at the ocean, Vera thought in pleasurable anticipation. For one week the world would seem to stop. *They both needed that*, Vera told herself.

Paul was exhausted from internecine battles at the school. He was so conscientious, so dedicated to improving the quality of his school – and encountering little success. And she, too, was tired. Not just from the demands of the business, she analysed. They lived in such tumultuous times. Just to turn on the television each night and watch the news was traumatic.

Let this be a calm summer, she prayed – remembering last summer, when George Wallace's defiant behaviour in Alabama had brought federal troops onto the campus of the University of Alabama. Remembering the riots in Harlem, Chicago, Birmingham, Atlanta. *Let everything work out peacefully with Laurie's voter-registration group down in Georgia.*

*

Laurie emerged from the discouragingly inadequate shower in the bathroom of the shabby frame house that was housing their group this summer. The sash of her short, terrycloth robe tight about her waist, clutching perspiration-soaked clothes and wet towel in her arms, she walked down the hall to the minuscule bedroom she shared with Adele and Marian, the Bennington junior who'd come down with the group this summer and was fast losing her starry-eyed attitude about their mission.

'Feel better?' Stretched on one of the cots that occupied most of the room, Adele glanced up from the magazine she was reading. Laurie noted that Marian had already left for her date with Chet, the senior from Howard University.

'I did for about five minutes. God, this heat is unbelievable!' Laurie collapsed on the cot that sat about ten inches from Adele's.

'It was just as bad last summer,' Adele recalled, 'but we were a year younger – and so wide-eyed about what we were doing.'

'I get the feeling this year that some of the group resent some of the others –' She paused, suddenly awkward. How could she express what she was thinking to Adele without sounding racist?

'Sugar, I know what you're thinking.' Adele's smile was rueful. 'I'm okay – up to a point – because I'm black. But some of the blacks look on these white college kids – like you – with something that smells of contempt.' Her voice was calm, but her eyes were furious. 'I want to knock their heads together. But then I realize what it is with them. They know all these white college kids – and they group me along with you – are going back to comfortable lives at the end of the summer.'

'I work as hard as anybody here,' Laurie said defensively, 'but Jock keeps picking on me any chance he gets.'

'Laurie, you know why,' Adele clucked. 'He's pissed because you won't sleep with him.'

Laurie stared at her in shock. 'I don't like him that way.' She'd never slept with anybody – but when she did, she'd have to love the guy.

'I heard him talking the other night.' Adele dropped her voice to a semblance of bass. '"That Laurie is such a phoney! Pretending she's so liberal and all – but she won't go to bed with me because I'm not lily-white." And why do you think Marian's flat on her back somewhere now with Chet? Because she's proving to herself – and to Chet – that she's not prejudiced. And that's nuts. Before the summer's over,' she predicted, 'there's going to be a real battle between Chet and Joe – because Joe was Marian's boyfriend back home and he figures he's being dumped because he's white. Which is true,' she summed up.

'What's all that got to do with voter-registration?' Laurie challenged impatiently.

'Something happened to the whole scene during the past school year. We were out of it. We didn't get a whiff. Last year white college kids were welcomed; now they're resented. The black workers feel they ought to control this fight – and here they have uppity white college students showing them up.'

'They ought to be grateful,' Laurie flared. 'We've done a lot to help.' She thought about the three workers in Mississippi – black James Chaney and white Michael Schwerner and Andrew Goodman – both New Yorkers – who just yesterday had been discovered murdered. An unnerving situation to their own group.

'The difference between black students and white students is that we don't have the white belief in the system,' Adele said with candour, identifying herself with the black workers. 'I hang in there, hoping it *will* work.'

Laurie was startled. She'd heard Frank – who'd been out with them last summer and now again this year – make cracks about how all his wealthy white parents cared about was making money. *They don't give a shit about segregation or poverty or urban crises.*

Dad worried that the draft was unfair to low-income families because they couldn't keep their sons in college and thereby earn draft-deferment. But she'd always been wrapped up in the belief that the American system was the best in the world. They'd been raised to believe that. Was it working just for middle and upper class families like her own? It was a disturbing thought.

At the beginning of orientation week at SUNY-Albany, sitting in her car – bursting with luggage, record albums, books, and Tracy's recently acquired guitar, Vera yelled to Tracy and David to join her.

'We're coming, we're coming,' Tracy called back breathlessly. 'Mom, you're compulsive about time.'

'I don't like to be late.' Vera was calm but defensive. 'Let's get moving.' *It had never occurred to either of David's parents to take on this chore, of course*, she thought in annoyance.

Her arms clutching a batch of LPs, Tracy was shoving herself across the front seat to allow room for David. The trunk and rear seat were loaded. Tracy's own car – *my precious treasure* – remained in the Kahn garage. There was a question as to whether she would be allowed to keep a car on campus during her freshman year.

'Tracy, why don't you put those in the back?'

'Trust my new Beatles album and the new Bob Dylan back there by themselves?' Tracy uttered a vocal rejection.

'Mrs Kahn, don't you sometimes think Tracy's kind of infantile for almost eighteen?' David said with a mixture of derision and deep affection.

Sometimes, Vera thought, she wasn't sure whether they behaved like brother and sister or an old married couple. And all too frequently she asked herself how far they'd gone together. She couldn't come out and say, 'Tracy, are you sleeping with David?' But the stories that circulated about some of their peers were unnerving.

She reminded herself yet again that she'd been only a few months older than Tracy when she'd first slept with Paul. But those were different times, chaotic times. And she'd seemed so much older than Tracy.

Vera deposited David first at his dorm, then drove Tracy to hers. She made a point of leaving as soon as Tracy's belongings were transferred from car to dorm room. She remembered Doris's admonition about this. 'When I went off to Barnard, I was embarrassed to death at the way Dad was so reluctant to leave. He kept hanging around as though I were about eight and he was terrified of leaving me alone.'

Driving back home – wistfully aware of the absence of Tracy and David – she tried to deal with the knowledge that for much of the year ahead both Tracy and Laurie would be away from home. *But it didn't mean the family was breaking up*, she derided her sense of loss. *They'd be home at intervals – on all the important holidays.* Still, driving back into town she fought against a wave of desolation.

Vera was enthralled on the October afternoon when Paul – home from his after-school group – phoned her at her office to tell her he'd just heard a TV news bulletin reporting that Martin Luther King, Jr was to receive the Nobel Peace Award.

'Paul, how wonderful! I wonder if Laurie knows yet?' Her immediate impulse was to phone Laurie in New York.

'I imagine the whole country will know by dinner time,' Paul said with a chuckle. 'But I can also imagine Laurie's response.' Paul's voice held a hint of warning. 'She'll be thrilled, of course – and then she'll point out that Alfred Nobel established the Nobel Peace Prize out of guilt for having unleashed all those deadly weapons on the world.'

'She'll simmer down, I hope, by the time she comes home for Thanksgiving.' Vera was uncharacteristically sarcastic. The wall between her and Laurie remained in place.

'I hope the radical blacks will be impressed by King's Nobel prize,' Paul said slowly. 'I hope they'll think in terms of non-violence.'

Vera knew he was troubled by the rising militant voices of black Muslims and what was being descried by white columnists as their black racism. And along with Paul, she was disturbed by Laurie's outspoken cynicism about what could and did happen in these United States. Everybody in this country was supposed to have the right to vote, but Laurie was discovering what a rough battle it was to make this come true.

This past summer Laurie had spent twenty-four hours in jail because of her determination to help blacks register to vote – but the man who murdered highly respected black leader Medger Evers roamed the streets a free man. She talked with blazing eloquence about being reviled by whites for her efforts to help blacks to register to vote. *Their legal right.* On two occasions she had personally experienced physical violence.

And Laurie was so upset about the American presence in Vietnam, Vera remembered. Slowing down in an unexpected burst of traffic, she could hear Laurie's voice in exasperated protest on her last evening home before returning to school:

'The government keeps sending troops to Vietnam to

protect it from the Viet Cong, but they do nothing to protect students who're fighting for the civil rights guaranteed by our Constitution!'

A few miles out of Eastwood – after a glance at her watch – she stopped at a gas station to phone Paul at the school. He had a free period now and his lunch period was coming up. She'd pick him up and take him off for lunch. Dad wasn't expecting her to come into the office until early afternoon.

Paul was waiting in the parking lot when she arrived.

'You're feeling like the mother bird who's seen her last little one fly out of the nest,' he jibed as he slid onto the seat beside her.

'Yeah.' Leave it to Paul to know her feelings at this moment, she thought with a surge of love.

'Let's have lunch at that place you discovered last month – the one sitting at the edge of the pond with the pair of swans. Let's be decadent and have a glass of wine with lunch.'

'You've persuaded me.' She followed his light mood with a sense of relief.

But over lunch, the conversation ultimately became serious. Paul, too, was distressed at seeing American soldiers going to Vietnam in increasing numbers.

'It's hard to swallow – this story that we're sending over only advisors. By the end of the year we're expecting to have over 23,000 Americans in Vietnam. Damn it, Vera, how can we pretend they're only advisors?'

'In the face of what happened last month at the Gulf of Tonkin, how can we say we're not fighting a war?' On August 4, Vera remembered – following reports that a North Vietnamese torpedo craft had attacked two US destroyers in the Gulf of Tonkin – US planes were ordered to bomb North Vietnam.

'And according to the polls, 85% of Americans

approved that,' Paul said disgustedly. 'We ought to get the hell out of Vietnam.'

'Don't let Dad hear you say that,' Vera warned. 'He's convinced that by sending troops to Vietnam we're saving the world from Communism.'

'Enough of this,' Paul ordered. 'What are we having for dessert?'

Later – after driving Paul back to the school and heading for her office – Vera felt enmeshed in depression. Where was the country heading? What was happening to so many of their college generation? So bright – so compassionate – and becoming so disillusioned.

Chapter Thirty

The day was cold and depressingly grey. Weather forecasters were predicting heavy snow by late evening. Paul was relieved when the bell rang at the end of the last period of the day. His mind wasn't on teaching today. He was upset over the battle with Vera last night. She admitted she was furious at the way he'd defended the student who'd burnt his draft card at a public demonstration last week. 'Paul, that's showing contempt for this country!'

Laurie would be home for the winter break sometime this afternoon. And Tracy was due in tomorrow evening, he comforted himself. He anticipated their arrival with deep pleasure. The house came alive when the girls were home.

A hand moved involuntarily to the pocket of his jacket, and his mood plunged into morbid apprehension. He pulled out the note that had been in his mailbox in the teachers' room. What the hell did Franklin want to see him about now? Another parent objecting to his bringing up the subject of drugs in the high school – so sure they had no such problem. How could they close their eyes to what was happening to their own kids?

All at once tense, he strode down the stairs to the floor below. He'd never liked the principal, but he had to keep up a facade of accepting his school policies – or resign. He wasn't ready to do that, he admitted. If he weren't teaching, what would he do with his life? If he resigned here, he'd have a rough time finding another spot in a commuting-area school. Franklin would make sure of that.

Masking his inner conflicts, he walked to the principal's office, decorated to reflect the Christmas season. He exchanged a few words with the school secretary, then was ushered inside.

'Sit down, Paul.' Franklin was brusque. He waited until Paul was seated, then continued. 'I've kept quiet about your after-school peace group, but in the current conditions I have to insist you drop it. It could have terrible repercussions.'

'There're a total of five in the group.' Paul struggled to appear calm. 'Four boys and one girl. That hardly presents a threat to anyone.'

'Drop it! I won't have my school being part of this insanity we see around us!' The other man's voice was shrill. 'These crazy kids fighting the draft! These stupid demonstrations! It's un-American.'

'It's freedom of speech.' Paul appeared almost detached. Inside he fumed. Now that LBJ had been elected for a full term of his own, what was he going to do about Vietnam? He'd campaigned as the peace candidate. But he remembered a November article in the *Wall Street Journal* that Laurie had sent him. The article suggested that the government was preparing an escalation of the war in Southeast Asia, and that was frightening. 'Clark, let's be glad that our young people are relating to what's happening in the world. We don't have the apathy we saw in students in the '50s. That's –'

'Bullshit,' Clark Franklin interrupted. 'Cancel the group. This school is not catering to those half-baked kids. That's not freedom of speech,' he scoffed. 'They're traitors to this country. I won't allow the school premises to be used for such purposes.'

Paul left the office. Of course, he could meet with the

kids in his own home, he thought in defiance. No, he couldn't. He rejected this immediately. Dad called the anti-Vietnam kids 'young hoodlums who've had it too good.' He'd have to disband the small group. To Dad the war in Vietnam was another battle against Communism.

Most Americans, he thought with recurrent apprehension, were proud that this country was rushing to the aid of the South Vietnamese government. On the surface it appeared a fine gesture. A Harris poll showed 85% approved. Even such liberals as Eugene McCarthy, Albert Gore, and George McGovern approved. After the trouble in the Gulf of Tonkin, the *Washington Post* had written: 'President Johnson has earned the gratitude of the free world.' But South Vietnam was not a democracy, he thought in repetitious rage. It had been ruled by a series of in-and-out unpopular dictators.

Paul drove home, impatient to talk with Vera about Franklin's insistence he disband his peace group. It hadn't begun as an anti-Vietnam movement, but now it would be considered just that. And damn it, why not? He *was* opposed to the war in Vietnam.

He glanced at his watch. It would be another two hours before Vera left the office. On impulse he decided to drop by and visit with Doris. If Doris weren't there, he could at least spend a little time with Neal. It had been a long time since his own kids were three years old, he thought nostalgically. He enjoyed his young nephew.

He saw Doris's car turn into the driveway as he approached the house. Thank God that Doris's life had taken this new path. It was as though she had been reborn when she met Phil.

'Hi!' Emerging from her car, Doris spied him. 'I didn't see you behind me.'

'I thought I'd pop in and yak for a while,' he called, drawing to a stop. 'Remember, you and Phil are coming over for dinner tomorrow night.' He left the car to join her on the stairs. 'But you'd better bring Neal or the girls will send you right home.'

'I wouldn't dare not bring him,' she said, chuckling. 'We saw them at Thanksgiving, but it seems so long ago.'

From inside the house came Neal's sweet, light voice. 'Mommie, Mommie!'

For a few moments they were caught up in greeting Neal. Then Mrs Ambrose coaxed him to join her in the kitchen for a treat.

'You look uptight,' Doris said when they were alone in her cosy den. 'Problems at school?'

'Same old story.' Paul dropped into a chair. 'I don't fit in with Clark Franklin's vision of what he refers to as *my school*. He ordered me to drop my peace group.'

'Because of the Vietnam business,' Doris assumed. Paul nodded. 'So you'll drop it for now,' she advised. 'How long can this craziness go on?'

'Too damn long.' Paul was grim.

'Tracy and I talked about it when she was home for Thanksgiving,' Doris told him and he stared at her in surprise. She hadn't said a word to him – but then, because of Dad, they tried to avoid the subject of the war in Vietnam. 'David was just registering for the draft. As long as he's in school, of course, he'll be deferred; but he keeps talking of dropping out of school, and she worries about that.'

'The deferment rules are a real problem,' Paul acknowledged. 'Laurie told me that Adele is close to some young student from NYU who's going to leave at the end of the school year to work for a while to save up for his senior year. Adele worries that he could be drafted.' His eyes reflected sympathy. 'It seems so rotten that families who can afford to keep their sons in school can be sure they won't be grabbed.'

'Watch the enrolment at the graduate schools surge,' Doris predicted. 'The poor will see their sons drafted. Not the middle class or the rich. Thank God Neal is so young.'

'I thank God both my kids are girls,' Paul confessed. He hesitated. 'I wish Vera understood how you and I feel about this war. Sometimes I'm sure she regards me as a traitor. Damn it, Doris, Vera and I have been through so much together. It scares me that something like this can put such distance between us. Sometimes she looks at me as though she's seeing a stranger. We've always been so close –'

'You'll be close again.' She managed a confident smile, yet Paul realized he'd startled her. 'You and Vera have always had something very special. Nothing can disturb that for long.'

'By the end of this year we'll have 23,000 troops in Vietnam. And there's gossip about a heavy escalation. How many of our kids will die over there? And I think of all the money going into the war that could be used to cut down poverty, improve our educational system. It's such a waste!'

'Let's go out to the kitchen. I'll put up coffee.'

'The universal consolation prize.' Paul laughed, but rose to his feet. 'What did people do before there was coffee?'

'They had tea,' Doris surmised. 'But where else in Eastwood can you get freshly ground, freshly perked coffee?'

Tracy glanced up at the night-dark sky – though it was barely five o'clock – while David stowed their valises in the back of his recently acquired Dodge.

'We should have left earlier,' she scolded. 'The snow's coming down like it's never going to stop.' Weathermen had predicted six to eight inches, she recalled.

'We'll be okay,' David soothed. 'We've got snow tyres – and they'll have the ploughs out on the roads by the time we hit the highway. Hey, this is a great car. I don't know what kind of pills my mother's on this month, but they sure make her happy. I never thought she'd give me my own wheels.' The Dodge – the family's second car – was being replaced by an expensive foreign sports car. 'We're only an hour and a half from home.'

'With the way the snow's coming down, it could be five hours,' she warned, climbing into the front seat.

'Warm enough?' David asked solicitously ten minutes later. The road ahead was one expanse of white, the trees on either side already edged with snow.

'I'm fine. You okay?'

'Yeah.' He was squinting now. 'The visibility is lousy. Turn on the radio, hunh?'

Tracy flipped the selector across the dial from station to station until she located a disc jockey offering a Beatles medley. Now she leaned back in pleasure. It was kind of nice, driving in heavy snow this way – warm inside, David close, the music great.

'We're not going to make any time this way,' David complained. Traffic was creeping over the treacherous road. 'You hungry?'

'Getting there,' Tracy admitted.

'Watch for a diner. We're running into home-bound people. If we start out thirty minutes later, we'll run into less traffic.'

Within fifteen minutes they were in a booth at a roadside diner, devouring mammoth hamburgers. The windows were steamed over. Bob Dylan's voice drifted from a nearby jukebox. A pair of truck drivers straddled stools at the counter. A couple with two small children occupied one booth. No other patrons were in the diner.

Tracy and David lingered over mugs of strong black

coffee, discussed plans for the days ahead. He was excited by the prospect of several days of skiing. New to skiing, she was ambivalent. In the privacy of their booth – at a far end of the diner – David's foot slid beneath the table to contact hers.

'You shouldn't be wearing that red sweater on a night like this,' he reproached. 'You make me so horny.'

Tracy giggled. 'You mean you're not complaining anymore that my boobs are so small?'

'I never complained.'

In his mind he had her sweater off, she guessed, his hands all over her. He knew just what excited her. He knew, also, the limits they'd decided on long ago – everything but . . .

'It's such a rotten night,' he said tentatively, his eyes sending an erotic message. 'We could stop at a motel, call your folks and mine and say we'll be home tomorrow.'

'I don't know –' But all at once her heart was pounding. Lots of the kids were sleeping together – no demarcation lines.

'No,' he contradicted himself. 'We've talked this through a hundred times. We're not ready for that yet.'

'There's the back seat of the car,' she reminded. 'We can play house within our limits.'

'Let's.' His face exuded anticipation. 'By our rules.'

Vera revelled in the presence of Laurie and Tracy in the house, though she was ever-conscious that the war in Vietnam – and this country's participation – only exacerbated Laurie's resentment that her own family manufactured guns. Ever since the tragic death of little Serena Robinson, Laurie had refused to go to the company's Christmas office party – where Joel loved to show off his grandchildren. This year, Tracy had concocted an excuse not to put in an appearance – because of the war, Vera surmised – and Joel was hurt. He loved his three grandchildren, but Tracy he adored.

At regular intervals David was on hand, good-humouredly accepting Joel's taunts about his long hair. *What's the matter with young guys these days? They all want to look like girls?* Laurie spent an amazing amount of time each day poring over textbooks. *Look, I know I have to make top grades or I'll never make it into med school.*

On a night when her parents and grandfather were absent from the house for the evening and David had left early to nurse a bad cold, Tracy prodded herself to invade Laurie's room to ask a question that had been invading her mind for weeks – ever since her roommate Claire said she'd gotten sick on morning glory seeds. Sure, she'd been reading the articles in the student newspapers about drugs – but whom did you *believe*?

'Laurie, I have to talk,' she said with a familiar flare of drama. 'It's important.'

'It's important for me to study,' Laurie said, but she laid aside her textbook. 'But what's your problem?' Exasperation gave way to resignation.

'You go to a big-city school. What about drugs on campus?'

Laurie thought for a moment. 'Sure, there're drugs on campus. Not as much at an all-girl campus as at co-ed schools. But it's a bad scene. Tracy, are you messing around with drugs?'

'No.' Tracy was startled at the accusation. 'Well, not really. I mean, everybody smokes pot now and then – but I'm scared of LSD and all the pills.'

'Everybody doesn't smoke pot,' Laurie refuted. 'Some, sure, but –'

'Haven't *you*?' Tracy challenged.

'At parties now and then,' Laurie conceded. 'You

know, when somebody starts passing around joints. But not on a regular basis.'

'David says it's cheaper than liquor and never makes you sick. He said his parents pass around joints at dinner parties.'

'Students are being suspended at some schools if they're caught with marijuana. I know a boy at Columbia who was turned over to the cops by somebody in his dorm for selling pills. He said he was working his way through school by dealing. Tracy, a lot of students brag about taking drugs – but they're faking. It makes them feel they're gaining status. When Dad was in college, he said students would brag about how much bourbon they could drink before they got sick. The ones who're heavy into the drug scene – and they're stupid – don't talk about it.'

'David and I talk about it a lot,' Tracy admitted. 'David got a copy of that summer edition of Harvard Review – about drugs and the mind – and the La Guardia Report on Marijuana that's been reprinted by some group that wants to see marijuana legalized. It claims pot is no worse than smoking a cigarette. But actually we're scared of most of the stuff that's floating around. Except for pot.'

'Who knows what that will do later on?' Laurie challenged. 'I don't think much is happening on a lot of campuses out of big cities. I think a lot of it's talk.' Laurie paused in seeming debate. 'Okay, so I hear a lot about drugs down at NYU – because it's so close to Greenwich Village. There's supposed to be a lot at Berkeley – and some at Columbia,' she conceded with a show of reluctance. 'I haven't got time for that crap,' she wound up bluntly. 'Nobody's going to tell me that a nickel bag is going to see me through a rough exam. Only cramming will do that.'

A week before Laurie was to return to school, Adele came up to visit. As always, Vera was delighted to see her. She listened with pleasure to the earnest discussions between Paul and Adele about the sad state of American education. Listening to them, she could brush aside her unease at Paul's attitude about the war in Vietnam. She couldn't understand this. He'd fought against the Nazis. He'd seen what happened to people deprived of democratic rights. How could he not support the fight to control the spread of Communism? *It wasn't like Paul.*

It unnerved her to feel this division between herself and Paul. The wall between Laurie and her had never been completely obliterated – and now there was this new wall shooting up between Paul and her. Sometimes Doris teased her – lovingly – about her passionate obsession for family. But family, she told herself defensively, was her most cherished possession.

Too quickly, Vera thought, the winter college break was over. Laurie and Tracy returned to school. She knew it was absurd – but each time the girls left Eastwood she was assaulted by panic – a fear that she would never see them again. Always she remembered those terrible minutes on *Kristallnacht* when she'd hidden in the Schmidts' apartment while Mama and Papa and Ernst were dragged away by the SS men.

'I should have taken time off from the office while the girls were home,' Vera reproached herself while she and Doris sat over coffee in the Kahn kitchen while the three men – Paul, Joel, and Phil – watched a basketball game on television.

'Don't feel guilty because you're working,' Doris ordered. 'Laurie and Tracy understand that you're important to the business. Even Dad admits that without you it would be a piddling operation.' Once shorn of Wayne's covert – illegal – sales, business had plummeted. Through Vera's efforts, the company had regained its earlier status.

'I've gotten all wrapped up in expanding the catalogue,'

Vera paused. 'Sometimes I wonder if Paul resents that.'

'Enough of this guilt shit,' Doris clucked. 'You're making a big contribution to the family finances. You've taken a load of responsibility off Dad's shoulders. You've –'

'Phil's doing great with the shop,' Vera broke in. 'And your helping with the buying has been a major asset.' Instinct had told her to enlarge in the women's-wear area – and it was paying off. 'Sometimes I think I get carried away with the potential of the catalogue market, but we're doing so well with it.'

'And you're a damn good mother,' Doris picked up. 'Laurie and Tracy weren't lying around the house expecting to be waited on hand and foot. Those days are gone forever.'

'Laurie seemed so tired when she first arrived,' Vera said lovingly. 'But pre-meds are all so worried about their grades. She said there are about forty or fifty thousand pre-med students applying each year for maybe twelve thousand places in medical schools. She lives in terror of being rejected.'

'She's bright. She'll make it.' Doris nodded with conviction.

'She frets that so much time is spent on studying subjects that she says have nothing to do with becoming a doctor. Why are the young always in such a rush?'

Doris chuckled. 'Honey, we were no different.'

'At eighteen I was worried about survival.' Vera was blunt. She paused for a moment. 'That's what David said,' she recalled uneasily. 'If he gets drafted, how does he know he'll make it home again?'

'WWII was a war that had to be fought.' Doris was suddenly serious. 'If anyone knows that, you do. This is a whole different ball game. It's –'

'You sound like Paul,' Vera reproached. Remembering Paul's passionate accusations to his father and herself last night while they were listening to the news. *Let's face facts. The Vietnam war is being fought because of economics. The United States wants to have a stake in Vietnam's rubber plantations, its rice fields, its timber. And the people over there are happy to work for almost nothing. They make designer jeans, TV parts – a long list of things. This war is being fought to make a few Americans richer. It's not going to help the poor or the middle class.*

'Paul and Phil are both sure we're going to see the draft numbers soar in the months ahead,' Doris said. 'The word is that we'll be shipping out a lot of troops.'

'Adele is upset that so many of the kids being drafted are poor blacks.' More and more these last weeks – though she admitted this to no one – Vera was torn between support of the fight to stop the spread of Communism in Southeast Asia and trepidation about the possible loss of American lives in the months ahead. 'And Tracy, of course, is nervous that David will drop out of school and lose his deferment.'

'I'm just grateful that Phil is too old and Neal is too young to be drafted.' But now Doris's face exuded distaste. 'If Wayne were alive, he'd be debating about which side – North or South Vietnam – to try to sell arms to. He'd have been in his glory.'

Vera was unnerved when – in February – President Johnson announced a major escalation of American participation in the Vietnam war. With Paul and Joel she listened to the news on television. The implication was that there would be sustained bombing of North Vietnam.

'We can't let the Communists take over all of Asia,'

Joel said with conviction. 'That's a major threat to the world.'

'Dad, we have no business in Vietnam,' Paul objected. 'We –'

'Paul, we must be concerned about the rest of the world,' Vera broke in urgently. 'If someone had intervened in Germany when Hitler began his rampage, think how many lives would have been saved.' *Papa and Mama and Ernst*, she thought in fresh anguish.

'It's not the Communists who're infiltrating South Vietnam that are causing the problems,' Paul said. 'The workers and the peasants want to rid themselves of vile dictators who rule their lives. It's a civil war – with the South Vietnamese wanting peace and self-determination. We're supporting the wrong people. Remember when Laurie wrote us about Mademoiselle Nhu's visit to Columbia – and how 300 students booed her?' Vera recalled that Mademoiselle Nhu was the wife of the head of the South Vietnamese secret police and sister-in-law of President Diem. 'This is the woman who made a joke of the Buddhist monks and their self-immolation in protest of religious persecution. She referred to these protests as barbecues!'

'Yesterday two of the workers at the factory told me their sons were being drafted,' Vera said softly. 'One's nineteen, the other twenty. It's awful to realize they could die in Vietnam.'

'Don't be so pessimistic,' Joel ordered. 'We send in our forces, this stupid war will be over in six months. Johnson's absolutely right in what he's doing.'

But Vera was beginning to question the validity of this war. Why were we supporting dictators? The reasons to fight in World War II had been so clear-cut. So necessary. It was a war that had to be fought. Why were they supporting unpopular dictators?

Each month 17,000 Americans were being drafted. Where would it end? She thought of David, whom Tracy loved. *Would he become a Vietnam casualty*?

Chapter Thirty-one

Vera struggled to avoid discussion of Vietnam in Joel's presence. She exhorted Paul to refrain from wrangling with his father when Joel praised LBJ's decision to ship 3500 marines to Vietnam early in March.

'We have to prevent the spread of Communism,' Joel repeated endlessly. 'We're the only major power other than Russia. It's our responsibility to keep the world free from dictatorships like Russia's. That's what Communism is – a dictatorship!'

Johnson's escalation of US participation in the Vietnam war accelerated protest demonstrations on campuses around the country. With Laurie and Tracy home for spring vacation, Vera lived in constant tension – ever watchful for volatile outbreaks between Joel and his granddaughters. David – often underfoot – was put on warning, also. But Joel was unexpectedly subdued when the news media told the world that a US spokesman in Saigon had confirmed an ugly rumour. Yes, South Vietnamese forces were using tear gas.

'That's unconscionable!' he raged after watching the evening news on television. 'You'll see – Congress will censure them for that. When something is wrong, I'll be the first to admit it. But these demonstrations on college campuses –' He clucked in disapproval, gazed grimly from Laurie to Tracy. 'They're just a handful of students.'

'But they have the *right* to speak,' Laurie picked up. 'Out at some college in Ohio, the campus police just stood by doing nothing when about 150 right-wing students ploughed into a handful of demonstrators, grabbed and burned their signs, then kicked them.'

'That was at Kent State,' Tracy nodded indignantly. 'David said, "What else can you expect in a conservative town?"'

Most people in this country, Vera surmised, were confused about the war. Like herself. *Was the government behaving immorally*? Or was it determined to assume its responsibilities – not only to its own people but the rest of the world as well?

She watched her father-in-law's bewilderment and pain with compassion. He saw his son and his grandchildren rebelling against what he considered cherished values – the belief that their country could do no wrong. Doris and Phil were careful to conceal their own fears that US involvement in the Vietnam war was wrong, she thought gratefully. Dad was seventy-three years old – and suddenly his deep-rooted beliefs of a lifetime were being challenged.

The uproar from Congressmen in reaction to the report of the use of tear gas by the South Vietnamese forces blended with the rage of many Americans over what was happening right at home – in Alabama. What had been planned as a four-day peaceful civil rights march from Selma, Alabama, to Montgomery – fifty miles away – erupted in violence when, on Sunday, March 6, Governor Wallace ordered the highway patrol to stop the marchers. State trooper cars lined the roadside. When the marchers did not agree to disperse within two minutes, troopers ploughed into the group with bullwhips and rubber tubing wrapped in barbed wire. Tear gas filled the air.

Vera and Paul witnessed the happening when the Sunday-evening movie they were watching – *Judgement at Nuremberg* – was interrupted so that ABC Television could provide a shocking film clip of what was happening in Selma. On Monday morning, the front pages of the newspapers across the country carried the story and graphic photographs of Selma's 'bloody Sunday.' Protest demonstrations took place from coast to coast. In Toronto, Canada, 2,000 people demonstrated.

'Johnson will come forward and submit a strong new voting-rights bill,' Paul predicted. 'Wait and see.'

Laurie reported that she would not be going down South this summer. She wanted to go to summer school in order to carry a light load in her senior year. 'I need to keep my grades up.' As always, she was anxious about being accepted at medical school.

'I don't know why she worries all the time,' Vera confided to Doris – trying to ignore her own anxieties. 'We know how bright she is.'

'Let's face it, Vera – there're a limited number of places in the medical schools.' Doris was realistic. 'And being a woman won't be an asset.'

'I'll feel better knowing that she's in school rather than chasing around down South with that voter-registration team,' Vera admitted. 'I don't think the summer classes will erupt into the *teach-ins* we're seeing everywhere now.'

Across the country, faculty members – usually the younger ones – were joining with students to protest the American intervention in Vietnam. The word had spread from campus to campus. The teach-ins – in the hundreds and held at night so as not to interfere with regular classes – often ran from 8:00 PM to 8:00 AM. It was a crusade to spread the word that the United States was fighting a war they were convinced was immoral.

'We have to spread the truth about why we're there!' Laurie said defensively when her grandfather made a pithy remark about 'these crazy students acting up on the campuses.' Later, she reported with triumph that the ‘teach-in’ at Columbia – Barnard was its sister college – had brought out over 2,500 students.

Paul said it was always at the elite schools that these rebellions began, Vera thought on this spring morning that seemed reluctant to discard winter cold. They’d listened to the radio news at breakfast about the latest incident. In a surge of restlessness – her mind reluctant to focus on business – she decided to go out for an early lunch. She reached for her black coat, fake fur-trimmed knitted hat, and purse. Checked that her gloves were in her coat pocket. Now she headed out of her office and down the hall to the front door.

‘How’s your grandson down in New York doing?’ She paused to chat for a moment with their janitor. Elijah had come to work for the company almost twenty years ago after being stranded in town when his car broke down. Widowed, he had three daughters and several granddaughters living in Harlem – and one grandson, who was his pride and joy.

‘Oh, he’s gonna be fine, Miss Vera.’ Elijah radiated pride. ‘He’s joined the army. He ain’t waitin’ to be drafted.’ All at once his face was solemn. ‘Best thing in the world for that boy to go into the army, gettin’ away from bad friends in that project where he lives. The army’ll make a man out of him.’

Not much was said in this town about the war in Vietnam, Vera reflected. People watched the television news, of course; but it was as though here in Eastwood they lived in another world. They were observers, Vera determined, watching the world go round. Only a handful extended their personal involvement beyond Eastwood.

Now and then you heard about a boy being drafted. Then it became personal. In her mind she heard Laurie’s frequently repeated taunt: *Not college students. They don’t worry about the draft*!

The chill outdoors was reminiscent of dead winter rather than spring, Vera thought, tugging at the collar of her coat. Then, drawing her knitted hat more closely about her head, she walked swiftly to the pleasant small café where she lunched regularly.

'You're early today.' Mary O'Brien's plain face lit up with a bright smile as Vera slid into a chair at her usual table. 'I'll get your cup of tea while you decide.' For Vera the Blue Lantern stocked Earl Grey teabags. Since the years in London, Vera had been addicted to Earl Grey.

She debated about the 'specials' with Mary, chose the split-pea soup and a small salad. Now she relaxed, sipped her tea, and waited for her luncheon to be served.

'I love that hat.' Breaking into her introspection, Mary placed a bowl of steaming split-pea soup before Vera.

'Thank you.' Vera smiled at her long-time waitress. Mary had been here for over fourteen years, she thought. Ever since her little boy – her only child – was old enough to be in school full-time. That was when her husband had walked out on her for a teenage sexpot. But Mary had rallied, found this job, devoted herself to raising her son.

'I got a hat almost like it over in Saratoga.' Mary's eyes were wistful as she gazed at Vera's near-perfect features, highlighted by the hat. 'I hope it looks as good on me as it does on you.'

'I'm sure it does,' Vera encouraged. A tiny white lie.

'I used to think that if I were pretty, my life would be wonderful. Then I understood that even beautiful movie stars weren't always happy. Oh, I didn't tell you my news.' Mary glowed. 'My boy Jimmy is going into the service this week. I'll miss him something awful, but he promises he'll write every chance he gets. I don't have to tell you how proud I am of him.'

Elijah's grandson had enlisted. Mary was sending her

son Jimmy – who'd gone to school with Tracy – off to Vietnam. Both so proud of them. Would *she* feel that way if she had a son? She'd thought she'd seen the end of war when she came to live in Eastwood, Vera remembered with an odd ache. Would the world ever exist in total peace? Paul's dream. Was that all it was ever to be? A dream?

It seemed to Vera that the teach-ins – and Tracy and David were enthusiastic about these – had brought a new closeness between Laurie and Tracy.

'Of course, they've always been close,' Vera said to Doris on a steamy July Sunday afternoon while the two women relaxed in the Kahns' air-conditioned den. Paul and Phil, along with little Neal, had gone off to watch a local baseball game. Joel was at a committee meeting of the Eastwood Chamber of Commerce. 'But there's something new there now.' Why did she feel that that new closeness made her an outsider? Ridiculous, she reproached herself.

'This is a generation like none other,' Doris mused. 'But I'm proud of them.'

'I can't believe that next year this time Laurie'll have her degree – and be on her way to med school.' Vera held up crossed fingers. 'I'm so happy that she knows what she wants to do with her life – but I wish she'd feel less harried all the time.'

'You wish she'd find time for a social life,' Doris said. 'Give her time, Vera. She's so young.'

Laurie came home from summer school for two weeks before returning to campus for the new school year. Adele – who'd spent the summer working in New York with a Harlem youth group – came with her. Much of the talk revolved around the recent riots in Watts, a low-income black community in Los Angeles. Lasting from August

11–16 the riots resulted in 35 deaths – all black – and hundreds of injuries, plus $200,000,000 in damages. It was carnage that had been watched around the world on TV.

'Watts is only the beginning,' Adele warned. 'Not just in Watts, but wherever blacks live in ghetto conditions. I look around Harlem and I'm scared of what's to come. I look at my own family – what exists of family,' she added caustically. 'Maybe in the South there are jobs for blacks, but not in big-city ghettos. And without jobs, there're no families. Mom was smart – and lucky. She got the two of us out of the inner city.'

'Your mom was a wonderful woman,' Laurie said with love.

'But look at my cousins – and their kids.' Adele pantomimed despair. 'For two generations now – all illegitimate. No fathers at home. They have no hope. Without hope, people have nothing.'

'The situation must change,' Vera said with determined optimism. 'Johnson vows to make changes.'

'This is a terrible time for the civil rights movement.' Adele's eyes reflected her inner desolation. 'When Martin Luther King went out to Watts to help calm things, the people there told him to go home – they didn't want his dreams. They want decent housing, jobs. The people in power out in California don't understand! And it's not much different in New York.'

'I think the whole world was shocked by what happened at Watts.' Vera flinched, recalling the nights of watching via television as a chunk of Los Angeles became a panorama of burning, looting, beatings, and killings. And each night her mind rushed back to the horror of *Kristallnacht* in Berlin, almost twenty-seven years ago. But this wasn't fanatical Nazis out for genocide. These were desperate people pushed beyond their limits.

Then once again Laurie and Tracy were off to school. Early in the new school year Paul reported that – as in suburban schools – students in the local schools were voicing dissatisfaction. A new, unexpected experience in the Eastwood school system.

'These kids are demanding more of some of the teachers – and by God, they have every right to,' Paul told Vera in the privacy of their bedroom. His father considered such talk disloyal to the town. 'Sherman and Logan give their students nothing – and the kids know it. But Franklin won't hear a word against them!'

'If they'd raise teacher salaries, they'd get more competent people,' Vera said bluntly.

'But nobody wants to raise taxes,' Paul countered. 'And it's not just the money. I was talking with Ted about it last night.' He grinned. 'The girls aren't tying up the phone for hours now – it's me. There's a lot of rebellion in high schools around the country from what I'm reading. Our standards are dropping so low, a lot of us are ashamed to be teaching. In our high school, Vera! The quality goes from excellent to disgustingly low. We've expanded our school population by twenty per cent in the last ten years, but we haven't added another classroom. And this is happening all over the country.'

'It would be helpful if Franklin weren't such an ass,' Vera sympathized.

'The bastard takes policy-making upon himself.' Paul grunted in frustration. 'That's not his job. The school board is supposed to make policy; the superintendent is supposed to administer. We don't have a superintendent of schools, so principals are supposedly administering. But damn it, they're not supposed to make policy.'

'Paul, why doesn't a group of teachers approach the school board and demand changes?'

'Because our principals have the school board in their

back pockets!' Paul exploded. *Why couldn't he talk with this fervour to the board*? 'Several PTA members tried to talk to Franklin. They got nowhere. All he cares about is that the teaching staff follow the lesson plans he approves. He doesn't give a shit how much the kids learn.'

'With this much foment, there has to be some action soon,' Vera said. If the girls were still in the Eastwood schools, she'd get out there and fight, she told herself impatiently. Once Neal was in school, Doris would fight. Doris's voice might have some value, she thought cynically. Doris *was* old family. Vera had just married into old family. After almost twenty years in Eastwood, she was still an outsider.

'The old-timers don't realize that a new breed of teachers is coming into the system. One that recognizes the problems and is ready to take them on. But dissenting voices have to grow louder.' Paul's anger seemed to have dissipated. 'We can't stay in a rut. We have to move ahead. Our time is coming, Vera.' A fresh hope welled in his eyes. 'It's destined.'

In the weeks ahead, Vera fought to break down the wall of gloom that threatened to enclose her. In her phone conversations with Laurie, she was ever-conscious of Laurie's anxiety about keeping up her grades this last year at college – and about medical school. Phone calls with Tracy revealed Tracy's anxieties about David's dropping out of school – exposing himself to the draft.

This was such a troubled time, she thought tiredly. The country was being torn apart by the battles over civil rights and by the anti-war movement. She was drained by constantly striving to avoid conflicts between Paul and his father over the escalating Vietnam war. And next week, the girls would be home for the long Thanksgiving weekend. She'd have to tell them not to bait their grandfather about Vietnam.

In a need to pull herself out of this mood of depression, Vera forced herself to focus on business. Here was a challenge she always welcomed. She'd thought much in the past months about expanding their mail-order business from a regional to national orientation. It was a major step – and Dad would balk at first, she warned herself. Yet he did trust her instincts.

They wouldn't be trying to compete with Sears Roebuck or Montgomery Ward, she rationalized. They'd sell sporting goods and sportswear, just as with their regional catalogue. They'd stress the service angle – every customer must be satisfied or the merchandise could be returned. And part of the deal, she decided with growing enthusiasm, would be to make the Eastwood shop the centrepiece of the mail-order business.

On a crisp, sunny morning she approached Joel on this expansion. As anticipated, he was uneasy.

'Vera, on a national basis? That'll cost a fortune!'

'We're standing still now,' she pointed out. 'It's time to move ahead. We can –'

'We can lose our shirts,' he broke in and Vera sensed he was unnerved.

'We offer smart merchandise at a sensible price,' she continued. 'With Doris and Phil handling the buying.' There, *that* pleased Dad. They'd be involving Doris as a buyer. Family. 'They have a knack for knowing what sells in the shop.'

'That's Eastwood,' he said warily.

'That's Middle America,' she corrected. 'Attractive but conservative styles. Merchandise that'll be good two years from now as well as today. If I had a crystal ball, I'd see mail-order catalogues growing into a tremendous business – and I don't mean just Sears Roebuck.'

'Let's think about it,' Joel hedged. 'That's big bucks. We'll talk more tonight.'

Joel was humming when he left her office, Vera noted. An unfailing sign that he was pleased by her latest direction for the business. He'd go along with the expansion.

On this Wednesday before Thanksgiving – with Laurie and Tracy due home late in the evening for the long weekend – Vera and Doris conferred in the den about the holiday dinner, determining what items on the menu Doris would bring, what Vera would prepare here at the house.

'David'll be having Thanksgiving dinner here with us,' Vera told Doris.

'So what else is new?' But Doris's chuckle was warm with affection.

'He'll leave around seven to meet his parents. They're going out to some swanky restaurant in Saratoga for the big dinner.' Vera's voice reeked with contempt.

'It always surprises me that restaurants are open on Thanksgiving Day.' Doris squinted in contemplation. 'It always seemed to me a holiday to celebrate at home.'

Both women tensed in alertness at the sound of a car driving up before the house. Paul had driven over to the Saratoga railroad station to pick up Laurie. *They couldn't be home yet*, Vera thought. And Tracy and David weren't due until late in the evening.

'It could be Phil.' Doris rose to her feet. 'I called the shop to tell him I was coming over here before dinner – and that we'd be eating a little late tonight.'

They heard the front door open and close.

'Vera?' Joel's voice was agitated. 'You home yet?'

'In the den, Dad.' Vera exchanged an anxious glance with Doris.

A moment later Joel appeared in the door. His face was drained of colour.

'Dad, what's happened?' Doris demanded.

He took a deep breath. 'You know Mary O'Brien, the waitress at the Blue Lantern?' *Everybody in Eastwood knew Mary.*

'What about Mary?' Vera's voice was sharp with anxiety.

'She just received word from the War Department. Her son Jim was killed in Vietnam.'

Vera stood immobile, frozen in shock. She remembered Jimmy as a shy, towheaded five-year-old, then an awkward, scrupulously polite teenager. She remembered him at high school graduation – self-conscious in his first real suit. He and Tracy had graduated the same year. He'd been in Paul's class. Dad had swung a job for Jimmy at the supermarket after graduation.

The Vietnam war had come home to them, she thought in anguish. All at once it was a personal war. An Eastwood boy had given his life.

This wasn't as it had been in World War II, she thought in sudden, dizzying comprehension. Mary O'Brien's only child had died in a war they barely understood. Why were American boys fighting in Vietnam? For whom? *How many more Americans would die before the war was over?*

Chapter Thirty-two

By late spring, Vera was caught up in Laurie's imminent graduation from Barnard. *How pleased Papa would have been*, she thought nostalgically. *And Mama*. Laurie would enter medical school in September – as Ernst had yearned to do.

Laurie's future monopolized her grandfather's conversation to the point where longtime friends were beginning to tease him about 'your granddaughter the doctor.' He'd never ceased being disappointed that Paul would not follow him in the business, Vera realized – though he found pleasure in Doris and Phil's activity in the expanding mail-order catalogue division, which was attracting national admiration.

With growing frequency Vera mused, *it was the business that saved her sanity*. She could escape problems at home by throwing herself into work. Kahn's Country Store – which Joel heralded as her creation – was becoming an institution, she acknowledged. Even a tourist attraction. Emphasizing women's wear had brought about major success.

She hadn't discussed it yet with Dad, but the next step was to open half-a-dozen stores around the country – all replicas of the one here. Phil was smart about building a recognizable image. He pointed out the importance of advertising, promotion. 'Hey, the shop's great – but you have to let the world know it's here.'

Though she was delighted when the girls came home for their spring break, this year Vera was oddly relieved when the vacation was over. Not because she didn't adore having Laurie and Tracy home, she acknowledged, but because she was upset over the soaring friction arising between her father-in-law and David, who was constantly underfoot when Tracy was home.

Tracy worried that David would be drafted. Especially now when he was letting his grades slide. In February, General Hershey told the local draft boards they could call up college students who fell in the lower-grades group. Also, a national exam would check on grades and general intelligence – and this, too, would be given over to the draft boards.

'Young people are going nuts these days,' Joel grumbled, settling himself in the den to watch TV with Vera and Paul on this first evening after the girls' return to school. 'And that David!' He grunted in disgust. 'All this crap about maybe burning his draft card. Kids like that ought to be thrown in jail! I don't know why Tracy lets him hang around her.'

'David makes a lot of noise,' Paul said evasively. 'So many of the kids do.' He didn't want to start up again with Dad, Vera understood.

'Not a lot of the kids,' Joel rejected grimly. 'It's always the same ones. A few rotten eggs make a lot of noise –' he pounced on Paul's choice of words. '– and suddenly they're the majority. I read the newspapers. The Gallup polls say that 72% of all students don't get involved in those crazy demonstrations.'

'But they're sympathetic. And every week more students are becoming involved. Look back in history, Dad,' Paul pleaded. 'How many colonists were crying out for independence in 1776? But the word spread and it became a mass outcry.'

'What would have happened in World War II?' Joel challenged, 'if our boys had reacted like these screwballs?

This country would have been overrun by the Nazis! We would have died in concentration camps.'

'Even in the late '30s college students were rejecting the draft,' Paul countered. 'That went out the window when they saw what the world was up against, but this war makes no sense!'

'Dad, why don't you go down to New York with Doris next week when she has that shooting for the Christmas catalogue?' Vera intervened, anxious to redirect the conversation. 'Maybe take her and Laurie out for dinner and to a play.'

Joel shook his head, grimaced in distaste.

'I don't like the city anymore. It was different years ago, when Paul was in college.' He exchanged a nostalgic smile with Paul. 'I'd be in New York on a business trip, and he'd come down from Columbia and we'd go for an Italian dinner in Greenwich Village and maybe see a play at that little Provincetown Playhouse. It wasn't exactly Broadway –'

'It was fun, Dad,' Paul agreed gently.

'But now, what I hear about Greenwich Village – it's a different world. Kids smoking marijuana, tripping, freaking out,' Joel said scornfully. 'LSD takes them to heaven.'

'Dad, where did you pick up that lingo?' Paul joshed.

'I read the *New York Times Magazine*, the national magazines,' Joel said with contempt. 'The whole world's going berserk.'

'We're all going down to New York for Laurie's graduation,' Vera declared. 'The three of us and Doris and Phil. Tracy'll be out of classes by then. She'll take care of Neal. You know Neal adores her.'

'And David will be there with Tracy,' Joel guessed. 'He's bad for her. He fills her head with nutty ideas. And that hair!' He snorted. 'Don't these kids ever go to a barber?'

'It's a phase,' Paul began cautiously. 'Every generation rebels.'

'My generation didn't run around with our hair hanging down our backs and dressed like slobs,' Joel shot back. 'We didn't talk about refusing to fight for our country. Your generation didn't do that.'

'Dad, I'm going to make reservations for us all at the Plaza,' Vera said, desperate to avoid another scene about David. 'We'll –'

'The Plaza?' Joel lifted an eyebrow. 'You're talking fancy money.' Then all at once he was grinning. 'But we can afford it. Sometimes I forget how well we're doing. Maybe you walked out on the business, Paul, but you brought the family the best thing that ever happened to it. Vera, you've got the business head I expected from Paul.'

On the sunny Thursday afternoon of June 2, the Kahn clan was part of the 12,000 spectators in the outdoor amphitheatre created by Low Memorial Library and adjacent structures at Columbia. Paul reached for Vera's hand while they watched the huge procession of blue-robed figures file to their seats. The music was 'March of the Earl of Oxford' by the sixteenth-century English composer, William Byrd.

'I'm so impressed,' Vera whispered, tears blurring her vision as 6,832 students prepared to receive a variety of degrees. 'I wish Papa and Mama could be here today! They'd be so proud.' For Papa, education had been supremely important. He'd given his life to continue teaching in Berlin. *Paul was so like him*, she thought, washed in tenderness.

Vera heard little of the speeches that followed. Her mind hurtled back in time to her last days in Berlin. The constant humiliations, the deprivations, the foreboding fears that became a reality. Papa would be sad that she had not gone on to college – but his granddaughters would have the degrees she wasn't able to acquire. She remembered the catty remarks of one of the faculty wives at a dinner party last week. 'Vera, I think it's amazing that you've gone so far without a college education.'

She was the only faculty wife in their group without a degree. This inescapable fact was constantly tossed at her. And she was the only one who held down a full-time job. The other faculty wives took care of their houses and children, did volunteer work. Only one – Dolores Aiken – complained about being bored with her existence. 'Damn it, Vera – that Friedan woman is so right. Women live in bondage.'

Many of these young women here, she told herself with satisfaction, would not settle for being housewives and mothers. They looked forward to careers. In Eastwood – in their small-town, middle-class world – she was an oddity. But times were changing. Women, too, were rebelling.

Paul didn't resent her working. Did he resent her earning a salary so much larger than his own? Their pay cheques went into a joint checking or savings account, along with the substantial bonuses that Dad insisted on giving her each year. The money question – who earned how much – never bothered Paul. *Or did it?*

Dolores complained regularly about being strapped for money, but she said Lance would be upset if she tried for a career. 'I might be able to do it in a large city, but not here in Eastwood. His precious masculinity would sag to the floor. His professional pride would suffer. But I can't refurnish my living room with his professional pride.'

'It's getting cloudy,' Paul whispered, banishing her introspection. 'I hope it doesn't start to rain before the exercises are over.'

As the exercises drew to a close at four-thirty, the sky became an ominous grey. As the blue-robed figures began the recessional, the first droplets of rain began to fall. Despite this, the crowd seemed to enjoy these final moments.

They'd go back to the Plaza and relax awhile, Vera planned. Then they'd drive down to Ratner's on Second Avenue for dinner. Dad had unexpectedly expressed an interest in a 'real Jewish meal.'

When I was a little boy, my father would sometimes take my mother and me to New York with him on buying trips – and we'd always go down to Ratner's on Second Avenue for dinner.

But the segment of Second Avenue to which Dad referred was no longer the Lower East Side. It had been reborn as the East Village, a special haven of the young. Laurie wrote about going down to the East Village to see Off-Broadway plays. Not in the grand, elegant playhouses where Dad as a small boy had seen the Yiddish stars of the early years of the century, but in tiny playhouses with primitive stages or simply a small 'playing area.'

Vera felt wrapped in warmth this evening as the family lingered over a sumptuous dinner that Doris warned would collectively add twenty pounds to their group. *Dad was in such high spirits*, she thought with pleasure. So often these days he seemed simultaneously bewildered, hurt, and distraught by the changes that coloured this decade.

Through the years, she'd nurtured a passionate obsession to hold the family together. She watched as so many of the young in Eastwood moved away from their families to distant places to come together perhaps once or twice a year. Of course, Laurie and Tracy were away at school now, but that was a temporary situation. She couldn't bear to envision a future where they lived in distant cities.

Unrealistic, yes, her mind rebuked – but this was her *family*, her *life*.

Thus far Dad had been able to block out – most of the time – the knowledge that Paul was an outspoken pacifist. *Pacifist*, he would partially accept, Vera interpreted. The anti-war movement, he abhorred. What had happened to patriotism, loyalty to one's country?

She worried about the hostility that broke out at disturbing moments between her father-in-law and Tracy – which had its roots in Tracy's closeness to David. Sometimes she feared that he would ban David from the house. How would she cope with that situation?

She worried, too, that Paul would – in an unwary moment – admit to his father that he was helping to organize a small, Albany-based We Won't Go group similar to several others being formed around the country. She didn't want to think how Dad would react to that.

Doris and Phil were smart. They didn't let on to Dad that they were harbouring doubts about the country's involvement in Vietnam. But what was most upsetting to her was that *she didn't honestly know how she felt about the war*.

Why did she keep vacillating? She listened to Paul and began to ask herself why American boys were fighting – and dying – in a tiny country halfway around the world. But then she remembered Hitler in Germany. How many lives would have been saved if this country had come in earlier to help stop his mad rampage?

She was haunted by the fear that what was happening in Vietnam would tear her family apart before it was over.

After two weeks at home, Laurie left to work with Adele for the summer on a Harlem youth programme. In September, Adele would teach at a private, experimental school in Harlem. She and Laurie would continue to share an apartment. Vera tried to close her mind to suspicions that the two girls would also be working in the New York City anti-war movement.

As usual, Paul would teach in summer school, but two nights a week he'd drive to Albany for meetings with the grassroots We Won't Go group. She was ever-fearful that his father would learn of this activity. Nor would it set well, she surmised, with Clark Franklin. Tracy had prodded David into joining her for a light summer session at school – her intent, to raise his grades and keep him out of the draft.

Paul carried around in his wallet an article Adele had given him from the *New York Times* that pleaded for public schooling for four-year-olds. '*It doesn't mean trying to push teaching ahead, it's to prepare all those kids who're not ready for the first grade*,' Adele wrote. Paul was enthusiastic about this, though realistically he saw little chance of its occurring on any impressive scale. Now Doris was running into serious financial problems in keeping her long-established three-to-four-year-old morning group in operation.

Vera struggled to bury herself in work. She was unnerved by reports from Vietnam, film footage shown on TV where US marines were torching peasant huts. She was uneasy when, late in the summer, Tracy and David drove up to Canada – presumably for a visit.

'What do you mean, Tracy's driving with David for a vacation in Quebec City?' Joel demanded in outrage. 'Are they married and we don't know about it?'

'Dad, you know how casual young people are today,' Vera soothed. 'They're going with a group,' she improvised. She didn't want to remember that Canada was becoming an escape hatch for draft-evaders. *But David hadn't been called up.*

In New York, Laurie rejoiced in her first year of med school. At last she was involved in subjects that were relevant to her future as a doctor. She knew even before her first class that anatomy would be rugged. 'You won't believe the memorization that's required,' she confessed to Adele at the end of her first month. But still, she revelled in being there.

Banished was her involvement in the Harlem youth group, the anti-war movement. School and study devoured every waking moment. Even when she went home for the long Thanksgiving weekend, she spent much of the time holed up in her room with textbooks.

'The first two years are all pre-clinical stuff,' she explained to Tracy on this weekend. 'Everything's in lecture halls and the labs. Just once in a while – the way I hear it – will we actually get into the hospital and make contact with doctors and patients.'

'I don't know what I want to do with my life.' Tracy sighed. 'I settled for an English major because that's what David chose. His parents are still screaming that he has to go to law school. They'd better be happy if he just stays in college long enough to get his BA.' She squinted inquisitively at Laurie. 'What about your social life?'

'Who has time for a social life?' Laurie countered. 'We're in class eight hours a day, five days a week. We're swamped with learning.'

To Tracy's astonishment, David said he wouldn't be able to have Thanksgiving dinner with her family.

'My folks got this crazy idea we should have Thanksgiving dinner together this year. At a restaurant, of course,' he drawled sarcastically. 'But I'll come over in the evening for pecan pie.'

The moment David walked into the house Tracy knew he was upset. She fretted while he exchanged small talk with her mother in the kitchen – over a huge slab of pie.

'I ate like a pig,' she announced impatiently. 'Let's go for a walk.'

'Let him finish his pie,' her mother scolded.

'What's bugging you?' she demanded as the front door to the house closed behind them.

'You won't believe what my parents have cooked up,' he warned.

'I'll believe it. Tell me.'

'They've worked some deal where I'll be like an exchange student – going to school in London for the next semester. *London, England*,' he emphasized grimly.

'David, that's so exciting!' Tracy's mind was conjuring up fascinating images.

'The school over there is on the trimester system. I have to leave right after Christmas and stay there until some time in July! I'll be earning two semesters under their system – and the school here will give me full credit. It took some manoeuvring, but my old man managed it.' He sighed. 'How do I get out of it?'

'You don't want to get out of it!' Tracy churned with anticipation. 'We have to fix it for me to go, too!'

'How?' David was intrigued by this prospect.

'I'll work on my folks,' she plotted.

'How?' David asked again, uneasy about the outcome.

'You know Mom and Dad – they're softies. I'll cry about how the two of them and Laurie have all been out of the country but I've never been anywhere except Canada – and Bermuda – and that's right here. It'll work.' She nodded confidently. 'You find out everything you can about how it was set up. The junior year is not exactly the time to be an exchange student,' she conceded, 'but I'd love it. My mother lived in London for a while. That's where she met my father. Laurie was born in London. Oh, David, it would be so cool!'

Tracy had expected it would be her father – always sentimental about London – who would help push through the arrangements for her to go to the college at the edge of London – where David, too, would be a student. But it was her mother who went all out to ensure that she could go, even though the new semester was so close at hand. Mom worried about the way Grandpa hit on David all the time, she surmised. Mom figured it would be helpful to have David out of sight for a while.

On schedule – two days before New Year's Day, 1967 – Tracy and David flew to London. Tracy was rapturous at the prospect of spending almost seven months in London. Mom was scared to death she'd get homesick, but that wouldn't happen. Besides, she'd take any bet that Mom would be over in London to visit before three months had passed.

'Call home once or twice a month,' her mother had ordered in the last moment of farewells. 'Collect.'

'Is there any other way?' Tracy'd bubbled.

On the overnight flight Tracy dozed, her head on David's shoulder. In these last couple of weeks, it seemed to her, David had grown up. All of a sudden it was David who was making decisions. During the spring break, they'd travel around Europe. Students travelled cheap, he insisted. They'd save their allowances, maybe even find jobs that didn't require work permits.

They'd send reports to the student newspaper about what was happening on campuses in Europe, David had decided. She'd sensed a new respect for David in her father's long conversations with him about the months ahead. Dad was so concerned about the quality of education – not only here at home but around the world. While the plane – wrapped in darkness – made its way across the Atlantic, she replayed in her mind scraps of talk with him about student rebellions.

'So many people here at home seem to consider it an American experience. It's happening all over the world. Italy, Germany, Sweden, Russia, Spain, Belgium, Japan, Formosa, Poland, Hungary, Czechoslovakia. I read somewhere that students have demonstrated even in Tanzania.'

Because David was with her, Tracy acknowledged to herself, she felt no fear about attending a school in a strange country, where she knew no one, living in a dorm where everybody knew one another except for herself. She felt an unexpected surge of sentiment at being here where her mother had lived in such trying times. Mom had been younger than she, had had to work to support herself.

Hand in hand with David she explored London. It wasn't the war-desecrated London Mom had known, she told herself while she and David stood before landmarks that she'd heard her parents describe in nostalgic detail. She wrote home with enthusiasm about how at London colleges students didn't encounter the heavy studying – except for exams – that American college students knew.

'Oh sure, we put in a lot of time studying and working – but it's not the classroom scene like at home. We go to some lectures but mainly tutorials with professors, one on one. David is just blossoming here.'

Late in February, Tracy received a letter from her mother.

'What did I tell you, David? Mom's coming here!' Presumably on business. *Just for a few days but it gives me a chance to see you.*

'Why didn't Dad come with you?' Tracy demanded when she and David met her mother at Heathrow. 'Doesn't he want to see London again? I mean, it was so important to your lives.' Belatedly, she remembered that Dad said Mom had a thing about going to London. But she'd gotten over the hang-up to come to see her, Tracy thought affectionately.

'I wanted him to come.' Vera's eyes were oddly wary. *This was traumatic for Mom – coming back to London*, Tracy thought compassionately. *Dad should be with her*. 'But he said he'd feel guilty if he took eight days off from his counselling group.'

It seemed to Tracy that her mother had barely arrived when they headed with her for Heathrow. She hadn't expected to feel this awful loneliness when Mom went home, she realized in astonishment.

'Have fun during your spring vacation,' her mother said tenderly. 'You can cover a lot of territory in three weeks.' Earlier she'd handed over a wad of cash to be transformed into traveller's cheques.

'I'll phone the Munches when we're in Copenhagen,' Tracy promised. It was so sweet, she thought, the way Mom exchanged letters two or three times a year with the family that had taken her in when she had had to run from Berlin. 'You'll write and tell them I'll call?'

'I'll write,' her mother promised.

But Tracy and David found their anticipation of travel in Europe eclipsed now by the escalation of the student movement at the London School of Economics. They knew that for months there had been dissension between students and administration at LSE. Students – some of the brightest in Great Britain – had been demanding a more democratic and free university.

Tracy and David had observed some earlier – milder – skirmishes where LSE students had paraded with banners that read: Berkeley, 1966; LSE, 1967 – We'll Bring This School to a Halt, Too. Some, Tracy recalled, had even gone on a hunger strike. Dad had told them that student rebellion was not an American phenomenon, Tracy remembered – but seeing this made his words real. They heard that one of the leaders of the student movement was an American graduate student from Denver named Marshall Bloom. There were 324 Americans at LSE.

On Monday, March 13, Tracy and David met her roommate – an ebullient student-activist named Audrey Sims – at a Lyons cafeteria for a cheap dinner before going to a Students' Union meeting.

'It's true!' Audrey told the other two when they'd settled themselves at a corner table. 'Students at LSE are sitting-in! It's a round-the-clock deal. In the main entrance hall – with a banner that says: Beware the Pedagogic Gerontocracy.'

'I thought LSE was supposed to be such a liberal school.' David was sombre. 'Why did they suspend Bloom and Adelstein for the rest of the school year just because they wanted to discuss university appointments?' Adelstein was president of the Students' Union.

Now their lives revolved around the sit-in at LSE. By Wednesday evening, 104 students had been suspended. The demonstrators were, in fact, in control of the university – though this was not their goal. They wanted a more democratic university.

At other schools sentiment ran high for a show of support. On Friday, March 17, 3,000 students marched through the City of London and the West End – Tracy and David among them. Students from Manchester, Leeds, Cambridge, and other schools joined forces – wearing yellow daffodils, the new symbol of their rebellion.

The Times called the demonstrations 'unprecedented in British university history.' Tracy revelled in being part of this. And in the course of this student rebellion, she arrived at a decision about her future – vague thus far despite her selection of a major.

'David, I know what I want to do with my life now. I want to teach – at the university level. I want to see changes made in our own education system.' She paused to giggle. 'I suppose you'll say I'm doing this because of my exposure to Dad and Adele.'

'I can settle for that, too,' David said seriously. 'We'll both teach at the same university. The academic life has a lot going for it.' He chuckled. 'By the time we're there, the situation will be cooler. Of course, my parents will be furious. They can't exactly bitch – because college professors are considered respectable – but they'll make ugly noises about the low salaries. In their eyes, that is.'

'We don't care about them,' Tracy shot back defiantly.

'No.' He surprised her with this admission. 'All of a sudden I realize I *don't* much care what my parents think. I used to – I wanted so badly to please them. But it doesn't matter anymore. Maybe you can say I've grown up.'

'Dad and Mom will be pleased,' Tracy said, her face luminous. 'Teaching is becoming a family tradition.' Instead of making guns. 'Oh wow, I can just imagine Dad's relief. I know he was scared to death I'd settle on something wildly unconventional.'

'Do you suppose this is the time to announce we're officially engaged?'

'No.' Tracy shook her head. 'That's *too* conventional!'

Early in the new year Laurie found herself reaching out for relaxation. Small groups began to form, with intermittent parties at a student's apartment – usually after a major exam. Through the college years she'd avoided any romantic attachments, but now she was flattered by the pursuit of male medical students.

'This guy Marty Stevens is really coming on strong,' she confided to Adele over a Sunday-morning breakfast in early April after a noisy party that had wound up in a maudlin singfest silenced by an irate neighbour. 'Look, how many women are there in my class? Ten in a class of well over a hundred. I'm convenient,' she rationalized, yet she felt a surge of excitement when she remembered how Marty had stopped dancing to kiss her in the shadowy corner of the living room. Every woman in their group – even the two wives of med students – was attracted to Marty. Sandy-haired, blue-eyed, with movie-star features, a lean, hard body, and a charismatic charm, Marty dominated any gathering, she thought in delicious abandonment to emotion.

'You like him?' Adele probed, shifting a piece of Nova from plate to bagel.

'I could if I let myself,' Laurie admitted. 'But of course, it might have been the tequila we were drinking last night. Yeah, I know,' she said, her chuckle self-mocking. 'I nurse one drink through the whole evening.' She'd sworn off drinking in her freshman year after witnessing the wholesale throwing up of first-year college students after drinking blasts.

'Let yourself,' Adele encouraged. 'But don't get pregnant.' All at once she was sombre. 'I was thinking – if Terry and I got married and right away I was pregnant, he'd be safe from the draft. Lots of guys are taking that route,' she reflected. 'But we sat down and talked about it and it wouldn't work for us. If Terry had a wife and kid, he'd never get his degree. I don't want to stop working. If we can keep this school running, we'll be helping some kids that would otherwise be lost.'

'Med students don't have much time for play,' Laurie pointed out. 'So if we have a little fun together, why not?'

Laurie told herself at the end of her first date with Marty Stevens that her life would forever be entangled with his. His father was a tax lawyer, his mother a psychologist. His parents had what Grandpa would call a mixed marriage: Marty's mother was Jewish; his father,

Protestant. Marty called himself an agnostic. Grandpa would be upset that she was going with someone who was only half-Jewish, she thought. Mom and Dad would understand.

Now she was with Marty every moment they could manage. At parties with their small group, at his comfortable one-bedroom apartment near the medical school, or occasionally at her apartment when Adele gave notice she would be with Terry in his tiny West Seventies studio. Marty couldn't understand why she was stalling on sleeping with him. It was no big deal these days.

'Look, if you're not ready, you keep saying *no*,' Adele advised. 'Of course, I stopped saying *no* to Terry a long time ago.'

'You don't like Marty.' Involuntarily Laurie gave voice to the suspicion that had been haunting her for weeks.

'Laurie, I've never seen the guy for more than three minutes,' Adele scolded. 'All I know is what you tell me.' She paused. 'I think he's hooked on becoming the richest doctor in Manhattan. You know me – that's a real turn-off.'

'He's ambitious,' Laurie corrected. But she felt a tinge of guilt as she remembered what he'd said when they'd first met. 'My old man's a tax lawyer. He said, "To hell with going to law school. I'm a tax lawyer, I know what sharp doctors make. *That's* the gravy train."'

'If he makes you happy, go for it.' Adele's smile was warm and loving, but her eyes – Laurie thought – were troubled.

On the last evening before leaving for home, Laurie went to a party at Marty's apartment. She remained after the others had left to help him clean up. She'd told Adele she might stay over at Marty's apartment – though he didn't know it.

'Let's leave the dishes in the sink,' he said, reaching for

her. 'I want to sublet this joint and get something with a dishwasher. My old man can afford it.'

'We've got one year behind us, three to go.' Her voice was unsteady because he was sliding one hand down the low neckline of her dress. He knew what that did to her, she thought, closing her eyes while the hand fondled the lush spill of a breast.

'I don't know if I could survive them without you.' His mouth was at her ear now. 'Honey, when are you going to grow up and show me you're a woman?'

'How about tonight?' she whispered. It was awful to think that she wouldn't see Marty until next fall. She was going home for the summer and just collapse. Adele understood she had to give everything of herself to med school now. No time for anything else. Marty was leaving for eight weeks in Europe with a college buddy.

'Fireworks are going off in my head.' His free hand closed in about her rump, prodding her body against his. 'No more stop lights,' he crooned. 'An express to paradise.'

They'd made passionate love so many times, she thought in soaring anticipation as he lifted her from her feet and carried her into the tiny bedroom, but tonight would be the ultimate moment. They undressed with impatient speed, swayed together in the triumphant knowledge there'd be no denial of themselves tonight. And then the gentle thrust of his hands on her shoulders in the darkened bedroom, and she felt herself falling upon the mattress. Hands reaching for the other, bodies moving with sudden urgency. And – almost too soon – it was over, the sounds of her own passion poignant in the silence.

'Relax, Laurie,' he soothed with smug reassurance. 'The night's just beginning.'

She'd known almost from their first meeting that she'd spend her life with Marty. Together they'd survive the next three years of med school, Laurie told herself – resting in his embrace. They'd intern at the same hospital. They'd set up practice together. Adele would see she was wrong about Marty. He wasn't 'a greedy bastard.' He was ambitious.

Chapter Thirty-three

Vera sprawled on a chaise on the screen porch of the Kahn house on this late August night that was breaking heat records. Since morning the air conditioning had provided only warm air. On Sundays in Eastwood nobody worked. Hopefully, the air conditioning would be repaired tomorrow. Amazing, she mused, how they became dependent on new creations of technology. Fifteen years ago, people took it for granted they'd swelter in summer – though, in truth, she'd been shocked at the discomfort of American summers after the years in London and Copenhagen.

From inside the house came the hum of a fan in Laurie's bedroom. She'd been on the phone for almost an hour with that friend from med school who was visiting Paris. What a phone bill that would be – but not theirs. Tracy and David were at his parents' summer house at Lake George. Dad didn't know his parents were somewhere in Europe.

She heard the muted tones of the TV in the den. Paul was watching the news. This was a summer of such extremes, she considered, tugging at the perspiration-soaked back of her blouse with one hand and smacking an errant mosquito on her sun-tanned leg with the other. The newspapers and magazines were full of articles about the Haight-Ashbury section of San Francisco, where young hippies were spreading the word that love was *in*. And the word was the same in New York City's East Village and in other major cities around the country.

But the *summer of love* was turning into a nightmare, she reflected, remembering the hordes of teenage runaways intent on joining the psychedelic paradise they thought existed in the East Village and the Haight-Ashbury.

This summer the country had seen the worst race-riots in its history – in more than 100 cities. The most devastating had been in Detroit and Newark. In five days of rioting, 45 people had been killed in Detroit. In Newark – also in a devastating five-day spell of violence – 26 people had died. Many more had been injured.

Laurie's accusation last night was seared into Vera's memory.

'When people can stop buying guns whenever they like – when guns are outlawed – we'll stop seeing kids shot down in the streets of urban ghettos!'

Thank God, Dad hadn't been home when she'd said that. He was already upset over all the talk in Washington about another gun-control bill. To him it was an infringement on the individual rights of every American.

She couldn't come out and say to Dad, 'Laurie's right. All those crying out for gun-control laws are right.' But she and Dad weren't villains because they manufactured guns, she told herself defensively – though in Laurie's mind they were tainted by this. Guns were necessary for keeping the peace. Without arms last month, Israel would have been annihilated – instead of winning the Six-Day War that had threatened its existence. If there had not been guns in the hands of good people, she would have been captured in that fishing village in Denmark and sent to a concentration camp. Those terrified moments, too, were seared into her memory.

Paul strolled onto the porch with a pitcher and a pair of glasses in tow.

'Try a glass of lemonade,' he coaxed, settling himself

on a chair beside her. 'It'll cool you off for a little while.'

'We've gotten so dependent on air conditioning.' Her smile was wry. 'But think of all the people who've never had it.'

'Laurie must be roasting up in her room.' He poured lemonade into two tall glasses. 'You think there's something serious between her and that med student who keeps calling?'

'These days how can you tell? They're all so casual.' Vera sighed. Instinct warned her not to ask questions. In her daughter's eyes she was the enemy, the enemy who manufactured small arms. 'And how serious can she get with all that schooling ahead of her?' She worried constantly about this. 'By the time she's in private practice she'll be close to thirty.'

'Women medical students do marry,' Paul pointed out after a moment. He knew exactly what she was thinking, Vera told herself in gratitude. He knew her anxiety about Laurie's future.

'It's tougher for a woman than a man,' Vera said, half expecting a challenge from Paul. 'A man can be a medical student, marry, have children. A woman medical student can marry – and pray not to get pregnant. There's no room in her life for a family. Med school's rough enough – but we've heard more than we'd like to know about the insane hours during the internship years.'

'Ah, you're worried about having to wait to become a grandmother,' Paul chided good-humouredly. 'You're forty-two years old and look thirty. Who'd ever believe anytime soon that you were a grandmother?'

'There's Tracy and David,' she reminded. 'We still have hopes.'

'When do you think Tracy and David'll get married?' He lifted one foot to rest on the chaise. Her sigh was eloquent. 'Don't they realize it would improve his draft status?'

'David says it's a miracle he hasn't been called up so far.'

'He won't go if he is called,' Paul predicted sombrely. 'And you know, I won't blame him.' His smile was quizzical. 'Honey, I'm still trying to figure you out. I know you hate this war. You realize we've gotten into something that never should have happened in the first place. But when Dad shoots off his mouth about draft-dodgers being the worst kind of traitors, you don't say a word.'

'Neither do you,' she said quietly. She didn't want to consider what would happen if Dad discovered Paul was counselling would-be draft-evaders in Albany. 'I don't think Dad will ever understand what's happening in South Vietnam. He sees this country as a defender of democracy, sworn to keep Communism from spreading around the world.'

'There's no democracy in South Vietnam!' A nerve quivered in his right eyelid. 'People here at home have to realize that.'

They both started guiltily at the sound of a car pulling into the driveway. Dad was coming home from one of his interminable meetings.

'I hated to leave my meeting,' Joel called to them. 'The air conditioning was great.'

Drained by the heat wave, he climbed the stairs to the porch with deliberate slowness. He had been over-conscious of his age since his longtime pharmacist friend fell and broke his hip four months ago, Vera thought. She and Doris had debated about giving him a surprise seventy-fifth birthday party, then decided against it. He didn't need to be reminded of the passing years. She'd scolded him when he'd bought himself a new car early in the year and talked about its 'seeing him through.' It was time he stopped looking at the calendar.

'Anything momentous at your civic meeting, Dad?' Paul joshed.

'Only five people showed up.' Joel lowered himself into a chair, reached for Paul's half-filled glass of lemonade. 'Nobody wants to stir in this weather.' He paused, listened to the sound of a typewriter in use in an upstairs bedroom. 'I thought Laurie came home for a rest. She's either on the phone, typing, or with her nose in a book.'

'You know Laurie – the perpetual worrier.' Vera smiled. 'She wants to start the new school-year ahead of the game. She'll be leaving day after tomorrow.' Already she felt a sense of loss. 'And Tracy comes home in the morning and leaves the next day, also.'

'I still have Neal to spoil.' Joel's face softened. Now he took Neal with him for target practice – as he had once taken Tracy. 'I waited a long time for a grandson, but it was worth it.'

Vera knew he was already envisioning the day when Neal would come into the business, to take over eventually what had begun six generations earlier. His big fear, she realized, was that he wouldn't live to see it. She wished there were some way she could make him understand that he should take each day at a time. Enjoy each day. It was from Dad, Vera mused, that Laurie had inherited her tendency to worry.

Laurie waited restlessly for a call from the airport. Marty had promised to phone the moment he was through Customs. She felt guilty about having left home two days earlier than she had to – lying to Mom and Dad. But she hadn't see Marty in ten weeks. *Ten weeks*. They needed these two days together before they were caught up in the old grind.

Adele had made a point of saying she'd sleep over at Terry's tonight and tomorrow night. Adele knew she felt more comfortable staying here than going to Marty's pad. It was kooky to feel that way. Why did it matter where they slept together? Marty didn't say anything about their getting married, but she understood he felt he had to get through med school before taking such a step.

Some of the students were married, she considered – staring out into the night. Some were just living together. Oddly, *she* wasn't ready for that. Anyhow, being together this way – whenever they could fit it into their schedules – was more practical. Med school and marriage could be a killer.

There were moments when the whole med school scene infuriated her, she admitted to herself in a rare moment of candour. They were constantly treated as though they were ten-year-olds. *We're just bodies there*, she railed inwardly, *for them to pour facts over. We're memorization machines, and then come the tests and we have to pour it back out to them. We're not supposed to think – or to have opinions. It's humiliating*. She accused in silence, knowing that other med students shared these feelings with her.

Her introspection was punctured when her eyes focused on the kerb below. A cab had pulled to a stop. The door was thrust open. Marty emerged. He hadn't stopped to phone. With a rush of excitement she darted to open the apartment door. He had a key. He didn't need to be buzzed in. She listened for the sound of the elevator rising to her floor. Then she spied Marty, charging up the stairs.

'Hey, baby! You look wonderful!' He rushed towards her, swept her into his arms.

'You said you'd call,' she scolded, laughter mingling with tears of pleasure.

'I got a lift into the city with this guy who had a limo

waiting,' he explained. 'No standing in a taxi line –'

'Are you hungry?' she asked while they moved arm-in-arm into the apartment.

'Just for you.' Marty stopped dead to kiss her with a passion that matched her own.

They made love, lay together in a torrent of conversation about his summer in Europe, her summer at home.

'Yeah, we've got to get real serious this year,' he said with pleased anticipation. 'No more fooling about whether to specialize – or in what to specialize.'

'No problem with us,' Laurie said, in love with life at this moment. 'We're both specializing.' She'd given this a lot of thought through the years. 'You in surgery, me in pediatrics.'

'Maybe you ought to give that some thought,' Marty suggested. 'Pediatrics is a nice, reliable field. Hell, there're always kids being born. But there's a hell of a lot more money in other areas. Take obstetrics. You know what you can bill a C-section for these days?' He whistled eloquently.

'Marty, I don't want to be an obstetrician.' All at once Laurie was uneasy. 'I want to be a pediatrician.'

'Consider orthopedic surgery,' he pursued, squinting in thought.

'No!' Laurie sat upright in bed. 'I know what I want to do with my life. I want to be a pediatrician.'

'Cool it,' he purred. 'Save all that energy for something important. We've got a lot of making up to do.'

With brutal suddenness she and Marty were caught up in the school rat race again. They quickly realized that their second year would be rougher than the first. Exams were coming along more heavily. Every waking moment was given over to studying. Bedtime was postponed to allow more time with the books. Their private lives were on hold. The only exceptions were the nights after an exam, when groups gathered at a student's apartment for what Marty labelled 'one hysterical blast.'

Now their small clique was expanding to include a woman student – Ava Benson – whose husband was divorcing her. 'He said I wasn't a wife anymore. I was a med school machine.' Ava encouraged Jeffrey Green – probably the brightest in their class, Laurie thought with respect – to join them on a snowy, early December night after a particularly rough exam.

'I'm not sure I can stay awake,' he warned, stifling a yawn. 'I haven't had a decent night's sleep in a month.'

'Sleep? What's that?' Laurie drawled. But she understood his feelings.

'Hey, we have to unwind now and then.' Marty dropped an arm possessively about Laurie's shoulders. 'Have a few beers, dance a little, sing.'

'Make love,' Ava added. 'Hey, what's that?'

'I'll show you, I'll show you,' their class clown offered quickly.

Normally at these parties they focused on grabbing as much fun as possible. Tonight – perhaps because the exam had been such a bitch and they all felt like such klutzes, Laurie mused – they were into talking. As usual, Marty dominated the group.

'Next year we'll be third-year students. That means we'll be spending most of our time in the hospital and clinics. We –'

'You just can't wait to parade around in a white coat with a stethoscope hanging around your neck,' Ava jibed. '"Calling Dr Kildare, calling Dr Kildare!"'

'Knock it off,' Marty ordered good-humouredly. 'But the time has come to zero in on where we're heading. The big deal on the scene now is subspecializing. That's where the loot's going to be! I'm settling on cardiac surgery. I'll have a house in Westchester and an in-ground pool in five years,' he boasted. 'From there on the sky's the limit.'

'Now that's a callous attitude,' Jeff drawled. 'What happened to public service?' He made a joke of it, yet Laurie sensed an undercurrent of seriousness in him.

'That's for the sucker brigade.' Marty shrugged. 'The missionary division. Look, I'm working my butt off – and there's worse to come. You know about those thirty-six-hour shifts when we're interning. The back-to-back shifts that keep popping up. We have to collect for all that shit! That's our reward, boys and girls.'

'What about Medicare and Medicaid?' Ava demanded. 'Doesn't that come under the heading of doctors' bonanza?'

'That's a whole social revolution,' Marty crowed. 'And with the shortage of doctors, we're in the driver's seat.'

'As soon as Congress started showing serious intent to pass Medicare and Medicaid, a lot of doctors began to double their fees,' Jeff said distastefully. 'Because they knew Medicare and Medicaid fees would be based on what doctors charged in the quarter or so before the bill went through.'

'That's smart,' Ava said, yet Laurie sensed an undertone of guilt in her voice.

'That's fraud,' Jeff retorted. 'And the hospitals are no better. Everybody knew a year ago there was a crisis in health care. Back in March there was a special Report to the President on Medical Care Prices – and it shows that hospital charges that had been rising between 6% and 8% for years went up 16.5% in 1963. And it's kept going up. And that same report said that the jump in doctors' fees last year was the largest in forty years.'

'Back home, folks are talking about awful doctor bills,' a student from Dallas admitted. 'They worry.'

'That's some doctors.' Laurie tried for an optimistic

note. 'We have this wonderful Dr Evans in Eastwood. I don't think he's raised his fees more than five dollars in the last ten years. Everybody in town loves that man.'

'Love doesn't put money in the bank,' Marty drawled. 'We've got special skills. Let people pay for them.'

She wished Marty wouldn't make it seem as though all they cared about was making a lot of money. Sure, there were some in their class who were outspoken about that – but there were others who came to medicine with other motives. Jeff Green, she suspected, would always regard medicine as a public service – and immediately she felt guilty at this thought. She wasn't putting down Marty, she told herself defensively. Marty talked a lot. He'd be a terrific surgeon once they survived their training.

Laurie was sprawled on the living room sofa, listening to the TV news about the 1,000 anti-war protesters who'd tried to close down the New York induction centre – among them Dr Spock and Allen Ginsberg – when Adele unlocked the door and came into the apartment with an expression that screamed *crisis*.

Laurie sat upright. 'Adele, what's happened?'

'Terry's been drafted. Yeah, I know –' She closed her eyes, dropped onto the sofa. 'We knew it could happen. This is his year to work instead of going to school.'

'What's he going to do?' Laurie felt her throat tighten in alarm.

'He's going into the service. You know Terry. He feels it's his responsibility to show he's a patriotic black.'

'But he's against the war,' Laurie protested.

'He thinks it's an immoral war,' Adele corrected tiredly. 'But it would be more immoral for him not to show himself a loyal American citizen. So we're going for blood tests tomorrow. We'll get married at City Hall on

Monday. I don't suppose you can get out of class?' Her smile was wistful.

'If you're getting married, I'll cut a class,' Laurie told her.

If Terry had been able to stay in school this year, he would have been deferred. He wouldn't be going to Vietnam.

Churning after yet another battle with Marty – one that hadn't been resolved in bed because there had been no time, Laurie hurried through the blustery night cold to the Tip Toe Inn. She was fifteen minutes late, she noted with impatience as she approached the entrance to the restaurant. Adele and Terry would be waiting for her. Because the three of them had such tight schedules later in the week, they'd chosen tonight for their wedding dinner. Over the weekend Adele and Terry were making a quick trip to North Carolina – so his mother and sisters could meet Adele and to give him a chance to see his family before his induction.

Inside the cosy warmth of the Tip Toe Inn, Laurie spied Adele and Terry at a corner table.

'My friends are over there,' she told the smiling hostess and made her way to their table. The dinner crowd was just beginning to appear.

'We had our blood tests,' Adele told Laurie and pulled up her sleeve to indicate a Band-Aid. 'We're on our way.'

Their waitress approached. For a few minutes they focused on ordering. Laurie made her decision quickly. Adele and Terry were in good-humoured debate.

This was all so unreal, Laurie thought – Adele and Terry getting married, Terry going into the service. And she felt drained from the row with Marty. He'd been bragging about how Medicare was such a gravy train for doctors.

'Laurie, stop being Alice in Wonderland. This is the real world. Take this guy in the apartment across from mine – fresh out of his residency. He's waiting for a penthouse pad to become available. He tells me how he can run up a scratch on a mild diabetic to *multiple lesions* and a three-hundred-dollar bill. He dabs on ointment, slaps on a Band-Aid, and *voilà*, a bill to Medicare for three hundred bucks.'

In contrast, she remembered Jeff's outrage when an aunt who went on Medicare suddenly found her ophthalmologist's bill for a routine annual checkup billowing to three times its normal size by listing her as a new patient.

'She's afraid to report him,' Jeff had said in frustration. 'He's been her doctor for almost thirty years. She's terrified of going to somebody new.'

Why couldn't she admit to herself that what she'd felt for Marty was dead? They couldn't keep fighting, then making up in bed. What kind of future did that hold for them? She couldn't make Marty over into an image she could accept – and she would never let herself become the kind of woman Marty wanted her to be.

In truth, she told herself bluntly, there was no place in a woman med student's life for emotional attachments. That was the price a woman paid for wanting to become a doctor. It didn't mean she had to live like a nun. Just no lasting relationships. What she wanted most in her life was to become a doctor. *A doctor like Dr Evans up in Eastwood*. He wasn't a vanishing breed, as Dad sometimes mourned. A whole new generation like herself and Jeff were coming along.

'What do you think, Laurie?' Terry's voice – blending cynicism with humour – brought her back to the present. 'Am I crazy to feel it's my obligation as a young black man to serve in Vietnam?'

'You know how I feel about Vietnam,' Laurie reminded.

'He's so tied up in civil rights he can't think of anything else,' Adele taunted, struggling to sound amused.

'I had a weird experience last night.' Terry squinted as he called up the memory. 'I met these two guys – both black, both just back from Vietnam. Two totally different reactions to the war. Both twenty-two, with a tour of duty behind them. One guy cursed Johnson for not letting them atom-bomb Hanoi . . . so sure he was there to save the world from Communism. He said he came back home and was going crazy. He landed a job, but got into a brawl with his boss, who said we didn't belong in Vietnam. He's signing up for another tour – going back to 'Nam.'

'He's one of those guys who thinks if he has a gun in his hand he has power.' Adele grunted in impatience. 'When will they realize that education – *learning* – is power? Not guns.'

'My mother brought up my sisters and me to feel that we owed all our allegiance to God and country. She'll be proud of me for going to Vietnam.' Terry's smile was gentle. 'She'll hurt because she'll be scared for me. But she taught us that things like serving in the military were part of our responsibility as Americans. She said that blacks – she still calls us *coloureds* – have to work hard to "show we can be as good as whites." '

'She's a dear, sweet woman, Terry – but too many of her generation accept that we aren't as good. Our generation *doesn't*.' Adele reached out to cover his hand with hers. 'But it kills me that if you'd have had the means to stay in school, you wouldn't be on your way to Vietnam.'

'This other vet – he came right out and said that the Vietnamese people want us out of there – they're just scared to come out and say it. He said what pisses him off most is that our government was lying to him. All that American propaganda about how democratic and honest the Vietnamese government is! He said his old man went all the way from North Africa, through Sicily, and into Italy in World War II – but they knew why they were there. And his own father –' Terry paused, his smile twisted in compassion '– can't understand why *he* wasn't happy serving his country.'

'At least, you'll be able to finish college under the GI Bill.' Adele was making a desperate effort to hide her own fears, Laurie interpreted. 'And there're some middle-class white kids with college backgrounds showing up at the induction centres now. It's no longer a mostly black, blue-collar army.'

Vera was shaken when she heard on the television news on January 5, that Dr Benjamin Spock – whose book on child care both she and Doris, along with millions of other mothers, considered a national treasure – had been indicted by the Federal government along with four others for counselling American young men in resisting the draft. This could happen to Paul.

'Vera, we've known this was a possibility,' he chided gently while they sat together in the den before a blazing fire in the grate.

'I don't want it to happen to you!' Her voice was uncharacteristically shrill.

'I'm not important enough to be dragged in,' Paul soothed. 'They're going after big names.'

'Do you think Dr Spock and the others will go to jail?' The prospect of Paul being jailed unnerved her.

'These are weird times,' he said after a moment. 'This all goes back to that letter published last October in the *New York Review of Books* and the *New Republic*, which pleaded for faculty support for draft-evaders. Dr Spock signed – with a long list of other people. Including,' he added wryly, 'two Nobel prize-winners, Linus Pauling and Albert Szent-Gyorgi, who contend that since the Vietnam war was never declared by Congress, it's unconstitutional.'

'Tracy doesn't say anything, but I know she's terrified that David will be drafted.' The latest figures showed 485,000 Americans in Vietnam. 'He graduates in June. He'll be losing his college deferment.' And graduate-school attendance wouldn't help. On February 23, that deferment had been abolished.

'He won't go,' Paul said gently.

'If he doesn't, he could go to jail,' Vera reminded. 'Either way – if he goes or he doesn't go – Tracy will be a wreck.' She hesitated. 'Paul, have you been talking to him?'

Paul seemed startled. 'Of course, I've been talking to him – every time he's in the house.'

'You know what I mean,' Vera pushed. 'Have you been advising him?'

'When the time comes, it's a decision he has to make himself. But I've pointed out his prerogatives. If he decides to resist, he can face the possibility of being jailed. It's happening. Or he can go to Canada.'

'Tracy would go with him.' Vera's face was drained of colour as she dwelt on this. Tracy and David in exile – that's what it would amount to, she thought in anguish. *When would they be able to return*?

'Paul!' Joel's voice vibrated through the house. 'Where the hell are you?'

'In the den,' Paul called, exchanging an anxious glance with Vera. 'He sounds terribly upset.'

'Paul, I can't believe what I've just heard.' Joel's voice preceded him into the den. Then he hovered in the doorway, his eyes brilliant with a blend of rage and disbelief.

'What did you just hear?' Vera strove for calm. *Something to do with Paul's draft-counselling*? 'Oh, you've heard about Dr Spock's being indicted,' she guessed with an effort at optimism.

'I heard about my own son heading a counselling group for draft-dodgers in Albany!' A vein pounded in Joel's forehead. 'Paul, tell me it isn't true!'

'I can't do that, Dad.' Paul managed an aura of calm.

It seemed to Vera that her father-in-law aged before her eyes. He stared at Paul as though he'd never seen him before . . . as though he were a contemptible stranger.

'You're disgracing the family.' Joel's voice trembled. 'I'll never be able to hold up my head in this town again! You're a traitor to our country!'

'There're a lot of Americans who don't feel that way. The climate's changing.' Paul strived to sound almost detached. 'This is something I have to do. I'm sorry that you're upset.'

'Kahns fought in the Civil War, in the Spanish American War, in World War I. They must be crying out in their graves for the dishonour you're bringing on them!'

Paul seemed to reel before this attack for an instant. 'Dad, try to understand.'

'How can I understand? I was so proud of you when you enlisted. I was afraid, yes – I admit that. There wasn't a day or night that I didn't pray you would come home to us. I didn't expect this of my son. We've always been loyal Americans. *We believed in our country*.'

'Our country is making a major mistake.' Paul hesitated, inhaled with an air of pain. 'I know how you feel about the antiwar movement. I respect that.' For a moment his eyes strayed to Vera. 'Vera and I will go to a motel tonight. We'll be out of your house as soon as possible.' He took a deep breath, exhaled as though with pain. 'I'm sorry, Dad.'

Chapter Thirty-four

Joel turned to Vera in shock and agonized bewilderment as Paul strode from the room. 'Vera, what have I done? I love you and Paul. My family's my life. I don't know what's happening in this world. Do you believe our country's doing a terrible thing to fight in Vietnam?' His eyes pleaded for understanding.

'For a long time I believed we were doing the right thing,' she said, groping for words. 'Most Americans believed that way. But a lot of us have come to believe – like Paul – that the war is not being fought for freedom in Vietnam. We're propping up tyrannical South Vietnamese dictators whom the people don't want to rule them. Millions of dollars that're being spent in Vietnam every week should be spent here at home – to alleviate poverty, improve our education system, fight crime.'

'President Kennedy thought we ought to fight in Vietnam. President Johnson keeps telling us that –'

'You know how deeply Paul feels about this,' Vera said gently. 'You know how bright and persevering he is. He said that way back in 1954 – when Kennedy was a senator from Massachusetts – he was against our involvement in Vietnam. In 1961 – when Johnson was Vice-President – he went to Vietnam and reported that "American combat troop involvement is not only not required, it is not desirable." In 1964, Paul said, liberal senators like Eugene McCarthy and George McGovern and Albert Gore approved of our sending Americans troops to Vietnam. But not now, Dad.' She churned with a need to make him understand. 'Those same senators are involved in the fight to get our troops out of Vietnam. We made a mistake. The important thing is to recognize that.'

'I can't worry about what's happening in Vietnam,' Joel said exhaustedly. 'I can worry only about what's happening with my family. Talk to Paul. I can't bear to see the two of you move out of this house. What would it be without you?' He spread his hands in a gesture of helplessness. 'Vera, talk to him.'

'I'll talk to him,' she promised. She, too, was shaken at the prospect of moving out of the house that had been home for over twenty-one years. 'We'll work this out.'

Vera went upstairs to their bedroom. Paul stood at a window – the drapes not yet drawn – and stared out into the blackness of the night.

'Paul, Dad's terribly upset,' she began.

'What can I do?' he challenged without turning away from the window. 'Deny everything I believe in?'

'He needs time. He doesn't want us to move out.'

'He's ashamed of me. He said I'm disgracing the family. How can I stay here?' He swung about to face her, his eyes reflecting his inner agony. 'Tell me. How can I stay here?'

'He's your father, and he loves you. You know how deeply he loves you.' She saw Paul flinch and knew he was remembering how his father had taken the blame for the accidental shooting of his mother. 'He's spent all his life with the conviction that his country can do no wrong. We have to be here for him.'

'How?'

'By staying here in the house. That's what he wants. It won't be easy. We'll have to take each day at a time. But he is your father, and we love him.'

'If Dad has heard about the group in Albany, it must be all over town now.' Paul crossed from the window to sit on the edge of the bed. 'I'll have to resign from the faculty.' His smile was lopsided. 'Before I'm fired.'

'That would be best,' Vera agreed.

'What will I do with my life?' Paul tried for cynical humour. 'I've been a teacher for twenty-one years.'

'You could go back to school, work for your doctorate,' Vera suggested.

'It's too late for that.' His smile was wry. 'And with all the rumpus on college campuses these days, I wouldn't be the type to appeal to the administrations. I'd never get hired.'

'I try so hard to understand what's happening in the minds of students these days.' Vera sighed. 'If my father were alive, he'd be so bewildered, so upset.'

'This generation of students is living with a situation no others faced,' Paul pointed out. 'The Cold War. But there's always been student rebellion. I remember back in the late '30s when Doris was in college and she went down to Manhattan to picket in the garment district with a bunch of girl students from fine old families. And there were American students who went off to fight with the Abraham Lincoln Brigade in the Spanish Civil War. Then came World War II – and all we thought about was war. That was our rebellion. Kids today worry about such tough problems – civil rights, Vietnam, all the changes that are occurring in the world. They feel a frightening insecurity and frustration. And remember, there's been a student population explosion since the end of World War II.'

'Young people today see college as their right – not a privilege for the well-fixed. And we need them college-educated,' Vera said with conviction. 'There's been a knowledge explosion, too. So much has been learned – and so fast. It's as though the world of science fiction has become a reality.'

'Kids in middle-class families have been raised to ask questions. And they're asking questions on campuses all over the world. I think,' Paul said humorously, 'that if I were teaching at the college level today I'd be in constant hot water.'

'Paul, you have so much to say – and you say it so well. Get back to writing. That's what you'll do with your life.'

'It'll mean a serious drop in income,' he warned. 'Not that we're suffering – considering your weekly pay cheque.'

'Focus on writing,' she reiterated. 'Run down to New York and talk with that group Adele is working with – you were so excited about what they're doing.' Adele had come up with Laurie this past Thanksgiving. 'And you do what you think is right about the draft-counselling. We just won't talk about it around Dad.'

'Vera, how would I survive without you?' Paul reached to pull her down beside him.

'We survive together,' she said softly. 'We're a family.'

Vera knew that in this pro-war town life was not easy these days for either Paul or his father. The news that Paul was heading a We Won't Go group had raced about town. To many local residents he was a pariah. Their current housekeeper – who had a nephew in Vietnam – quit. Her replacement – another Irene – cared only about her three cats. 'I don't think they'll be drafted,' Paul said with an effort at levity.

Paul and his father had made a silent pact. They could discuss any matter in this house except the war in Vietnam. Vera had heard her father-in-law in terse conversation on the phone with a friend. 'What Paul does is his business. I don't want to talk about it.'

She watched anxiously for repercussions when Tracy

came home for a weekend and announced that she and David would not be here for the spring break. They would join hordes of other young college students who were going to campaign for Eugene McCarthy, who'd announced formally at a press conference last November 30 that he would seek the Democratic nomination.

'He's the peace candidate,' Tracy electioneered earnestly. 'This is my first chance to vote for a president. I want my first vote to help put Gene in the White House!'

Alone in their room Vera and Paul discussed the coming primaries.

'There's the smell of change in the air,' Paul observed. 'You can almost hear people's minds ticking. A lot of those who wanted to keep us in Vietnam are switching sides. The Tet offensive was brutal. It was demoralizing to American forces. For the first time ever, we have to consider that we could lose a war. We can't fight a guerrilla enemy and win.'

'It's weird how little things can switch individual thinking,' Vera said slowly. 'I can't get out of my mind that item in the newspapers. You know –' She couldn't bring herself to give it voice.

Paul nodded. 'You mean the Associated Press report on what that American artillery officer said – after we shelled the hell out of Ben Tre in the Mekong Delta. *We had to destroy it in order to save it.*' Paul grimaced in revulsion, contemplating the additional half-million Vietnamese who became refugees after this action that reduced their homes to rubble.

'What will forever remain in my memory,' Vera said, tensing, 'is that film we saw on television where a Viet Cong officer was captured and beaten, then brought to the head of the South Vietnamese national police – and this executioner reaches for his pistol and shoots him in the head. It was horrible.' She shivered.

'Millions of Americans saw that film. I think it helped to change a lot of minds. I think a lot of people are changing from hawks to doves.'

The next two months, Vera thought in retrospect, were the most harrowing in all the years she'd been in this country. In the March 12 primary in New Hampshire, LBJ led Eugene McCarthy by less than one full percentage point. Four days later, Robert Kennedy announced that he, too, was a candidate for the Democratic nomination. On March 31, President Johnson told the American people that he would not seek another term.

On April 4, Martin Luther King was assassinated in Memphis, Tennessee. Riots erupted in over one hundred cities. Twelve people were killed in Washington, DC, another twenty-five in other cities. In Washington, DC, fires were set in the downtown shopping area as well as in the ghettoes. In New York City, a courageous Mayor Lindsay kept the cool by walking through Harlem streets to plead for calm.

On Tuesday evening, April 23, Vera was shocked when she switched on the TV news to discover that pandemonium existed on the Columbia campus. Columbia and Barnard students had taken over Hamilton Hall and had now moved into Low Library.

Joel was outraged. 'It's a damn Communist plot!' he railed. 'All these college demonstrations around the country! Better they should be fighting in Vietnam!'

Vera motioned for silence from Paul. 'Let me call Laurie and see what she has to say about all this.'

'The medical school is way uptown,' Paul reminded. 'This is all happening on the main campus.'

Laurie was full of sympathy for the demonstrators.

'It has been building up for a long time,' she told her mother. 'Back in February there was a demonstration about recruiters from Dow Chemical – you know – the napalm-makers – being on campus. The students are upset about Vietnam and about the draft and now this business about building a new gym on *public land*. The community – meaning Harlem blacks – will be able to use it only at certain times. This after Columbia – the Great Landlord – is responsible for evicting maybe ten thousand poor blacks in Harlem. It was the final straw.'

Assiduously following the TV news about the trouble on the Columbia campus, Vera learned – along with the rest of the country – that the following night students from the school of architecture took over Avery Hall. After midnight on Thursday, the police were brought onto campus.

The Columbia rioting continued late into May, when most students planned to leave for home. The evening before Laurie was to leave, she met Marty for dinner. She argued with him in soaring heat at their favourite Italian restaurant, just around the corner from his apartment. But tonight she felt no inclination to go up to his apartment, though after tomorrow they wouldn't see each other for weeks. She was increasingly unnerved about the way they fought.

'Marty, how can you be so callous?' Since the first day of the riots on campus he'd been contemptuous and arrogant about the students – and faculty – who were part of the action.

'They're a bunch of shitheads to carry on this way,' Marty said scornfully. 'What'll it gain them? They'll come back to school next semester to find the main campus loaded with security cops, but nothing will change.'

'You're so wrapped up in yourself, Marty.' She was forcing herself to face realizations she'd dodged for months. 'You don't give a damn about the rest of the world.'

'The rest of the world doesn't give a damn about me. We have to look out for what's good for *us*. Like you,

Laurie. Why can't you admit it's smart to prepare yourself for subspecialization? That's going to be the big deal tomorrow. Honey –' His voice softened. His knee sought under the table for hers. 'You're such a sentimental slob. But you're *my* sentimental slob, and I can't bear sitting here and not being able to hold you close. What do you say we forget about coffee and make a wild dash for the apartment?' His eyes dwelt on the lush rise of her breasts with a hunger that all at once was replicated in her.

'Marty, we need to talk –' But already she wavered.

'Later we'll talk,' he promised and lifted a hand to signal their waiter.

Vera was wistful that Tracy and David had not bothered to hang around for graduation. She'd been there for Laurie's graduation, and she'd hoped to be there for Tracy's. Sentimental occasions were – to her – a reinforcement of the togetherness of family. Tracy had been home for just one night, and then yesterday morning she and David had left to join other young volunteers who yearned to see Gene McCarthy win the presidential election in November.

The early June evening was fragrant with the scent of grass mowed late in the afternoon drifting into the den as Vera talked with Laurie in New York. Laurie would be home for a week, bringing Adele with her, and then go back to work with the group of dedicated young doctors who manned a storefront clinic in Harlem.

'What does Adele hear from her husband?' Vera asked sympathetically.

'Terry tries to be cheerful, but she says his bitterness shows through. Oh, she'll just stay in Eastwood for a couple of days, Mom. She wants to be here in case mail comes from Terry.'

'We'll be glad to have her as long as she feels comfortable.' Vera remembered her own anguished wait for letters from Paul during World War II. Her whole life had revolved around those letters.

Off the phone she checked her watch. It was just nine-forty – another twenty minutes before the ten o'clock news would be on TV. She settled herself on the sofa, reached for the current issue of *Newsweek*. Paul was at a counselling session with a local high school graduate who expected to be drafted any day. For counselling sessions here in Eastwood Paul utilized the den in Doris and Phil's house.

Dad had driven over to Cambridge to visit a friend who'd just bought an antique revolver. He'd probably come home with cake from King's, she thought indulgently. And Paul would be home soon, too. She'd put up a pot of coffee.

With coffee on the range, Vera returned to the den. Almost simultaneously she heard two cars pull into the driveway. Dad and Paul, she decided and went out to the foyer to greet them. She was glad Dad had gone over to Cambridge to see his friend. He was avoiding some of his usual evening meetings because of the caustic remarks about Paul that came his way.

'You stopped by King's,' she accused as Joel – with Paul right behind him – walked into the house with the familiar bakery box in tow. 'And I just happen to have put up a fresh pot of coffee.'

Joel launched into a rapt description of the Colt revolver that his friend had acquired.

'Where did he find this?' Vera asked. To Dad antique guns were precious jewels.

'You two go on into the den,' Paul ordered – relieved, Vera knew, that Dad hadn't asked where he'd been. 'I'll rustle up the coffee.' He reached for the box from King's and headed for the kitchen.

'Frank bought it from a private owner,' Joel said in high spirits. 'Somebody his brother down in New York was acquainted with.'

'Is Frank still giving his wife a hard time about his diabetes?' Vera asked with a flicker of humour. The doctor repeatedly told Frank his diabetes was so mild that he required no medication, just an abstinence from sugar. He put her through a three-degree at each meal about its contents, though he was known to ignore the presence of sugar when dining out at his favourite restaurants.

'You know Frank.' Joel chuckled. 'Now that he has Medicare, he's very careful about his health.' Joel seemed all at once grim as he settled himself on the sofa. 'I'm pissed,' he said in an occasional moment of vulgarity. 'He had this little scratch on his ankle – from a playful kitten they've just acquired. So he goes to his family doctor – a young guy who just took over from the old one. He looks at the scratch. "It's nothing," he says, puts on a bit of ointment and a Band-Aid – and when Frank sees the bill, it reads $300 for multiple lacerations. Now tell me, how is something like Medicare going to work with bastards like that on the loose?'

'Not all doctors are like that.' But Vera was shocked. 'You know Laurie won't ever be that way.'

'He's heard other stories.' Joel was grim. 'What's happened to ethics in this country?'

Vera reported on her conversation with Laurie. Paul returned with a tray bearing coffee mugs and a plate of King's locally famous apple fritters.

'Turn on the TV,' he told Vera. 'It's time for the news.'

Vera complied, then returned to the sofa. As she'd expected, primary election returns were of top interest on this Tuesday evening, June 4.

'Tracy's going to be so disappointed,' Paul said

sympathetically. 'Bobby Kennedy's beat McCarthy in a third primary.'

'There're still about nine weeks before the Democratic Convention.' Vera refused to abandon hope. 'Gene might just make it.'

After watching the late news, Vera and Paul went up to their bedroom. Joel remained before the TV set in search of a '40s movie, his latest addiction. They were about to retire for the night when Joel called up in obvious agitation.

'Get down here,' he yelled. 'It's happening again!'

Just past midnight Los Angeles time – fresh from the triumph of winning the important California primary – Robert Kennedy had been shot in a corridor of the Ambassador Hotel's Empire Room.

Vera and Paul sat with Joel in numbed silence while a TV newscaster reported the happenings. At 1:44 AM Robert Kennedy was pronounced dead. He had been assassinated by a snub-nosed Iver-Johnson revolver.

With anguish – listening to the morning news on the radio – Vera remembered that Kahn Firearms manufactured a revolver similar to the one that had killed Robert Kennedy. Lyndon Johnson had just condemned the nation's 'insane traffic in guns'. How would she ever make Laurie – and possibly now Tracy – understand that they were not in an evil business?

Laurie waited for Tracy at the entrance to the Charleston Gardens in B. Altman's in New York. What was so urgent that Tracy had come all the way down here to talk about with her? But then Tracy was always so dramatic, she coddled her unease. She wished the pair of women sitting beside her on the seating circle – both wearing the new 'midi' length that looked so dowdy beside the popular 'mini' and was sure to disappear shortly – would shut up. All this endless talk of the SAT grades of their sons, who'd be leaving for college in two or three days. So smug that college would keep them out of what David called the *Vietnam Annihilation Factory*.

She'd worked all summer with the storefront clinic in Harlem because she considered that a part of her medical education. Sometimes she felt guilty at the way she allowed that to dominate her life. Tracy and David had campaigned for Gene McCarthy right up to the Democratic Convention in Chicago over the last weekend. Like everybody she knew, they'd been shocked and horrified by the assassination of Robert Kennedy. But they hadn't even hung around for their college degrees. They'd gone from their final classes to the campaign trail.

God, what a massacre the Chicago Convention had been! Over 700 hurt – not just college kids but convention delegates, clergymen, middle-aged professional people fighting for what they believed in, even newsmen there to report on the convention. Over 200 cops, too, had been injured. But this time Mayor Daly's police had demonstrated their brutality – well-known to black residents of the city's West Side and South Side – before the world. They couldn't hide from the TV cameras.

Marty was due back from France tonight. He'd gone there to take some special classes meant to glamorize his training background. She suspected he'd been more interested in the partying – though he'd written that students in France clamoured for news about what was happening on American college campuses. He should have spent the summer working at one of the storefront clinics with her. This year he hadn't burnt up the trans-Atlantic phone wires with calls to her. She'd been too busy to notice until he mentioned it. '*I can't believe I'm breaking my butt this way during vacation. But hey, it adds glamour to the degree when I get it.*'

She had been startled when she'd walked into the clinic that first morning to find Jeff Green there – but later, she told herself she should have known he'd be involved in something in public service. They'd been warned they'd work long, exhausting hours – and that was the way it'd been throughout the summer. She was pleased at the warm friendship that had developed between Jeff and herself.

Most nights they ended up in the Broadway cafeteria near her apartment. His own was in the low '90s, a few blocks above hers. Mostly they talked shop – both exhilarated by the hands-on experience they were acquiring at the clinic. But she'd learned that his mother had taken a flier as a Red Cross worker during World War II, met his father, got pregnant, got married – and four years later divorced his father.

His mother had re-married twice since then. He'd seen her once in the past five years. He'd been shipped off to boarding school at ten when she was on her second divorce. His father and grandparents had fought futilely for custody. His father was a writer who'd won critical acclaim – but little money – with his first novel.

'He was on his way to becoming an alcoholic when he died in a car smash-up. I was thirteen. But my grandparents were always there for me. I went to them during most school vacations. They died within six months of each other during my senior year in high school.'

He was proud that he was getting through medical school with no financial help from his mother, though it was clear she was in an upper income bracket. He talked about his grandparents, and she talked about her grandfather – even confessing to the barrier between them because of his business. Jeff had understood. She remembered that first evening when they'd sat for two hours at a corner table in the brightly lighted cafeteria and exchanged confidences.

'My mother comes from an old Boston family. Once my father was out of his Air Force uniform and scrounging for a job to support us, she decided the romance had gone out of their marriage. He was a warm, compassionate man – but always frustrated that he couldn't keep his family together. My mother – and her family – were ashamed that my father's parents were immigrants from Russia. They ran a mom-and-pop grocery store on the Lower East Side. To my mother I was her Big Mistake. To my grandparents I was their treasure – but she would never give them custody. But they had so much love. It's their money that's seeing me through med school.'

At different times during the summer she'd brought Jeff up to the apartment for dinner with Adele and herself. Adele had liked him immediately. In a way, Laurie thought, the three of them had common goals. Last night they'd had dinner at the apartment and talked about Terry in Vietnam and Adele's problems with the mother of a teenager in her summer group.

'I'm furious at the militant welfare-mothers who pop out one kid after another – six, seven, eight. Why don't they stop having babies? With three or four – or more – fathers involved. And then I'm ashamed of my rage because I know what they've come from. We've failed them in our system.'

'You did well for yourself,' Jeff had said gently.

'I was lucky. Mom got us out of the ghetto and into another world. But not everybody is strong like Mom was.'

'Look, this is the generation that has to work to change the system,' Jeff had said.

'Hi!' Tracy's voice intruded on her thoughts . . . faintly breathless because Tracy never walked – she always ran. 'I'm not late, am I?'

'I'm early.' Laurie rose to her feet. There were only

two people ahead of them in the line at the entrance to the Charleston Gardens, she noted. The lunch crowd had eased off. 'So what's up?'

'The shit is about to hit the fan,' Tracy said with a flippancy her eyes belied . . . using one of her grandfather's favourite expressions in moments of crisis. 'David just got his draft notice.'

Chapter Thirty-five

'Ooh –' Laurie froze in place.

'We're next,' Tracy said, shoving her towards the entrance to the Charleston Gardens. She anticipated the hostess's question. 'Non-smoking, please.'

They followed the hostess through the maze of tables in the huge, high-ceilinged restaurant with its faded, massive murals that were designed to lend a flavour of antebellum Charleston gardens. She led them to a table for two that flanked the wall.

'What's David going to do?' Laurie asked when they were seated, ignoring the menu.

'Wait,' Tracy ordered, her eyes betraying her tension. 'I'm having the chunky chicken salad on a roll. What about you?'

'I'll have the same,' Laurie said, annoyed by this derailment. 'Tell me about David.'

Laurie frowned as a genial waitress approached, entailing another delay. Then they were alone again.

'Well?' Laurie prodded.

'David talked a long time with Dad last night.' Tracy's eyes were eloquent. 'Then *we* talked on the phone till after midnight. *David got his draft notice.*'

'Oh, Tracy –'

'He wanted to rip it up and mail it to his draft board. He said they can't arrest everybody that does that.' She paused. 'Sometimes I think he wants to be arrested – that it'll be making a statement.'

'Dad says the number of indictments for draft-evasion

are going up,' Laurie recalled uneasily. 'Of course, they'd have to catch David first.'

'I don't want David to go to jail!' Tracy's voice was a ferocious whisper. 'I've heard too much about what goes on in prisons. The fights between the inmates, the gang-rapes. He could get up to five years!'

'There's Canada,' Laurie pointed out. Of course, David knew that. 'A lot of draftees are running up there.'

'I convinced David he mustn't take a chance on going to jail.' She took a deep, laboured breath. 'So we're going to Canada.'

'*We*?' Laurie was startled.

'I wouldn't let him go alone.' Tracy stared at her in reproof. 'I told you – we've gone over the options. Canada's the only way out.'

'You don't know when you'll be able to come back home.' Laurie felt a coldness invade her. *Would David ever be able to come home without facing a prison term*?

'I want to be with David. I guess that's all I've ever wanted. We've talked to Dad about the way to handle this. He's a good counsellor, Laurie.' Her face was luminous with love. 'It's a breeze to get into Canada. We just cross over as tourists. All we need is ID. We have our drivers' licences and passports – either one is enough. Under Canadian law, draft-evaders can't be extradited. We'll go in as tourists and later switch to *landed immigrant* status.'

'Give up your American citizenship?' Laurie gaped in disbelief. 'Tracy, you can't do that!'

'We won't be giving up our American citizenship. Being admitted as a *landed immigrant* just means we have a legal right to be there on a permanent basis. Living there for five years gives us the right to apply for Canadian citizenship.' Tracy paused, squinting in thought. 'We can ask for *student entry certificates*, but they have to be renewed every year. Anyhow, for now we're just driving up as visitors – and we'll apply for whatever we decide after we're there. It's okay to do that,' she insisted because Laurie seemed distraught. 'Anyhow, I told David to meet us at the Madison Avenue entrance at two o'clock. He'll explain everything to you.'

'What do Mom and Dad say about this?' Laurie demanded.

'They don't know. We want you to tell them tonight – once we've crossed into Canada. David thinks Montreal is the best bet for us, and –'

'How're you going to live?' Laurie broke in. *They were two babes in the woods – so bloody impractical! They'd never had to take responsibility for their own lives*, she thought impatiently. 'Do you and David have money to last awhile?'

'We're driving up in my car. David's out at a used-car dealer in Queens now to sell his. That'll last us for two or three months.'

'It's an old car.' Laurie was grim. Mom and Dad were going to hit the ceiling!

'We'll have no trouble finding jobs.' Tracy was determinedly cheerful. 'With a college degree, it's a snap. We've checked it out. There are all those groups up there waiting to help draft evaders. The Canadian Friends Service, the Central Committee for Conscientious Objectors, the Fellowship of Reconciliation of Canada – several church groups.' A wisp of a smile brightened her face. 'The biggest magazine in Canada – *MacLeans*, I think it's called – ran an editorial headed "Draft Dodgers are Refugees Not Criminals."'

'Can't you understand? Our government doesn't feel that way! David might never be able to come back here!' But Laurie knew there was no stopping Tracy and David. 'You could be exiles for the rest of your lives. You'll –'

'We'll play it by ear,' Tracy interrupted. 'And it's not so far from Eastwood that you can't come up and see us. Tell Mom and Dad – and Grandpa – not to worry.' She managed a wry smile. 'Somewhere along the road, David and I will get married.'

Laurie dreaded the call she must make home on Tracy's behalf, yet in a corner of her mind she suspected the family would not be totally surprised. Upset, yes – but not surprised. Certainly not Dad. But David's response when she'd asked him if he'd told his parents still ricocheted in her mind.

'You know my parents, Laurie. They flipped out, washed me out of their lives. They don't want to hear from me anymore. Dad said, "If I were a religious Jew, I'd say *Kaddish* for you."'

Now Laurie paced restlessly about the small living room of her Manhattan apartment. Shouldn't Marty's flight have arrived by now? Why didn't he call?

They were halfway through med school, she thought with momentary satisfaction. But everybody said the third year of med school was when you realized how little you really knew. This was the year you started your clinical rotations, started doing presentations. You learned to call each patient by his or her first name.

It would be weird to call a patient in Grandpa's age bracket by his or her first name, she thought in a whimsical moment. And this was the year you had to learn to deal with your emotions. It wasn't easy to know a patient you were seeing had no chance of survival.

Marty kept saying you had to learn to keep a distance from patients. *Hell, you have no time for compassion!* Her mind travelled to Dr Evans – that most compassionate of doctors. Dad said he was a vanishing breed. She hoped that wasn't so.

She started at the sound of the elevator drawing to a stop at their floor. She heard the elevator door slide open with its peculiar hissing sound and darted to open the apartment door. Last year he hadn't bothered to call – he'd come straight here from the airport.

'Hey, baby, I brought a bottle of bubbly with me,' Marty effervesced, charging towards her. 'Where'll it be tonight – your place or mine?'

'Adele's always obliging,' she reminded, running into his arms. 'She's staying over at a friend's house.'

'Oh baby, I can't wait.'

They moved into the apartment, locked the door behind them, clung together in a passionate embrace. In a corner of her mind she was startled to sense that something was missing in their relationship tonight. Was it the scent of perfume that clung to his jacket? Definitely a woman's perfume . . . that must have been overpowering in its intensity eight or nine hours ago when he'd said farewell in Paris.

'I'll get some glasses,' she said, forcing an air of conviviality. Was it a surprise to her that Marty had played around in Paris? No!

'It has to chill first,' he reproached. 'Like me. All the way back on the plane I kept thinking about our reunion. It's been a long time, baby.'

'You chose it,' she said involuntarily.

'Are you pissed at me for going to Paris?' He clucked in reproach. 'Honey, it's going to pay off when we set up offices.' He was full of talk about a group practice now. 'You know, the glamour touch.'

'I've never thought of medicine as being a glamorous field.' Why wasn't she responding to Marty as she had before he went away? He was doing all the provocative little things that used to arouse her to such heights.

'Enough of conversation.' He pulled his mouth away

from her ear, his hand from within the neckline of her blouse. 'Let's go into the bedroom and make ourselves comfortable. I've got such a hunger for you.' A huskiness in his voice that should be setting her teeth on edge.

She was conscious of a strange sense of guilt that she wasn't responding to his efforts; then, all at once, she felt a tidal wave of excitement. It was going to be all right.

'Oh wow, you know how to give a guy a real welcome,' he crooned. 'How could I have stayed away so long?'

But it wasn't the way it used to be, Laurie tormented herself.

'Let me get the champagne,' she said suddenly and reached for the shortie nightie that lay across the foot of the bed.

'Okay, so we'll take a break,' he drawled. 'Do you have today's *New York Times* around?' he called after her as she walked to the door.

'Yeah. You want to read the news *now*?' She turned around curiously.

'I was driving a Citroën in Paris. It was great. I want to see if the New York City dealer advertises.'

'You're going to try to buy a Citroën? Your folks will spring for that?'

'I might push them into a little action. They know the kind of money I'll be making once we're out of training.' His smile was dazzling.

'Marty, is that all you think of?' She'd said that a lot of times in the past, but all at once she was revolted by his attitude. Fragments of conversation with Jeff darted across her mind. *A lot of people think doctors are money-grubbers. Why must we be in the top one-half of one per cent of earners in this country*?

'You pick up some strange ideas from that roommate of yours,' he drawled. 'In her field she can't do any better.

We can. We're going to break our butts till we're out there practising – but I mean to make up for every lousy, rotten minute. We've got skills people need – and they have to pay for them.' *How many times must she listen to him say that*?

'I don't think we're on the same wavelength, Marty.' She stared coldly at him. 'I want something more than a Citroën or a co-op on Park Avenue. I want the feeling I'm making a contribution on this earth.'

'You sound like a road company Mother Theresa,' he mocked, all at once hostile. He reached for the clump of clothes that lay on the floor beside the bed and began to dress. 'When you get your mind straightened out, call me.'

Laurie told herself she'd be so caught up in her first hospital rotation – with the traumatic responsibilities this involved – that she'd have little time to think about her break with Marty. She knew it was permanent. *How could she have been so blind*? No, she hadn't been blind, she taunted herself. She'd known what Marty was, but had been too infatuated to admit it. She'd scolded him over and over again about his attitude towards medicine as though he were a naughty little boy. But this summer – working with Jeff – she'd been pushed into blunt recognition.

She could live without Marty. She didn't need a man in her life. A woman in the medical profession was better off alone. There was no room in your life to be a *woman*. Even now, she worried about how she dressed when she was on the wards. If a woman dressed smartly, she didn't look *serious*.

A woman in medicine had to make a choice, she told herself. An occasional woman doctor could have it all – a career plus family. But the odds were against it. More than anything else in the world, she wanted to be a terrific pediatrician. She didn't need Marty. *She didn't need any man in her life.*

Tracy was sombre as they headed for Westchester to pick up the north-bound New York State Thruway – with David at the wheel of her car. They'd both expected more money from the sale of his car. Still, they'd manage, she reassured herself for the hundredth time.

'How long will it take us to reach Montreal?' she asked.

'About eight hours. Don't worry that it'll be so late when we arrive,' he added quickly. 'There're plenty of motels around.'

'But Expo 67 is open again this year,' she reminded him. 'There'll still be a lot of tourists up there.'

'If there're any problems, I have phone numbers to call. We won't have to sleep in the car.' He took a hand from the wheel to grope for hers. 'We've got lots of people on our side up there.'

David said McGill in Montreal was a great school – and they might get fellowships. Later, they'd figure out how to handle going back to school. But right now, they had to pull their lives together and get into a holding pattern.

With the Customs barrier into Canada still a hundred miles distant, Tracy on impulse suggested they spend the night on US soil, then drive up into Canada in the morning.

'Okay.' An unfamiliar wariness that seemed to mask alarm infiltrated his voice. 'You want to think some more before we become exiles?' Humour was meant to hide his unease.

'David, no!' She was shocked that he could suspect this. 'It's just that I want us to sleep together the whole way – without our rules – on home territory. It's kind of like our wedding night.' She dropped her head onto his shoulder. 'So the ceremony will come later.'

'As soon as we can arrange it,' he said firmly. 'You make your mother and dad understand that.'

'So we'll stop at the first classy diner we see,' she ordered. 'We'll have burgers and coffee – no steaks,' she teased. 'Not on our budgets. Then we'll ask about the nearest Howard Johnson's.'

'Maybe we could skip the diner.' A sudden urgency in his voice now.

'No,' she insisted. 'You're going to need your strength.' She reached with one hand to stroke his thigh. 'And keep your eyes on the road!'

Vera struggled to hold on to her shaky semblance of acceptance. The three of them – she and Paul and Dad – had been waiting for the late-night TV news to come on when Laurie phoned and dropped her bomb.

'What are you going to do about it?' Joel demanded. 'Vera, go up to Montreal and find Tracy! Make her understand she can't ruin her life this way!'

'We can't do that, Dad,' Vera said gently. 'We have to respect her decisions.' But she was unnerved at the thought of Tracy in Canada. It wasn't like when she was at school – when she'd be coming home at intervals. 'She's not a child anymore.'

'She's behaving like a child,' Joel shot back. 'Paul, you have to do something. She can't stay up there in Montreal with that hippy!'

'David's not a hippy,' Paul said. 'That's a different breed. Along with a lot of others his age, he's grown up believing in values that he doesn't see his family – or much of our society – recognizing. He's insecure and rebellious.'

'God, Paul, how can you make excuses for them?' Joel shook his head in bewilderment. 'Your daughter runs off to Canada to live with a draft-dodger – and you make excuses for both of them? When will we see Tracy again?' A plaintive note of fear pushed through his belligerence.

'We've always known Tracy and David would be married.' Vera struggled for calm. 'They'll be married up in Montreal. We'll go up to see them regularly; it's only a four-hour drive from here. We have to let them work out their lives as they see fit.' *But why couldn't Tracy have called and told her what was happening? Why had she had to hear it from Laurie?*

'*You'll* go to Montreal to see them,' Joel told Vera and Paul. 'If my granddaughter wants to see me, she'll have to come to Eastwood.'

Tracy sat with a street map of Montreal spread across her lap while David drove at a slow pace along sun-splashed Dorchester Street in search of a tourist home for their first nights in Montreal – until they could locate permanently. She studied the paperback tourist guide they'd picked up in New York.

'What about this place?' she asked David. The past three houses they'd tried were at capacity, but the area offered a feast of tourist homes. It was close to 11:00 AM – probably check-out time.

'Is it listed?' David asked.

What he meant was, is it cheap? *He was so uptight about money*, she worried. 'Doubles are $8.00 a night. Of course, the book was published two years ago, and with Expo 67 the rates could be jumping.'

David pulled up before the rambling white house of indeterminate age. The sign out front indicated they could expect free parking, large rooms – either with private baths or hand basins – and there were TV sets for rent.

'It's not the Waldorf,' Tracy flipped, 'but it could be home for a few nights.'

They left the car and walked hand in hand towards the entrance. Mom and Dad must know by now, Tracy told herself. She'd said they were going out to visit a friend from school whose family had a beach house at Wainscott at the far end of Long Island. That they needed to unwind after the awfulness of the Chicago Convention. By now Laurie had called them.

The landlady was friendly but businesslike. She showed them the one double room still available. David winced at the $12.00 a night rental – but with people still coming in on vacation to see Expo 67, what else could they expect? Tracy reasoned.

They paid up front for two nights, then went out to park the car per instructions and brought their light gear to the house. Later, she'd ask Mom to ship more of her clothes and books and records up here, Tracy comforted herself. There was no way of knowing how long they'd have to stay. People back home were already talking about amnesty for draft-evaders, yet instinct warned her they could be here for a long haul.

'Let's go check with the group that'll help us find an apartment,' David said with an air of bravado. 'We have to get this show on the road.'

They left the house and returned to the car. It was so weird, Tracy thought, knowing they were in a foreign country and they *had* to stay here. It wasn't like those months at school in London. Then they'd known that come late July they'd be at Heathrow and waiting for their flight home.

'Let's play today.' Her smile managed to appear dazzling. 'It's our honeymoon. Didn't you register us as David and Tracy Marcus? So the ceremony comes later.'

'Okay.' He followed her lead. 'We'll go out to Expo 67. It's not a fair,' he reminded her, quoting the tour book. 'It's an exhibition. The city of Montreal literally created a new island to house it. We park and take the Metro out there,' he recalled. 'I hear it's real cool.'

Today they'd play. Tomorrow they'd get down to the business of being residents of Montreal. Tracy ordered herself to dismiss the truant doubts that tiptoed across her mind. How would they feel – six months or a year from now – about not being able to go home even for a weekend?

When would they be able to go home?

Chapter Thirty-six

Despite his efforts to conceal this, Vera knew Paul was as anxious as she about Tracy's future. Then, late in September, Tracy phoned to say that she and David were applying for admission to the graduate school at McGill University.

'We'll be able to start in the January term,' she said with clear enthusiasm. 'Would you believe it? After all David's swearing he wouldn't go to law school, that's what he's hoping to do. And I want a master's – at least – in education. How's that for a shocker?'

'Darling, it sounds wonderful,' Vera said with relief. 'But you'll need money. You and David will need money,' she amended. 'Dad and I will –'

'We'll be able to save some between now and January,' Tracy interrupted. 'And if we change from student visas to landed immigrant, then we'll be eligible for financial aid.'

'You keep your student visas,' Vera insisted. 'Dad and I will provide whatever financial aid you and David need.' Hadn't Tracy said she and David would be married 'somewhere along the way'? David was family.

'Hold on, Mom.' Tracy was in consultation with David. Vera waited impatiently. She knew it was absurd, but she didn't want them to be landed immigrants. That seemed so final. 'Mom?' Tracy returned to the phone.

'Yes, darling?' Vera's heart was pounding.

'I talked to David. He says you and Dad are wonderful – and he promises he'll pay you back some day. Thanks,

Mom,' she whispered. 'And let me thank Dad, too.'

A week later Tracy phoned to say that she and David had been married.

'By the rabbi of the oldest synagogue in Canada,' Tracy told her. Paul joined in on an extension in their bedroom. 'It was founded in Montreal in 1768. We thought about a civil ceremony, but we knew you and Dad – and Grandpa – would want us to have a religious ceremony. Don't bother telling David's family.' Hurt mingled with cynicism in her voice. 'His mother hung up on him the first time he tried to call from up here.'

'Neither of you need David's parents.' Paul joined the conversation. 'It's their loss – not yours.'

'Tell Grandpa we had our wedding dinner at Ben's Delicatessen. It's kind of a landmark here in Montreal. Great smoked beef sandwiches on rye, borscht, cheese-cake, and tea. Tell him we went there because we knew it was a place he'd love – and we kind of felt as though he were sitting there with us.'

'I'll tell him,' Vera promised. She knew Tracy missed the special closeness she'd shared with her grandfather before he became so hostile to David.

'Tell him David's had a real haircut. He looks gorgeous.' Tracy suppressed an incipient giggle. 'I think he feels naked.'

A letter from Tracy early in November enlightened her parents on a most unusual situation in London – a city she knew they both loved.

'I just received this wild letter from Audrey.' Her room-mate when she was at school in London, Vera recognized. 'I can't imagine something like this happening in London, but there was this really super long-planned Vietnam peace demonstration on Sunday, October 27. They were expecting 200,000 to show up. There had been two earlier ones, but nothing like this! Before it even happened, the newspapers were calling it the *October Revolution*. They said the National Gallery, the National Portrait Gallery, and the Tate Gallery would be closed that whole weekend. All the entrances to the Houses of Parliament would be sealed. The British transport police had cancelled weekend leaves and put everybody on standby. American troops in Great Britain – all twenty-six thousand – have orders to stay out of London.'

Vera paused, shook her head in dismay. 'It goes on and on. Can you believe this is happening in our London?'

'The whole world's changing,' Paul replied.

'The police in London aren't even armed,' Vera recalled. 'But perhaps that's good.' *Laurie would say that*, she thought involuntarily.

'What does Tracy say about the actual demonstration?' Paul prodded, and Vera returned to scan Tracy's long letter.

'Despite all the fears and preparations, I gather it was comparatively peaceful. Only about forty demonstrators and six policemen were injured – and nobody was seriously hurt. Forty-three people were arrested – eight of them students.'

'Vera, we ought to take a month off and visit London together. It was so important in our lives.' Paul's face was nostalgic. 'Maybe next summer?'

'I'd love to see London again. Just to walk the streets and know there'd be no bombs. To see all its beauty without the old fears.' Vera, too, was caught up in remembrance. 'When life is on a more even keel, we'll go back to London,' she promised. Yet in a corner of her mind she knew she couldn't go back to London with Paul. Going to see Tracy and David had been different. Going with Paul would be a walk into the past. It would shove her back into years she couldn't bear to face – the years in Copenhagen, the horror of *Kristallnacht*.

Vera was especially conscious of Tracy's absence with the approach of Thanksgiving. While *she* was free to come home, Vera knew she'd never leave David alone on Thanksgiving. Holidays must be poignant occasions for the kids who'd run from the draft to live in Canada, she thought compassionately. She brushed from her mind Mary O'Brien's bitter accusation a few days ago. *How can folks talk about amnesty for those draft-dodgers – when boys like my son lie dead in Vietnam*? Though the bitter-cold weather was on its way, she and Paul should fly up to Montreal to spend a weekend with Tracy and David. Maybe next month, she thought with a flurry of anticipation.

On Thanksgiving morning, Doris came over immediately after breakfast to help with the dinner preparations – always prepared by family now. Paul was upstairs, finishing up an article for the small magazine that was publishing him regularly. His father had gone to help a local group deliver Thanksgiving baskets to several elderly shut-ins. Later Phil and Neal would arrive. There was a soothing quietness about the house on occasions like this, Vera thought sentimentally.

'Who's this fellow Laurie's bringing home?' Doris questioned, settling down to a cup of coffee with Vera, a provocative glint in her eyes.

'Doris, I warned you,' Vera reminded good-humouredly. 'Laurie wanted it understood Jeff is a good *friend*. No romance,' she emphasized. 'He's a fellow med student who was going to be alone on Thanksgiving – and you know Laurie. Right away she ordered him to come home with her.'

'What about the other fellow – the one you said used to call her from Paris?'

'Laurie never let on there was anything serious – and I never dared pry.' Always Vera felt herself on thin ice with Laurie – loved but not *liked*. 'But that was summer before last. This past summer – the little while she was home – there were no calls. But don't you make any bright remarks.'

'I won't. I promise.'

'I've been getting all that garbage from her about how there's no room in a woman med student's life for romance. All she thinks about is finishing med school and going on into her residency.' Vera sighed. 'I know, women are pushing off marriage these days. I know that plenty of women lead happy, successful lives without a man.' She managed a wry smile. 'I've read all those feminist articles you shove at me.'

'But you want grandchildren,' Doris joshed. 'Hey, look how long I'm going to have to wait – and I'm almost eight years older than you.'

'Of course, Jeff's name creeps into the conversation a lot,' Vera conceded. 'But then, these days, women can have close men friends without a physical attraction being involved. She keeps saying he thinks a lot the way she does.'

'Un-hunh.' Doris nodded knowingly.

'Doris, knock it off.' But truant hope welled in Vera. To her, happiness meant *family*. She yearned to see her daughters with husbands and children. At least, Tracy was halfway there. Though Dad was unhappy about Tracy's marriage, she and Paul were pleased.

By late morning Phil had arrived with Neal, Paul had come downstairs, and Joel had returned from delivering the baskets. They gathered in the den to watch the Macy's Thanksgiving Day Parade because this had become a ritual for Neal, who had to be constantly urged to sit an acceptable distance from the screen. 'Why do all kids think they have to climb into the set?' Joel had complained good-humouredly through the years – first with Laurie and Tracy, now with Neal.

Neal was such a darling boy, Vera thought. They were all inclined to spoil him, though Doris warned against this. Phil was enthralled that Neal had asked for piano lessons and was already showing promise.

Just past noon, Paul left the house to drive to the Saratoga railroad station to meet Laurie and Jeff. Almost on sight, Vera decided she liked Jeff Green. He was warm, bright, compassionate. And he was fascinated when Paul talked about Dr Evans and the reverence with which the ageing doctor was held in Eastwood.

'Dr Evans is a holdover from another era,' Joel told him with obvious affection. 'He's been in this town for forty-eight years. Other doctors came and went – Dr Evans belonged to us.'

In a flurry of high spirits, the three women brought the traditional Thanksgiving dinner to the table. Yet Vera was pointedly aware of Tracy's absence. Laurie knew not to ask about Tracy and David in her grandfather's presence. That would just bring on a tirade of recrimination. Yet Vera suspected that her father-in-law was having fresh doubts about the Vietnam war – and that he was troubled by this. It was not in what he said – it was the way he looked when they watched TV news programmes.

Nixon – who'd won the election by the slimmest margin since 1912, narrower even than his loss to JFK in 1960 – talked about carrying out his campaign promise to end the war in Vietnam. It was now the longest war in American history, and Americans were increasingly disenchanted. Once the war was over, Vera thought with shaky optimism, the president would offer amnesty to the thousands of draft-evaders who'd sought sanctuary in Canada and Sweden and other countries. *Wouldn't he*?

The conversation at the dinner table was peppered with reminiscences of other Thanksgivings. Jeff talked poignantly about the Thanksgivings that he'd been allowed to spend with his grandparents. Paul remembered Thanksgivings in Europe during World War II. *Hell, there was no way we could eat Spam and pretend it was turkey.* Vera and Paul recalled a Thanksgiving they'd shared in war-torn, ration-racked London.

While the three women served pecan pie and coffee, the men discussed the need in this country for a national health insurance programme.

'We're the only industrialized country on this planet – except for South Africa – that doesn't provide its people with guaranteed health care. And what we offer people without money is so damned demeaning,' Jeff said urgently. 'Decent health care should be the right of every person in this country.'

'There's too much waste,' Phil said. 'Too much inefficiency.'

'But when people talk about changing the system, they don't mean better treatment,' Jeff pointed out, his voice deepening with contempt. 'They're only talking about saving money.'

'When I was a kid,' Phil reminisced, 'people thought about hospitals as being institutions of mercy. They've become big business.'

'Truman fought for national health insurance – to be funded by payroll deductions. But the plan got nowhere, though he kept trying for years,' Joel recalled. 'But at least Johnson pushed Medicare through. Senior citizens are grateful for that.'

'But what about the rest of the population?' Jeff asked with impatience. 'Don't they –'

'Enough shop talk,' Doris interrupted, sitting down at the table again. 'If anybody wants seconds of pie, there's a whole pecan we haven't even started.'

Involuntarily Vera remembered that Tracy always took seconds of pecan pie. Where were Tracy and David right now? *They must be homesick*, she thought in anguish – *so far away from home and family on this special holiday*. All those kids who couldn't bring themselves to fight an immoral war. *She and Paul would go up to Montreal to see Tracy and David late next month*, she resolved. Maybe between Christmas and New Year's – when everything was slow with the business.

On Friday morning Vera came awake slowly, conscious of the comforting sounds of heat coming up in the radiators. She felt a surge of contentment. Laurie was home. She and Jeff would be returning to school on Sunday evening, but for now she was here. Her mind hurtled back through the years to that day in October 1944 when Paul had arrived at their London apartment on a five-day leave. It was the first time he saw Laurie. Oh yes, a few days could be very precious when they brought loved ones together.

She heard the sound of water running in the bathroom. Paul was showering. Through the years of teaching, he'd acquired the habit of rising early. Another few minutes here under the blankets, she promised herself, then she'd get up.

When she and Paul arrived at the breakfast table, they found her father-in-law and Jeff already there – in lively conversation over steaming cups of coffee. Laurie would be sleeping late, she surmised indulgently.

'I'm taking Jeff over to meet Dr Evans,' Joel announced in rare high spirits. Sometimes Vera worried that Paul and Doris had encouraged him to withdraw from the business the way he had. He kept up all his civic activities, but often she felt he was enduring a rudderless existence. 'You know how Doc is always moaning about the new crop of doctors . . . how they're all after fancy, big city or rich suburban practices, when small towns and rural areas are crying for new doctors.'

'You'll like Dr Evans,' Vera assured Jeff. But in a corner of her mind she questioned Joel's motive for taking Jeff to meet Dr Evans. He was harbouring some sweet hope that – once Jeff finished medical school and his residency – he would come to Eastwood to share Dr Evans' practice. Dr Evans was a good doctor and a wonderful man. Nobody here in town wanted to consider that one day – only a few years hence – the years would catch up with him.

Arriving at the house from the office at the end of the working day, Vera heard voices in the den. She found the three men and Laurie – as she'd expected – watching the six o'clock news on television. She sat down to join them. At the commercial break, Joel switched the volume to a murmur and turned to her.

'Guess what we fixed up,' he said jubilantly. 'For the school's intercession Jeff's coming to stay with us. He's going to spend those weeks working with Dr Evans. What Doc calls real *hands-on* experience. These two guys were made for each other.'

Involuntarily Vera turned to Laurie. Her throat tightened in alarm. Laurie was upset that Jeff would be here in the house for almost a month. All at once she understood – as Laurie did. *Dad was trying to play matchmaker between Laurie and Jeff.* If there could have been anything – and deep in her heart she'd harboured a wistful hope – he'd just destroyed that chance.

Vera and Paul decided to drive to Montreal – as she had planned – in the interim between Christmas and New Year's. It was a perfect time, they agreed. Laurie and Jeff would be at the house with Dad. Though his health was good, they worried about his frequent depressions.

Doris had tried to talk to him about seeing a therapist, but he'd erupted in rage. Still, Dad was enjoying Jeff's presence at the house, Vera told herself – the little time he was there. Jeff spent most of his daytime hours and even some evenings with Dr Evans.

Dad warned them they might be caught in a heavy Canadian snowstorm this time of year.

'The highways are kept in great shape,' Paul said optimistically. 'We can drive up in five hours.'

They were in the car by eight o'clock on departure morning, anticipated arriving in Montreal in time for a late lunch. Expecting harsh winter winds and biting cold, they dressed accordingly, though they knew that much of Montreal's population found it possible to live an almost subterranean life in the months when the temperature plummeted to staggering lowness. Tracy had written with awe about Underground Montreal, which roamed for two-and-a-half miles and offered a dazzling array of boutiques, grocery stores, restaurants, a church, a discotheque, and a Metro station.

They arrived in Montreal to feel only a mild breeze that carried a hint of rain.

'Can you believe it?' Paul marvelled while they listened to a local weather report on the car radio. 'It's 38 degrees!'

'Let's find the hotel,' Vera said, impatient to see Tracy. 'The kids will be waiting for us there.' She'd rejected their offer to relinquish their bedroom to spend three nights in sleeping bags.

Astonished by the lack of traffic congestion – because Montreal separated pedestrians, cars, and electric trains – they followed Tracy's instructions and arrived at the elegant Queen Elizabeth on Dorchester Boulevard. With the car in parking facilities, they sought out the palatial black-marble-pillared lobby of the *Queen E* – as Tracy had referred to it.

'Oh God, Paul, will we ever find them here?' Vera said in sudden panic as she viewed the busy area.

'Mom!' Tracy's voice reached her and she spied a waving hand.

'There they are!' Clutching their over-sized valise in one hand, Paul reached for Vera's arm with the other.

'Mom, you're really here!' Vera saw the relief in her younger daughter's eyes as they clung together. 'It seems like forever!'

Tracy turned to embrace her father while David and her mother exchanged a warm hug.

'Let me take your luggage.' Almost shy in this first encounter as a son-in-law, David reached for Paul's valise.

'You're probably starving,' Tracy effervesced. 'Get registered, send up your luggage, and let's go somewhere for lunch.'

'Somewhere very special,' Vera decreed, rejoicing in this reunion. Yet already she had concluded that Tracy was lonely – not happy – in this self-imposed exile. She remembered her own first months in Copenhagen. She'd loved the Munches, was so grateful for their kindness – but had felt such desolation at living in a strange country.

After a brief consultation with David, Tracy decided that they would lunch at Le Café – one of eleven restaurants within the huge hotel complex.

'From there we can go straight to the Place Ville Marie,' she explained with an almost hysterical gaiety. 'That's the Underground Montreal that I wrote you about. We don't have to go out into the street – there's a direct indoor passageway.'

Tracy and David had managed to take the day off from their respective jobs – though they'd be leaving shortly to begin graduate studies at McGill. They were determined to show Vera and Paul as much as was humanly possible today. They visited the Place Ville Marie – where Vera was awed by the network of escalators. In the

Underground – all of which had been completed only within the past four years – they boarded a Metro for their next destination. Vera and Paul were impressed by the blue-and-white Metro cars, which rolled along in awesome quietness and were devoid of the graffiti so familiar in the New York City subway system.

In the light, late-afternoon drizzle they admired the Montreal skyline, pierced in recent years by a series of high-rises.

'The Stock Exchange wanted to build a fifty-seven-storey skyscraper, but the city planning department would only allow forty-seven,' David told them. 'And they only allow construction on 40% of the land, so they'll never have those huge clusters of tall towers like in New York.'

Vera was touched by Tracy and David's insistence that they have dinner *at home*. It was as though, she thought lovingly, they wanted to convince Paul and her that they had a real home here in Montreal. The apartment was tiny but cheerful. The four carried on lively conversation while together Tracy and David prepared a substantial, tasty meal.

'Where did you two learn to cook like this?' Paul asked in genuine admiration.

Tracy giggled. 'We used something called a cookbook. It's real easy if you pay attention.'

The three days in Montreal sped past. Vera and Paul took photographs of the ancient synagogue where Tracy and David had been married. They drove to the top of Mount Royal to gaze down at the winding St Lawrence and to visit historic St Joseph's Oratory. They saw both Old Montreal and the exciting modern Montreal. They visited McGill University – austere structures of brick and Quebec grey stone, campus elms stark and forbidding. Yet the sprawling university grounds – surrounded by the city – seemed an oasis of quiet in the midst of urban bustle.

Vera constantly was conscious of American young men – some with wives and babies – who'd come here in flight from the draft. They were lonely, she thought compassionately. They missed family and home. And Canadian culture was slightly different – more formal, more conservative.

On their fourth morning in Montreal – overcast and with a serious drop in temperature – Vera and Paul headed back for Eastwood. They'd shared a bittersweet breakfast with Tracy and David before retrieving their car. Tracy's last words lingered in Vera's mind. *Mom, come up again soon. Montreal's not really that far from Eastwood.*

Tracy had contrived a few moments of whispered conference with her before breakfast. Paul's fiftieth birthday was approaching, and Tracy wished advice about an appropriate birthday present. *At this point*, Vera thought grimly, *it would probably be wisest just to forget the birthday*.

Paul had made rueful remarks in the last weeks about reaching fifty with few accomplishments to show for those years. So he wasn't earning much money from his writing – he was building up a following, gaining respect in the educational community. That should count for a lot. And even his counselling draft-evaders had lost its sting with so many Americans convinced that the action in Vietnam was a tremendous error.

'It looks as though the sun's going to break through.' Paul intruded on her introspection. 'That's a good omen.'

'The good omen,' Vera said with unfamiliar brusqueness, 'is when President Nixon keeps his promise to pull our troops out of Vietnam.' She paused, took a laboured breath. 'And when he announces amnesty for the kids who ran to Canada and Sweden.'

'Tracy and David are going back to school,' he pointed out gently. 'That's a good omen for the future.'

'But when will they be allowed to come back home?' Her voice was taut with anguish. 'Tracy's so lonely up there.'

Paul hesitated. 'It was a choice she made, Vera.'

'Because she's so loyal to David. But she's miserable.'

'Did she say that?' Paul challenged.

'Couldn't you feel it?' Of course he could. His eyes told her so. 'It broke my heart to say goodbye. Leaving her up there in a strange country when she wants so much to come home.'

'Nothing in life comes without a price tag. Tracy made a decision. All those American kids up in Canada knew what they were doing.'

'I know what it's like to live in exile.' A bitterness that had long lain buried in Vera's subconscious pushed through the surface. 'I remember.'

'Tracy's not living in exile.'

'What else can you call it?' Vera shot back, attacked by memories of Copenhagen, of the loneliness of a London without Paul.

Paul's hands tightened on the wheel. 'She went up there of her own volition. She's with David. She hasn't lost her family. This isn't a rehash of *Kristallnacht*. For God's sake, Vera, when are you going to learn to let go of the past?'

Vera sat very still and silent. As with all husbands and wives, she and Paul had argued on occasions through the years. They'd been through heated battles. But she had never heard that undertone of resentment directed at her before.

Paul was upset, she tried to comfort herself. He didn't

mean to be nasty. He worried about the flood of draft-age boys he'd counselled. Many of them had gone to Canada. He was asking himself if he had done the right thing.

She wasn't living in the past, she told herself defensively. Yet her mind taunted her with the knowledge that each time Laurie or Tracy went off to school, she felt a terrifying sense of loss. She dreaded the day when Laurie or Tracy would settle permanently in a town or city away from Eastwood. It would be as though she were losing her family for a second time.

Every day of her existence on this planet, she lived with the agonizing memory of hovering behind the closed door of the Schmidts' flat while she listened to the shouting on the floor above, heard her father's rebellious retorts to the SS troopers as he and Mama and Ernst were being dragged down the stairs and off into the night. To their deaths.

Without being aware of it, was she being blind to Paul's needs? *Was she in danger of losing him, too? Was it to come to pass as in her nightmares? Was she once again meant to lose those nearest and dearest to her?*

Chapter Thirty-seven

By spring Laurie was already worrying about where she would spend her internship and residency. She meant to heed Jeff's advice to try for a big-city hospital – *where you experience every kind of medical emergency.* An inner-city hospital, she'd narrowed this down, where interns and residents were desperately needed.

Along with Jeff, she was experiencing all the frustrations of a third-year medical student. This was the year of unpredictability. The year when both admitted to a guilt that they were, in truth, using patients to further their own knowledge. And always they were conscious of a feeling of inadequacy.

On this early April morning, Laurie awoke with an instant realization that this was Adele's twenty-fifth birthday. They went through their usual 'happy birthday' routine, then hurried off in their separate directions. Laurie had already plotted with Jeff – providing no emergency arose in conflict – to bring home Chinese take-out and a small birthday cake as a surprise party for Adele.

She was on medical rotation. This was the rotation that filled her with the most insecurity. Here the patients in her care were mostly elderly and she was struggling to cope with putting IVs into fragile and delicate skin. She felt a stab of remorse each time a patient winced in pain.

Early on her rounds she was grateful that today seemed less horrendous than yesterday. And then she went into the room of a woman who had been admitted three days earlier. A vital, vivacious woman about her grandfather's age and with whom she'd felt an instant rapport. Right away she understood that something sombre had occurred. Her doctor and a resident were involved in a work-up. She appeared close to tears. Laurie crossed to take her hand, smiled reassuringly. That was expected of a third-year medical student. But while the doctor and resident continued their work-up, the woman lifted her face to Laurie's.

'It's cancer, they told me.' Her voice choked. 'They can't operate.'

Laurie's hand tightened on the patient's. Tears spilled over and poured down her cheeks. *A doctor was not supposed to cry.*

At the end of the relentlessly long day, Laurie hurried to meet Jeff as pre-arranged.

'Okay, you made it,' he said exuberantly, then paused. 'Rough day?'

'I did the unforgivable,' she told him in a tortured whisper. 'I cried when a patient told me she was going to die.'

'Let's get out of here,' he said gently.

Walking through the balmy early evening, they talked about the special problems ahead of them.

'I couldn't stand the callous attitude of that doctor,' Laurie admitted. 'And I know he's a good doctor. I've seen him be so kind with patients. But he just walked away and left this woman with the resident and me.'

'He knew he couldn't do any more for her,' Jeff pointed out. 'He went on to his next patient. And residents –' Jeff's smile was rueful. 'Residents don't have time to be compassionate.'

'If I can't be compassionate, I don't want to be a doctor,' Laurie said angrily, tears welling in her eyes again.

'Knock it off,' Jeff ordered. 'We have to learn to take the bad with the good. Right now we have a birthday party to organize.'

The phone was ringing in the apartment when Laurie unlocked the door. Jeff balanced the bags from the Chinese take-out restaurant with the minuscule birthday cake they'd bought at Cake Master's. With the door open, Laurie rushed to pick up the phone. The caller was Adele.

'Hi.' Adele's voice came to her in that special tone that said she'd run up against problems at school. 'I called to warn you not to expect me home for dinner. I'll grab a hamburger and coffee here at school. We're having a meeting that'll probably go on until ten or eleven – with some irate politicians.'

'Oh, Adele. On your birthday?' Laurie was exasperated.

'If you brought home Chinese, save some for me. I'll need resuscitation.'

Laurie and Jeff dug into dinner with an effort at enthusiasm. The leftovers went into the refrigerator.

'We'll light the birthday candles, eat a chunk of cake, and toast Adele with coffee,' Jeff ordered. 'We'll save a piece of cake for Adele, of course.'

Jeff knew she felt miserable, Laurie thought. And she'd seen him cut up over a lost patient, she remembered. But he hadn't cried with his patient.

'If Adele is going to put in all the crazy hours plus the headaches she has with teaching, she might as well have gone to medical school,' he joked. 'At least, she'd be seeing decent money at the end of the trail.'

'Adele isn't in teaching for the money,' Laurie shot back.

'And I'm not in medicine for the money,' Jeff retorted.

'I didn't mean it like that,' Laurie apologized. 'I'm just so damn tired. I feel so helpless. Like today with that sweet woman at the hospital. She came in so perky and in love with life.' Her voice dropped to a whisper. 'And I felt so helpless.'

'Doctors can help only up to a point,' Jeff began and stopped short as tears spilled onto her cheeks. 'Honey, you can't make the whole world well and happy.'

All at once she was in Jeff's arms, and he was murmuring endearments. He lifted her face to his, brought his mouth down to hers. Almost in a trance she responded.

'What are we doing?' she asked breathlessly when his mouth left hers, his arms still holding her close.

'What I've wanted to do for such a long time.'

'This is crazy, you know.' But she wanted him to hold her. She wanted him to make love to her.

'So let's be crazy,' he whispered.

Laurie brushed away reality, abandoned herself to emotion. She uttered a faint chuckle of amused derision when he lifted her in his arms, then almost tripped over the coffee table in his impatience to carry her into the bedroom.

'Jeff, what about the door?' she asked in sudden alarm minutes later – after they'd explored each other's nakedness with sensuous pleasure.

'You always lock and put on the chain the minute you come in,' he reminded. 'And Adele's at a meeting.'

'I wouldn't want Margie next door to barge in to borrow coffee,' she said huskily.

'This is our own private world,' he promised, moving with her in passionate rhythm. 'Forget about Margie, forget about Adele, forget about the hospital . . .'

At last they lay motionless, legs entangled, his face against hers.

'I knew it would be great. But not this great,' he said with an air of exultant exhaustion.

'It was crazy.' *How had it happened?* But Laurie was conscious of a feeling of total relaxation.

'Crazy,' he acknowledged.

'There's no future in this,' she warned. 'Nothing permanent.'

'I know,' he agreed. 'We've got our futures plotted for years ahead. Another year of med school, four years of residency. I head for a small-town practice, you to a ghetto hospital. We'll be worlds apart. But for now,' he said quietly, 'we can have something we both need to help us through the training period. No ties. No obligations.'

'And we can still be friends?' Laurie persisted. 'You and Adele are my very best friends in this world.'

'We can still be friends,' he promised and pulled himself above her again. 'But for now, will you please shut up?' he pleaded lovingly. 'More action and less words.'

On a mid-April Friday – with the first signs of spring on display in Eastwood – Vera and Paul headed for Montreal for a three-day weekend with Tracy and David. Vera had tried futilely to persuade Joel to go up with them.

'If Tracy wants to see me, let her come to Eastwood,' he said. '*She* can come home if she likes,' he emphasized.

But he'd self-consciously prepared a *care package* for her: A collection of edible goodies he knew Tracy adored. And they took with them, also, the news that Doris and Phil would be going up with Neal for a week as soon as school closed.

'Let's don't mention that we're working with a group that's petitioning Congress for an amnesty bill,' Paul warned when they stopped in a diner for coffee. 'We mustn't give them false hopes.'

'That's all you think it is – false hopes?' *She hadn't meant to sound hostile*, she thought guiltily. *Why were she and Paul bickering so much these days*?

'Not false,' he corrected himself. 'Just that it could be a long time in coming.'

'Tracy's not going to admit it, but I *know* she's homesick. I hear it in her voice every time we speak on the phone. I feel so helpless.'

'Vera, you can't fix everything.' She was conscious of a hint of impatience in his voice. *Because he was uptight – about Vietnam, about the state of education in this country*, she told herself. *When would he learn to unwind?* 'Right now, Tracy and David are focused on their schooling,' he went on determinedly. 'That's important.'

'I wish we could persuade her to come home for a week or two this summer.' Vera sighed. 'There's no real reason why she can't. And Dad would be so pleased.'

'She's not going to leave David. And there's nothing you can do to make Dad approve of her running off to Canada.'

She shouldn't have mentioned the barrier between Dad and Tracy, Vera reproached herself. It had made him remember his own tenuous situation with Dad. All his life Paul had been so eager to please his father. How could she make Paul understand he *wasn't* a failure?

By the time they approached Canadian Customs, the weather had turned blustery and cold. Ominous clumps of clouds hovered in the sky.

'Snow by nightfall,' Paul predicted while they waited for the always-swift clearance at Customs.

'This late in April?' Vera lifted an eyebrow in doubt.

'In Canada, yes,' he reminded. 'But the roads will be cleared by the time we leave.'

On their arrival in Montreal, they went directly to the hotel, registered, then headed for Tracy and David's apartment. They let themselves in with the key Tracy had mailed and prepared to wait for the other two to arrive from their respective classes.

'Why don't I run down to the deli near here?' Paul suggested. 'I'll pick up dinner makings. We'll eat in the apartment. No need to run around in this weather.' Already snow was beginning to fall.

Moments after Paul left, Vera was startled by the ringing of the phone. She hesitated a moment, then reached for the receiver.

'Hello.'

'Vera, I couldn't wait to tell you!' Doris's voice was electric. 'Dad was just talking with one of his buddies who follows everything in Congress – and he said that Congressman Koch from New York City has introduced a bill that'll offer amnesty for draft-evaders. All criminal prosecutions will be wiped off the slate. If it goes through, David and Tracy can come home!'

'I don't understand.' Vera forced herself to be realistic. 'They're still drafting men.'

'The way Dad understands it, there'll be a new interpretation of CO status. If a draftee can prove he's opposed to a particular war on moral or philosophical grounds, then he'll be classified as a CO and will do noncombatant or civilian service for two years. Even those in jail or pending criminal prosecution will be eligible for this. Of course, it hasn't been passed yet.'

'What are its chances?' Vera asked. *Dad had told Doris about the bill*, her mind computed. *Dad was so anxious for Tracy to come home.*

'Who can tell?' Doris admitted and paused. 'Phil doesn't think it'll be passed. But at least, people are thinking in that direction. Not just little groups like yours, but those right up there in Congress.'

'I'll tell the kids,' Vera said after a moment. 'But they'll understand it's just the first efforts.' *Amnesty. What a beautiful word.*

Over huge pastrami sandwiches and mounds of coleslaw and potato salad, Vera and Paul discussed the Koch bill with Tracy and David. Only now did they drop their masks and admit to yearnings to go home.

'Sure, some of the guys – and their wives – say they don't want to go back until the whole society in the United States changes,' David said seriously. 'But most of those we know – like ourselves – are dying to go home.'

As Paul had feared, the Koch bill did not go through, though Koch made it clear this was not the end of his efforts. Vera and Paul felt encouraged when on June 8, President Nixon announced that, by the end of August, 25,000 US troops would be withdrawn from Vietnam.

'That's the beginning of the end,' Paul said enthusiastically.

'From your mouth to God's ear,' Vera whispered, borrowing a phrase learned years ago from Fiona.

Vera was in high spirits when Laurie came home for a week at the end of school and brought Jeff and Adele with her. Now she learned that Jeff would remain in Eastwood for the summer – living at the Kahn house at Joel's insistence – while Laurie returned to work at the Harlem clinic again. Adele would be involved in a Harlem project for inner-city children. For a breathtaking few hours – on their first arrival – she'd convinced herself that the relationship between Laurie and Jeff had deepened beyond friendship.

'I tell you, Jeff's sure to come back here to go into practice with Doc Evans,' Joel confided with satisfaction. 'Now why can't Laurie see the light and team up with him?' A glint in his eyes said he meant more than a professional arrangement. *But Laurie and Jeff were pulled in opposite directions.*

Vera focused on making this week a warm and loving occasion. Even Dad, she thought with relief, seemed to be emerging from his constant depression. He'd watched

Adele grow up; she was like family. He took pleasure in listening to the earnest discussions between Adele and Paul about the future of American education.

'Paul, you think you know what it's like teaching in a ghetto school,' Adele told him on the evening before she and Laurie were to return to New York. Earlier there had been a family dinner. Doris and Phil had left with Neal because it was now past his bedtime. Jeff had gone on a house-call with Dr Evans. Laurie was in the kitchen preparing a late round of coffee. The others gathered in the den for more conversation. 'You have to be there to know. We spend almost 70% of our time just trying to keep order in the classroom. We're constantly on the watch to defuse violence. And the traffic in drugs is not getting better – it's getting worse. Oh, sure,' she drawled, faintly teasing. 'You're having problems even here. Doris told me how the kids are fighting against the new dress codes.'

'That's not what worries me in our schools, Adele. It's the quality of the education. This is not a rich suburban community. We're dealing here with serious budget cuts. We have a few dedicated teachers in the system; they go out and buy supplies with their own money because they can't bear to see the kids cheated.'

'The kids in Eastwood come to school prepared to learn,' Adele said with quiet intensity. 'Ghetto kids arrive with few of the skills they need to make it in the school world. God knows, some of us try – but it's not enough.'

'I think that the unsung heroes of this country are our school-teachers,' Vera said softly. 'Teachers like you two.' She turned from Adele to Paul. 'Because you care and you're trying to make the system better. You're making a contribution.' She paused. 'Sometimes I envy you.'

Joel seemed startled. Dismayed. 'Vera, you're a successful woman. You're head of a major business. You should envy no one.'

'I think that I've always felt guilty that I'm alive.' Vera spoke compulsively – from the heart. 'I stood by while my mother and father and brother were marched off to their deaths – and I did nothing.'

'Vera, you were thirteen years old. What could you have done?' Paul challenged.

'You've been a fine wife and mother. You've been the centre of this family,' Joel declared. 'You've made the business successful beyond my fondest dreams.'

'I didn't mean to sound maudlin,' Vera apologized, all at once self-conscious. *Why had she said that?* 'It's just that today is my parents' wedding anniversary. Every year I remember. It was always such a joyous celebration in our house.'

Paul reached for her hand. 'As *our* anniversary is in *this* house.' Walking into the den with a tray of coffee-filled mugs, Laurie smiled at this show of affection.

'You talk about making a contribution, Vera.' Joel reached for a mug of coffee, rose to his feet as though propelled by a need for action. 'You're doing that. Kahns have been in business in this town for five generations. We've been there to serve when our country needed us – going back to the Civil War. We –'

'Grandpa, if there were no guns, there could be no wars,' Laurie broke in passionately. 'There'd be less crime. There'd –'

'Laurie, grow up!' Joel bristled. 'Guns help keep the peace. They –'

'Like now, with half-a-million Americans fighting in Vietnam?' she demanded. 'With more than 33,000 dead and many more wounded? With no guns, Tracy wouldn't be hiding away with David in Canada!'

'Stop it, you two!' Vera was pale, her voice strident.

She was aware of Paul's supplicating glance in her direction, but she couldn't let Dad and Laurie stand here and tear each other apart. 'We don't have to agree on everything.' She was struggling for calm. 'Dad's entitled to his opinions, Laurie. And Dad, we have to respect Laurie's opinions. Now no more talk about guns.'

But her family was divided, she told herself in anguish. *How could she ever bring them back together again?*

Chapter Thirty-eight

Vera was touched by Joel's pleasure at having Jeff in the house for the summer, though in truth most of his waking hours were spent in Dr Evans' company. Then, over the Fourth of July weekend, Joel confided that he was launching a secret campaign.

'Next June, Doc Evans will have been serving this town fifty years. Let's have a surprise banquet in his honour. Isn't it time we told him how much he's loved and appreciated in this town?'

'Dad, I think it's a wonderful idea.' Tears filled her eyes. Almost everybody in Eastwood had a special story to tell about Dr Evans. 'But I don't know how long you'll be able to keep it a secret.'

'I'm setting up a committee. You and Doris will be on it. Another eight or ten people from different walks of life.' Joel radiated excitement. 'I know it's a long way off, but this has to be something spectacular. Maybe we can have it in the school gym. What do you think?'

Now Vera and Joel debated the initial steps in arranging for the banquet. When Paul arrived home from delivering a talk to a parent/teacher organization in a nearby community, he joined enthusiastically in the discussion. *This would be so good for Dad*, Vera told herself. The family had worried about his depression in these last months. This would pull him out of it.

Again this summer Paul talked to Vera about their going to London for two or three weeks in the early fall. *When the tourist hordes will be gone*. But – fighting guilt that she was keeping him from something he yearned to do – she pointed out that she couldn't take off more than three or four days from the business. Besides, going to London with Paul was an unnerving prospect – a journey into the past that she was afraid to face.

'We'll be going up to Montreal at the end of the month,' she hedged. 'We promised the kids that we'd see Expo 67 with them.' For the third year, Expo 67 was open to the public.

Doris and Phil would be driving up next month. Tracy was hurt and disappointed that her grandfather refused to visit, though he often talked with her on the telephone. He never asked about David. It was as though she were away at school and alone. He was proud that she was at McGill. Impatient to earn graduate degrees, both Tracy and David were taking summer classes.

On a steamy night in late August, Vera came home after a late conference at the office to find Paul and Joel in the den, sitting on the edge of their chairs while they watched a news bulletin on TV.

'Vera, you won't believe what happened!' Joel's face was flushed, his shoulders hunched in shock. 'A United States infantry company in the Rice Bowl –' Vietnam, she understood, '– just refused direct orders to advance! For hours,' he stressed, 'until some veteran with his head on straight convinced them they had to fight!'

'They'd been fighting a hellish battle for five days,' Paul reproached. 'And now they were expected to go into a labyrinth of North Vietnamese bunkers to bring out the bodies of Americans killed in a helicopter crash?'

'But whoever heard of an American soldier refusing to obey an order?' Joel blustered. 'Would *you* have done it? No!'

'In World War II, we knew we were fighting against horrible evil. The whole world saw Hitler as a menace to humanity. Those kids in Vietnam – and most of them are kids,' Paul interjected, '– they *know* the crap we've fed them about fighting for democracy in Vietnam was a crock of shit. They're angry that American leaders have been lying to them. Sure, in the beginning a lot of them felt they were fighting to save the world from Communism, but that didn't last long.'

'How do you know all this?' Joel challenged defensively.

'It's like we've talked about before.' Vera contrived an aura of calm. 'Six years ago even liberals like Al Gore and George McGovern and Gene McCarthy were in favour of our going into Vietnam, but then they realized there is no democracy in Vietnam.'

'Dad, the world agrees that the North Vietnamese were responsible for the terrorism and guerrilla war in South Vietnam,' Paul continued. 'But Ngo Dinh Diem became an oppressive dictator. The US government urged him to change his policies. He refused. Then –'

'I know all this,' Joel interrupted impatiently, yet Vera sensed a new defensiveness in him. 'He and his brother were assassinated by the military *junta*. The new government abolished martial law, promised free elections later.'

'Dad, the South Vietnamese government has gone through a series of changes, but it remains a dictatorship. Innocent civilians – children, women, old men – are being butchered for no reason. *We don't belong there.*'

'I don't want to talk about it anymore.' Joel was brusque. 'Enough already.'

Yet Vera took hope in her suspicion that her father-in-law was at last feeling doubts about the American presence in Vietnam.

Vera looked forward to Laurie's coming home for a few days before the beginning of the new school-year, her final year in med school. She was disappointed when Laurie cut her stay short by two days with vague talk about needing to get reoriented in the school routine.

Would the wall between Laurie and herself – and Laurie and Dad – ever be abolished? she asked herself in recurrent anguish. She knew what would make the difference. All she had to tell Laurie was that she and Dad had decided to close down Kahn Firearms Company – that henceforth, they'd operate only the mail-order catalogue and the chain of shops. *No guns on sale in the shops.* But to lay Kahn Firearms to rest would destroy Dad.

With a sense of loss Vera watched from the porch as Laurie and Jeff settled themselves in the old-model but still reliable Dodge that Dr Evans had insisted on giving Jeff as a reward for his summer work. Already she was impatient for the Thanksgiving weekend, when they'd be home. Already, she admonished herself, she was thinking of Jeff as a son-in-law when both Laurie and Jeff were frank about scheduling their futures in opposite directions.

In the vintage Dodge, Laurie rested her head against Jeff's shoulder as they travelled south on Route 22.

'Hey, I missed you,' Jeff said softly. 'Busy as hell, but I missed you.'

'I missed you, too,' Laurie admitted. 'Whom else can I gripe to? It was a long, hot summer.' She paused. 'That's the phrase journalists use to describe ghetto rioting. This summer was fairly calm in that respect. Oh, we dealt with a lot of heroin overdoses and stab wounds and gunshot wounds, but not on the scale of what's happened in earlier years.'

'This is the year – again – of the anti-war movement,' he speculated. 'I think of guys like Terry – fighting in Vietnam – and I feel a kind of guilt that as a med student

I'm exempt from the draft.' His smile was wry. 'A lot of grad students were caught in the new ruling this year. Since most grad students are over 21, they're right near the top of the draft boards' lists.' Laurie understood that the draft boards were obligated to take the oldest men on the available lists.

'This year's going to be wild,' Laurie predicted. 'All of a sudden we're *almost there* – heading for playing at being real doctors when we feel so damned inadequate.'

'It's a long drive into Manhattan,' Jeff said with a studied casualness that got her instant attention. 'What do you say we find a cosy but inexpensive little motel and have ourselves a real reunion?'

'Are you propositioning me, doctor?' Laurie drawled. Sometimes she worried that Jeff was playing a game, that he was hoping this would be for the long haul. She'd learned that the one thing in life she could count on was her work. Nothing could come before career.

'Don't play coy, doctor,' he admonished. 'Do we stop or don't we?'

'We stop,' Laurie told him.

She was all turned on because they hadn't made love in such a long time, she told herself – conscious of an impatience to be in his arms, to be filled with him. It wasn't *Jeff*, she forced herself to rationalize. She was young, healthy, female – she had needs.

Fleetingly, she dwelt on the knowledge that Jeff was going into his last year of med school. After that, he would be eligible for the draft. Interns and residents were serving in Vietnam. But she didn't want to think about that.

On October 11, the presidents of five Ivy League colleges called on Nixon to accelerate plans to bring American troops home from Vietnam – warning of the imminent

Moratorium. Four days later, millions of Americans across the country – in hundreds of towns and cities – took off from jobs and schools to take part in the first Vietnam Moratorium Day. Laurie phoned from New York to report that, along with college absenteeism, 90% of the city's high school students were cutting classes.

There were mass meetings, candlelight processions, prayer meetings. Church bells rang out through the land. Many demonstrators wore black armbands in memory of Americans who had died in Vietnam. This was unlike other demonstrations in that it was not held over a weekend, nor only in a handful of major cities. Advance advertisements in the *New York Times* listed Republican Senators Mark Hatfield and Charles Goodell along with the expected Democratic names.

At the scheduled time, Vera left the office to join Paul at the small local gathering.

'I have to do it, Dad,' she told her father-in-law, who watched sombrely while three employees in the plant withdrew along with her to demonstrate.

'I know,' he said. With resignation or approval? Vera asked herself.

At dinner that evening, Vera observed that her father-in-law was abnormally silent. Even when they went into the den to watch the evening news, he made no comment.

'I think it's shitty the way TV provided no prime-time live coverage,' Paul groused. 'Just this late-night wrap-up. And don't tell me it isn't because of pressure from the White House.'

'Dad, would you like some hot chocolate?' Vera asked solicitously. He'd been complaining about insomnia, she remembered.

'That would be good.' He managed a wisp of a smile.

Dad was trying to deal with the anti-war movement, Vera interpreted. It was so difficult for him to admit the country had made a bad mistake – possibly an immoral mistake – in sending Americans to fight in Vietnam. A fragment of a letter from Terry that Adele had read to her lingered in her mind. 'This is a bloody civil war. We don't belong here. Is our government so afraid to admit they've lost a war that they'll keep us here till we're all dead?'

On November 3, Nixon addressed the nation on TV to report that the North Vietnamese had rejected the secret peace proposals the government had been offering them. Now he asked for support for his plans to *Vietnamese* the war.

'Meaning what?' Vera asked without stopping to think.

'Meaning, let the Vietnamese fight their war. Let Americans come home,' Paul supplied.

'Maybe then Tracy'll come home.' Vera felt a surge of optimism.

'That doesn't mean amnesty for draft-dodgers,' Joel warned. 'But Tracy's not a draft-dodger.' A glaze seemed to cover his eyes, Vera thought. 'I don't know why she can't come home for a visit.'

'Go up with us the next time,' Vera urged. Dad refused to recognize that Tracy was showing support for David by not coming home for a brief visit. Tracy had always been tenaciously loyal. 'She wants so much to see you.'

'If Tracy wants to see her grandfather, let her come home.' His brusqueness was to mask his yearning to see his adored grandchild. He loved Laurie and Neal, Vera reassured herself, but his relationship with Tracy was special. Joel paused. 'We won't stop her from going back. She knows that.'

The following evening Tracy phoned from Montreal. Vera heard an electric excitement in her voice.

'Laurie called a little while ago,' Tracy bubbled. 'She said she and Adele are going down to Washington for the second Vietnam Moratorium. It's not going to be just another demonstration. This will be a three-day deal – on November 13, 14, and 15 – focusing on Washington DC. I've talked with David about it and he understands. I'm flying down to New York to meet them and –'

'What about school?' Vera interrupted, all at once anxious. A three-day demonstration could involve violence.

'I have no classes on Thursday – that's the thirteenth. I can handle missing one day.'

'Tracy, it sounds dangerous.' Vera was assaulted by images of police in riot gear using tear gas to break up the crowds.

'It's a demonstration for peace,' Tracy reminded. 'The New Mobilization Committee – they're coordinating the whole deal – won't let any radical group take over. Mom, I have to go.'

'Be careful, darling.' Vera's throat tightened.

'We'll be fine,' Tracy insisted. 'Oh, I'll leave Washington late Saturday afternoon by train. I'll let you know when I'll arrive in Saratoga.' *Tracy was coming home*, Vera realized with sudden joy. 'I can get a late-evening plane out of Albany on Sunday night, so I'll be home for a little bit,' she wound up breathlessly.

'Tracy, that's wonderful! Be sure and call to give us your arrival time. It'll be so good to have you home even for a little while.'

Vera counted the days until Tracy would arrive in Eastwood. Paul – and Doris and Phil – kept assuring her there'd be no violence at the three-day demonstration. Newspapers predicted it would be the largest that had ever taken place in Washington DC.

'I don't know why they have to demonstrate,' Joel grumbled, though Vera knew he was elated at the prospect of seeing Tracy. 'Nixon's made it clear he means to bring an end to the war.'

'These young people want it to end now,' Paul said bluntly.

On November 11, Veterans Day was observed throughout the nation. Nixon's *Silent Majority* – those who approved of his handling of the Vietnam War – used the occasion for their own demonstrations. Thousands displayed flags, turned on their car headlights, lighted the porches of their homes. It wasn't the war they were supporting, Paul pointed out to Vera. It was Nixon's way of trying to end the war: 'Peace – but peace with honour.' *But how many more people must die for that peace with honour*, Vera asked herself.

For Vera and Paul, Veterans Day was always an occasion for reminiscing. They'd been actively part of World War II. They'd experienced firsthand the devastation and loss of life that are always part of war. Vera's thoughts focused on *Kristallnacht* and the deaths of her parents and her brother – and on neighbours in London who had died under Nazi attack. Paul remembered the mission when Chuck – his Columbia buddy – had crashed in flames. He and Chuck had thought themselves invincible.

On Wednesday evening November 12, David drove Tracy to the airport at Dorval.

'Look,' he said tensely while they waited for her flight to be announced, 'if you decide to stay in Eastwood, I'll understand.'

'How can you even think of that?' she scolded. 'You know I'm coming back. Home is wherever you are.'

Laurie and Jeff met her flight in New York. They were full of reports about the three-day demonstration. At least 250,000 – most of them young people – were expected to participate.

'And leave it to Jeff,' she said with tender mockery. 'Always so efficient. Everybody's so edgy about where they'll stay in Washington, but weeks ago he reserved rooms for us at the Statler Hilton. *At student rates*,' she wound up triumphantly. 'We're paying thirteen bucks a night rather than the usual $24 to $26.'

At Laurie and Adele's apartment, the four of them talked till past midnight, when Jeff broke up the discussion.

'We want to be in the car tomorrow by 7:00 AM,' he reminded. 'Traffic is going to be hellish.'

The next morning – right on schedule – they headed south, ebullient yet solemn about the purpose of the occasion. The day was cold and grey with the threat of rain. By the time they arrived in Washington, the traffic jams were horrendous. At the hotel they were able to make arrangements for parking, settled in their two rooms – Adele and Tracy in one, Laurie and Jeff in the adjoining room. Then they headed out to join the crowds of young people – in the familiar uniforms of jeans, heavy sweaters, school jackets, and ponchos – that milled about the streets. An endless parade of cars drove at a five-mile-an-hour pace though the streets.

'A lot of guys will be in sleeping bags tonight,' Jeff prophesied, eyeing the equipment carried by many. He chuckled. 'We're getting too old for that.'

'Mom worried about violence here,' Tracy said as they strolled near the White House, where five students were handing out candy corn and gum. Someone else told them that St Mark's Episcopal Church had become a reception centre for demonstrators. 'They're giving out free sandwiches and coffee there. It's real groovy.'

Others told them that 35,000 troops were standing by 'to keep the peace.'

'Don't they know peace is what this is all about?' Tracy demanded.

At twilight – while seven drummers beat a funereal roll

– the opening event of the demonstration began: The March against Death, an event that was predicted to continue through the night and far into Friday. Thousands of demonstrators would march – in single file – the four miles from Arlington National Cemetery to the foot of Capitol Hill. Each would wear a placard about the neck that bore the name of someone who had died in Vietnam or the name of a community that had been destroyed.

In her room at the Statler Hilton, Adele prepared with Tracy's help the placards which each of the four of them was to wear. Her placard would carry the name of Terry's high school buddy who had died in the Tet Offensive. Laurie's remembered the brother of a Barnard friend. Jeff's bore the name of a remote village – where only civilians had remained – that had been wiped out. Tracy's placard remembered Mary O'Brien's son Jimmy, with whom she'd gone to school.

Jeff appeared in the doorway. 'I brought candles.' He held out four in his hand. 'It's dark already. We'll need them.'

Half an hour later, the four of them joined the candle-lit line at Arlington. Rumours told them that the march would probably last right into Saturday morning. Slowly the line moved forward in single file. In the course of the four-mile walk, Tracy was conscious of the crowds of onlookers – many of them in tears. She was here for all those who had died, she told herself, fighting not to cry. *For the soldiers and the civilians.*

At last their group approached the foot of Capitol Hill. There, each name was read aloud and its placard placed in a huge, flag-draped coffin. Tracy wished David could be here with her. In his heart he was.

On Friday the crowds swelled. Reports were that students across the nation were cutting classes in high schools and colleges. Those who could were arriving here to share in the main event tomorrow. By midafternoon a thunderstorm had hit the area, but this did nothing to lessen the enthusiasm of the crowds. Word circulated triumphantly about the hordes of celebrities who were present.

In the evening – with the March of Death continuing – an hour-long service called Liturgy for Peace was held at the 3,000 seat National Cathedral, where there was standing room only. By midnight, reports indicated that more than 40,000 were participating in the march from Arlington to Capitol Hill. And circulars were making the rounds to report that Senate Democratic Leader Mike Mansfield had only praise for the demonstrators. *I applaud the order, dignity and decorum of the demonstrators. These youngsters are our children, our neighbours, our friends. The only sorrow is they can't vote – they can only protest.*

Saturday activities began with a nine o'clock memorial service on the Mall. Then in the sharp morning chill the demonstrators – the police estimated a crowd of 250,000; the Mobilization Committee put the figure close to 800,000 – began the one-mile march down Pennsylvania Avenue to the Washington Monument. The marchers were led by Eugene McCarthy, Coretta King, Arlo Guthrie, and Dr Benjamin Spock. The atmosphere was festive, in contrast to the poignant March of Death that had begun on Thursday evening and had continued for almost forty hours.

The rally began at the monument at noon. In addition to the array of eloquent anti-war speakers, there was much music on the programme – mostly folk and rock, plus a brilliant monologue by Dick Gregory. Pete Seeger brought the crowd to its feet as he sang 'Bring Them Home.' And the crowd responded with 'Give Peace a Chance.' At close to 4:00 PM, Jeff nudged the other three in his group to begin to seek a path through the crowds.

'Let's get on the road before the mass exodus begins,' he ordered. 'Otherwise it'll take us till midnight to get back to New York!'

Exhilarated at having been part of an historic event, they settled themselves in the car for the ride back to New York.

'Turn on the radio,' Tracy ordered Jeff. 'Let's hear what's happening in other places!'

She hid her anxiety as they hit pockets of sluggish traffic. If she missed her train, there wouldn't be another until tomorrow. She wanted so much to be home – even for only twenty-four hours. She didn't want to miss one precious hour.

Kids like themselves whom they'd met in Montreal said it got easier after the first year – but that wasn't true. Would she and David ever be able to go home again? How would they survive – living in exile forever?

Chapter Thirty-nine

Vera was conscious of the Sunday morning quiet as she sat across the breakfast table from Tracy. A cosy warmth pervaded the room, fragrant with the aroma of freshly brewed coffee. The windows were steamed over, providing an aura of strangely pleasant isolation from the rest of the world. Last evening – with the whole family together except for Laurie – had filled her with such contentment.

This early breakfast was an oasis of time she would treasure, she thought while Tracy talked effervescently – despite barely five hours sleep – about the past three days in Washington, DC.

'It was one of the most exciting times in my life,' Tracy declared, only now smothering a yawn. 'You and Dad should have come down, too.' She paused. 'You didn't because of Grandpa,' she guessed.

'We talked about it,' Vera confessed. 'Do you remember when you and David went with Dad and me and Doris and Phil to the civil rights march and we heard Martin Luther King give his I-have-a-dream speech? You were only sixteen,' she reflected.

'Sure I remember. David and I kept talking about it for months. We were so proud to have been there.' All at once Tracy was sombre. 'Grandpa was glad to see me, but he didn't even ask about David.'

'This is a bad time for him.' Vera's eyes pleaded for compassion. 'But I see him coming around to our view about Vietnam.' Polls showed that most Americans were now against the war. 'And he's been upset about the 1968

Gun Control Law. To him it's a denial of freedom.'

'Can't he understand that it'll save lives?' Tracy asked passionately. 'Mom, what do we have to do to make him realize that the violence in this country is going to get worse if we don't get tougher on gun ownership? Adele said that –'

'Darling, please,' Vera broke in. 'Don't talk about guns around Grandpa.' *Here it was again*, she thought painfully. Tracy and Laurie's resentment that she and Dad were part of the firearms business. But couldn't they understand that even if she were able to persuade Dad to close up that part of the company – and he would *never* accept that – then others would increase their own production to meet the demand? 'He's so thrilled to have you here.'

'As long as I don't talk about David or about guns.' For a moment Tracy radiated open hostility. 'Okay, I'll be good,' she relented.

'I'll tell Mary O'Brien that you memorialized Jimmy at the march,' Vera said. 'She'll be pleased.'

'Maybe I should go over to the Blue Lantern later and tell her myself,' Tracy said on impulse. 'Does she work on Sundays?'

'In the morning. For the early-breakfast people and the after-church crowd. Shall we go over now? Grandpa and Dad will sleep late.' They had stayed up long past the time when Doris and Phil left with Neal. Oh, it had been wonderful to have them all together! If Laurie had been there, too, it would have been perfect. 'There won't be many people at the Blue Lantern this early on a Sunday morning.'

'Let's go,' Tracy said enthusiastically.

At this early hour it seemed as though all of Eastwood were asleep. The streets were almost deserted, shops closed. At the Blue Lantern, a trio of men occupied stools at the counter. The tables were deserted. Vera saw Mary O'Brien's face light up as she and Tracy walked into the small, modest restaurant. People in Eastwood knew that Tracy was studying at McGill. The fact that she had gone to Canada with David and that they were married was never mentioned. Again, because of Dad, Vera conceded. This was still a Republican town; most residents followed Nixon's lead on Vietnam with unquestioning devotion.

'We've had breakfast,' Vera told Mary apologetically, 'but your coffee's always so good we thought we'd drop in for another cup. And –' she hesitated a moment, knowing that pleasure would blend with pain at the mention of Jimmy '– Tracy was down in Washington, DC, along with Laurie, for the second Vietnam Moratorium demonstration.' She saw Mary's face tighten. 'She was telling me about the very touching march that lasted for forty hours – people marching with placards about their necks honouring someone who had died in Vietnam – or a devastated South Vietnam community.'

'I wore a placard with Jimmy's name on it, and –' Tracy stopped short, startled by Mary's glare of rage.

'That was a terrible thing to do!' Mary spoke through clenched teeth. 'Using my son's name for something that's disgracing this country! Jimmy wouldn't have liked that one bit!' Pale and distraught, Mary stalked away from their table.

'I thought she'd be pleased,' Tracy whispered, shaken by Mary's reaction. 'It was meant to honour Jimmy's memory.'

'I guess we just didn't realize that some people would take it in a different way.' Vera tried for a conciliatory smile.

'Jeff said there would be people who'd feel that way,' Tracy said after a moment. 'He heard somebody in our hotel lobby say that we were making a mockery of all those who'd died in the Vietnam war. That we were saying they'd all died for nothing. I can't see it that way.'

Vera and Tracy sat sipping their coffee in silence – each caught up in private reverie. Mary approached their table again, without a word refilled their cups, and returned the carafe to its customary place behind the counter.

'What can I say to her?' Tracy was desolate.

'Just let it be,' Vera whispered. 'And don't let it spoil your memory of those three days. You were making an important statement.'

'David and I don't socialize with other Americans up there,' Tracy said. 'We don't have time for the meetings and all.' She gestured vaguely. 'Between school and our part-time jobs. And we've signed up for six hours a week of volunteer work at a literacy centre.'

'There's a lot of talk already about amnesty,' Vera began encouragingly.

'Mom, that's a long way off,' Tracy interrupted. 'I was talking with Dad about it last night. But we'll have to wait. I won't let David come home and face a prison sentence.'

Vera glanced up to see Mary approaching their table again. She braced herself for ugly words.

'I'm sorry I talked that way,' Mary said softly. 'It hurts me to think that Jimmy died for nothing. He wrote me just weeks before – before it happened. He said he couldn't stand what they were doing to the people over there. He said we should get out of Vietnam before more died.' Her voice broke. 'It was nothing. Jimmy died for nothing.'

'Mary, no,' Vera insisted, searching for words of comfort. 'His country called, and he answered. He was a hero. You can be proud of him.'

'My baby died for nothing,' Mary repeated. 'Unless this teaches us not to let it happen again this way.'

Within twenty-four hours, a shocking account of American activities in Vietnam burst forth on TV screens and on the front pages of newspapers throughout the country. A newspaper journalist had broken the story of an early-morning massacre at My Lai. A company of 60 to 70 US infantrymen – acting under orders – had moved into the village of My Lai and in a twenty minute massacre burnt down the wooden huts, dynamited the brick one, and shot down the inhabitants – women, children, old men – as they tried to escape.

'I don't believe this,' Joel gasped as they watched the evening newscast. 'I don't believe this!'

'It's inhuman,' Vera whispered, her mind hurtling back to the memory of Hitler's concentration camps revealed to a shocked world after V-E Day.

Now they learned that the massacre had occurred in March of the previous year and would have remained secret except that a conscience-stricken Vietnam veteran – now a college student – had felt compelled to report what he'd heard from men who had been at My Lai. He wrote a stream of impassioned letters to Congressmen, even to the President. A probe had led to formal charges – and now the world learned about what *Time Magazine* labelled 'My Lai: An American Tragedy.'

Television and radio news, newspapers and magazines pursued this American atrocity in the days ahead. Vera was astonished by her father-in-law's obsessive pursuit of every item about My Lai.

'Dad can't believe American soldiers could behave that way,' Paul reminded her. 'He's looking for a way to accept what happened at My Lai.'

Then Joel came to them with a self-conscious, agonized admission.

'We made a terrible mistake in going into Vietnam. It took the kids to understand,' he said sombrely. 'They saw what diehards like me refused to see. I didn't want to believe our country could make a mistake. But we did – and the sooner we get the hell out of Vietnam, the better I'll feel.'

'Amen,' Vera said softly.

Joel paused in thought. 'The weather's on the rough side right now. But next time you talk with Tracy, you tell her I'll be up to visit sometime in the spring. And I expect her and David to take me to Ben's for one of those smoked beef sandwiches she keeps raving about. And tell David to make sure he has a haircut before I get there.'

Vera and Paul anxiously watched for Nixon's announcements about the withdrawal of troops from Vietnam. Paul was realistic, she told herself – he knew there could be no amnesty until every American serviceman was back home. On December 15, Nixon announced that another 50,000 troops would be withdrawn from Vietnam early in the coming year.

'It's slow, but it's coming.' Paul tried to be optimistic. 'We're getting out of Vietnam.'

'But how many more will die before it happens?' Vera countered.

The mood of the country was tainted by bitterness and disillusionment. A new decade was approaching. *Let it be better than the present one*, Vera prayed. *What did she want of this new year*? she asked herself a few days before its arrival – when the house held a spurious serenity for her because Laurie was home and had brought Adele and Jeff with her for ten days. The three of them would return to New York on New Year's Day.

What did she want? she asked herself again. To see Tracy and David back in Eastwood. When their nightmare exile was over, they wanted to live somewhere in the area, for which she was grateful. And she yearned to see Laurie happy in her profession. In June she'd have her medical degree. In July she'd begin her internship – along with Jeff – at Bellevue. Then she planned to practise in a ghetto area. Not here in Eastwood. Was this to be a nation of scattered families?

As always when Adele was in the house, education dominated much of the evening conversation. *Paul enjoyed verbal-wrestling with Adele*, Vera thought indulgently. And Adele was ecstatic that he had mentioned her work at the small Harlem school in his recent article. He was encouraging her to write an article about her current project.

Paul was frustrated that those in power were doing nothing to improve the educational system in Eastwood. He'd tried so hard through his years of teaching. Still, he relished his small success in writing about education, Vera comforted herself. The occasional lecturing. *Not much money, but I feel I'm reaching people.*

Vera sensed, too, that Paul was astonished and pleased by his father's glow of pride each time another article appeared with his byline. She'd seen her father-in-law pull the current article from his jacket pocket to show off to friends. It was important to Paul to feel he had not disappointed his father.

Now – two hours before the arrival of 1970 – Vera sat in her favourite lounge chair in the living room and listened while Paul and Adele talked shop. Phil sat at the piano, playing in muted volume the medley of George Gershwin music that had become part of their New Year's Eve celebrations. At moments in the course of the chess game he was playing with Neal, Joel hummed snatches of Gershwin. Laurie was sprawled in a lounge chair, absorbed in another Steinbeck novel.

Doris appeared in the entrance with a tray of hot apple cider. Vera rose to her feet and crossed the room to help her distribute the cinnamon-spiked beverage. *What were Tracy and David doing at this moment*? she wondered wistfully. All the American kids forced into exile.

'All right, I do sound like Nixon,' Paul conceded to Adele. 'I *don't* think we're getting as much as we should for the bucks we're spending on education.'

'We're not getting enough bucks,' Adele shot back.

'More money means higher taxes and everybody gets upset.' Paul was sombre. 'We need a school system here that understands the needs of today's kids. Here in Eastwood schools haven't changed in fifty years. Too many of our schools haven't changed in fifty years.'

'When are you going to sit down and write that book you talked about?' Adele asked zealously. *What book*? Vera asked herself. Paul had never talked to her about a book. 'You have such insight into educational problems. Put aside the articles, focus on bringing it all together in a book. Education is at a crisis point in this country.'

'I can't waste all that time on a book. On a gamble,' Paul hedged.

'Yes, you can!' Vera's voice was electric. Paul was worried about the loss of income from his articles and the lecturing. Had they drifted so far apart that he couldn't talk to her about this? In earlier years there had been nothing they couldn't sit down and work out together. He had confided in Adele about writing a book – *not in her*.

'It'll take a lot of discipline.' Doris joined in, making this sound more of a challenge than a warning.

'Your brother has discipline,' Joel said, and Vera saw Paul's glow of amazement. 'If he wants to do something, he does it.'

'Paul, it's an obligation,' Vera said softly. 'Take the time off and write the book.'

Paul hesitated. 'I'm not sure I can.'

'You can,' Vera insisted. All at once it was as though she and Paul were alone in the room. 'Remember what you said to me all those years ago in London, when you came to me after V-E Day?' Her eyes searched his. 'You said, "If this world is to see lasting peace, we're going to have to educate the people." That's been your whole goal in life. And now you have a chance – a *responsibility* – to do your share in that monumental job.'

'So it's settled.' Joel broke into the poignant moment between Paul and Vera, startling her. She hadn't been aware that he was listening. 'Put yourself on a work schedule. Set up the guest room as your office. You've got a book to write.'

'Somewhere along the line,' Adele said, 'spend time at my school – which God knows, isn't perfect. But see the difference between it and most other ghetto schools. We still have to watch for drugs,' she granted, 'and we've got kids with major problems. But our kids don't have to ask for passes to go to the bathroom. Or to the library. We don't have teachers and students on patrol duty.'

Now Vera screened out the lively conversation erupting around her. She had not been the best of wives these last few years, she rebuked herself. She'd allowed herself to become too wrapped up in the business – because that had been the way to fight her own demons.

This summer she and Paul would go to London together for two or three weeks, she decided. But already road blocks were zooming into place in her mind. To go to London was to remember what she needed to put behind her. To remember *Kristallnacht*.

Chapter Forty

Vera was astonished at the efforts required to organize the banquet in Dr Evans' honour. Joel and Doris took on increasing responsibility in their determination to make this a memorable event.

'I doubt it's a secret any longer,' Phil said at a family dinner late in March, 'but Doc's cool about it. He's not letting on he knows a thing.'

'How's the song coming?' Joel asked. Phil was writing a song for the occasion.

'It's coming. Not quite the way I want it yet, but I'll get there. Hey, didn't I have a song that made it into an Off-Broadway musical?' he demanded with a wink.

At the end of March, Joel flew to Montreal to spend four days with Tracy and David.

'Canada's been good for David,' Joel commented on his return. 'Got himself a decent haircut. He'd never make it as a hippie now.'

Vera kept remembering how Congressman Koch from New York had gone to Canada at the end of December to talk with draft-evaders in Montreal, Toronto, and Ottawa. He wanted very much to see an amnesty bill passed by Congress. But Paul kept warning her it wouldn't be soon.

In New York Laurie was ever-conscious that she was on the verge of graduating from medical school, that in July she was to start her internship. Though there were four years of internship and residency ahead of them, she could not forget that at the end of those years she and Jeff would head off in opposite directions.

She'd allowed herself to become too dependent on Jeff, she admonished herself. A bad move! They'd been great for each other through med school – and it would be the same for the next four years. But the time would come when she would have to stand on her own two feet and carry on alone.

Mom said that Dr Evans talked about bringing in a second doctor in addition to Jeff – probably a pediatrician – because Eastwood was growing. More young people were staying in Eastwood these days. Most of that was due to the extra jobs the family was creating these days. Grandpa was proud that the company had been written up in a leading trade journal because of the good working conditions and benefits it provided its employees. She was, as ever, astonished at the way Mom kept expanding the business. *But Mom and Grandpa still sold guns*, she thought in distaste.

During the spring break at school, she and Jeff drove up to Eastwood for a brief visit. She was oddly uncomfortable at the way Jeff seemed to have joined the family, she confessed to Adele on their return.

'They're losing a daughter but gaining a son,' Adele flipped, but her eyes were sympathetic.

'They're not losing me,' Laurie contradicted. 'So won't be practising in Eastwood. I'm still in the family. And I made it clear long ago that Mom and Dad were not to regard Jeff as a son-in-law. I know what I want to do with my life. Almost as far back as I can remember, I knew I wanted to be a doctor.'

'I think you're nuts to let Jeff get away. Hey, it's late and we both have to be up at six,' Adele said abruptly. 'Let's cut the crap and go to sleep.'

As usual on Monday afternoon, Laurie checked the

mailbox before heading up to their apartment. It was stuffed – meaning Adele hadn't come home yet. She unlocked the box, pulled out the usual assortment of ads, bills, and catalogues. She smiled when she saw the letter for Adele from Terry. Adele would be in a great mood tonight.

She was sprawled in the living room lounge chair with a mug of peppermint tea at her elbow when Adele arrived twenty minutes later.

'Don't sit down,' she told her, smiling. 'You have a letter from Terry on the table.'

'Oh, I need that today!' Adele crossed to the table for the envelope. 'It's been a real bitch. We've acquired a new kid who thinks it's groovy to pack a gun along with his school books. He's pissed because we told him that was a no-no.'

'Tea?' Laurie asked as Adele dropped onto the corner of the sofa and ripped open the envelope. 'I've a pot of water boiling.'

'The real thing,' Adele ordered. 'None of the herb stuff.'

'Coming right up.'

'Oh, God!' Laurie froze in her tracks at Adele's sudden exclamation. 'Oh, Laurie, I don't believe it's really happening!' Adele's face was incandescent. 'Terry says he'll be coming home – on rotation or something – in June!'

To celebrate, Laurie and Adele went out to dinner at the new Chinese restaurant a few blocks from their apartment.

'Chinese fits right into my budget,' Adele said as they walked through the sharp April chill to Broadway. 'I thought I'd be able to save money on this job – but no way.'

'Not if you keep spending half your salary on supplies for your class,' Laurie pointed out.

'I keep meaning to put money in the bank every month,'

Adele said. 'You know, to have a nest egg to fall back on when I get pregnant and have to be out of work for a while. Terry says as soon as he's out of the service and into a decent job, he wants us to have a kid.' She paused, squinted in thought. 'You know, for the first year that Terry was in Vietnam, I was scared to death he'd be killed.' Involuntarily Laurie tensed. In a few weeks Jeff would be eligible for the draft. The word was that they needed doctors like crazy. She didn't want to think about Jeff in Vietnam. 'But Terry says that the guys who last through the first three or four months are the ones that are likely to survive. He says that after that you develop a sixth sense. At first you're not cool – you do stupid things. Oh Laurie, I can't wait to see him.' Her face crinkled in laughter. 'He's going to be one tired old boy when I get hold of him!'

Each day Adele came home with a fresh idea about redecorating the apartment. It was taken for granted that Laurie would move in with Jeff while Terry was home.

'I don't understand this rotation bit,' Laurie said on a late April Friday while she and Adele helped Jeff prepare a spaghetti dinner for the three of them at his tiny apartment. 'They can't send him back to Vietnam, can they? Nixon says he's winding down the war in Vietnam. Troops are being brought home.'

'Probably he'll remain in the service but here at home until the whole deal's over,' Jeff suggested brightly. 'It's not going as fast as a lot of us would like.'

'Oh, I had a letter from Mom today,' Laurie told Jeff. 'Nobody's making a pretence anymore about the banquet for Dr Evans being a secret. He said he wants you there, Jeff. He wants to introduce you to the community.'

'I won't be practising for four more years,' Jeff protested, but he appeared pleased. 'I think it's great that the town's giving him that banquet. It must be wonderful to know you've spent fifty years tending to a community and that your service is truly appreciated.'

'In fifty years we'll be attending a banquet for you,' Adele declared.

'Right,' Laurie picked up. 'Adele and Terry will be there – maybe with a grandchild or two.' *Why was Jeff looking at her that way*? 'And I'll take time off from my practice in Harlem or Bed-Stuy to join them.' No time in a woman doctor's life for children or grandchildren. She'd realized that long ago.

'I forgot to pick up wine.' Jeff clucked in disgust. 'Which one of you volunteers to run down to the liquor store? I'm buying. I can't leave my sauce,' he pointed out, stirring the spaghetti sauce for which he'd become famous among money-short med students. 'Flip for it.'

The day had been long and hectic. God, she'd be glad to be out of this nine-to-five school-grind, Laurie thought as she reached for the keys for her apartment door. She closed her mind to the knowledge that starting in July with her internship, her hours would often be longer and even more gruelling. While she dealt with the second lock – because Manhattan had become a city requiring double and even triple locks – she heard the sharp ring of the phone inside.

She pushed the door wide, rushed inside to pick up the phone.

'Hello.'

'Is this Laurie Kahn?' a crisp voice at the other end inquired.

'Yes, it is.'

'This is Detective Rogers,' he identified himself. 'I'm sorry to report that there's been a shooting at the Lancester Special School. The victim – Adele Garrett – carried ID which listed you as next of kin.'

'How is she?' Laurie's heart was pounding. 'Where is she?'

Disbelieving, Laurie listened to the detective's report, wrote down directions.

'Thank you. I'll be at the hospital in twenty minutes!' White with shock, trembling, she disconnected the caller and dialled Jeff's number. She waited impatiently for him to respond. *Where the hell was he*?

'Hello.'

'Jeff, something awful's happened! I can't believe –'

'Calm down, Laurie,' he ordered. 'Now tell me.'

Her words tumbling over one another, she told him what little she knew. Of course, they were aware of violence in the schools – but, somehow, they had never expected it to happen at Adele's school. Hadn't Adele bragged about how they were keeping their kids under control?

'I'll pick you up in a cab in front of your house in five minutes,' Jeff told her. 'She's going to be all right.'

At the hospital, Laurie saw the nurse's start of astonishment when she presented herself at the emergency room.

'Adele considers me next of kin,' Laurie explained shakily. 'We're close friends. Like sisters.'

'She's in surgery,' the nurse told them.

'Where shall we wait?' Jeff asked.

The nurse gave them directions and they sought the bank of elevators. On the surgical floor – too anxious to sit – they paced about the waiting area, talking in muted tones about the shooting, until at last they sat in mutual exhaustion. Moments later, Laurie saw a door swing open, and a surgically garbed man emerged.

'There's the doctor!' She leapt to her feet along with Jeff. Her heart was pounding.

'We're waiting for word about Adele Garrett,' Jeff told him. 'The shooting victim.'

'I'm sorry,' the surgeon said with perfunctory compassion. If he were surprised that they were white, he concealed it. 'She never regained consciousness. She died on the operating table.'

'Oh, my God!' This was insane. Shock merged with rage in her. Terry was coming home – but Adele was dead?

In a daze, Laurie heard Jeff identify themselves as fourth-year medical students. She heard him ask the necessary – practical – questions. Holding her hand tightly in his, he led her outside and hailed a cab for them.

'We'll call Mom,' Laurie whispered. 'We'll need money for Adele's funeral.' Her voice broke. 'Jeff, how could it have happened?'

But she knew how it had happened. The police had told them. Adele had tried to take a gun away from a student who was threatening a 15-year-old girl who had rejected him. The new kid she'd said was a big problem, Laurie guessed. He and Adele had struggled. The gun went off. Adele was shot in the head.

Too numb to cry yet, Vera put down the phone, walked to the sofa, sat at the edge of one corner. *Adele was dead.* This was unreal. Last night Adele and Paul had talked on the phone for almost an hour about a new experiment in her school. He was to drive down to New York to discuss it further with her principal. Now they must rush to New York to arrange for her funeral.

Vera's mind catapulted back through the years – twenty-four years ago – to the morning she and Doris had gone to the railroad station to pick up Fiona and Adele. She'd been so happy that Laurie would have a friend right in the house – and the two little girls had been so pleased with each other. She remembered the childhood illnesses – which had naturally passed from one to the other of the three little girls in the household. She remembered the terrible day when they'd learned that Fiona had been killed by a hit-and-run driver in New York – and her futile efforts to persuade Fiona's mother to let Adele stay with them.

'Vera?' She was startled from her painful reverie by Paul's voice.

'In the den, Paul.'

In a daze – trying to accept ugly reality – Vera told him what had happened, aware of his shock, knowing the memories this would evoke in him. He'd been six years old when he saw his mother crumple to the floor and die of a gunshot wound.

'We'll have to go right down there,' he said, his eyes reflecting his pain. 'I can't believe it, Vera.'

'I know.' She lost her perilous hold on composure. 'Paul, she was twenty-six years old. Terry's scheduled to come home in June. She's been so happy with her teaching.' *Guns again. Guns spreading tragedy among the innocent.*

Paul reached to pull her close. 'We knew there's violence in the schools – but I'd thought Adele's school was free of it. It's something we read about or see on TV news reports.'

'Can you imagine what Laurie's going through?' Vera's mind charged back through the years – to the moment she and Paul had rushed into the Robinson house to find Laurie hovering over seven-year-old Serena Robinson, killed by a gun fired by her small brother. *'How can it be happening this way again?'*

'Laurie'll need us.' Paul glanced at his watch. 'We should be in the car in an hour.'

'I told her we'd be there tonight. She wants us to stay in her apartment – she'll sleep on the sofa. Jeff's with her,' she added. *Thank God for Jeff.*

'Tell Irene to get dinner on the table as fast as she can,' Paul said. 'I'll have to make a couple of calls. We'll probably be down there three or four days.'

'I'll phone Eve at home.' Eve was her long-time administrative assistant. 'She'll make calls, reschedule some appointments.'

'You talk to Irene. I'll go upstairs and start to pack.' He drew her close. 'It's rough,' he said gently. 'Adele was like a member of the family.'

Joel returned to the house minutes before Irene prepared to serve dinner. Paul brought him into the den, reported the tragic news. Joel stood frozen in shock for a moment, his face ashen.

'Those kids are animals!' he blazed. 'She never should have taught in a ghetto school. She knew the crime statistics there!' He turned to Vera. 'How's Laurie taking it?'

'She's devastated.' Vera flinched. 'All those years ago, Serena – and now Adele.'

She knew that Joel was remembering his wife's death. Was this a terrible retribution for the family's manufacturing guns?

'Laurie's going to say we're responsible for this.' Joel was all at once defensive. 'We built the gun that creep used to kill Adele?' he blustered. 'That's bullshit!'

'We'll never change the way Laurie feels about guns. I know it, and you know it.' Vera was fighting for calm. She'd lost one family on *Kristallnacht*. She mustn't spend the rest of her life fearing to lose again. 'I suspect Tracy, too, isn't comfortable that her family is in the business of –'

'Vera, what do the kids want from me?' Joel's voice was strident. He turned accusingly to Paul. 'It's not just Laurie and Tracy. You and Doris have always been ashamed of what your father does for a living. But for generations, Kahns have built guns. *For sportsmen*. And when our country needed arms, we helped supply them. We considered it our duty. We –'

'Dad, nobody has a right to tell you to close your business,' Vera broke in. 'If you did, that wouldn't stop the flow of guns into cities and towns across the country. And you've been an honourable man,' she said gently. 'But the gun situation is going berserk these days. Guns are falling into the hands of dangerous people. Where did a fifteen-year-old boy get hold of a gun?'

'You're talking gun control?' Joel sputtered. 'Guns are necessary to keep peace in the world. To –'

'Dad, you're talking about another era. Do you know how many lives are lost each year because of guns in the wrong hands? Adele would be alive today if that crazy kid hadn't been able to buy a gun!' Her voice was harsh with grief. 'Our crime rate wouldn't be escalating like mad.'

'Vera, Irene wants to serve dinner,' Paul interrupted. 'Let's eat and get in the car.'

'Dad, I'm not telling you to give up the business,' Vera reiterated. 'Guns are important.' In a corner of her mind she remembered the little fishing village in Copenhagen and how guns had saved her life. She remembered how she'd told Paul – when he'd left her in London – that she wished she had a gun to keep under her pillow. Guns had meant protection to her then. And in a corner of her mind she heard Paul's recrimination only two years ago: *For God's sake, Vera, when are you going to learn to let go of the past?* 'But today, guns must be regulated,' she insisted, moving into uncharted areas. 'I think there's a road we can take that will let us keep the business in operation and yet bring the family together again. I think we can do it, Dad.'

'What road?' Joel was wary, yet Vera felt a humility in him, a yearning to mend fences. He loathed this under-the-surface conflict with every member of the family except her. 'What can we do?'

'We'll talk about it when Paul and I get back from New York,' she said gently, feeling his anguish. 'It'll take some negotiations.'

'I'll come down to New York for Adele's funeral,' Joel told her. 'You let me know when to come.'

In the next four days, Laurie was grateful that Jeff never left her side. Along with her mother and father, he took over the myriad details of laying Adele to rest. He notified her estranged family. He wrote Terry. Her grandfather and Doris came down for the funeral. Tracy and David wired flowers. And always Jeff was there beside her.

Walking into the church for Adele's funeral service, Laurie told herself she must make Jeff understand she wanted him to be part of her life forever. He'd played the game according to the rules she'd drawn, accepted what she allowed herself to offer him. But in her heart she'd felt Jeff loved her for the long haul – even while she denied permanence to her own love.

Was she right? Would Jeff always be there for her? All at once it was terribly important to know. Adele would be pleased, she thought with a fresh surge of grief that Adele could never know. She could hear Adele's voice scolding her. *Laurie, you and Jeff are made for each other. Like Terry and me.*

The pews of the church were quickly filled. Others gathered together at the rear. The church that had been so dear to Adele's mother and grandmother, Laurie remembered. She saw clusters of Adele's students – their feelings of loss etched on their young faces – clinging together at the rear of the church. The girls in tears, the boys shamefacedly wet-eyed. Oh yes, Adele had been much loved, would be missed.

With Adele laid to rest beside her mother in a Queens cemetery, her adopted family headed back to their car. Caught up in memories of Adele, Laurie said little on the long drive into Manhattan. She was vaguely conscious of the quiet conversation among the others. Then the car was emerging from the Queens Midtown Tunnel.

'We'll go downtown to Ratner's on Second Avenue for an early dinner,' her father said, circling around the FDR Drive. 'Okay, Dad?'

'That'll be nice, Paul.'

When they left the car at the parking lot on East 5th Street, Laurie fell into step with Jeff behind the others.

'Jeff, I could never have survived this without you,' she whispered. 'I don't think I can survive life without you.'

She lifted her eyes to his, saw his face light up as he comprehended her message.

'Ever since those first weeks in med school, I knew I wanted to spend the rest of my life with you.' He reached for her hand. 'But I was always afraid to push.'

'It won't bother you to share your practice with your wife?' She asked coyly.

'You can call yourself *Dr Kahn*,' he replied lovingly, 'but we'll know you're *Laurie Green*, also.'

'We've got three weeks between graduation and beginning our internship.' Her smile was shaky. 'I know a June wedding is awfully traditional –'

'Let's be traditional.' He squeezed her hand. 'Your family will like that.'

'Will it be wrong?' All at once doubts invaded her. 'I mean, so soon after Adele –'

'Adele would approve. She knew we belong together.'

'You're sure?'

'I'm sure.'

*

Several days after their graduation from the Columbia College of Physicians and Surgeons, Laurie and Jeff were married in the summer-flower-bedecked living room of the Kahn house. A glorious fragrance permeated the air. Phil sat at the piano now and played Mendelssohn's Wedding March as Laurie – flanked by her mother and father – walked to the improvised *chuppah*, where Jeff waited for her.

In a semi-circle of chairs arranged for the occasion, Joel sat between Doris and Tracy. With a sweetly solemn expression Neal sat next to his mother.

While Laurie and Jeff stood before the rabbi, Vera and Paul joined the others in the semi-circle of chairs. The rabbi began the service. Vera reached out for Paul's hand. Her eyes strayed to Tracy. How sad that David could not be here with them today. Jeff's mother wasn't here. He had pointed out that he had no knowledge of her whereabouts. 'I doubt that she would have bothered to come, anyway,' he'd said.

Earlier Terry had phoned to give Laurie and Jeff his congratulations and good wishes. They understood he couldn't bring himself to attend the wedding, just two-and-a-half years after his own City Hall marriage to Adele – where they had been in attendance.

The day would arrive, Vera promised herself, when Tracy and David could come home again. And today she allowed herself hope for a true reconciliation with Laurie and Tracy – a bringing together of the family. She and Dad had worked so hard for this. Please God, let Laurie and Tracy understand that they *could* be a whole family.

And then the rabbi was saying the magic words. 'I now pronounce you husband and wife.'

There was a flurry of embraces, an air of festivity that was marked, too, by sadness because Adele was not there to share the occasion with them.

'All right,' Joel said jovially at last, exchanging a meaningful glance with Vera. 'Let's go into the dining room and this wonderful dinner that's been prepared for us.'

They took their places at the dining table – extended to holiday length. Under the table Vera's foot reached for comforting contact with Paul's. Her eyes met Doris's across the table. Paul and Doris – along with Phil – knew of the extended conferences she and Dad had had with their lawyers. Was she being overly optimistic to believe that at long last family differences would be erased? As much as she, Dad wanted this. Would Laurie and Tracy accept what they had to offer? *Was it too late*?

When the wedding cake had been cut and served, Joel tapped on his champagne goblet for silence, cleared his throat self-consciously, and announced, 'We have a special announcement to make. A momentous decision that is, in part, a tribute to Adele's memory. Adele's death made us understand what had to be done. Vera,' he said gently, 'tell them.'

'We've been working with our lawyers to make some changes in the business,' Vera said, speaking to Laurie and Tracy. 'We've broken it up. Your grandfather and I feel this is something we must do. Kahn Firearms is now one company. The catalogue division and the chain of stores are another.' She paused, took a deep breath. The girls didn't understand yet. 'As of this date, all the profits from Kahn Firearms will go into a fund to support a gun-control group.' She paused again, watching her daughters' astonishment as they assimilated what she had said. 'Paul, you explain it to Laurie and Tracy.'

'To close the gun division would throw a lot of people here in town out of work,' Paul began. 'You know how your grandfather would feel about that. And it wouldn't stop some other firm from picking up the business we'd be turning down. It would be of no real value. Then your mother and grandfather decided to take the gun-division profits and funnel them into a special fund to fight for gun control. The Kahn family will be fighting in a small way against crime on the streets and for a peaceful world.'

'Mom! Oh, Mom!' Radiant, Laurie left her seat to rush to her mother while Tracy turned to embrace her grandfather.

'That's a double wedding present,' Tracy said exuberantly, reaching now to kiss her mother while Laurie moved to hug her grandfather. 'It's for David and me, too. Oh, thank you! Thank you!'

She didn't have to be afraid anymore. Vera felt herself wrapped in a precious serenity. Her family was together again. They would always be together. *At last she could put Kristallnacht behind her.*

Epilogue

The weather – this late January of 1977 – was approaching blizzard proportions in upstate New York. The Kahn house was surrounded by a blanket of snow. The towering trees – edged in white – swayed with a spurious air of fragility. Approaching dusk lent an aura of drama to the winter landscape.

In the living room Paul crouched before a blazing fire in the grate, added additional logs out of exuberance rather than necessity.

'Paul, when will the man with the snowplough be here?' Vera hovered in the doorway. Her eyes – her whole demeanour – exuded a joy that seemed to infiltrate the whole house. 'The driveway should be cleared by the time Dad and Phil return from Albany with Tracy and David.'

'He'll be here any minute,' Paul soothed, rising to his feet. 'Anyhow, the kids' plane came in twenty-five minutes late because of the storm. It'll be at least an hour before they arrive.'

'Vera –' Doris's voice filtered down the hall from the kitchen '– I'm putting the yams into the oven now.' For this festive reunion-dinner, Irene had been given the day off.

'Great,' Vera called back. 'And put up some cider – Laurie and Jeff should be here any minute with Cathy. They'll appreciate a warm-up.'

'I hope Cathy likes the little panda bear I picked up for her.' Paul reached into a breakfront drawer to bring out the latest stuffed animal he'd bought for his three-year-old granddaughter.

'She'll love it. And I hope Laurie and Jeff can get through one evening without a house call,' Vera said with mock reproach. In truth, she was happy that Eastwood's new pair of doctors – with Dr Evans finally accepting retirement – belonged to that vanishing breed of doctors who still made house calls.

'Shall I turn on the news?' Paul asked tentatively.

'Not now,' Vera vetoed. 'I want just to glory in the news we had last week.'

On January 21 – the day after his inauguration – President Carter had made it his first official business to issue an unconditional pardon to almost all men who had peacefully resisted the draft during the Vietnam war. Meant to ease the divisiveness of the war, the announcement had brought about vociferous controversy – though Vera blocked this from her mind. It was enough to know that Tracy and David were coming home.

Various veterans' organizations were upset about the pardon. Senator Barry Goldwater called it 'the most disgraceful thing a President has ever done,' but the parents and wives of those pardoned offered a heartfelt thanks. Some pro-amnesty groups admitted to disappointment that the pardons didn't extend to military deserters – of which there were about 100,000. In addition to the thousands who'd fled to Canada, Sweden, and other countries, the pardon included 250,000 men who'd never registered for the draft.

Tracy and David would be here for this long-awaited reunion but must return to Montreal to wind up their affairs. In six weeks they would be home on a permanent basis. The knowledge was a glorious chorus that sang in Vera's mind.

Tracy and David's child would be born on American

soil, Vera reminded herself with recurrent joy. They didn't know yet, but Dad was buying them a house as a belated wedding gift. A house they would choose. Only to Paul had Vera confessed that she was grateful that David's parents had deserted Eastwood – *too provincial for words* – to move to Albany. But Tracy and David's child – to be named Ernest if a boy, Ernestine if a girl – would not lack for love, she told herself with pride.

'Aunt Vera, where do you want the logs?' His face ruddy from the cold, Neal stood in the doorway, his arms loaded with birch logs.

'Here, let me help you.' Paul crossed to take a share of his logs. 'You look like you're studying to play Santa Claus,' he joshed. 'Or the town drunk.'

'Hey, Uncle Paul, did I tell you what happened in current events class yesterday?' Neal's newly baritone voice echoed with pride. 'We have to do a report on your new book!' Paul's second book had just been published.

'Great,' Paul approved, exchanging a warm glance with Vera.

In time Tracy would teach in the Eastwood school system, Vera told herself. David would be active with Paul in managing the Kahn Fund for Gun Control, utilizing his law training on an in-person basis rather than the long-distance efforts necessary until now. Already Joel was nudging him to become active in local politics once he and Tracy were legal residents – reminding him that his great-grandfather-in-law had been a much-loved mayor of Eastwood.

Then Laurie and Jeff arrived with effervescent little Cathy. The atmosphere crackled with high spirits as Vera and Doris handed out cinnamon-stick spiked mugs of hot apple cider. Hearing the sounds of the snowplough clearing the driveway, Vera smiled. Sooner than they'd expected, Joel and Phil arrived with Tracy and David.

'Darling, you're enormous,' Vera laughed through tears of pleasure, patting Tracy's extended stomach. 'Are you sure you have four months to go?'

'You'll have to be patient, Grandma,' David kidded, clutching Vera in a warm embrace.

'You're probably starving,' Doris said. 'Vera, let's get this show on the road.'

The family gathered about the newly acquired dinner table, large enough to seat a dozen. *They'd be twelve when Tracy's child was born*, Vera thought tenderly. Her family. Her *wonderful* family.

'Paul,' Vera whispered while the others listened absorbedly to a story David was relating about their lives in Montreal. 'I've just decided that we'll expand our trip to London this year.' Each year now, she and Paul spent three weeks in London. 'I want to go to Berlin.' She saw his start of astonishment. 'To see where Mama and Papa and Ernst are buried.'

All these years later she could hear Mrs Munch's voice telling her what had happened to her family in Berlin. *Your father was shot to death on Kristallnacht. Your mother and brother died in Oranienburg-Sachsenhausen. Through special channels Herr Schmidt was able to collect their ashes. The ashes were buried in synagogue ground.*

'We'll visit the synagogue where Mama and Papa and Ernst are buried,' she said softly. 'We'll say a prayer for them.'

But there was a new serenity about her, a new peace in her heart. At last, she told herself, she could truly put *Kristallnacht* into the past.